BECOMING
MALLORY

A NOVEL

ELAINE EVANS

To Samantha, my daughter and personal Mallory.
Remember, *you are worthy.*

AUTHOR'S NOTE

Becoming Mallory is a coming-of-age novel that centers on a family coming to terms with their daughter's autism diagnosis as well as her anxiety and depression. The story, although inspirational, contains elements that may be sensitive for some readers. Depictions of anxiety and depression, self-harm tendencies, and suicidal thoughts (no attempt), are present in the novel. Readers who are sensitive to these themes, please take note.

Prologue

Mallory

They say autism is a superpower, but I disagree.

Trust me when I say I'm not feeling super right now as I lie in this hospital bed. Autism has brought me nothing but pain, anxiety, depression, and confusion. All I want is to be normal. I'm thinking at seventeen, desiring to be a regular teenager, accepted by society, and not having to recoil at someone else's touch isn't too much to ask.

I mean, is it?

I shift in the cramped bed, adjusting the thin white sheet, and look over at my mom. She's asleep in a blue plastic chair next to my bed, and it looks uncomfortable. Yet she hasn't left my side since "that night." As I watch her chest rise and fall under the scratchy blanket the hospital gave her, I can't help but feel a tremendous amount of guilt. I'm sure she'd rather be anywhere else but here in this barren hospital room designed to keep me safe during my stay.

Which is smart.

Because I don't trust myself anymore.

But that's my mom. My parents are two of the most amazing people you'll ever meet. I've put them through enough worry to last three lifetimes. I don't deserve them. Or my brother. Or anyone, for that matter. And especially not *him*.

I wonder what he's doing right now. Does he miss me? Is he thinking about me as much as I am about him? Did he ever love me?

The guilt and loneliness are too much, so I look away from my mom and turn back over to stare at the blank white ceiling. I've stared at it for so long these past twenty-four hours that I have its imperfections memorized.

This room is cold. My life is cold.

Will I ever get better?

Will I ever have a life? A real life? Free of worry, anxiety, and depression?

Will I ever see him again?

Will autism always control me?

When?

When will I become Mallory?

The Early Years

1

THE BEGINNING

Laura

PREGNANT

Yep, that's what the little white stick in my hand says.

Three minutes.

That's how long it took to find out our lives were about to become so much bigger.

I'm sitting on the edge of my bed, staring at the closet in front of me. I did *not* want to find out if I was pregnant in my bathroom. Somehow, that always seemed weird to me, learning you're going to have a baby in the same place your toilet lives.

No, thank you.

So, I brought the test into my bedroom before I looked at it. To the comfort of my room, the softness of my handmade quilt. This is where I needed to be. I also didn't want the two-lines-means-positive tests. I had to see the word looking back at me. No guessing game this time around.

Not that I didn't know what the result would be. Deep down, I knew. I had none of the typical PMS symptoms that signaled the start of my period. No bloating, no backache, no sore breasts, no heavy feeling in my legs. Nothing. To be honest, my physical body feels great.

Only twice before have I felt this way in my life. Once was with my first son, Eli. His ashes are becoming one with the earth at my favorite park. The second time is sitting at my feet, playing with his dump trunk in his zip-up footie dinosaur pajamas, oblivious to the fact that he's going to become a big brother. Our plan was for Jake, our ten-month-old, to be an only child.

Surprise!

My heart feels heavy as I stroke his head with a gentle touch. "Sorry, Bubba." He tilts his head back to look at me, and a dimple appears on his cheek. I'm sure he's wondering why I haven't gotten him breakfast yet.

See, clueless.

I glance at the test again. "Yep, still pregnant." As if saying it out loud helps with my realization. It doesn't. Was I hoping it would change?

I don't want to admit it, but deep down I was hoping it would. This isn't a part of our plan. Talk about a life detour.

I toss the test on my bed (Ew! Note to self: wash the bedding later). I grip the edge of my quilt, feeling the texture beneath my fingertips as my knees bounce. I rub my temples as the questions swirl around in my head.

How did this happen? Okay, I know the answer to this one.

How am I going to tell Scott?

How will he react?

How are we going to afford this?

How am I going to handle having two kids under the age of two?

So. Many. Questions.

I have enough feeling in my legs to stand and take the cordless phone from its base on the side of my dresser.

Time to call Scott. He's working, unaware his life's about to change with one call from his pregnant wife.

Poor guy.

I weigh my options, staring at the phone in my hand, contemplating whether it'd be best to tell him now or wait till he gets home. I jerk my head as the decision comes immediately. It has to be now. It'll drive me mad otherwise, and I don't want this to be the longest day of my life.

Nope. Not happening.

I dial Scott's cell number, pausing between each button, trying to draw it out as much as possible. I put the phone up to my ear and wait for it to ring. He'll pick up. He only left for work an hour ago, and it's very unusual for me to call him during the day, except for my daily lunch call or barring something horrible happening. I decide this fits into the latter category.

Ring, Ring ... Ring, Ring ... Ring, Ring...

Nervous energy sends me pacing around the room, chewing my fingernail while I wait for him to answer.

Ring, Ring ... Ring, Ring...

"Oh, my God! Answer the—"

"Hey, babe!"

Finally!

"Sorry, the phone was all the way over on the other side of the room. Everything okay?" He's screaming over the usual job site commotion in the background. Drills drilling, hammers hammering, people yelling, and loud music. Chaos fills my ear. Scott's in construction, and unless he's at lunch when I call, this is what I hear.

"I need to talk to you about something important. Are you able to step away?"

"Um, sure. Give me a sec," he says with a slight quiver in his voice. I hear the construction background noise fade. Then it's gone. "Alright, I'm outside. You're freaking me out, Laura. I don't like the way your voice sounds."

Okay, here it goes.

I take a deep breath, my throat tightening as I close my eyes. "Scott, I'm pregnant."

I can hear him breathing on the other end of the line. Waiting for him to say something, to say anything, feels like an eternity. When I can't take it anymore, I blurt out, "I was going to wait until you got home, but I just couldn't. I needed—"

"Are you okay?" He cuts me off, his voice steady and calm. The question doesn't surprise me. This is Scott. My rock. Always worried about me, caring about me, loving me.

"I'm fine, I guess. A little shocked."

Lie. I knew.

I pause and peer down at Jake. He's still playing with his dump truck, not a care in the world. A tinge of jealousy swells inside of me for my ten-month-old baby. My attention returns to my husband, who still hasn't told me how he feels about the news. "Scott, what are we going to do?"

He lets out a hearty chuckle. "What do you mean, 'What are we going to do?' We're going to have a baby!" When I hear the joy in his voice, my worries fade. I drop my shoulders, and a feeling of contentment washes over me. If I had waited, I would have regretted it, so I'm glad I told him immediately.

He's walking back into the construction site because the commotion is getting louder. I walk into the kitchen to make coffee since my caffeine headache is screaming at me. While washing my hands, I realize he hasn't said anything. "Scott, you still there?"

"Yeah, babe, I'm here. Hold on one second." He turns down the radio and clears his throat. "Hey, guys! Listen up, I have an announcement to make." The drills and hammers stop, and the talking fades. My husband has a deep, commanding voice, so when he raises it, everyone stands and turns to hear what he has to say. I can hear the silence both on the other end of the phone and in my house as I wait to hear what comes next. Scott takes a deep breath. The anticipation is thick ... then it happens.

"I'M GOING TO BE A DAD! AGAIN!"

What I hear next is amazing. The whoops, the yelling of 'Congrats, dude!', the clapping, the high fives. I rest the phone between my head and shoulder as I make my coffee and listen to my husband say 'Thanks, man' a million times. Jake follows me into the kitchen, abandoning his dump truck. He walks closer to me and pulls on my pajama pants. He's ready for his breakfast.

"Hey, Bubba. You're hungry, huh?" I turn my attention back to Scott and the congratulatory party happening in my ear. "Hun, I gotta go. I'm so relieved you're happy."

"Happy? I'm thrilled! I mean, what if it's a girl?"

And for the first time since I woke up this morning, a huge smile comes across my face.

2

NINE MONTHS LATER

Laura

It's early in the morning on a humid August day in 2007. I'm back at the same hospital where I delivered Jake, in an operating room, ready to deliver our precious daughter. I'm laid out on my back; my arms are out to my side, and it's bone-chilling cold. A faint odor of hospital-grade disinfectant hangs in the air. I'm a nurse, and I will never get used to that smell.

Tubes are everywhere, needles are in my arm, draping on top and in front of me, as well as doctors and nurses moving around each other. It looks like they are doing a choreographed dance. They are swaying through the room with speed and grace, making sure not to knock over the plethora of equipment that is everywhere. It's impressive. A well-oiled machine is what my dad would say. Even though it's organized, it's still chaotic and nerve-wracking. I can't believe I am about to have my second C-section in less than two years.

I close my eyes to block out all the commotion and calm my nerves as I wait for Scott to come in all gowned up. As I do, my mind wonders, and I fantasize about our daughter. Gosh, I can't wait to meet her! The same questions that have swirled in my head for months are still there.

Who will she look like?

Will she be a well-behaved baby?

Will she have a lot of hair?

Will Mallory be healthy?

Mallory.

That's what we named her. Like so many couples before us, we struggled with finding that perfect name. We wanted it to be different but not weird. Obviously, there's a fine line. I mean, this is serious business, naming another human being. Since I named Jake, we agreed Scott would name our newest addition. He was determined to find one that meant something special. A name that would set her apart, and he was serious about it.

I remember that day with fondness. The day when Scott finally decided what name would follow our daughter for the rest of her life.

It was a gloomy Sunday afternoon in the spring, and I felt the warmth of Scott's legs as I rested my feet on him while re-reading What to Expect When You're Expecting for the second time in less than two years. He was sitting and reading a baby name book as if he was studying for a final exam in college.

"How about Victoria?" he inquired. "It means 'victory.'"

"Nah," I said, dismissing the suggestion. "Then people will want to call her Vicky or Tori. You know how I feel about nicknames."

"True. You hate them." He continued to read as I placed my book on the coffee table and watched the rain drip down the windowpane. Jake was sound asleep. He always fought me on his afternoon nap, but the rain that day would knock out even the most stubborn napper. I rubbed my stomach in slow circles, and she kicked me so hard I swore she was mad at me.

This girl is going to be tough. I smiled. Feeling my kids kick and move inside me is my favorite part of being pregnant. I felt so happy and content even though we had been at the name game for over an hour.

"Okay, I got one!" he proclaimed as he sat up a little straighter and grabbed my ankle, holding it tight. "Stella! It means 'star.'" He glanced my way, his eyes wide, searching for my approval.

"That's kinda pretty..." Then, my eyes shot up as something dawned on me. "Wait a second. Didn't you date a girl in high school named Stella?"

"Oh yeah! That red-headed girl that lived down the street from me." He glanced up, and the corners of his mouth were twitching in a smirk. I wasn't so sure I wanted to know what he was remembering about cute Stella down the street.

"Hey!" I playfully kicked him in the leg as he laughed. "That one is out for sure."

He sighed, tossed the book on the coffee table, and grabbed the remote to watch TV. "My head is spinning. Let's pick this up later. We have time, right?" He tapped his hand on my knee and then rested it there. I nodded, turning my head to the sound of the rain, and dozed off. I'm not sure how long I had my eyes closed when Scott gently nudged my leg.

"Hey, Laura. Wake up." I rubbed my eyes as he pointed to the TV. He was watching re-runs of Family Ties, which I found strange, to say the least. But it was a Sunday afternoon after football season, and there was nothing on TV worth watching. Well, other than Family Ties re-runs on Nickelodeon. "How about Mallory? I don't know what the meaning is, but I like it. I like it a lot. What do you think?" He looked over at me, and I knew this was it. The way it rolled off his tongue, the way his eyes gleamed, the excitement in his voice. For whatever reason, this name was speaking to him. And after all, it was his choice. Mallory, the oldest daughter on a sitcom that I watched growing up in the eighties and loved, was now going to be the name of the beautiful person growing inside of me.

It was perfect.

"Hey, babe." Scott's voice jolts me back to the here and now. He places a gentle kiss on my forehead as a warm smile crosses his lips. In an instant, everyone else in the delivery room seems to disappear, and all I can feel is the warmth of his presence.

The hospital staff covered Scott head to toe in the usual support person's surgical uniform. A funny blue thing that resembles a shower cap covers his full head of brown hair. The surgical mask makes his brown eyes appear even bigger than they already are. A yellow robe that ties at the waist hits above his knees because of his six-foot-four frame. Gloves for his hands and blue covers for his shoes complete the sterile ensemble. His complexion, tanned from the summer sun, is pale. There is a tightness around his eyes, and his hands are shaking. I know this look.

He's full of fear.

This is exactly how he appeared when I delivered Jake. After Jake was born and I cuddled him in the recovery room, I remember asking Scott what he was thinking when he was next to me, waiting for his son to be born. He said, "Well, if anything were to go wrong, I could lose my son and wife all at once. The thought of that was terrifying." I'm assuming, with how he appears right now, his feelings haven't changed. *Gosh, I love this man.* He leans in and kisses me gently on the lips after the forehead peck. His lips are stiff.

"Hey, sweetie. Thanks for coming. Love the outfit," I joke, trying to lighten the mood.

"Thanks," he says with a forced snicker. He wears a tight grin as he glances at me with a pale, nervous look. On impulse, he places his palm on my head and rubs his thumb on my forehead.

"Did you bring any wine?" We share a laugh, as the fear and tension seem to dissipate, if only for a moment.

"Man, don't I wish. Some Wild Turkey would be nice right about now." He takes my hand in his and squeezes it. "It's going to be fine," he says with soft words. I could feel the trembling of his hands and the clamminess of his skin. "I saw Dr. McMurray out in the hall. He said that he was going to be in soon." He glances around the room, taking in the weird surroundings. "You ready for this?" He winks.

"As ready as I'll ever be. Who is here?" When Jake was born, it felt like every person we had ever met was at the hospital. He was the first-born grandchild on both sides, so everyone was excited. This time around, we asked for only the grandparents.

"Let's see. My mom, your mom and dad, your brother, my brother, and Cousin Johnny, of course."

No one listened.

"And Jake is coming later, right?"

"Yep. My mom is going to pick him up from daycare around three o'clock and bring him right over."

"I can't wait for him to meet her." A nurse comes up and asks me to verify my name and date of birth for the one-millionth time. I guess this should bring me some measure of comfort. I know from working as a nurse that this is the standard operating procedure. In the past, I always thought patients were being ridiculous when they looked annoyed when we would ask them. Now I get it ... it's irritating. "Laura Givens. March 18th, 1975."

"Perfect. We are going to be starting soon." She taps my arm and, in the most enthusiastic cheerleader voice, says, "You've got this, momma!" I wonder how many times she has said these same words to a worried, expectant mother this week alone. Probably a lot. But she was right because Dr. McMurray walks in right away wearing almost the same get-up as Scott.

"Hey there, Laura! You ready to get this show on the road?" He's standing right behind Scott and gives me a thumbs-up. Dr. McMurray has been my OB-GYN since I was sixteen, and he is always so happy and jovial. He is the perfect doctor.

"Yes, sir! I'm ready."

"Alright then. Let's deliver you a baby!"

And with that, the well-oiled machine dances.

"You are the most beautiful baby girl I have ever seen," I whisper to Mallory as I gently stroke the top of her head, her baby-soft skin feeling like silk. I can feel her warmth in my arms as she sleeps without a care in the world. She's perfect. I know every parent says that about their child, but she is. Staring at her as I lie in the hospital bed, I get some answers to the questions I was asking myself in the operating room.

Who will she look like? My mother. Mallory has my mom's round face, wide-set eyes of a brownish-green color that will more than likely turn brown, and her turned-up nose. Ten long fingers and ten toes. In short, she's gorgeous, just like my mom.

Will she be a well-behaved baby? So far, so good. She hasn't made so much as a peep.

Will she have a lot of hair? Yes! It's dark blonde, silky soft, fine, and shiny. Perfect baby hair that you can't help but touch.

Will Mallory be healthy? I pray she is. Both physically and emotionally.

I stare at her with all the wonder and awe that any new mother has. What will her life be like? Who will she marry, what career will she choose, and who will her friends be? I glance at Scott, who is sitting in the hospital's signature blue recliner, and he's beaming at me. "What?" I ask, my eyes crinkling with a smile.

"What are you thinking?" he asks as he rests his chin on his hand.

"Oh, you know, the usual stuff," I say as I continue to stroke her hair. "Just wondering what her life will be like."

"It's gonna be interesting, that's for sure."

"No doubt." I study her, and she's a blank slate. A whole new life, ready to begin.

"Can you believe what became of that day when you walked into Home Depot?" Scott asks. My mind immediately catapults back in time. My dad sent me, a nineteen-year-old girl, to Home Depot to get a Swivel P-trap because he was working on the sink. I sulked about going, of course. I had no clue what I was looking for, and that's when I saw Scott. All six foot four of him in an orange smock. His strong jawline, broad shoulders, brown hair, and whiskey-colored eyes just about threw me backward.

He was working and professional, of course, much to my disappointment. We exchanged flirty smiles and a longing glance, but that was it. He sold me my pipe and sent me on my way.

Once I got home, though, my dad informed me that the pipe was the wrong size. I raced back to the store (to get the correct pipe size, of course) and found him. When I handed him the bag of pipe and told him it was the wrong size, Scott's exact words were, "I know." He admitted later that same night—our first date—that he took a chance of selling me the wrong pipe, hoping I would return when his shift was close to over.

It couldn't have worked out better if he planned it. After that first night, we dated for a year and a half, got married, and ten years later had Jake. Now, here we are.

I tear my eyes away from Mallory and admire my husband. "That day changed my life."

He swipes a piece of hair off of my forehead. "Mine too," he whispers.

Scott takes Mallory for me so that I can shower. Once I'm done, I find them both sleeping. Scott's head is cocked to the side, a position that I know he will regret later. It takes me a while to get back into bed, but once I do, I position myself so that I can stare at two of the most important people in my life. I feel a sense of contentment, like nothing could be more perfect. I doze off as I watch them. Thoughts of the future dance around in my head.

I can't help but hope it will be peaceful and trouble-free.

3

FIFTEEN MONTHS LATER

Laura

T he first few months of Mallory's life were a blur.

The chaos started the day we came home from the hospital. The visits from friends and family, the lack of sleep, along with breastfeeding. Then there were the diapers. I felt like I was drowning in Pampers. I knew having two kids under the age of two would be taxing, but to be honest, I had no clue. When friends would ask how it was going, I always told them to imagine having a set of twins. Except one of them is walking, talking, and learning to go pee in the potty, while the other needs to be fed every two hours.

But at the same time, I really felt like I had a handle on this. I had already done all of this baby stuff with Jake. I totally had it all under control.

I was so cocky because raising two children so close together in age was a challenge.

In the beginning, and as Mallory got older, Scott and I had a great routine. I would get up with Mallory during the week for her nightly feedings. Then, on the weekends, Scott would take over so I could catch up on sleep. There was nothing I loved more than waking up on a Sunday and seeing my husband lying on the couch, knees bent, with Mallory up against his thighs. He would contort his face in a host of funny ways as he pretended to bite her sockless feet. She would let out a belly laugh as if it was the funniest thing in the universe. And that's because, to her, it was.

Before I knew it, it was time for me to return to my job as a nurse. Life was running full steam ahead, and we were riding with it. In the blink of an eye, Mallory was fifteen months old, and Jake was almost three years old. For Jake, his big milestones started and never stopped. And since they are so close in age, I know what to expect.

So, it surprises me that Mallory is lagging. She's almost a year and a half and isn't showing any signs of walking. She also isn't talking. Not one word. No Momma. No Dada. Nothing even comes close to a word in the English language. Only sounds. Not that I am comparing her to Jake. But I have read the baby books, the mommy blogs, and all the parenting websites. Some of them even twice. And in the beginning, she did everything on time.

Smiles at parents. Two months old. *Check.*

Rolls over. Four months. *Check.*

Sits without support. Six months. *Check.*

Starts crawling. Eight months. *Check.*

Waves bye-bye. Ten months. *Check.*

But after ten months, the long-awaited, special moments that all parents expect felt like they would never come. Scott and I would talk about it here and there, and we always came up with the same answer. *She's not her big brother.* And every Google search would offer the same reassuring words. 'Kids progress at their own rate.' I took comfort in that and remained patient.

It's late afternoon on a Tuesday in mid-November. It's the time of year in Ohio when you can feel winter knocking on the door. The days become chillier, the sound of the furnace running becomes a familiar background noise, and the winter coats come out of storage. Next up, shoveling snow.

I'm making dinner when Scott calls.

"Hey, babe! Just calling to say I'm on my way home." Every day, he calls to give me a heads-up. It's incredibly sweet.

"Great! How far out are you?"

"Maybe ten or fifteen minutes, depending on traffic. I'm starving! What's for dinner?"

"You're favorite ... Spaghetti and Meatballs."

"Great! See ya shortly. Love ya."

Monday through Friday, we have the same conversation. The only thing that changes is the dinner option for the evening. You would think it would get old after all this time, but it doesn't. I anticipate this phone call every single day.

Ten minutes later, I'm finishing up dinner as he walks through the door that connects the garage to the kitchen. This is the favorite part of my day ... when the family is all together again. We eat dinner and play with the kids and then it's bath time. After that, we read to them. Each in their bed, and before you know it, the time comes to put them down for the night.

Strike that.

My favorite part of the day is when the kids are in bed. Then, it's time for Scott and me to be alone in a nice, quiet house. But right now, it's about to get loud.

"Hey, guys! Daddy's home!" Scott's booming voice fills the room when he walks in the door. He loves to see the kids running in to greet him. This may be the favorite part of *his* day.

Jake comes running from the living room like a bat out of hell, his feet padding on the floor. "DADDY!" he yells as he jumps and wraps himself around Scott's legs.

"Hey, buddy!" He rubs Jake's hair, making a mess of it. Scott would always say that he wanted kids so that he could have a family. He wasn't a fan of the infant stage. But this he loves. He adores playing and interacting with them and being their human jungle gym.

"Daddy, I got a new twuck. Wanna see it?" Another new truck from Grammie, Scott's mom. His bedroom is overflowing with them, thanks to the love of his grandparents.

"You bet I do. Let me say hi to your mommy and sister first." I see Mallory crawling toward the kitchen, her knees sliding as she attempts to grip the slick marble floor. She may not walk, but man, can she crawl fast! I swear that's why she isn't walking yet. Why bother with walking when she can get there faster by crawling? She's not behind in her milestones. She's smart and thinks outside of the box.

Yep, nothing to worry about.

Scott walks over to me and kisses me on the cheek, his lips cold from the outside. "Hey, babe."

"Hey, sweetie. How was your day?" I ask as I turn off the burner and wipe my hands on the kitchen towel that hangs from the oven door.

"Tiring but good. We got a lot accomplished on the Miller job." I smile and give a slight nod, pretending I understand what the Miller job is, even though I'm clueless. He studies Mallory, then turns back to me. "Any attempt at walking today?" I lower my gaze and shake my head. He rubs my back. A gesture that says, 'It's okay.'

He leans down and scoops Mallory up, and I hear the smack of his kiss on her forehead. "How's my Mal Pal?" Yep, you heard right. A stinking nickname. I hate nicknames, but this one I love.

Mallory doesn't answer Scott. She says nothing because there are no words yet, either. But something's different. I stare in confusion and notice that Mallory won't look Scott in the eye.

Has she always done that? I turn back to the task at hand: dinner. As I stir the sauce, the aroma of garlic and basil fills the air, causing me to pause and think about this one for a second. I make a split-second decision to put that thought out of my mind as I tap the wooden spoon on the edge of the pot and sit it down on the spoon rest.

Stop reading into everything. She's probably just tired.

Scott places Mallory on his hip. "How much longer till dinner's ready? It smells amazing." He leans over the bubbling pot of sauce and dips his finger in to get a taste.

"Hey!" I snicker as I playfully smack his hand away. "It's almost ready. Give me about ten minutes."

"Sounds good. We will talk about Mallory later," he says as he winks at me.

Good grief, what could he want to talk about?

I know the issues at hand. Repeating the same conversation over and over changes nothing.

Jake pulls on Scott's pant leg. "Daddy. Let's go see my twuck. Huwy!" He takes off, racing out of the kitchen and up the steps to his room.

"Alright! Let's go!" In pursuit of Jake, Scott lifts Mallory up and out as if she's taking flight. She giggles as they follow Jake to his room. I set the table for dinner and wonder what the night's conversation will bring. *I'm not sure I am up for this.*

4

Laura

"Finally, the kids are asleep," I say with a sigh of relief as I plop down on the couch. I turn to Scott, but he isn't paying attention.

He's out cold.

The nightly routine is complete, and Scott and I are finally alone for the night. Well, technically, *I'm* alone for the night. Scott's in dreamland. I choose not to disturb him and make myself comfortable. I throw a blanket over my legs to read a book that's supposed to be the best thriller of 2008. It's a pleasant distraction from all the will-she or won't-she talk. Fortunately, Scott dozed off while watching basketball, and I no longer have to endure a discussion about the great walking/talking debate. His head drops, then it bobs back up again. His arms are crossed over his chest, and his snoring is mixing with the sound of the game. The long day of work has caught up to him.

We decided at dinner to talk to the doctor about Mallory at her upcoming physical appointment, which is next week. Although, I'm pretty sure I know how the discussion will go. He's old school and has the wait-and-see approach, which I appreciate. Mallory will do things when she is ready. It's everyone else that wants to push things. And I know that it all comes from a place of love. For me, though, I would rather sit back and enjoy my daughter.

Is this something I should worry about, though?

The constant back-and-forth feelings that I have about all of it can make my head spin. However, tonight, I am putting all these thoughts aside, and I'm going to lie here next to Scott and enjoy my book.

The ear-splitting sound of the phone ringing suddenly interrupts my peaceful evening. I throw the blanket off my legs and jump to answer it because I don't want the kids to wake up.

"Who in the world is calling at this hour?" I say out loud as I search for the phone with a sense of urgency. Not that eight o'clock is late. But in the world of sleeping toddlers, it might as well be one in the morning. I'm frantic as I survey around the room, lifting pillows, searching under the couch, and shoving my hand between the cushions.

Where is it?

"Who is calling now?" Scott sighs heavily with annoyance that the ringing phone has woken him up. He scoots his body down further onto the couch, lays his head back on the cushions, and dozes off again.

After it rings seven times, I find the phone under the coffee table on the other side of the room. "Hello," I answer curtly.

"Hi, honey." It's my mom.

Why in the world is she calling now? She knows our routine.

"I know it's late. I didn't wake the kids, did I?" My mom is talking in a low voice. As if the kids can hear her through the phone.

"Oh, hey, Mom. No, you didn't. Is everything okay? You never call in the evening." I'm struggling to keep my cool and not let my annoyance show.

"Yes, everything is fine, sweetie. I just wanted to call you when the kids are down so I can have your full attention. I need to talk to you about something. It's about Mallory."

Great. Here we go again.

My mom is especially worried about Mallory and wants to talk about it constantly. She looks up articles and talks to her friends about it. I've had such a nice day today; I don't want it to end with another conversation about Mallory's walking and talking, or lack thereof. I thought this discussion was going to come from Scott. But she is my mom, and I don't want to be disrespectful, so I'm going to humor her.

"Sure, Mom. What's up?" I say as I try to sprinkle in a dose of cheerfulness.

"Remember when I told you I was going to lunch with my friend Sylvie?"

"Mm-hm," I murmur as I head to the kitchen, not wanting to wake up Scott, so I tidy up as I talk to her. Placing the phone between my cheek and shoulder, I unload the dishwasher.

"Well, we got to talking about Mallory, and I was telling her how she seems delayed in some of her milestones. She felt so bad. Well, Sylvie told me about her husband's granddaughter, who has autism. And—"

"Wait. Did you say autism?" I immediately stop, the two plates I'm holding clattering in my hand. The word feels like a knife to my heart.

My mom can't think Mallory has autism. Can she?

"I did. As I was saying, Sylvie's husband's granddaughter has autism, and she was telling me some symptoms. Laura, honey, Mallory has some of these symptoms. Just the other day, she—"

"Mom, you can't be serious?" I ask as I interrupt her again. "Autistic kids are ... well, they aren't Mallory. They flap their arms and ... and do other things." I can't focus as I close the dishwasher door before I even finish unloading. I grab a sponge from the sink and take my frustrations out on the kids' handprint smudges on the refrigerator door.

"Laura, honey, please listen to me. She isn't walking. She isn't talking. Something is different," she pleads.

"I know that, Mom." I'm trying hard to keep it together. "I'm with her every day, sometimes all day long. I know my daughter, and she doesn't have—"

"Have you ever noticed that when you call her name or try to talk to her, she never looks you in the eye? Ever." This time, she interrupts me. "Or how she always cries when there are loud noises?" My mom's voice at first was full of desperation, but now it's forceful and assertive.

I stop to think about this for a second. I lean against the counter and cross my arms over my chest. Does she do these things? Have I missed these cues? I did notice the eye thing earlier with Scott.

Is it possible?

I shake my head and quickly dismiss these thoughts. It's not possible. I know my mom means well. She loves Mallory, but she is way off base.

"Look, Mom." I try my hardest to sound sensitive to my mom's worries. "I know you're concerned. But there is no way that Mallory is autistic. It's just not possible. I feel bad for Sylvie's husband's granddaughter, but that's not the reality we are dealing with. Scott and I decided we would talk about everything at her next well visit with her doctor. I'm sure she just needs more time, that's all. I appreciate your concern, I really do." As much as I feel she is mistaken, I meant the last part. My mom loves her granddaughter.

"Okay. I understand. I just love Mallory so much. You know that."

"I know you do. She has the toys to prove it," I say, trying to lighten the mood, and it works because my mom chuckles.

"I'll never stop spoiling those kids!"

"I hope not." Before she can offer more advice from Sylvie, I decide to wrap this up. "I gotta go, Mom. I need to do some things before bed." Not true. My book is the only thing demanding my time, but I need this conversation to be over.

"Okay, sweetie. Could you do me one favor, though?"

I close my eyes tightly and press my fingers against the bridge of my nose. "Sure, name it."

"I'm going to email you an article about autism in toddlers. Will you promise me to at least look it over?"

I sigh in defeat. "Sure, Mom. I promise. Send it over."

"Great!" A wave of excitement washes over her as if she has won a minor victory. "Good night, honey. I love you."

"Love you too, Mom." I hang up the phone and sit it down on the kitchen counter. I lower my head and grip the island, feeling the cool, smooth texture of the granite. This brief conversation with my mom has me confused. As if I wasn't worried about Mallory enough, now my mom has me wondering if Mallory has autism. "Great. One more thing to worry about," I say out loud.

My conversation with my mom, as well as talking to myself, must have woken up Scott because he is walking into the kitchen.

"What are you worried about?" he says through a yawn, leans against the counter next to me, and starts rubbing my back.

"My mom just called me, and she thinks Mallory has autism." He stops rubbing as he glances at me and tilts his head to the side.

"What? Autism? Where did that come from?"

"I know, right? Apparently, Sylvie's husband's granddaughter has it, so now my mom thinks Mallory does. She is going to send me an article to read."

"Well, it can't hurt to look it over, I guess. You know, to make her happy. But there is no way Mallory is autistic. That's impossible," he says as he shakes his head. It's reassuring to know that we agree.

He yawns again as he stretches his arms over his head, his hands almost touching the ceiling. "I'm going to head off to bed. Today wore me out, and I need to get up at the butt crack of dawn tomorrow." He brushes my cheek with a kiss. "Good night, babe."

"Good night, sweetie." His footsteps echo as he heads toward the stairs.

I turn off the light in the kitchen and head back into the living room. I grab my book, drape my favorite warm and fuzzy blanket over my legs, and settle in on the couch, getting ready to get lost in a fictional world. Before I read, I notice the laptop on the other side of the room. Knowing my mom, she hit send on that email as soon as we hung up. I stare at it and question myself. What if my mom is right? Mallory cries when there is a lot of commotion in the house. She doesn't look us in the eye. Well, sometimes she does.

Could there be something to this? I shake my head. *Nah. It's just not possible.*

I open the novel and decide to see what all the fuss is about with this thriller. I begin reading, but I don't get very far. After only a chapter, I slap the book down on my lap. I glance at the laptop out of the corner of my eye, debating whether to read the email. I glare at it longer than I should. With a deep breath, I refocus my attention back to the book in front of me.

The article from my mom will remain unread. For now, at least.

5

THE NEXT DAY

Scott

"Goodbye, babe," I whisper to Laura as I kiss her on the cheek. She mumbles something in her sleep as she turns over, grabs the duvet cover, and tucks it under her chin. Even asleep, she's beautiful as her brown hair feathers out over her pillow. The puffy duvet covers half of her face. I would saw off my arm to stay in bed with her right now and not leave to go to a construction site full of sweaty men and women. However, duty calls, and staying in bed with my wife doesn't pay the bills. Which is unfortunate.

It's five o'clock in the morning, and I have a huge workday ahead of me. I try to be as quiet as possible as I tip-toe out of the bedroom. I walk down the hall to peek into Jake's and Mallory's rooms. Both are the craziest sleepers. They look like contortionists. Jake's lying on his back with one leg wrapped around the other, which is making his hips twist in the strangest way. His arms are over his head with his face buried into his pillow.

How do kids sleep like that?

I mean seriously. I would need a year's worth of chiropractor appointments to recover from one night's sleep in that position. Yet, they are warm and (somewhat) comfortable. What more could I ask for?

Once I'm in the kitchen, I see the phone still sitting on the island where Laura left it last night. It's the only thing on the empty granite, other than a ceramic bowl of bananas. Although I need to discuss that phone call with Laura, my focus for now is on today's job. My stomach's grumbling, so I hastily grab a granola bar and banana before heading towards my truck. As the garage door creaks open and the night chill fills the garage, I think back to what Laura said last night.

Autism.

Laura's mom thinks Mallory may have autism. It's so ridiculous.

I will say this about my mother-in-law. She is not a meddler, and she never sticks her nose where it doesn't belong. Ever. So, the fact she called and vocalized this is shocking. It tells me she must believe it.

I try once again to refocus my thoughts. Laura and I can talk about this later. I put on my work boots, grab my tool belt and keys, and manage to leave waking no one. I pull my truck out onto the dark and quiet street, and I turn on the radio. Sports talk sounds like an excellent distraction. I love to hear all the so-called experts tear apart the game performances from the day before. I scan the neighborhood as I drive past. Very few houses have lights on. The streetlights hum with an electrical buzz, adding to the surreal feeling of the early morning. In about an hour, this little corner of the world will wake up, including my wife.

I know she is going to wake up thinking about that phone call.

UGH! Come on, Scott! Start thinking about the job today!

I try to put it out of my mind as I pull into Starbucks for coffee. Every other morning, Johnny and I take turns getting coffee for one another. I like mine black and bitter. Today, his is a vanilla latte made with sweet cream, extra foam, and a splash of cinnamon. His fancy, sugar-filled drinks are absolutely ridiculous, and the guys on the job mock him about them daily. He couldn't care less.

Johnny and I are more than cousins. He's my best friend and more of a brother to me than my own brother. We are close in age, only two months apart. We went through school together, got into trouble together, tried smoking together (first and only time because, gross); anything you can think of, we did it together. He was the best man at my wedding (much to my brother's dismay, but that's a story for another day), and we are now business partners. He is my ride-or-die.

I pull up to the job site and see Johnny, arms crossed and appearing relaxed, leaning up against his pristine, white truck. I get out and hand him his weird, fancy drink.

He gets a huge smile on his face. "Hello, sweet nectar of the Gods," he gleams, and I can see his breath in the air on exhale. He takes a long sip.

"Oh, please. That drink is nothing but sugar. God disapproves, trust me."

"Not true. God wants us happy. *This* drink makes me happy. It also wakes me up and gets me ready to work. Which, in turn, makes you happy. So, see, God approves."

I chuckle and continue to drink my black and bitter goodness.

We stand there, drinking our coffee and letting it seep into our brains so we can think clearly before the employees arrive. Givens Construction is growing by leaps and bounds. Faster than either of us has ever expected. We have an army of skilled guys and gals on staff. So many that we can build anything your heart desires. And build it close to perfection. The job we are currently on is a massive addition to a house and a new garage. And this is just one job of many. We have five others going on simultaneously all over town. Johnny and I will meet here, give assignments to the guys, then check in on the other sites and lend a hand if needed. It's a lot to juggle, but we get it done.

We sip our coffee in silence, which stretches on longer than usual, and I can tell Johnny's picking up on my lack of conversation. On a normal morning, I'm talking about this job or that job or asking him about whatever flavor of the month he is dating. This morning, though, I'm quiet as a church mouse. He keeps giving me side glances because the dude can read me like a book.

"You okay this morning? You don't seem like yourself," he asks as he takes another sip. One thing my family is not: height challenged. I'm six foot four, and Johnny has a half-inch on me. A fact he never lets me forget when he has the chance.

"I'm good," I deadpan as I peer straight ahead out into the night.

"Laura mad at ya, huh? What did you do this time?"

"No! Of course not. Why do you always assume I did something wrong?"

"Because you usually do."

He's not wrong. I tend to put my foot in my mouth. A lot. And I am a huge instigator. He takes another sip, and the only sound is passing traffic. I take a deep breath and decide to tell him.

"So, Laura's mom called last night. She seems to think Mallory has autism."

"Mm. That's um ... wow. Did she say why?" he asks as he turns and chucks his empty coffee into the bed of his truck. It lands with a thud on the mountain of empty Starbucks cups. He grabs his tool belt and hoists it over his shoulder.

"I didn't have time to ask. She called pretty late, and I went to bed right after. But I mean, you know what's going on." I glance at his truck bed. "By the way, when are you going to clean out this truck? It's disgusting." Johnny always washes and waxes his truck to perfection. On the outside. But inside is a disaster. Much like him.

"I'll get to it and stop trying to change the subject that you started," he says as he pokes me in the arm.

"Fine," I roll my eyes. We are making our way to the area that will soon house a new garage. I stop and think before I continue. "I don't know, man. It's completely off base. There is no way Mallory has autism. There has to be something else going on, right?"

Am I actually asking my single, wife-less, child-less, full-of-himself cousin his opinion? I guess I am.

Johnny stops walking and turns in my direction. "Are you asking my opinion? I'm not used to this. I'm going to need a minute to process."

"Haha. Hilarious. I mean, I guess I am. You spend a lot of time with Mal Pal."

"I do. Love that little squirt," he says as his lips turn up into a grin. Johnny loves my kids as if they were his own.

"Okay, well, what do you think could be going on?" I can't believe I'm asking him. But he is my best friend. He won't hold any punches. I hold my breath while I wait for his answer, and butterflies erupt in my gut. His opinion matters to me, and we've always had each other's backs.

"I think it's a possibility, yes," he says without even a hint of doubt or hesitation in his voice.

Whoa. Wait a second. Was I expecting him to say that?

No way. He is supposed to be on my side.

"Seriously?" I ask, my voice sounding unsteady. I take a step backward.

"Yes. Seriously. Why not? It could be one possibility for her issues. It would benefit your whole family to leave no stone unturned. Look into it." He puts his tool belt on, the leather creaking softly as he cinches it around his waist.

"Okay. Wow. I can't believe you think Mallory has autism," I say as I shake my head. My body feels stiff, and my heart is racing. I clench my hands into fists.

He studies me, his brow furrows in confusion. "Dude, are you mad? Look, you asked me. I didn't say she has it. I just said explore it as a possibility. That's all."

"Well, you weren't supposed to say that!" I yell, my deep voice reverberating through the early morning. I shock myself with the anger swelling inside of me. I asked for his opinion, so why am I so mad?

My outburst startles Johnny, and he flinches. He's as taken aback as I am by my reaction to this. "Scott, man. I will not tell you what you want to hear just to make you feel better. I'm not. Never have and never will. Your ego is big enough as it is." He walks ahead of me, but then he pauses. He turns back, and I can almost hear him trying to think of what he wants to say. "But you need to ask yourself why Mallory possibly having autism bothers you so much."

Now I'm really mad. Because deep down, I know he's right.

Why does the idea of Mallory having autism bother me?

I can't let my mind go there. I refuse to think that this could be a possibility. And even though I wanted Johnny's opinion, I never thought he would disagree with me. Is that what I wanted when I asked him? Validation? It's unfair to expect him to always agree with me, but dang it, I need an ally here.

"Okay, forget I asked *you* anything." I wave him off and turn to walk back to my truck. "I should have known better than to ask your opinion."

"What in the heck is that supposed to mean?" He marches after me, the sound of gravel crunching under his feet.

I turn to face him and point my finger at him. "It means what could you know about raising a kid? You haven't had as much as a two-week-long relationship in years. You know nothing about having a family. You're the furthest thing from a father."

I flinch because I've even startled myself with that sucker punch. That was below the belt, and I know it.

This is a weakness of mine. I turn to insults when I get mad or know I'm in the wrong. Right now, I immediately regret my words. Johnny wants a family more than anything. He may come across as a player, but it's all an act because all he wants to do is settle down and have kids.

Johnny's body tenses up, and he stands frozen, mouth gaping. He pauses and points his finger at me. "Never ask for my opinion about this again. Ever," he hisses at me. His chest is rising and falling with heavy breaths. He marches back toward his truck as he tears off his tool belt and throws it into the cab, and it makes an enormous thud. I watch as he rounds his truck and gets in. Before shutting his door, he proclaims, "I'm going to head to the Bowen job. You and your attitude can handle this on your own. Good luck." He doesn't turn to look at me as he slams the door so hard his truck shakes. He starts the engine, peels out, and heads out into the darkness with nothing but dust and gravel left in his wake.

Well, crap. I did it again.

This is my usual MO. Open mouth, insert foot, hurt those I care about. God, I have to stop doing this. I rub my hand on my neck because I need to get myself together. One by one, truck headlights fill the area with light because all the crew is arriving for work. And thanks to my outburst, my work here doubled.

Great job, Scott.

As the day wears on, my guilt is getting the best of me, as it should. So, after lunch, I text Johnny.

> **Me:** Hey man. That was uncool of me. Sorry. Your fancy coffee is on me all next week.

With a sigh, I hit send and wait for his response.

In usual Johnny's fashion, he makes me sweat it out. His reply comes five hours later.

Johnny: A week??? Ha! One month and all is forgiven.

Johnny: Jerk.

He's not wrong. I am a jerk.

6

FOUR YEARS LATER

Mallory

"SAY CHEESE!"

My Nana points her new pink phone at us. Me, my mommy, daddy, and my brother Jake are standing in front of the big tree. It's my first day of kindergarten, and I'm five years old.

And I'm scared.

It's Jake's first day, too. He is going into second grade. He's a pro and really smart. I'm not smart enough for this.

"Mallory, honey, look over here at Nana," my Nana says. Mommy taps me on the shoulder, which I don't like. I'm having one of my "don't touch me days." I don't like to be touched. Touching feels weird. It always has.

"Look over at Nana, sweetie, and smile." I try to listen to Mommy. I really do. But I don't like to look people in the eye. It's hard for me. It's confusing. But I know Mommy and Nana won't stop until I do.

Oh, hey! A squirrel! It's behind Nana, and it's trying to bury a nut. It's probably soft to touch. I like to touch soft things. I'll watch the squirrel and smile. Then Nana will think I'm smiling at her.

It's so hot outside. I hate to feel hot. I like winter. Winter is coming, but the leaves have to change color first. I like it when that happens. It's pretty.

"Cheese!" we all say together. Nana walks over to show Mommy the picture. My stomach is hurting because I hope I tricked them, and they will think I was looking at Nana. I look over at where the squirrel was, and he's gone. That makes me sad. I won't be able to walk over to him and try to touch him. I need to touch something soft today.

My mommy smiles at Nana. It must have worked! Mommy's happy with the picture. "Looks great, Mom! Thanks. Can you text me a copy?" Mommy asks and hands Nana her phone. I don't know what "text" means.

"Sure, honey," Nana says. Nana, Mommy, and Grammie start talking about something, but I never understand their conversations, so I walk away. I try to find my brother. Him and Daddy are talking and laughing. My daddy doesn't talk or laugh with me a whole lot. Only sometimes. I don't know why. I feel different from other kids, but my brother isn't. Jake talks to everyone. Maybe that's it. I guess I'll just stand here and wait. I'll play with my shirt.

Now we have to take pictures with Nana and Grammie. I don't want to take any more pictures. Plus, the squirrel is gone, so I don't know what to look at. And now the socks in my shoes are bothering me. The line across my toe is itching. I hate it, and I wish I could take them off. I like the feel of the grass under my feet. It makes me happy and less nervous.

I do like my new school clothes. They are cool. My shirt has Hello Kitty on it, and it's pink. My shorts are pink too. My lunch box and backpack have Barbie on them. I love pink. It's a pretty color, and it doesn't hurt my eyes. My shoes are pink with a white plastic toe. My brother said they are called Chucks, I think. I like them because they don't pinch my toes like other shoes do.

School is going to be scary, I think. I wonder if it will be loud because I hate loud noises and places. I don't want to talk to the other kids. Talking to people is hard.

I wish I knew why I feel like this.

I heard Mommy and Daddy talking to each other yesterday. Mommy is worried because I can't write my name. I cry when I try to do it, and then Mommy's sad. I hate it when Mommy's sad. I don't know why I can't do it.

We are finally done taking pictures. Nana and Grammie are leaving, and they hug me. I feel like I'm being squished, so I pull away. Jake smiles when he gets hugs. I wonder if he feels squished.

They get in their cars and drive away. "Bye, Nana! Bye, Grammie!" Jake and I say. They both honk their horns, and it's so loud. I cover my ears.

"Mallory, are you okay?" my mommy asks me. I shake my head. I don't want to talk. The sun is shining on my face. I don't like it. Mommy and Daddy grab our stuff, and we walk to the garage. I guess that means we are leaving now. For school. I want to cry, but I can't. Jake will make fun of me.

I don't want to go. Mommy grabs my hand. I pull my hand away. I don't want to be touched. She looks at me. I think I made her sad.

"You ready for the first day, buddy?" Daddy asks Jake. He didn't ask me.

"Yeah!" Jake jumps and yells as he runs for the car. He's so loud all the time. My stomach hurts again. Now, I want to hold my mommy's hand. I take it. She smiles.

We all walk to the garage. Daddy looks at Mommy, and I think he's worried. There are lines on his forehead. "You look tired, babe."

"I am. I didn't sleep well last night. I guess I was all keyed up about today, you know?" *Why didn't my mommy sleep good?* I'm worried. Is she sick? Is she going to die?

Daddy taps on the buttons that open the garage door. It makes a weird boop sound that I don't like. The garage door makes a creaking noise. I let go of Mommy's hand and cover my ears again.

I get in the car very fast because I like the car. It's quiet in here. Mommy helps me with my seatbelt. Daddy helps Jake.

"I can do it, Daddy. I'm in second grade now!" Jake says loudly.

"You're right! Sorry, bud. My bad," Daddy says, and then he laughs. Why is that funny? I don't understand.

"I'm nervous," Mommy says, then she shuts my door. "Do you think she will be okay?" Daddy shuts his door. They are talking to each other, but I can't hear them. I don't know what they are saying. I'm so nervous I start to chew on my shirt.

"Why are you eating your shirt, Mallory?" Jake asks me. "Stop it. It's weird."

I stop. Why is that weird? I'm nervous. I like to chew on things when I get nervous.

"Are you nervous?" I ask Jake.

He shrugs his shoulder. "A little." So if Jake's nervous, why doesn't he chew on things?

Mommy and Daddy get in the car. They are still talking. "Yes, I do," Daddy says. "I think that being with other kids and getting help from the teacher will push her a little. Being at school is exactly what she needs, babe. You'll see."

The teacher will push me?! And Mommy will see it! I don't like that. I hope my teacher doesn't push me. Now I'm more nervous. I feel like I want to cry.

"You're probably right," Mommy says. I look at Mommy and Daddy. I wait for them to tell me why my teacher will push me. But they don't.

Daddy starts the car. My mommy turns around and looks at me and Jake. "Alright. You both all buckled in and are ready to go?" She sounds so happy. I smile because I like it when everyone is happy.

"Let's go!" Jake screams again.

"Okay, guys. Let's do this!" Daddy says. He looks at Mommy. "It's going to be fine." He winks at her. She smiles. I smile, too, because Mommy is happy.

Now, we are pulling down the driveway. My stomach hurts more. I stop smiling. I look out the window at the grass.

The squirrel is back. I wish I could stay home with him.

He's soft.

7

eee

SEVEN MONTHS LATER

Laura

Time is a thief. Especially when you have school-aged kids, because before we knew it, fall had faded into winter, and winter morphed into spring, which means it's time for the second parent/teacher conference of the year.

Scott is out of town for a huge construction job, so I am flying solo to these conferences in late March. It's a rainy and dreary day, which is the usual March weather in Ohio. I walk the long pathway that leads to the school's entrance, tightening the belt on my coat one last time. Once inside, I pass the sign that says, 'Welcome Parents!' and I turn left to make my way to my kids' classrooms.

Liberty Elementary School is your typical school built in the sixties and in desperate need of a remodel. It's all on one level and is a labyrinth of hallways and smells like part mold, part old books. That old school smell you never forget as an adult.

First on my schedule is Jake, and I receive the same report I do every conference. He's excelling, reading at an advanced level, and he's well-behaved. Easy.

What has me on edge is Mallory's conference, and her room is across the hall from Jake's. There are parents in with her teacher, Mrs. Saad, so I glance around the hallway, trying to figure out what to do with myself while I wait. Along the wall, there is a row of wooden chairs leading to her classroom door. I pick one and sit down, the chair creaking as I settle in.

I think back to the first day of school in September. Mallory was so with-drawn that morning. I really had hoped that she would be eager about going to school. But she wasn't. She was quiet and reserved. Sending her off to this place was one of the hardest things I have ever done. At five years old, I was worried we had maybe sent her too soon. Waiting a year would have been okay. Yet here we are.

Mallory's conference in the fall went well. Mrs. Saad was getting to know her students, so there wasn't much to say. However, it has been seven months since school started, so I'm sure she will have more of an opinion because Mallory is struggling. I help her with her homework night after night, and it's always the same routine. She drags herself to the kitchen table. We start. She struggles, and she cries. Wash, rinse, repeat.

And forget about learning to read because she has no interest in that whatso-ever. And even though this is only kindergarten schoolwork … for her, it feels so much bigger and harder than that. Her memory of what she is learning is short. And this leads to tears every night at the dining room table.

I'm entering this conference with low expectations, bracing myself for dis-appointment.

The parents ahead of me in the classroom are taking up some of my time with their never-ending conversation. I can hear muffled laughs from behind the classroom door. I check the time as I tap my foot.

How long have they been in there?

I need to focus my attention on something to distract my mind. As I wait, I turn to consider some artwork that hangs on the wall behind me. Masterpieces hung with pride. I know Mallory loves art class, so I stand to find hers. My eyes pass along each watercolor. One of them looks like a sunset. One is a painting of a giraffe. Or is it? I can't tell.

I continue to admire all the pictures and view all the students' names. I scan them all, but I can't find Mallory's. I count all the artwork hanging in perfect rows. Twenty-two. There are twenty-three kids in Mallory's class.

Where is my daughter's picture?

As I continue to search, I hear the door open, and the other family walks out of the room. They exchange goodbyes with Mrs. Saad as they all shake hands. The parents walk down the hallway to leave, and we make brief eye contact, nodding at each other.

Mrs. Saad's voice fills the hallway as she glances in my direction. "Mrs. Givens?" My thoughts get broken up when I hear my name. I twist around and show off my wide, cheerful smile.

"Yes, hi," I say as I approach her, my arm extends to shake her hand. Mrs. Saad is a middle-aged woman in her late fifties. She's shorter, with dark hair, and she has glasses that sit on top of her head. She looks tired and worn out, with dark circles under her eyes. I'm sure those eyes have seen a lot.

"Thank you so much for coming tonight. Follow me this way," she says as she leads me into her classroom. I'm hit with a wave of nostalgia as I inhale the familiar smell of crayons and Elmer's glue.

She leads me to a red circular table in one of the four corners of the room. There's a sign above it that says, 'Learning Center.' The chairs are small and of different primary colors. I pick the green chair since it's my favorite color. Plus, I'm hoping that it will bring me some good vibes for this visit.

I take a quick scan of the room. On the opposite side is the 'Reading Corner.' Mrs. Saad's desk is in another corner of the room. It's perfect and organized. The last corner is the 'Free Time Station.' It's full of bins upon bins of toys. The middle of the room houses all the students' desks. And, of course, no classroom is complete without the traditional alphabet that lines the top of the wall above the chalkboard.

Mrs. Saad sits down and pulls out a file from a stack she has in front of her. I notice it has Mallory's name on it, but something else catches my eye. There is a red X next to her last name. A feeling of dread settles in the pit of my stomach because it seems like they flagged her file.

"Mrs. Givens, let me start by saying that Mallory is a joy to have in class." Her face radiates warmth as she starts, and I can tell she means what she's saying. "Mallory is so kind and helpful. Especially with me." I nod my head in

acknowledgment, my lips purse in a warm smile as she continues. I rub my hands
together nervously on the top of the desk. "However—"

"Oh, boy..." I cut her off, and I don't even know why.

She tries to comfort me by gently placing her hand on top of mine. "It's okay,
Mrs. Givens. Don't worry. Mallory isn't in any kind of disciplinary trouble."

I wasn't worried about that.

"But I have some concerns that I would like to discuss with you." She opens
the manila folder and hands me some of Mallory's work. It's only four papers.
I slide them from across the table and scan them over. Two of them are almost
completely blank, and the work done on them is illegible. No work is complete
on the third paper, which looks like sight word practice. There are only drawings and doodles. I'm not surprised. The fourth and final one is her artwork.
The drawing that wasn't hanging with the other students' in the hallway. It's
beautiful. I feel a wave of pride wash over me as I trace the lines of the flower she
painted.

She fixes her eyes on me as I examine it. "Her painting is amazing, isn't it?" I
sit silently and nod my head as tears form in my eyes. "Mallory is a very talented
artist. As a former art teacher, I can see her potential."

I shake my head to compose myself and hold back my tears. I clear my throat.
"You said you had some concerns, though?" I ask because I want her to cut to
the chase but also dreading what is about to come next.

"I do. Mallory has been exhibiting some behaviors that I want to bring to
your attention." Her voice grows a little deeper, taking on a more serious tone.

"Like what?"

"Well, for starters, Mallory never interacts or socializes with the other students. She eats her lunch here with me because she can't handle the noise
of the lunchroom. That's when she helps me the most. She is an exceptional
organizer!" She chuckles, and I feel the corners of my mouth tugging upwards
into a smile. "Do you see those bottom four rows of books over there on the
bookshelf?" She points to the opposite corner of the room, otherwise known as
the 'Reading Corner.' A cozy little nook that has a large tent that is full of puffy
bean bag chairs and pillows. Two bookshelves are to the right of it and are full of

easy readers. I drag my attention to the bookshelf, and the books are in perfect order. On the first shelf, they are organized by height. Tallest to shortest. The next ones are by color. The third row, by height. Fourth row, color.

"Mallory organizes those books every single day at lunch. She rotates them daily. And when the kids take them from the shelf to read, she watches them like a hawk to make sure they are put back in the right place." I'm still looking at the shelf as she describes my daughter's daily activities. I turn my attention back to the teacher as she continues. "Mallory also gets hyper-focused on things. When she sets her mind on something, she cannot and will not stop talking or obsessing about it." She pauses. "Mrs. Givens, has Mallory ever exhibited these types of behaviors at home?"

I stop and think for a second before I answer her. Mallory's stuffed animals in her room are all color-coordinated. When the TV is loud at home, it bothers her, and she covers her ears. She talks a lot about one certain subject. Like the time we told the kids we were going to buy them a special gift if they kept their rooms clean for a month straight. She knew what gift she wanted and didn't stop talking about it for the whole four weeks. That was a long month.

"No, not really." I lie, feeling my heart twist with guilt. *Why did I just do that?* Was it a feeling of embarrassment or, perhaps, a hint of pride?

Mrs. Saad nods (knowing I'm not being truthful) and pulls out a piece of paper from the manila folder. The top reads, 'School-Aged Autism Checklist.' She slides it across the table, and I pull it toward me. The left side of the paper is a column for teachers and the right for parents. I freeze as my eyes lock with hers.

"Do you think Mallory has autism?" I ask as my voice trembles, which catches me off guard.

"I think there is a possibility, yes." I take a moment to let her answer settle in. *Here we go again.*

First my mom a few years ago, and now Mallory's teacher.

"And, Mrs. Givens," she continues, "I'm not talking about the non-verbal type of autism. The autism spectrum is very broad. I suspect she may be on the higher end of the spectrum." She rests her calming hand back on mine. "I don't want to alarm you or upset you. But as her teacher, I feel it's my responsibility to bring this to your attention. That's why I wanted to give you this check-off list."

I glance at it again and notice that she has already completed her side of the list. Red checks, as far as the eye could see. The parent side, which I guess is where I come in, is blank.

"So, do you want me to fill this out and give it back to you? Then what?" My brain is spinning, and confusion sets in as I try to figure out what she expects of me.

"No, there is no need for that. The ball is in your court now. I recommend filling it out because no one knows your daughter better than you do, Mrs. Givens. No one. Now, if you decide we should test her for autism...."

Her voice trails off. She's talking to me, her words drifting through the air, but I'm too lost in my own thoughts to pay attention. It's like I am in a trance because her words sound muddled and hallowed. I thought she was going to talk to me about Mallory's lack of interest in learning how to read, not this.

She hands me a brochure for an institute that specializes in having children tested for autism. She explains her concern about Mallory's academic progress but feels it's more important to explore the other issue she brought up. Also, she talks about how talented she feels Mallory is in art, so she is going to assign Mallory to a classroom for kids gifted in the arts. I think I agree with this, but the room feels like it's tightening around me, so I'm not sure.

The conference ends, we exchange pleasantries, and I forget to thank her for all her hard work. I can feel her watching me walk down the hallway that somehow feels smaller than it was before. Moving through the school, I walk past parent after parent, classroom after classroom, until I finally reach my car. I'm thankful the rain has stopped, and I notice a rainbow in the sky. Normally, I get giddy at the sight of a rainbow, but today, I feel nothing.

With robotic motions, I put on my seatbelt, rest my elbow on the car door, and gaze out the window. I toss the papers she gave me on the passenger seat as I try to process the conversation we had. A weird sensation comes over me, and it's a strange feeling of detachment, like I observed that whole conference from a distance.

Questions swirl around in my head, and I have a full-on conversation with myself in the parking lot of the school.

What just happened? Your daughter's teacher thinks she has autism, that's what.

Should I tell Scott? I'll wait till he gets home in two days. No need to worry or upset him.

Do I fill out the checklist form? Ugh. I guess I should. I'll wait a few days.

Is Mrs. Saad right?

I don't have an answer for that last one. I am convinced that there must be another explanation. Something other than autism.

I pick up the pamphlet and study it, feeling the smooth paper under my fingertips. I crumble it up and throw it on the dashboard with force. My anger wells up, and I'm mad, but at who or what, I don't know. With my hands gripping the steering wheel, I close my eyes, trying to collect my thoughts and calm myself down. After a few seconds, I surrender to what seems to be my new reality. I study the balled-up pamphlet. Heaving a defeated sigh, I grab it, smooth it out, and stick it in my purse.

I try to gather myself together as I turn on the car. While I take a deep breath and smooth out my hair, I turn on some music to distract myself. I pull out of the school and drive the short distance home. Before I go into the house, I fish the pamphlet out and peek at it.

Nope. Can't process this right now.

As I shove it back in my purse, I decide to keep it and promise myself to look at it ... soon. I pull the visor down to check my appearance in the mirror before I go into the house. I'm shocked at what I see because I must have been crying on the way home, made clear by my red, puffy eyes, but I don't remember. So much for trying to play it cool.

I grab my purse and walk into the house to relieve my mom of babysitting duties. I decide not to tell her she and Mrs. Saad agree about Mallory because

I'm not sure I have the energy to handle the barrage of questions that would come my way.

As an attempt to empty my mind of the day's events, I spend the rest of the evening with my babies. We play a fun game of hide-and-seek, color together, then start our bedtime routine. I talk to Scott, who is laughing and relaying to me a Johnny story. Thankfully, it seems he has forgotten about the conference because he doesn't ask about it. I pour myself a glass of wine and settle in for the night on the couch, ready to see what *The Real Housewives* are up to. As I reach for the remote, I see my laptop across the room, and I remember the email that my mom sent to me all those years ago.

Did I ever read it?

I sit my wine on the coffee table, the burgundy liquid sloshing in the glass. Retrieving my computer, I make myself comfortable on the couch, propping my feet up and resting the laptop on my lap. I open my email and locate the folder I saved it under, scrolling until I find the five-year-old article.

When I finally do, I take a deep breath, a quick sip of wine for courage, and I click.

8

TWO DAYS LATER

Scott

"What are you reading over there?"

I glance over at my wife, lying on the couch with her face in a book as usual. I don't get the fascination she has with reading. She claims reading takes her into other worlds and helps her escape. My escape is being in my living room at the end of the day, watching whatever sport is on TV while sitting on my couch with a glass of bourbon. I read enough in school to last me a lifetime. Unless it's a job estimate or instructions on a new tool I've bought, I'm not interested.

"It's so good," she says as she turns the page with excitement. "The main male character is about to tell his long-lost love, who just came back into his life, that he married someone else. *And* that someone else is her former best friend."

"So yeah, just like the other hundreds of books you've read," I counter, my tone dripping with sarcasm.

"Hey!" She throws her pillow at me from across the room. I catch it with ease and place it behind my head.

"Thanks. I needed another pillow." I give her a sly, suggestive wink and a flirtatious smile.

"I like to read. So, sue me," she says as she closes the book and crosses the room. She stops, standing in front of me, and extends her hand. "Mind if I join you? I've missed you." This is also my escape. Having my wife in my arms. The kids sleeping in their beds only adds to the allure.

"No need to ask." I take her hand and pull her down next to me as she lets out a squeal. Holding her close, I feel the softness of her skin and the weight of her body against mine as she nestles her head into my chest. The smell of her coconut shampoo assaults my nose. I've been out of town on a construction job for the last few days, and, man, do I miss her and the kids when I'm gone. Johnny says I'm always on edge and crabby when we go out of town for jobs, and he's right. I'm miserable because I'm not near the three people who ground me the most.

I gently run my fingers along her arm as she slings her leg over mine. Goosebumps erupt on her smooth skin as she sinks deeper and deeper into me. Our bodies come together in a way that feels like a perfect puzzle.

She feels like home.

"How was everything while I was gone?" I whisper.

"Good. Nothing special happened. I had an awful day at work yesterday. Phoebe got fired, so we were down a nurse." I listen as she tells me all about Phoebe administering the wrong medication to a patient and how she left in a blaze of glory.

"Wait. Weren't the kids' conferences a few days ago?" I inquire, lifting my head to look at her. "How did they go?" I try to always come to these conferences. Mostly for support but also to show the teachers that Laura and I are a team. Which we are, of course. I know most dads don't care, or they think that this is only the wife's job.

I'm not that husband or dad.

When I ask her this, though, her body becomes rigid, and she hesitates to answer, shifting with unease.

Did something happen at the conference?

I fix my gaze on her. "Did you hear me, sweetie? How was the conference?" She wiggles away from me, stands up, and gathers up my empty bourbon glass and potato chip bag.

"Um ... yeah. They went great." She makes her way into the kitchen, tosses the chip bag in the garbage (Wait! That still had chips in it!), and sits my bourbon glass in the sink. I watch her from the back of the couch. She's acting strange. I mean, she threw away perfectly good chips.

She continues. "Jake is, of course, acing all his classes and work." She's now scrubbing the sink like she's mad at it. I can hear the squeak of the sponge on the stainless steel, so it's obviously already clean. Laura always cleans or has to busy herself with something when she's stressed.

"What about Mallory's?" I ask, fearful of her answer.

"Oh, you know, the usual." She tosses the sponge in the sink. "Mrs. Saad knows she's struggling, so they are going to work with her some more. That's all." She now has her face in the fridge. I can hear the clinking and clanking of glass as she checks the expiration dates on bottles of ketchup and mustard.

Why is she so stressed? It feels as if she is holding something back from me. But is she? I mean, normally, I am with her at these conferences, so I'm sure she would have told me if anything happened, even though I was out of town. Maybe there isn't anything to tell.

"Hey, so do you still want this hot sauce? It expires in"—she peers at the bottle—"ten days." Turning her attention toward me over the fridge door, holding the bottle of hot sauce in the air, she's tense.

Yeah. Definitely acting strange.

I stare at her as she glares at me with wide eyes, waiting for my response.

Do I pursue this? Is she holding out on me?

I don't know. Mallory is struggling, and it has gotten more noticeable. I see it, even though I don't talk about it. Even with Laura. For whatever reason, it's a conversation we don't tackle. Deep down, we both know why. Is it avoidance, or maybe denial? Who knows?

On impulse, I decide to hold back and not press the issue. I trust Laura, and I know she would tell me if something was off. Besides, I haven't seen my wife in three days, and I missed her so much.

"Nah. You can pitch it," I say as I get up from the couch and head in her direction. I swear I'm like a moth to a flame with my wife. Plus, she's so dang cute right now. She pulled her hair into a messy bun, and she's wearing black leggings with an oversized Ohio State t-shirt and no makeup. Her toenails are painted a blood red. My favorite. I come from behind her, shut the refrigerator door, and turn her around, placing my hands on her waist as she rests her hands on my chest. I kiss her tenderly.

"Let's say we go upstairs," I whisper in her ear, getting another whiff of coconut, hoping she gets my meaning.

She grasps my hand in hers, leading me up the stairs with a gentle tug. And just like that, I forgot what we were talking about.

Man, did I miss my wife.

9

FIVE MONTHS LATER

Laura

"Hey, sweetie! Did you have fun?"

"I did, Mommy! So much fun!"

If someone can see my face right now, I'm sure my eyes are beaming, coupled with a massive sense of relief. Mallory climbs into the back seat of the car and throws her pink sparkling backpack, Dora the Explorer sleeping bag, and pillow on the seat next to her. The excitement in her voice is contagious.

It seems surreal, but I'm picking Mallory up from her very first sleepover. A friend of mine, Amanda, called last week and asked if Mallory could come over and spend the night with her daughter Hailey and a few of her friends. It thrilled me that Amanda was thoughtful enough to include Mallory. Amanda and I have been friends for years, and our daughters are the same age.

But of course, I was nervous about the idea since, even at six years old, Mallory's social skills aren't the best. However, after talking it over with Scott, we asked Mallory and left the decision to her. We sat with her the week prior and asked her if she wanted to go. Her eagerness took us by surprise and filled us with hope.

"This is so good, Laura," Scott had said after we asked her. "I know she will grow out of all her little quirks. I can feel it happening. Being with other kids is exactly what she needs." Scott is trying hard to be optimistic. He has been hoping and even praying that somehow Mallory's quirks will magically go away. He grasps at every straw as some sort of sign that all our concerns will disappear and Mallory will be okay. It's as if he can't fully accept Mallory for who she is and feels the need to change her.

Despite this, the day we asked Mallory, I went to bed relieved, wondering if he was right. Mallory never wanted to be with kids her age, or people in general, for that matter. Yet here we were.

In usual Mallory fashion, she became obsessed with the sleepover and talked about it non-stop for the entire week. The sheer volume of questions was mind-numbing.

"Is it time for the sweepover yet, Mommy?"

"Hey, Mommy, when is my sweepover?"

"Mommy, when do we weave for the sweepover?"

"Can I take Saige with me?"

Saige is Mallory's American Girl doll, and she loves her! Saige comes with us everywhere. Into stores and restaurants, she even eats dinner with us in her own chair that attaches to the dining room table. Every American Girl doll has a story. Saige is an artist and a horse lover, which is why Mallory begged us to buy her because both are Mallory's new obsession.

"Mommy, don't go yet. I have to buckle in Saige." She carefully buckles the seat belt around Saige, her tongue hanging out in concentration. I hear it click in place. "Okay, Mommy, we are weady."

"Alright, awesome. Let's get going." I put the car in reverse and pull out of Amanda's driveway. As I pull onto the street, I honk and wave at Amanda as she stands on her front porch waving back.

"We are having pizza for dinner. How does that sound?" I ask as I turn out of Amanda's development.

"Yummy!" I glance at Mallory in the rear-view mirror, and she is stroking Saige's red hair. She loves to touch anything soft. Since Saige's hair feels like silk, she runs her small hand over it like Saige is her pet cat.

I pull onto the highway, heading for home. We have about a fifteen-minute drive ahead of us before we get to the pizza shop to pick up dinner. I'm tapping my fingers on the steering wheel, dying to know how this all went.

"So, sweetie, you said you had fun. What did you guys do?" Time to play twenty questions with a six-year-old.

"Pwayed."

"That sounds like fun. What did you play?"

"American Girl dolls. She has wots of dem, Mommy." Sometimes, her minor speech impediment is so cute when she talks. I love it when she says, 'wots' instead of 'lots.'

"Wow! That sounds exciting. How many does she have?" I ask this on purpose because I want to hear her say it again.

"A wot. I don't wemember. But they also had wots of candy." I laugh, secretly proud of myself. I got a double 'wot' this time.

"Were there any Smarties?" I ask because this is her favorite candy, and I'm sure she ate massive amounts of the small pastel-colored discs of sugar.

"Yes! Wots of them!"

We have another one!

When I let out a sigh of satisfaction, I feel a wave of relief wash over me. Scott was spot on. Mallory being with other girls seems to have done some good.

I stop asking questions, and I put on Mallory's favorite CD. We both start singing along to a song about dinosaurs as I drive down I-80. Her sweet little singing voice is filling the car. The sun is hanging lower in the sky since summer is ending. Tonight, my whole family will be back under one roof, eating pizza and watching a movie, and it all sounds next to perfect.

As I pull into the pizza shop, my cell phone pings. I put the car in park, turn off the ignition, and grab my phone out of my purse. It's a text from Amanda.

Amanda: Hey! Thanks for allowing Mallory to stay over! We all
had a great time. Would I be able

> to call you later? Maybe after
> dinner?

I read the text twice. What in the world could she want to talk about? I just left her house. Mallory said she had a great time. I text back.

Me: Sure! How about 7:00?

Amanda: Great! Talk to ya then!

I throw my phone back into my purse and stare at the entrance of the pizza shop.

What in the world does she want to talk about?

I shake my head free of my worry as Mallory, Saige, and I head in to get our dinner. I open the door. *DING!* The small bell above the door alerts the whole restaurant that we are there. The smell of freshly baked dough and spicy pepperoni fills the air. As I stand at the counter waiting for the blue-haired girl to get our food, I'm looking forward to the family time we are going to have this evening. I refuse to allow my thoughts to get the best of me and ruin my good mood.

However, the blue-haired girl is taking forever, and I can feel my mind racing as I wait.

Ugh. I've already failed.

— ele —

I'm so mad at myself.

I can't believe I ate four pieces of greasy pepperoni pizza. Stress eating at its best. At the sink, I rinse the dishes with anger, as if the plates have personally offended me and forced me to eat that much. As I load the dishwasher, I glance at the clock and notice it's almost seven. I exhale deeply, and my mind races with possibilities of what Amanda wants to talk about. I'm sure if Mallory left something behind, she would have said that in the text. Or did she get sick while she was there? Too many Smarties?

Nah. She would have called me when it happened if that was the case.

Scott notices I am preoccupied and wraps his arm around my waist as I stand at the sink, lost in my thoughts. He rests his chin on my shoulder and tightens his arms around me with a squeeze.

"What's wrong, babe? I can tell something is on your mind. You ate four pieces, so it must be big."

He knows me so well that I can't help but chuckle at how easily he can read my mind. "Oh, you know me. Always overthinking."

He clenches my waist and spins me around so we are face to face. "What's up? Is it the slumber party? I mean, Mallory hasn't shut up about all the American Girl dolls since she walked in the door. It's driving Jake up a wall."

"Yeah, I noticed his many eye rolls." I turn away from his gaze, my eyes settling on the smooth marble floor. "No, it's not that. Or maybe it is. Amanda texted me and wants to call me tonight at seven."

He furrows his brow. "Hm. Wonder what she wants to talk about."

"No clue. Based on what Mallory said, everything went great." I loosen myself from his grasp and turn my attention back to the dishes in the sink. "I'm sure it's nothing." I wave my hand in front of my face. "Maybe she wants to get a playdate together or something."

Scott kisses the top of my head. "I'm sure that's all it is." He smacks my butt and heads back into the living room but then stops and turns around. "Have I ever told you how cute you are in that apron?"

After eighteen years of marriage, that man can still make me blush like a teenager. I can feel my cheeks get hot, and I'm sure they are turning a pretty pink lemonade color.

I smooth out the front of the apron with my hands. "What ... you mean this old thing?" He laughs, then winks at me before heading back into the living room.

Yep. We are putting the kids to bed early tonight.

I take off the apron and hang it on a hook next to the counter as I glance at the clock on the stove. Six-fifty-nine. I know my phone will ring any second because Amanda is never late. I've known her since nursing school, and she is nothing if not prompt. She never missed a class and was never late for work. Heck, she even delivered her daughter on her due date. She and I work at different hospitals, but we have maintained contact over the years and even more so now because of Facebook.

Just then, I hear my ringtone, and I dig through my purse, feeling the vibration of my phone. As I fish it out, I notice Scott is busy watching Toy Story III with the kids, so I know I can have an uninterrupted conversation. A rarity in this house. I stare at the screen for a second or two, take a deep breath to steady myself, and finally hit the green button.

"Hey, Amanda! Right on time, as always."

"Oh, you know me so well! I hate to be late." She laughs so loud I have to jerk my phone away from my ear. She seems nervous.

"Let me say Mallory has not stopped talking about the sleepover since I picked her up. She had so much fun. Thanks so much for inviting her."

"Great! I am so relieved to hear you say that. Honestly, that's why I'm calling. I was so worried she didn't have fun."

Wait, what? She didn't think she had fun.

That makes little sense because Mallory hasn't stopped talking about it. "Why is that?" I close my eyes, knowing deep down what she's going to say. The tension mounts as I pace and gnaw at my thumb in the quiet kitchen.

"I mean, don't worry. She was fantastic and so, so sweet. But Laura, she kept completely to herself. Like, the entire time. I tried so hard to get her to play with the other girls. But all she wanted to do was sit on the upper bunk of the bunk bed and play with Hailey's American Girl dolls. Like, that's it. The whole time, that is all she did. Laura, I even had a hard time getting her to eat dinner last night and breakfast this morning. She was so focused on only the dolls. This morning, I asked her if she wanted to eat in the kitchen with the other girls, and she said no. Well, actually, she said 'No, fank you.' So cute. Anyway, I ended up bringing her pancakes, which she ate in bed. I was so worried since she was only eating Smarties. Hailey thought maybe she was sick or something." She pauses and takes a breath. "I was so torn about saying something, but I thought you should know. Mostly, I wanted to talk to you to make sure she had fun. Because if she didn't, I would feel terrible."

As Amanda tells the story of Mallory's first sleepover, a wave of emotion washes over me. I stop pacing because my feet are now rooted to the kitchen floor, tears pooling in my eyes. I'm numb, and all I'm aware of is the desire to end this phone call with Amanda and digest what she's told me. One thing is for sure: I'm keeping my worries about autism to myself. First, it's none of her business. And second, it would only worry her, and she would tell all our friends about it. Amanda is punctual and an amazing nurse, but she is also a gossip.

Ever since my conference with Mallory's teacher and reading the article from my mom, my suspicions have been growing. The only thing I haven't done is the check-off list Mrs. Saad gave me. I'm scared to see the red check marks because if I'm being honest with myself, I know there will be a lot.

"Laura, are you still there?" Her question knocks me back to reality.

"Oh, yeah, sorry. Amanda, thanks so much for telling me this. And let me put your mind at ease. Mallory had a great time. She is so in love with her new American Girl doll that I'm sure she had a brain aneurysm when she saw Hailey's collection. Dolls are her favorite thing." Not true. That would be painting and horses, followed by Saige.

"Oh, good! That makes me feel so much better!" There is a long pause, the seconds ticking by, neither of us knowing what to say next. "Okay, great!" She breaks the awkward silence. "So, I better let you get back to your family. It was so nice talking to you last week, and thanks again for letting Mallory stay. Hopefully, we can get the girls together soon." I know she is only saying this out of kindness and doesn't mean it. Especially after what she finished telling me. I'm not naïve. I know this was Hailey and Mallory's one and only play date.

"Yes, it was nice catching up last week. And anytime you want to have Mallory over again, call me, and we can work something out."

We say our goodbyes, and I hang up, slowly placing the phone on the kitchen counter. I'm leaning on the sink, squeezing the top of my nose with my fingers, trying to process everything. I take a moment to think back.

Last month, I showed Scott a Facebook post Amanda made about her and Hailey at the American Girl Doll store. We couldn't believe Amanda had bought Hailey another doll. I knew she had a ton already because Amanda posted about it every time she bought one. She loves to Facebook brag. "Those things aren't cheap," Scott had said. I remember Mallory sitting in the living room, and it dawns on me. Mallory remembered that conversation.

Gosh darn you, Facebook!

When Scott and I asked her if she wanted to sleep over at Hailey's house, of course, she was excited. She would get to play with all those dolls. Man, she is a smart kid! She can't remember the answer to one plus one, but this she keeps tucked away in the memory bank. I can't help but laugh quietly to myself.

I grab a bottle of wine and open it. When I reach into the cabinet to grab a wine glass, a wave of sadness hits me. Mallory said in the car, and about a thousand times at home, how much fun she had. Yet, she spent the entire twenty-four hours at Amanda's house alone. Playing by herself and never interacting with the other girls. For most kids, this would make them feel lonely and sad. But not my Mallory. The peace and quiet of being alone without the need to play with other children is something she finds enjoyable. Being forced to play and interact with others is overwhelming for her.

I'm relieved that Amanda didn't force Mallory to spend time with the other girls. I know my daughter. She would have cried and freaked out. She obviously saw Mallory was content and happy, so she left her alone. Amanda may be a huge gossip, but she was kind to my daughter and gave her a great first sleepover experience. I will always be grateful for that.

Right here and now, it's decided. I am going to talk to Scott and see if he is on board with getting Mallory tested for autism. After the movie, I will fill out the paper Mrs. Saad gave me so he can see how many autism markers she has.

But before all of that, I am going to pour myself a nice big glass of wine, head into the living room, sit on the couch with my family, and watch Andy give away Woody, Buzz, and all his other beloved toys to Bonnie.

That scene always makes me cry. It feels like a good way to hide my tears.

10

Laura

"Mmm ... this is nice," I moan as Scott runs his fingers along my arm, making my whole body tingle. I was worried Mallory would be up till the wee hours of the morning since she ate so much candy at Amanda's. But thank goodness, she was out like a light.

Scott and I have been lying under a sea of blankets as we talked for at least an hour. Neither of us wants to move, even though we both know we have to go to bed.

"She must have had a lot of fun. I bet they ran around Amanda's house like banshees. Screaming their heads off like little girls do when they get together. Pack mentality," Scott chuckles. I roll my eyes as I watch him laugh at his own joke.

"Well, that's the thing, babe. When Amanda called me earlier, that's what she wanted to talk about." Why I'm bringing this up now, when we are having such a lovely evening, is beyond me.

He lifts his arm and rests his elbow on his pillow. "Oh, really? What did she say? I was going to ask you about it, but we kinda got distracted." A playful smirk spreads across his face as he waggles his eyebrows.

"Stop!" I playfully slap his strong bicep, my favorite part of his body. "I'm being serious. She said that Mallory played alone the entire time. She never hung out with the other girls, not once. The only thing she wanted to do was play with Hailey's American Girl dolls. Amanda said she tried everything to coax her along, but nothing worked. She said that Mallory seemed obsessed with the dolls."

"Well, that's not too hard to believe. She loves her doll."

"But, babe"—I'm up on my elbow now, looking him square in the eye—"Mallory told me in the car that she had a blast. She has been talking about it all night long. Don't you think it's a little strange that her idea of fun is being alone in a house full of girls her age playing games, tie-dying shirts, and making cupcakes? These are things six-year-old girls love to do. She found more fun being alone than not being alone."

Scott lets the question dangle in the air for a second or two. His expression is unreadable. "So, she didn't play with the other girls? At all?" His eyes are downcast, his face full of uncertainty and fear as he starts picking at a non-existent spot on the bed sheet.

"No. Not once. Amanda said that she even brought her breakfast in bed because she wouldn't leave the room the dolls were in. I'm concerned, Scott."

"Concerned? Why?" His eyes shoot up, and his body tenses. "Maybe she was just excited because she loves her doll and had a chance to play with more of them. Maybe she felt uncomfortable. I don't know. Don't overthink this, honey." He kisses me on the forehead, and the weight of the mattress shifts as he gets out of bed. I watch as he pulls on his boxers. I turn over and lie on my back, staring up at the ceiling fan as it moves, sending a chill in the air. There is a massive knot in my stomach because not only is he dismissing my concerns, but he is accusing me of overthinking. Which, yeah, okay ... I do that. A lot. But this feels different. I decide I'm going to say it, so I sit up, the duvet rustling around me as I hold it to my chest. I take a deep, steadying breath.

Here goes nothing.

"Scott, I think there is a possibility Mallory may have autism." Scott freezes on his way to the bathroom. The statement hangs in the air, causing a silence that seems to stretch on for an eternity. He slowly turns, and I can feel his eyes on me.

"You *cannot* be serious?" he asks between gritted teeth.

I sit up a little straighter. "I am. There are just too many red flags. Or red check marks."

"What are you talking about, red check marks?" Confusion washes over his face as his eyebrows pinch together. I pull out the check-off list Mrs. Saad had given me from my nightstand drawer. While Scott was reading to Jake at bedtime, I filled it out. My tallies matched up with Mrs. Saad's, plus a few extras. Scott walks over to my side of the bed, and I hand him the paper. He studies it for a quick minute, then looks at me, frowning. "What in the heck is this?" he asks as he firmly grips the paper.

"Mallory's teacher gave that to me at her conference in the spring. She feels there is a chance Mallory has autism. Not the non-verbal kind. More on the higher end of the spectrum. I didn't want to believe it either, but then I read the article my mom sent to me a few years ago. Remember when she called me and had her suspicions?" He nods his head as he listens to me, yet his eyes never leave the checklist. "Anyway, I have been thinking, and she might have it. You have to admit she is showing some signs. I mean, look at the list." I choke out the last request, begging him to hear me.

Scott's shoulders slump in disappointment. "You never told me Mallory's teacher talked to you about this. When I asked you about the conference, you said it went well, but I could tell you were holding something back." He breaks eye contact with me and lowers his gaze to the floor. "Why didn't you say anything?" I can see the hurt etched in his furrowed brows.

I should have told him.

A wave of guilt hits me. "You're right. I'm sorry. I should have told you. But I didn't think you would agree. Plus, if I'm being honest, I wanted to avoid this"—I wave my finger between us—"having this conversation."

Without a second thought, he crumples the paper and chucks it in my direction. I hear it whoosh through the air before it hits the bed. He points his finger at me, his eyes boring into mine. "You can throw that in the trash," he hisses. "This is ridiculous, and you know it." He's lowering his voice yet is speaking with anger. He doesn't want to wake the kids but wants to get his point across. "Mrs. Saad does not know *my* daughter," he points to his chest as he takes steps to get closer to me. "I know Mallory, and she is fine, Laura. You are being paranoid and letting her teacher, your mom, and the internet get inside your head." He points to his temple, then back to me. "Just stop."

Well, that escalated quickly. Hurt to anger in a blink of an eye.

I'm filled with shock by his reaction, but I am not backing down. Scott has never talked to me like this before, and I won't put up with it. With force, I smack his hand away. "Get your finger out of my face! How dare you! I am coming to you about this because I love *our* daughter, and somehow, I'm the bad guy."

He lowers his head and shakes it in disgust as he crosses his arms over his chest. There is a long pause, and the silence is deafening. He brings his gaze back to mine. "So, was this your plan tonight?" he asks as he waves his hand over the messy bed. "Sleep with me, get me in a good mood, then spring this on me? Did you think you could butter me up and then talk to me about getting her tested because I know you, Laura? I know that's what you want to do." He jabs his finger toward me again, the air between us tense.

I'm staring at him in disbelief, and I can feel my throat tightening with emotion, but I refuse to cry. We've never argued like this before. I guess you could call it a whisper fight because that's what we are doing, hiding the screaming among hushed words. It's taking every fiber of my being to not lash out at him. I cannot believe he is accusing me of using sex to get what I want. As if I have manipulated this whole evening to get him on board. And to get what? Medical treatment for Mallory. Help for our daughter.

Unbelievable.

I'm seething as I hold the duvet so tight in my hand that my knuckles are turning white. I feel my pulse quicken as I glance away and exhale deeply before I speak, fearful I'll say something I will regret later.

Calm down. Take a deep breath.

I lift my head, tilt my chin up, and lock my gaze onto his. "Yes, Scott, you're right. Not about the sex; *that* was because I love you. The testing, though? That is *exactly* what I want to do. And I would love it if you were on board."

I'm calm, yet I have such conviction in my voice that I surprise myself. He shakes his head in disbelief and then turns on his heels, heading toward the bathroom. Before he enters, he straightens up and, without glancing back at me, says, "Absolutely not." He grabs the handle and yanks the door shut, causing the framed pictures on the walls to rattle.

Well, there you go.

I can't say that I'm surprised that he wasn't with me on this, but that. I wasn't expecting that reaction. It's hard to determine what's causing so much anger in him: me wanting to get her tested or not telling him about the conference, which I admit I should have. Either way, this evening didn't end the way I thought.

Hurling myself out of bed, I throw on my softest pajamas and walk downstairs while I clumsily arrange my hair in a messy bun. I'm shocked, sad, but most of all, angry. I keep replaying our fight in my head. His reaction tells me all I need to know about how he feels. He knows. He knows something isn't right with Mallory, and that outburst is him lashing out because of denial. As angry as I am at him for talking to me the way he did, I decide to give him some time to cool off.

Once I enter the kitchen, I reach for a glass from the cabinet and turn on the faucet. I hear the soothing sound of the water running from the tap as I fill the glass to the brim. As I drink, I see my purse out of the corner of my eye resting on the kitchen island. I sit my glass in the sink and go over to find the pamphlet Mrs. Saad had given me for the testing institute. It's still somewhat crinkled, so I smooth it out with my hands, head over to the fridge, and hang it up using a magnet. I stand there in the kitchen, with only the light above the sink illuminating the space, staring at the pamphlet. The sound of crickets outside fills the air as I feel a wave of determination wash over me.

I'm calling them first thing in the morning.

And no one, not even Scott, is going to stop me.

After I turn on the security alarm and double check we locked the house up for the evening, I head upstairs. I'm taking slow, deliberate steps because I'm in no hurry to go back to the bedroom. When I open the already ajar door, Scott is lying in bed on his side, but I'm not sure if he is sleeping. The duvet is tucked under his arm, covering his body. I can see his bare shoulder rising and falling. Deciding to say nothing, I crawl into bed and pull the covers up to my chin, feeling the weight of the blankets comforting me.

The bed feels cold and empty, even though he is lying beside me. A stark contrast to the warmth and passion it held two hours ago. I turn in the opposite direction and reach up to turn off the lamp on my nightstand, clouding the room in darkness.

Will I even get any sleep tonight?

I feel the mattress shift as Scott turns over. His warm arm wraps around my waist as he pulls me toward him. He's spooning me now, so I grab his arm as he squeezes me and then kisses me on the shoulder.

I can feel his warm breath as he whispers in my ear, "I'm so sorry." His soft lips kiss my shoulder again. "So sorry."

"Me too." I pause, not knowing if I want to say this now or let him see the fridge in the morning. I make a split-second decision, and before I know it, the words are spilling out of my mouth. "But Scott, I'm getting her tested," I whisper back. I hear him take a deep breath.

"I know."

11

Scott

I hold Laura close to my body, feeling her warmth until she drifts off to sleep.

Me? No sleep here. I'm lying here at two-thirty in the morning, seething with anger at myself and unable to take my eyes off the ceiling. How can I sleep after I acted the way I did? I apologized, of course, but Laura didn't deserve that. She's only trying to do the right thing for Mallory. She will forgive me because that's the type of woman she is. A classic Scott episode, lashing out because someone didn't agree with what I said.

Ugh. Why am I like this? I think I need therapy.

With a sigh, I roll over, give my pillow a few angry smacks, and curl up on my side, breathing in the scent of Laura's shampoo as I try to fall asleep. I grab my phone to check the time. Two-thirty-five. If I fall asleep right now, I can get three hours. Maybe I'll try counting sheep.

Three o'clock. *I bet lying on my other side will help.*

Three-thirty. *God, it's so hot in here!*

Four o'clock. *Is it raining outside? Great. That's going to screw up the job today.*

Four-thirty. *I hope Johnny remembers it's his turn for coffee.*

Five o'clock. *I can't believe Laura thinks Mallory is autistic.*

I slam my arms down on the duvet cover in frustration. *That's it. I surrender.*

It's time to throw in the towel. I can already feel the exhaustion of a long workday without sleep.

I ease the covers off me, the fabric rustling softly as I swing my legs to get out of bed, careful not to wake Laura. The chair in the corner of the room is cluttered with my work clothes, so I grab them and make my way to the office to change.

My brain won't quit, and I can't help but revisit the conversation I had with Laura last night.

Autism. *She thinks Mallory has autism.*

It's unbelievable. My baby girl is not autistic. She's different in her own beautiful way. And for some reason, this whole thing sparks some kind of anger in me I can't place. I'm mad. At what or who, I do not know at this point. Mad at Laura's mom for stirring the pot those few years ago. Mad at Mallory's teacher for presenting this to my wife. Still somewhat mad at Laura for wanting to pursue this. I'm also mad at myself for the way I treated Laura. I'm not sure I'll ever be able to forgive myself.

I can feel the intensity of my anger rising as I shove my legs into my jeans, pulling them up as if they have wronged me somehow.

Why doesn't anyone see this my way?

She's young, and she will grow out of this, I know it. But of course, everyone has to have a diagnosis attached to everything these days. It's annoying. I grab my shirt from the office chair and shove it over my body, tugging it down firmly.

I have to push this anger back down. Laura and I need to work through this because I can't stomach the idea of going through another argument.

No way. I shake my head as I put on my socks.

So yeah, it's decided. Ignoring it and hoping it will blow over is my strategy of choice. Everyone just needs time and space. Time to see Mallory grow and then they will see. She will not let us down. I know it.

After coming up with my plan of attack (which I admit is full-on avoidance), I walk down the hallway, the carpet feeling plush beneath my feet. I pass Jake's room and peek in. Of course, he's sleeping like the dead. The kid could sleep through a tornado. I chuckle silently to myself as I close the door, and the hinges creak. I cringe, hoping I didn't wake him.

Next is Mallory's room. I peek in with the intent of just looking, but something pulls me in. Because of everything, I feel a desire to be near her. Her room is dark, with only her Barbie night light illuminating the space. I have never seen so much pink in all my life. Pink walls, pink bedding, pink stuffed animals, and she is sleeping in pink pajamas that have cotton candy all over them. Pink is everywhere. It's like a bubble gum factory has thrown up in here. But she loves it, which means I love it.

On light feet, I walk over to her bed and crouch down beside her. Her eyes are fluttering, which I hope means she's having the best dream ever. I mean, what do six-year-olds dream about, anyway?

Mallory's always had dark blonde hair with curls in the end, but now it's changing into a chestnut brown. Right before our eyes, she is blossoming, and it's a privilege to witness.

I stroke her cheek, and her skin is baby soft under my callused fingers. With a gentle touch, I push her silky hair off her forehead. I could stay in this Pep-to-Bismal pink room and stare at her all day as she sleeps. My outburst toward Laura yesterday wasn't because I don't love and care about the well-being of my daughter. Far from it. I would put my life on the line and walk through fire if it meant protecting her; maybe this is what I'm facing now. A need to protect her. To fix whatever is wrong or going on. I'm her dad, and that's my job.

However, I know my wife. She will do what she thinks is best for Mallory as well. Even though I'm not comfortable with the idea.

My body tells me it's time to get up from this position. *Getting older sucks.* I stand slowly as my knees crack and pop on the way up. Then I lean down and kiss her on the forehead.

"See ya later, baby girl. I love you," I whisper as I spin around to leave her room, and GEEZ! Laura is standing in the doorway, causing me to jump out of my skin. I place my hand over my heart and suck in a breath. She laughs at my reaction.

"Sorry," she apologizes as she quietly chuckles. "I didn't mean to scare you."

I place my finger up to my mouth to signal her to be quiet as I shoo her out of the room and shut the door. "Well, you did, stalker. What the heck? Were you spying on me?" I ask once we are out in the hallway.

"No, of course not. You just looked so cute watching her sleep. All protective." She wraps her arms around my waist and gives me a hug with a loving gaze. "I liked it," she purrs.

Well, well. It looks as if she has forgiven me and remembers the better part of last night.

Thank God.

I return her embrace as I wrap my arms around her. I lean down and kiss her, one that should only be shared in the bedroom. We break apart, and her big, beautiful eyes meet mine, surrounded by her soft, dark eyelashes.

God, my wife is gorgeous.

I smirk and tease, "You need to brush your teeth."

"Hey!" She gently smacks me on the chest. "I just woke up, okay."

We walk to the kitchen to start our typical morning dance. Her, starting coffee and making herself some breakfast and lunch for work. Me, checking my emails before I leave for the day. Normally, we are chatty, but today, the air is heavy with an awkward silence. Finally, she pours herself some coffee and leans against the counter, the steam billowing up from the mug in her hands as she studies me.

I can feel her gaze on me, so I peer up from my laptop. "First you stare at me upstairs, now you're ogling me over your morning coffee. Is there a booger hanging out of my nose, or are you just thinking about that good morning kiss?" I'm being cheeky since I know what she wants to talk about.

"Haha. Cute," she says sarcastically, then she pauses. "Do you want to talk about last night? *Should* we talk about last night?" She places her coffee cup down and grips the edge of the counter with both hands.

I pause before I say anything and take a second to decide how I want to approach this. Drumming my fingers on the smooth granite kitchen island, releasing a low, steady breath, I choke out the words. "Laura, honey, I don't want to argue about this. It's pretty clear where we both stand, and I respect your wishes to get her tested. I do. I just don't agree with it. I'm sorry."

We linger in the moment, each of us waiting for the other to be the first to talk first. I can hear the ticking of the living room clock. Laura finally speaks up.

"Okay, then." She nods as she turns around and dumps her full cup of coffee in the sink. "I understand. I'm going to head upstairs to get ready for work," she says as she rinses out her favorite mug. "If you're gone by the time I get back, I hope you have a great day."

She doesn't even turn around to kiss me goodbye. I watch her leave the kitchen, her feet padding softly against the floor as she heads upstairs.

Well, I guess that was better than yelling at each other.

This tension between us isn't sitting right with me.

I take a second to refocus my thoughts on the email I was sending, bidding on an upcoming job. I hit send and close the laptop. When I look up, I notice a wrinkled pamphlet stuck to the refrigerator door with a magnet. I squint to try and read where it's from. "The Global Autism Institute Center for Treatment and Diagnosis," I read out loud to myself. My stool scraps along the marble floor as I stand and walk to the refrigerator. I remove the magnet and scan it as I turn it over in my hand. Laura has circled the phone number to call for new appointments.

I quickly hang it back up as if holding it in my hand is me agreeing with whatever happens next.

That's what I'm wondering, though.

What is going to happen next?

12

_ee_

ONE YEAR LATER

Laura

Global Autism Institute Center for Treatment and Diagnosis

September 14, 2014

RE: **Givens, Mallory**
DOB: 08/01/2007
PATIENT ID: 2651255
DOS: 10/01/2014

To the Parent or Guardian of Mallory Givens,

It was my pleasure to see your daughter, Mallory, in my clinic on 10/01/2014. Mallory was a joy to meet with. She charmed our staff with her eagerness and infectious personality. As you are aware, the reason for her visit to our center was regarding your concerns about possible autism. The symptoms Mallory presented with are listed below:

- Lack of eye contact

- Repetitive behaviors

- Obsessive thoughts/behaviors

- Lack of social skills

- Sensory issues

- PICA/eating of non-food items.

While in the clinic, Mallory met with our team of specialists in the field, including myself, different therapists, as well as our staff psychologist and psychiatrist. After our initial examinations of Mallory, we met collectively as a group to discuss her specific case and needs. Her official diagnosis is below for your records:

- Autism Spectrum Disorder/Level 1

In the past, this diagnosis went by the name 'Aspergers.' However, as of 2013, the names of the diagnoses have changed.

In accordance with her diagnosis, our team has decided that Mallory would benefit from the following therapies:

- Cognitive Behavior Therapy

- Speech Therapy

- Occupational Therapy

- ABA Therapy

- In school IEP

Feel free to call our appointment center at the number listed in the informational packet provided to you during your visit to set up these therapies. We will be happy to work with your schedule.

Thank you for using the Global Autism Institute for the diagnosis and care of your daughter. We look forward to working with you in the future!

Sincerely,

Phillip VanPatrick, Ph.D

Well, there you have it.

I lay the letter down on the kitchen island, and the torn envelope it came in rustles beside it. I keep my eyes on it, my finger tapping an impatient rhythm on the kitchen counter. Turning my gaze to the ceiling, my pulse quickens, my head is warm, and a knot of anxiety forms in my stomach.

I'm not surprised by the letter. I gathered with the team of doctors a week after Mallory was tested, and I felt the weight of their words as they shared the results. They supported me and patiently answered all my questions with understanding. And trust me, there were a lot of questions. However, even after that appointment and knowing what the outcome was going to be, having this letter in my hands makes it all that more final.

"Mallory has autism," I say out loud to no one in my quiet, dimly lit kitchen.

After I say the words, a sense of peace and acceptance fills me, and the reality of the situation sinks in. My seven-year-old daughter has autism. She has special needs. A disability. No matter the label, the truth is our lives are about to become much more complex.

My eyes wonder to the pile of mail that Scott had sifted through when he got off work. Ten different pieces of mail, all opened, except this one. The fact that he left the one addressed to 'The Parent or Guardian of Mallory Givens' unopened speaks volumes.

He is still trying to make sense of this whole thing. We haven't argued about Mallory's autism since that night in the bedroom a year ago. We also haven't talked about it ... at all. I provided him with the space I thought he needed. Thinking—no, hoping—it would help him accept our new reality. But now the space feels about as big as the Milky Way. Everything has been business as usual, of course, but there is tension between us. Something unspoken. And that unspoken word is 'autism.'

Scott knew we had the appointment. It took us a year to get in, which is unreal. I was astounded when I called the appointment center on my lunch break the day after our disagreement and they informed me the wait was that long. It was discouraging and upsetting, but most of all, the wait was excruciating. I made sure I had the appointment written on a Post-it and stuck it to the refrigerator so that Scott could see it. I hoped it would start a conversation, or he would ask questions. So often, I wondered how many times he opened that refrigerator door in a year. How many times did he see that yellow square piece of paper? Yet, he said nothing. Any mention or acknowledgment of it would have made me happy. Even a quick, 'Wow. I can't believe that appointment is two months away.' Instead, there was nothing.

I asked myself ... Was I overreacting? But somehow, that small, yellow piece of paper has caused an immense amount of tension between us. I just want something from him. Instead, after an entire year, I've got nothing. Scott made skirting around the issue an art form.

Then, to make matters worse, more troubling behaviors surfaced with Mallory. Her sensory issues increased. She can't have seams in her socks, tags in her clothes, nothing tight around her waist, and no scratchy fabrics. She's also begun tapping her fingers on her leg when she is upset. Which is a lot. And to put the cherry on top of this whole situation, we struggled through another school year.

I need my husband's calming presence to steady me during this turbulent time. I need his unconditional love, his infectious optimism, and his steadfast strength. He's present in every aspect of our lives, except this one. I feel so alone. So utterly and completely alone.

Scott's entrance into the kitchen jolts me from my thoughts.

Speak of the devil.

"Hey, babe! I didn't hear you come home. How was your day?" His cheerfulness is exaggerated. He is aware of what is in the envelope, and he's putting on a sunny demeanor to dodge it.

I fold the letter and quickly stuff it back into the envelope. "Hey, sweetie," I say as I lean into him and feel his lips brush against my cheek. "It was okay, I guess. How was your day?" I slide the envelope across the counter and tuck it under the stack of mail. He's scrutinizing my every move. I know he doesn't want to see or talk about it, so I hide it. I tuck it away like we have been doing with our feelings for over a year.

"What's that?" He inquires as he cocks his head to the side and his eyebrows raise, stretching out his arm toward the mound of envelopes.

"Oh, nothing important," I say, grabbing the mail before he can get to it, then placing it in the metallic mail bin that sits on the edge of the counter. I put in twelve exhausting hours of work today, accepted four admissions, and experienced two instances of being puked on by a patient. I don't have the energy for this dance tonight. The letter from our daughter's developmental pediatrician is still fresh in my mind. So, I can't stand here and act like everything is normal, talk to Scott as if nothing has changed, or pretend I'm not about to be inundated with therapy visits. What I need is to get out of this kitchen and go to a quiet place to gather my thoughts.

"I've had a long day, babe," I say as I turn to face him and place my hand on his chest. I can feel his heart beating under my palm. "So, I think I am going to go upstairs, say hi to the kids, and then take a long hot bubble bath."

Instead of paying attention to me, he fixes his eyes on the mail bin. I can hear the scratching sound of his hand against his stubble as he rubs his face. "Okay. I understand. I'll bring you a glass of wine. Sound good?"

"Sounds perfect," I say as I pat his chest and head toward the stairs.

Alcohol sounds like a fantastic idea.

13

Laura

A s I drag my exhausted legs up the stairs, I can hear my kids laughing in the distance. I'm eager to see them.

Jake retells his school day with enthusiasm, while Mallory excitedly describes Saige's imaginary journey. I can have the worst workday in the world, but being with these two beautiful humans is my everything. They bring me back to myself and remind me that getting puked on twice is worth it.

I head to the bedroom, shutting the door behind me with a soft click. The anticipation of how wonderful this bath is going to be is making me feel relaxed with each step I take. I sit on the edge of the bathtub and turn on the faucet. I listen to the sound of the running water, tapping my fingers under the stream until it reaches the perfect temperature. A nice cross between warm and scalding off my skin is my sweet spot. As I add the bubble bath, the tropical smell of mangos hits me. The bathroom fills up with steam, and the heat coming off the bath water already eases my sore muscles. I take off the hospital-issued scrubs since mine are in the trash bin at work, covered in room 305 B's vomit. I toss them in a heap on the floor right next to the laundry basket.

As soon as I dip my toe into the bath, I realize I forgot my phone in my purse.

With an annoyed sigh, I turn off the water, grab my robe from the back of the bathroom door, and make my way back into the kitchen. I round the corner of the stairs and stop dead. The letter from the doctor is lying flat on the island.

On light feet, I walk into the kitchen, feeling the chill of the tile against my bare feet. I see Scott sitting at the dining room table. His back is to me, shoulders slumped, head hanging, his elbows are resting on the table, and his hands are on top of his head. I linger for a moment and watch him. I know he read the letter.

Do I approach him? Should I ask him if he read it?

I'm frozen. The air in the room is so still that it feels like it is pressing down on my shoulders. On a normal evening, Scott is relaxing and sitting on the couch, watching TV with a glass of bourbon. But tonight, all I can hear is him breathing as I watch his back rise and fall.

Not knowing what to do, I reach for my purse to get my phone, trying to be as quiet as possible. I slowly slide it across the counter, but the big brass buckle on the handle makes a noise as it scrapes along the granite. He turns around, and the telltale signs of crying are there: his eyes are puffy, red, and watery.

I feel like I should approach him, put my arms around him, and tell him it's going to be okay. Assure him we will get through this. But I don't. I can't muster the energy to fight about this, so I remain silent.

Giving him a shy smile, I quickly fish my phone out of my purse. "I forgot my phone," I say as I hold it up. He nods, and the chair creaks as he turns back around. I let out a heavy sigh, my footsteps echoing in the stairwell as I make my way back.

Space, he needs space.

Eventually, though, the space needs to be filled.

I sit in the bathtub with my phone propped up on the tray that stretches across the tub. The lights are dim, and there are three different candles burning to make the bathroom smell like a citrus grove. Despite my best efforts, I can't seem to make my mind settle and relax. Normally, when I take a bath, I immerse myself in a book.

But not tonight.

Oh, don't get me wrong, I'm reading. But instead of a book, it's article after article about the different therapies Mallory will need. I feel like a fish out of water even though I did all the autism research over a year ago. I know everything that there is to know about autism, but these therapies ... this is a whole different ballpark. I wish I had my glass of wine, but I'm sure Scott's lost in his thoughts and forgot.

A few minutes later, I hear the hinges of the door as it opens. Within seconds, Scott is standing in the bathroom's doorway, holding a glass of Merlot. When I'm standing next to him, Scott's presence is commanding. He towers over me and is the sturdy tree that protects me from any storm. But tonight, something is different. He lacks the confidence his stature always brings when he enters a room. Grief-stricken eyes stare back at me, and I can feel the weight of sadness on his shoulders. Sometimes, no matter how big you are physically, feelings of being overwhelmed can make you feel small. That's what stands over me right now. A man who feels helpless and small.

"Hey, babe," I say softly. "Where are the kids?"

"Playing in Jake's room, I think," he says as he hands me the glass of wine. He closes the toilet seat and sits. "Sorry it took me a minute to bring this up."

"It's okay. No biggie," I say as I take a sip. The alcohol burns, and I feel the warmth as it goes down. The glass clinks against the tray, and I glance over at him. He is staring straight ahead with his elbows resting on his knees. I can tell he wants to say something because he's wringing his hands together. He slowly turns his attention to me.

"Why didn't you tell me about the letter? Why hide it from me?"

He doesn't appear angry, which is unexpected after our argument last year. Spending over twenty years together, I can tell what mood he's in the minute I see his face. But at this moment, I have nothing. It's unnerving since I have no idea what turn this conversation is going to take.

"I wasn't hiding it from you," I begin. "Well, not really. I would have shown you, eventually. You had to have seen it when you got the mail after work."

"When? When would you have shown me? Or talk to me about the visit?" Now I can read the lines on his forehead, and I see his wide eyes. He's hurt. But he doesn't get to be hurt. He's fully aware why I haven't talked to him about this. I'm the one that's hurt. So, I decide to remind him why.

I slide my tray down the length of the tub as I turn to face him and hear the water lapping against the sides of the tub. I place my bubble-covered arms on the edge. "Scott, come on. You have been avoiding this since day one, and you know it. You've seen me reading articles about autism. You knew we had the appointment scheduled, but did you ask me anything about it? No, you didn't. Do you know how bad that hurt *me*? I gave you space after our fight last year, but we need to talk about this. I mean, you see her, right? Do you? Do you look at Mallory? Like, do you really observe her? Because if you did, you would know. There is no denying it. That letter that sits on the counter. It's just confirmation." He lowers his eyes away from mine. "Scott, *please* look at me?"

He walks out of the bathroom without even glancing at my desperate face. I try to grab any part of him as he stands up. "Scott, honey…"

Nope. I'm done. He doesn't get to have more space.

"Scott," I plead as I get out of the tub. I know he hasn't left the bedroom because I didn't hear the door open. I wrap a towel around my warm body that's still covered in bubbles as I follow him into the bedroom. "We need to talk about this."

"You're right, we do," he says as he sits on the chair in the bedroom's corner. "We need a second opinion."

Dear Lord.

I stand in front of him, water dripping off my body, soaking the carpet under my feet. I throw my hand in the air and slap it on my leg in disbelief. "You can't be serious?" I snap back. "Scott, this institute is one of the best in the country. The doctor that signed that letter has a doctorate, for crying out loud. What more could another testing center tell us? What else do you need to accept this?"

"I don't know, okay!" he shouts. I flinch, his voice echoing as he lifts slightly out of the chair. His eyes are wide, and his hands are trembling. He turns away from me and peers at the world outside our window.

I kneel in front of him and place my hands on the rough fabric of his jeans. He looks at my hands and softens his tone as he takes in a shaky breath. "I fix things, Laura. I build things for a living. Then, if there is a problem, like with my crew, I fix it." He pauses before he continues. I rub my thumb lightly on his knee. "But my daughter ... I can't fix her. I can't make her better, and it scares the heck out of me. So, I avoided it. Thinking that maybe she just needed time."

He glances back out the window to gather his thoughts. "I'm her father, Laura," he says as he points to himself. "I'm supposed to protect her. She's my little girl." His voice trembles, and his chin quivers. "And I can't fix her. It's tearing me up. It's *eating* me up inside."

I can't help myself. I climb into his lap, and he grabs hold of me around the waist, pulls me to him, and buries his head into my wet shoulder. And weeps. I wrap my arms around him and stroke his hair as he lets out his grief.

This is the moment when you realize your child won't have a "normal" way of life. You know deep down that her life will be harder, people will be cruel, and there is nothing you can do to prevent that from happening. I have been through this same pain one year prior, so I know exactly what he is feeling.

He continues to hold me, and that space that has been there for over a year is finally closing. He composes himself and pulls back. His eyes are red and bloodshot. "What are we going to do?"

"We are going to be there for our daughter," I declare as I look him in the eye and cup his face in my hands, the stubble rough to my touch. "Scott, honey, Mallory doesn't need to be fixed. She needs our love, our help, and our support. But what I need from you is to hear you say it. This needs to be real for you, so you need to say it out loud."

"Say what?" he whispers as we touch our foreheads together.

"You need to say, 'Mallory has autism.'"

We don't move, and I can see his labored breathing. He pulls his forehead away from mine, glances out the window again, then turns his attention back to me. His eyes light up with his usual confidence.

"Mallory, my beautiful, vivacious, and amazing daughter, has autism." He lets out a deep breath, and his lips tick upward into a small smile. "Phew. That wasn't so bad."

I kiss him quickly, and he grabs my face and returns the kiss with a deep, lingering intensity. This isn't a kiss that has passion attached to it. It's a kiss that has strength behind it. A kiss that pulls us back together and makes us whole again. He pulls my face away and scans it. He wipes a stray hair from my cheek. "I'm so sorry, babe. I should have been there for you. But I'm here now. I think seeing that Post-it, then seeing that letter, and saying the words just now is what scared me the most. Acknowledging any of it would have made it real. If I just ignored it ... ignoring it ... well..." he lowers his head in shame. "Ignoring it meant it wasn't happening. I know that sounds ridiculous. But all I managed to accomplish was create a rift between us, and then I wasn't there for you ... or Mallory." He trails off, then he raises his head, and his eyes meet mine. They are full of regret and pleading. "Please, forgive me."

"Of course, I forgive you," I whisper. His powerful arms wrap around my waist as I hug him close. We embrace the warmth of our bodies, releasing the tension of all the unspoken words this past year.

We let go as he takes hold of my hands, places them in my lap, and squeezes twice. A gentle smile spreads across his face as he slides his hand along my jaw. His eyes are now shining and locked on mine, and in a voice dripping with confidence, he says, "Now, let's go give our daughter the best life possible. Can we do that together?"

"Let's do this," I answer with a smile. My rock, my strength, has made his way back to me. Together, there is nothing we can't do.

Just then, a single solid knock on the door breaks up our moment. "Mommy, are you in there?"

It's Jake. I'm sure he's wondering where his parents disappeared. "Sure, honey, come on in," I say as I turn to face the door.

He walks in and stops as he cocks his head to the side. "Mommy, why are you sitting on Daddy's lap covered in bubbles?"

14

NINE MONTHS LATER

Scott

"Are we there yet?" Jake's question rings out from the back seat so high-pitched and whiny it grates on my ears.

I'm positive I've heard Jake ask the same question fifteen times in the last hour. And we are only four hours into a ten-hour drive to North Carolina to see my brother.

You could say this trip is a gift to us as a family. We have all come to terms with the diagnosis of autism. After I wrapped my head around the contents of the letter, we finally told Jake. He was confused and asked a lot of questions, which is typical of him, but he handled it well. Nothing has changed for the two of them. Not yet, anyway.

Now it feels like our lives are consumed with many types of therapy appointments, IEP meetings (don't even get me started on that fiasco), and extra tutoring for Mallory. It's been an overwhelming amount of stress. So, this vacation is a much-needed break from the busyness that has become our life. It's June, and another school year has come and gone. Now, it's officially summer, and we are all ready to cut loose and have some fun.

"Okay, buddy, you need to stop asking. We talked about how this was going to be a long drive, remember," I remind him as I watch him through the rearview mirror. "You have plenty to keep you busy."

He lets out a huff, shifts in his seat, and crosses his arms over his chest. "I know. I'm just so *bored.*"

I glance at Laura, who is peacefully sleeping, her head swaying gently with the motion of the car. *No help there, I guess.*

This entire conversation with Jake reminds me of my brother. His whiny voice would echo through the car when we went on trips like this, driving me up the wall. He and his wife, Shayla, moved to the beach about a year ago, almost immediately after getting married. It devastated my mom when they left. The city of Wilmington offered her an amazing job, and I can't blame them for taking it.

Did I mention that Kyle is also my mother's favorite? Of course, she would never say it out loud. What mother would? But I know it's true. Kyle can do no wrong in my mom's eyes. He's the baby of the family, and there were different expectations for him compared to me.

I had to mow the grass every spring, summer, and fall. He had to keep his room clean.

I had to shovel the drive every time it snowed. He had to make his bed.

I had to wash the family car inside and out every week. Kyle had to vacuum the house (which I know he skimped on).

I decided not to go to college, which disappointed my mom. Kyle got his degree and had a gigantic party to celebrate.

Needless to say, this has all led to a lot of tension between him and me over the years. We support and love each other, of course, but we barely speak. We are not close ... at all. That's why I was so surprised when his wife Shayla called Laura to invite us to spend a week at the beach with them (he didn't call me. Did you notice that? Nope. Sent his wife to do it. Typical.). We all chipped in and rented a huge house right on the shore.

They invited Johnny too, but he couldn't make it. Which I was wholly disappointed about. Johnny has always acted as a buffer between Kyle and me. I'm going to be anxious without him there. I feel my heart beating fast at the thought of a possible argument with my brother. We only agreed to this trip so the kids could have an ocean experience. Playing in the waves, building sandcastles, collecting sea shells. I can put my differences with my brother aside for my kids. I hope.

"Here, Jake," Mallory says as she reaches across the back seat to extend her coloring book to her brother. "Color with me." I see Mallory trying to hand him her pouch of markers. She must have heard the strain in my and Jake's voices because Mallory becomes anxious in tense situations. And she will do anything necessary to diffuse the problem.

Jake shoves it away. "No, Mallory. I'm too old to color," he snaps back as he slouches in his seat and looks out the window. When did nine years old become too old to color?

This is going to be a long six hours.

I can hear the markers clinking together as Mallory turns her attention back to her coloring and sifts through the colors. "Daddy, I don't have to hug Uncle Kyle or Aunt Shay, do I?" I knew this question was coming. I glance at Mallory in the mirror and see her tapping her leg, which is also bouncing.

"No, of course not, honey. Remember, I talked to Uncle Kyle about it? So, no worries."

"Okay," she says without so much as a glance at me.

Mallory has been stressing about this for months, ever since we told the kids we were coming on this trip. That's because Uncle Kyle and Aunt Shayla are not on the Hug List.

Mallory often feels overwhelmed by the feeling of being touched, a common struggle for many on the spectrum. It's part of her sensory issues. Her personal space is just that, personal. She doesn't like hugs, shaking hands, or even snuggles. And sometimes, this even includes Laura and me, which can be difficult. Fist bumps are okay, though. We fist bump a lot, and I can't get enough of them. But, if you are on the Hug List, well, then you are golden.

The Hug List is Mallory's list of people she will give hugs to. The list is small. It's Laura, myself, her brother, her grandparents, and, well, that's it. Those hugs are precious and rare moments. But when we get one, it's incredible because we know they don't come naturally to her.

When I talked to Kyle to finalize everything before we left, I told him about the Hug List. Of course, he didn't understand and had to be all *Kyle* about it. Because Kyle knows best. Did I mention he is also a know-it-all?

"What do you mean I can't hug my niece? That's ridiculous, Scott. I haven't seen her in like forever," Kyle replied when I explained it all to him the day before we left.

"Kyle, I know it's unusual."

"Um ... yeah, it's weird."

"Hey! It may be weird to us, but it's very important to Mallory. Can you respect that, please?" I implored while I was packing the car. Holding the phone between my ear and shoulder, I was getting angrier by the second. I yanked the suitcases from the ground and threw them into the car. Why does he always have this effect on me?

"Well, maybe you could talk to her and explain to her that her uncle and aunt have missed her and want to hug her. You're the parent. Tell her what's expected of her." Then, I knew what was coming next. "I tell you what, when Shay and I have kids, we won't let them walk all over us. Nope. Won't happen." He isn't even a father yet and has it all figured out already.

God, why is he such a jerk? I wish Johnny was coming. He's on coffee duty for a month. I know he isn't coming because he hates Kyle. Can't say I blame him.

"Okay, yeah. Call me when it happens and let me know how it's a cakewalk for you. Can't wait to hear all about it," I said as I tried to slam down the trunk. After three attempts, it finally shut, and now nothing fit right. Which meant I would have to repack it later. Great.

"Alright, fine." he huffed. "I'll tell Shay, and we won't hug her. Happy now?"

I trudged back toward the house, my breath getting heavier with each step, and the air felt thick with tension. If that's even possible through a phone call.

"So, is this part of her so-called autism?" I froze because I couldn't believe he asked this question. I don't know if I could contain myself if I saw him face-to-face. Whenever I'm about to retaliate against my brother, I recall the sound of my mom's voice reminding me to think twice. I'm aware that our dislike for one another makes her sad, and I would never want to cause her any distress.

I closed my eyes and pinched the bridge of my nose, inhaling deeply before I answered him.

Mom.

Mom.

Mom.

"It's not 'so-called,' Kyle. She has autism," I said through gritted teeth as I walked into the house and saw Laura. She could read the frustration on my face and mouthed, 'Who is that?' I mouthed back to her, 'Kyle.' She rolled her eyes.

"I mean, I know you told me that's what the doctor said, but maybe he is some kind of voodoo quack that doesn't know what he's talking about. I mean, I would never settle if it was my kid. You should get a second opinion." I stared up at the ceiling, chewing on my bottom lip as he spewed his crap.

"Kyle, we aren't settling —" I stopped and closed my eyes, trying to quell my anger that was bubbling up. Laura sensed it also because she walked up beside me and started rubbing my back to calm me. She knows how much my brother grates on my nerves. "Look. I had a hard time accepting all of this, too. But it's our reality now. As your brother, I am asking for you to respect Mallory on this one. Please."

"Alright, man, whatever. It's weird is all I'm saying," he said with contempt in his voice.

"And you'll tell Shay?" I implored.

"Um ... of course I will. Geez. Would you calm down about this? You're always so serious all the time. You need this vaca to relax some. Autism isn't that big of a deal. Give it time. You'll see." Of course, he said this. I needed to wrap up the conversation fast before I made a comment I'd later regret.

"Okay. On that note, I'm going to go. See you in about twenty-four hours."

"Yep! Drive safe." With that, the phone went dead. I pulled it away from my ear and stared at it, and one thought came to my head. What does Shayla see in him?

The breathtaking view of the rolling mountains of West Virginia brings me back to the present as I drive. Country music plays from the radio as we wind our way through the highway, the only station available in the remote area. Up one mountain and down another.

It's only a week. The last time Kyle and I were under the same roof for an entire week was right before I moved out. Despite that, I can do this.

For my kids.

For my wife.

For our family.

15

Laura

"WHOA!" Jake exclaims as he grabs my arm. He has taken his first steps onto the sand, hearing the gentle lull of the Atlantic Ocean rolling in front of him. It's huge, powerful, yet peaceful. He stops, his eyes wide with excitement. "This is *way* better than Marshall Lake!"

I chuckle. "You're right, bud. This is way better."

After ten long hours in the car, we arrived in Wilmington, and the summer breeze was a welcome relief. The sun is setting, and it paints the ocean a beautiful pinkish color. The air smells salty, the wind is warm on my skin, and the sound of the waves is repetitive and soothing.

Man, I love the ocean.

Scott and I have been looking forward to bringing the kids here for months. This is their first trip to the ocean, and after seeing Jake's reaction, the long drive was worth it. The way he looks at the open water with such wonderment and awe makes you want to be a kid again.

"Come on, guys! Let's go!" Scott's feet pound the sand as he runs toward the ocean shore. Jake and Mallory run after him, their legs pumping at full force. Mallory lets out an excited squeal, which I think was supposed to be a laugh. They take off their shoes, and all three of them run toward the water, and as a wave comes in, they scamper away. The same thing happens over and over. Run toward the ocean, a wave comes, run away.

I sit down, take off my flip-flops, and wiggle my pink-painted toes in the sand as I watch the three people I care about most in this entire world get lost in the ocean's beauty. Scott loves the water and anything associated with it. Boating, swimming, surfing, fishing ... he has tried it and done it all. He says the sound of the ocean soothes him like nothing else.

Which is why Scott wanted to stop here first before we went to the beach house. His body was stiff the whole drive down, and I could tell from his nervous gaze that he was anxious about spending time with his brother. They are like oil and water ... they don't mix. And never will.

He relayed to me the conversation he had last night with his brother, then promised he would be on his best behavior.

I can only hope and trust that he will try his best, as this week will be taxing. I put all of that out of my mind as I watch my family play in the waves. Curling up into a ball, I wrap my arms around my knees and tilt my head to the sky, feeling the warmth of the sun on my face.

"Come on, Mommy!" I see Mallory standing next to me, her hand outstretched toward me. I get up and wipe the sand off my butt as I head toward my daughter. We race together toward the ocean, the sunlight reflecting off the waves. Then, turn around and run away before the wave catches us. The sound of Mallory's laughter fills the air.

"You made it!" Shayla greets us at the door with arms wide open. Her feet barely touch the ground as she jumps with excitement, her braids swinging in tandem. I wish I had an ounce of her energy to get me through the day. She encases me in a hug and squeezes tight. Next is Scott, then Jake.

I turn to search for Mallory, and when I see her, my heart drops. I can hear her heavy breathing and see her body tense up. Her eyes are wide, and I know she is scared and trying to stay calm. Getting hugged by someone she doesn't know or isn't on the Hug List is like a death sentence for her.

However, Kyle must have filled Shayla in on the situation. She squats down to get to eye level with Mallory. "Hey, Mallory. I missed you, and it's so nice to see you again. How about a pinkie shake instead of a hug?" She extends out her pinkie to Mallory. The woman who was jumping and squealing seconds ago is now talking in a low, soft voice. Mallory's posture changes instantly, her shoulders drop, and a smile spreads across her face as if someone has flipped a switch. Then she does something that is so shocking it blows me backward. She looks Shayla in the eye.

"Yes, that would be good. Can it be our secret handshake?" Mallory asks as she extends her delicate pinkie, wraps it around Shayla's, and shakes.

"Heck yeah, it can be!" And in an instant, my sister-in-law has a new buddy. Autistic kids can have a hard time with attachment. But when they feel a connection with a person, they do just that. They connect. And it's the most genuine thing in the world.

Shayla stands and sends me a knowing smile before her fingertips tap my arm lightly. The small gesture feels as if she is saying, 'I understand, and I got this.'

A booming voice comes out of the kitchen. "There's my family!" Hurricane Kyle enters the scene. "Where's my big brother at?" Scott steps forward, and Kyle claps him hard on the back in a hearty guy hug. Mallory turns her head away from the outburst and takes two steps backward. Shayla notices Mallory's sudden change, so she walks over to her and whispers something in Mallory's ear. I have no idea what, but Mallory's eyes fill with delight. She's giggling, grabbing Shayla's hand, and heading toward the kitchen with her new buddy.

"Hey, little brother," Scott says with a weak smile and obvious tension in his shoulders. "Thanks for inviting us down here."

"Of course! I figured you needed the break from hammering nails into wood, ya know?" He fakes a laugh while pretending to wield an imaginary hammer before smacking Scott on the back. Kyle has always demeaned Scott's construction business and skills hidden under the guise of a joke. Much to Scott's irritation. Kyle loves to bring up Scott's lack of a college degree any chance he gets.

Scott doesn't miss a beat and keeps his cool. "Well, it's a little more than that, but you're right. This trip will be an enjoyable break." He shoots me a look, his posture growing straighter as I give him a subtle smile. I can tell he is proud of himself for not reacting.

After we find our rooms, do some unpacking, and eat dinner, we all make our way to the back deck that overlooks the ocean. The view is spectacular, and I can feel myself getting excited about the week ahead as I watch Scott build a fire. The air is filled with the smell of wood smoke and the sound of laughter as the adults sip their drinks and the kids make s'mores around the fire pit.

So far, so good. It's been three hours, and the terrible twosome are being cordial.

Only a week left.

Three hours is apparently too long for Kyle.

"So, Johnny couldn't make it, huh? That must have bummed you out?" Kyle questions Scott while he savors his third glass of bourbon. Kyle has always envied Scott and Johnny's relationship. I guess he has enough liquid courage in him to poke the bear.

Scott's chest heaves before he answers. "Yep. It was a bummer. But it's all good. I'm excited to spend some time with you guys." He glances over his shoulder at Shayla, who is busy helping the kids make their s'mores. Mallory is mesmerized by her aunt, her face glowing with delight as she hangs on to Shayla's every word. "It's wonderful seeing Mallory getting attached to someone like this," Scott says as he watches his daughter giggle at whatever Shayla has said.

"Mm-hm," Kyle takes another sip. "Well, I told Shay to be extra nice to Mallory. You know, because we have to and all."

Crap. What the heck, Kyle?

Scott sets his rocks glass down on the table and bends at the waist, sitting with his elbows on his knees. "What in the heck does that mean, Kyle? Are you just doing us a favor? You know, out of the kindness of your heart."

"Dear God, you are so sensitive. Lighten up. You know what I mean," Kyle says as he takes another sip of his drink. Scott remains still, listening to the waves as he considers what to do next.

"Nope ... can't say that I do. Enlighten me." Scott claps his hands together.

Kyle sighs heavily, his head rolling back in exasperation. "I mean, since she is"—he air quotes—"special."

A few moments of conversation, and that was it. Scott bolts out of his chair, his finger jabbing in Kyle's direction. "You're damn right she is special. She is more special to this family than you will ever be."

The small outburst catches Shayla's attention. She can feel the palpable tension in the air and sense the situation is deteriorating. She quickly ushers the kids into the house, their chatter growing fainter as they make their way to the TV.

Kyle slams his glass down, bourbon spilling from the side. He's now on his feet, swaying a little from all the alcohol, and they are standing inches from each other, eye to eye. "Oh, here we go!" Kyle shouts. "Let's hear how special you are, Scott. Scott, the golden boy. Scott, with the huge successful construction business he owns with his *cousin* and *best friend*. Scott, with the perfect life. Scott, who has always been Mom's favorite! Scott, who now has the special needs kid, so she needs all the attention! Let's all bend over backward for Scott and his retarded daughter!!"

The next thing I know, I hear a loud crack as my husband's fist connects with Kyle's jaw. Kyle's head snaps back, and the rest of his body follows. The punch knocks him backward a few feet, and he lands on the deck with a loud crash, breaking a small patio table on impact. Shayla yells in shock and jumps, hurrying over to her husband. I sprint over to Scott and grab him with both hands, trying to pull him away from his brother. Scott's determined strides make my efforts seem like nothing as he stomps over to Kyle, grabbing his shirt. His arm is coiled backward, ready to strike yet again. The scene is total chaos and feels as if it's happening in slow motion. Kyle meekly curls up into a ball, his hands held up in surrender.

"Scott, please!!" Kyle cries out, desperation in his voice. "Stop!"

Scott steps back and lowers his arms, his chest heaving as he continues to loom over his brother. He looks at me, then into the house at the kids. They are blissfully unaware, their eyes glued to the TV screen as Scott hesitates, contemplating his next move. He mumbles something under his breath, kicks my chair, then marches down the deck steps and onto the beach, leaving footprints on his way to the shore. I turn my attention back to the scene, and I see Shayla's nostrils flaring, her breathing becoming more rapid. I'm half expecting her to yell, but she focuses her eyes on her husband, and I realize that her anger isn't directed at me or Scott.

Kyle is still lying on the deck, and his eyes are wide and blinking rapidly. Blood is dripping from a cut on his lip, which is red and already starting to swell. I have seen my husband get mad, but I have never seen him lay a finger on anyone. However, I have a feeling that punch had years of pent-up frustration attached to it. I peer out at the dark ocean, and I can faintly make out Scott in the distance. I pivot to look at Kyle and Shayla, then back to the shoreline. Deciding that I need to be with my husband, I turn to walk to the beach.

"Laura, no!" Shayla's voice booms in the night, startling me and stopping me in my tracks. "Stay right here."

She stands, taking in the sight of her husband. "Kyle, get up!"

Slowly, Kyle steadies himself on the Adirondack and stands to his feet, dabbing blood from his lip as he does. He turns his head, his eyes meeting hers as she gets close to him. "I have never yelled at you, and I have never told you what to do, but enough is enough with you two. I cannot believe you used that disgusting word!" She gestures to the shoreline. "Now, I want you to go down to the water and apologize to your brother."

"What! He hit me, Shay! He started it!"

Shayla raises her hand in protest. "Just stop!" She jabs her finger into his chest. "You know you started this. My God, Kyle, you sound like a toddler! You demeaned your niece ... to his face! And called her the worst thing you could ever say!" She stops and gazes around her, hands on her hips. She takes a long, deep breath. "Now, I know Laura will agree with me when I say that Scott has been in the wrong tonight by hitting you."

Correct. Well, kinda. Kyle did use the "R" word.

She continues. "But for the sake of this family, you two need to work this out. Mallory needs us to be united and in her corner. She needs her uncle to be by her side. This means you and Scott need to work this out and come to some sort of understanding. We can't have you two at each other's throats every time we are together. Imagine how that will stress her out. Mallory will hate and resent you. Is that what you want? For heaven's sake, you don't need to be close. Just be brothers."

Kyle's gaze slowly shifts downward, his hands settling on his hips. I can tell she has hit a nerve. "Now go down to that beach and talk to your brother. Then, when you are done, you will go into this house and spend some time with that wonderful little girl in there. Because if you do, you will see how special she really is. And that's because of her"—she points at me—"and because of him." She gestures in Scott's direction, and I can see her hand shaking.

She shoves his shoulder. "Now go! Laura and I will be in the house with the kids, waiting for you two. And don't step one foot in this house until both of you can act like adults, and I suggest you do because it's going to rain tonight. I would hate to sleep on the deck if I were you two."

Game. Set. Match.

I really, really like Shayla.

Kyle rubs the back of his neck and walks past me. He gets to the steps that lead down to the shore and pauses as he glances over his shoulder, remorse filling his face. "I'm so sorry, Laura."

I nod to him, the chill of the shore breeze rustling his hair as he walks toward his older brother. Shayla and I watch as he stops next to Scott. Standing side by side, with their hands in their pockets, they look identical from behind.

"Dang, Shay. *That* was amazing!" I glance at her, the wind blowing my hair and partially obscuring my view of her chocolate-brown skin. I sweep it away with a single motion.

"Thanks," she says with a shy smile. "It needed to be said. Mallory needs us to be united."

As I observe this woman I barely know, my heart fills with a deep respect for her.

I can't help the soft, satisfied hum that escapes my lips as a small smile appears. "You're right, she does."

We gaze back out at the shore. Scott and Kyle are talking calmly. A victory for sure, even if it's small. Shayla releases a sigh of relief. She whirls around to face me, her eyes bright with curiosity as she pops her hip out and rests her hand on it. "Did I see you bring ingredients to make margaritas?"

I let out a hearty laugh, understanding her meaning. "You did."

She flicks her thumb in the house's direction and smirks. "I don't know about you, but I need one. Like, now."

Scott and Kyle spend three hours in the dark, trying to work through decades of resentment and jealousy. Shayla and I spend three hours with a pitcher of margaritas, becoming fast friends. I'm pretty sure we have more fun.

With kids crashed out on the couch sound asleep, I'm in the kitchen washing away any evidence of our alcohol-induced bonding session. Shayla is covering the kids with blankets when the door to the back deck creaks open. Scott and Kyle walk in, and, to my surprise, they appear lighter, happier even. The blood on Kyle's face has dried to his chin, and his lip is double the size it was three hours ago. Shayla stands from her position near the couch, her eyes darting between them, her face stoic. "You guys cool?"

Scott flashes me a warm, fleeting smile before turning to his brother, his expression suddenly more serious. "Yeah, we will be. It's a start."

"Good." Shayla utters a content sigh as she makes her way to her husband and embraces him. After a few seconds, she starts searching for the First Aid Kit from under the kitchen sink.

Scott walks over to his brother and slaps him on the back. "Now go wash your face, little brother. It looks like you were in a fight."

Kyle chuckles as Shayla tends to his lip. "Yeah, you should see the other guy."

Scott pauses. "I bet he's pretty broken up, too."

16

TWO AND A HALF YEARS LATER

Scott

"Honey, your leg is shaking like a leaf," Laura says as she touches my knee, making me aware of the nervous twitch.

Laura's right, it is. I'm a nervous wreck.

The engine of my truck rumbles as we drive to the school to meet with some of Mallory's teachers. Laura and I have called these meetings because we have noticed a steady decline in Mallory's schoolwork and learning. Mallory is putting in the extra effort, yet her grades are falling. When the school year started—fifth grade—there were barely any signs of homework tears, but they have returned in full force.

One year ago, we decided to get Mallory tested for dyslexia. It did not surprise us when the developmental pediatrician informed us that our suspicions were spot on. However, the other discoveries they shared with us did. Mallory experiences mathematical dyslexia and a disability that makes it difficult for her to write and speak fluently. I've tried to remember the official names of them all. I gave up a while ago.

We made the school aware, and they promised to give Mallory the one-on-one attention she needed. Her teacher last year was a godsend. She got the ball rolling quickly, making sure Mallory had everything she needed to get started. However, now that she's in fifth grade, something isn't clicking. She's regressing, and we are here to find out what could be going on.

"Let's be honest. These things are no fun. You remember that first IEP meeting, right?" I ask.

"You mean the meeting we shall never speak of again? Yeah, I remember," she snickers. "But these meetings are a necessary evil. We need to sort this out."

When it comes to getting the help Mallory needs, don't get in my wife's way. Her inner mama bear is always lying in wait, ready to protect her cubs. And trust me, that bear is something else.

And, believe it or not, Mallory has another crusader on her side as of late.

Her Uncle Kyle. Shocking, I know.

And it's not only Kyle but also Shayla. Ever since our vacation a little over two years ago, the three of them have become best friends.

After that trip, they were honored to become a part of the Hug List. And Kyle has dove into everything about autism and dyslexia, so now he's an expert, of course. Honestly, he drives me nuts with it sometimes. He's still a know-it-all, but if he's going to be a self-designated expert on anything, I'm glad it's my daughter.

About a year ago, he and Shayla moved back home, much to my mother's delight. And honestly, it's been nice. He, Johnny, and I have gotten closer, and we hang out. A lot. Laura calls us the three musketeers. As a professor at Ohio Northeastern, Kyle's been a tremendous help in finding Mallory the resources she needs. He's not only giving advice but also providing instruction on how to tackle this school dilemma.

Kyle and I being civil? Who would have thunk it? Certainly not me.

As I'm thinking about this turn of events with my brother, my phone pings with a text message. I grab it from the middle console and hand it to Laura. "Can you read that, hon? It may be Johnny about the job."

I watch as she grabs my phone, her fingers tapping in the unlock code. "It's from Kyle. Interesting. Want me to read it?"

I nod as I make the turn onto the street Mallory's school is on. Buses are passing us, full of eager kids to be going home.

"It says, 'Good luck today, big brother. Remember, you and Laura hold all the cards. Don't let these teachers walk all over you. You got this! Mal Pal deserves it!'"

Man, have we come a long way.

Laura closes out my phone and sets it back on the console. "He's right, you know."

I grunt out a sigh because I'm about to say the unthinkable. "He is." I can see the amusement in Laura's eyes as her smirk widens, knowing how much it pains me to say that.

I pull into the school's parking lot, kill the truck's engine, and look over at my wife.

"You ready?" she asks while she slings her purse over her shoulder and puts her hand on the handle to open the door.

I am ready to watch my wife shine.

——ele——

Well, that was a disaster.

I shut the door behind us as we enter the hallway, and I look at my wife.

"Okay, babe. What in the ever-loving heck was that? What was her deal?" I glance back at the door. "I wonder if we should report her."

"I know, right? I have not liked her since day one. She has always had an attitude, and I could tell it annoyed her she had to deal with Mallory. She just wants a classroom full of perfect students. Mallory takes time and doesn't fit into her dream classroom. I've always known that, but I had no idea she wasn't sending her to her classes." Laura is standing with her hands on her hips. "It took everything in me to not chew her up and spit her out."

"Oh, I think in your own way, you did," I joke. "And besides, never trust a person who loves animal print that much. Like, geez." And I'm not exaggerating. Mrs. Malone's classroom looked like a cheetah exploded on every square inch. It was hurting my eyes.

"Obnoxious, isn't it?" Laura laughs while taking my hand and leading the way down the small, musty-smelling hallway.

Our first meeting with Mallory's teacher did not go as expected. Mrs. Malone was defensive, dismissive of our concerns, and told us *we* didn't work enough with Mallory at home. To top it off, we found out that she wasn't sending Mallory to her special ed classes regularly.

My wife saw red.

But Laura kept her cool. She put Mrs. Malone in her place by kindly explaining (sprinkled with a dose of passive aggression) Mallory's rights under the IDEA Act. Laura showed grace under pressure yet stood her ground like the mama bear she is. She was not about to let this teacher push our daughter aside. Not gonna lie, this version of my wife is sexy.

Laura squeezes my hand twice. "Well, we aren't done yet. Now, it's time to meet with Mrs. Rawlings. Her intervention specialist."

"And can I expect this same passive-aggressive version of my wife in this meeting? Because she's kinda hot."

Laura's laughter rings out, and she playfully nudges me at my side. "Haha. Very funny." I chuckle to myself. "No, Mrs. Rawlings should be good. She has always been Mallory's advocate in the school. I'm sure this will go well."

We arrive at room 215. I fix my gaze on Laura, and I can feel the understanding between us, even without words, as she nods.

I knock on the door.

17

Laura

M rs. Rawlings is sitting across from us, the smell of her strong perfume lingering in the air. Her eyes are kind, and her smile is warm. She's been a part of my daughter's team since the beginning, and I'm so thankful to her.

With the end of the school year quickly approaching, I know that Mrs. Malone will only be Mallory's teacher for the next few weeks. *Thank God.* But Mrs. Rawlings will follow Mallory until she is in middle school, which is another year. I'm positive she has some kind of plan in place to help my girl.

We sit in her classroom and chat casually before getting down to business. But honestly, my mind is all over the place. After the last disaster, I'm wondering what to expect with this meeting.

This is Scott's first time meeting Mrs. Rawlings and, as always, he is bringing his A game. Before I know it, Mrs. Rawlings' booming laugh fills the room as she and Scott exchange some kind of story.

"Well, I can see where Mallory gets her sense of humor from," she says, coming down from her laughter. I'll have to ask later what they were talking about.

"Oh, don't I know it?" I say as I look at my husband, and he grins back. He's going the extra mile to make sure this meeting is successful after the last one.

Get the teacher in a good mood. *Check.*

"So, what brings you two in here today? Mrs. Givens, I know you mentioned on the phone that you were concerned that Mallory is regressing," Mrs. Rawlings asks, grabbing her reading glasses.

"Yes, that's correct." I pull out the papers that I showed to Mrs. Malone in the last meeting, showcasing Mallory's regression, and recap our concerns. "As you can see, her grades have gone downhill considerably in the last few months. Scott and I are very concerned."

Scott shifts in his seat and speaks up. "Also, we just finished a meeting with her teacher, Mrs. Malone, and she told us she has been too busy to send Mallory to her special classes. We were upset to hear that."

"Well, of course, that is disheartening. I was wondering why Mallory's attendance in my class was becoming sporadic." She grabs a pen from her desk and a Post-it note. She scribbles something on it. "I will make a note of that and make sure that doesn't happen with my other students."

Wait? Her other students? What about Mallory?

"I want the two of you to know that I am aware of Mallory's recent struggles. I have noticed her decline, and I wonder if a more one-on-one attention would work better for her."

Now, we are getting somewhere. I like this.

Scott's eyes light up, and he leans forward in his seat, clearly in agreement. "I like the sound of that!"

"I do, too. I have wondered about that for a while now. Are you able to make that happen?" I inquire, my stomach in knots as I await her reply.

"That's what I was going to say next," Mrs. Rawlings continues, "even though I think that is what she needs, it's virtually impossible to bring it to fruition."

Scott and I shoot each other a puzzled glance. *I mean, isn't she the one that just suggested it?*

"However, I wonder though, with Mallory's host of issues and learning difficulties, if it's time that we accept the fact that she will be one of those adults that will need to have everything read to her for the rest of her life."

Did she seriously just say that?

I'm speechless. This one comment extinguishes the light-hearted nature of the visit. My body is rigid, my eyes blinking as I try to process her words.

Is this coming from the person who is supposed to be my child's advocate in this school?

Mrs. Rawlings breaks the silence. "Now, I know this can be hard to—"

Scott raises his hand and interrupts her. "Hold on. Are you saying that my eleven-year-old daughter is going to be illiterate as an adult?" he shoots back. Scott's light-hearted charm is gone, thrown away.

Mrs. Rawlings' gaze shoots between Scott and me. She notices the tension in the air and realizes she has said something wrong, so she frantically tries to undo the damage.

"No. No! That's not what I meant. What I meant—"

Scott cuts her off again. "But in a roundabout way, that's what you said."

A wave of realization hits me. The school is at a loss for what to do with Mallory. They have given up trying to help her. They stopped sending her to her classes, convinced that she was unable to learn how to read or write. Mallory's IEP clearly states that they cannot hold her back, so they stopped caring and will move her from grade to grade. All the while, she suffers academically.

This is not okay with us.

Mrs. Rawlings doesn't respond to Scott's words, her eyes wide with shock.

Scott turns to me, his face dripping with concern, silently asking me with his eyes, 'Are you okay?' *I'm not.* I try to hold back the tears, but my eyes sting, so I lower my gaze, hoping the teacher won't notice. Scott senses my hurt and takes control.

He stands and slides his chair in, the sound of its legs scraping against the floor echoing in the silent room. "Well, I think it's safe to say that this meeting is over." He turns to me and holds out his hand. "Come on, honey, let's go home to our kids."

Scott takes my shaking hand in his and squeezes twice. Our non-verbal communication to each other that all will be okay. "You have a nice evening, Mrs. Rawlings." With his hand in mine, he guides me out the door, leaving Mallory's teacher wide-eyed in shock. I don't even say goodbye. The fact that she has no clue how saying something like that can affect a child's parents is beyond me.

We walk down the hall, our hands tightly clasped together, the only sound is our shoes hitting the old, stained floor. We make it to the truck and get in, still in a daze. He places his keys in the ignition but hesitates before turning them, the sound of his breathing filling the air. Instead, he turns, and his eyes lock with mine. "What are you thinking?"

"Honestly?" I ask.

He nods.

"I'm thinking I should have smacked her."

We both let out a laugh, and it fills the truck, enough to break the tension. After a few moments, the reality of the situation comes crashing back.

"Scott, what are we going to do? Should we send her to another district?"

"No. I mean, maybe. I don't know. But she is not returning to this school next year. That's for sure."

I nod in agreement as I turn to look out the window.

Scott's eyes light up as if he has an idea, and he abruptly sits up straighter. "Alright, I think I know what to do. Now, honey, hear me out as I say this," he starts, and a comforting feeling comes over me as he intertwines his fingers with mine. "I think what Mrs. Rawlings said about Mallory needing one-on-one help is what she needs."

"But you heard her. They will not agree to that."

"I know. But ... now, I know this may sound crazy," he pauses, "but what if we homeschooled her?"

I stare at him and blink slowly. "You can't be serious?"

"I am! Look, I really feel this can be the only way to get her up to speed. The construction business is booming. You could quit your job—"

"I'm sorry...what!?" I exclaim as I draw my head back and shake it in disbelief.

"Now, hold on. Let me finish. We don't need your income right now. You could quit your job and give Mallory the attention she needs. Just for a year or two. We can get her on track, then that will give us time to explore our options. In the meantime, she can finish out the school year here, and that will give you the entire summer to prepare. I'm sure Kyle would help with anything you could need."

I can't believe he is on board with this. Scott's suggestion of homeschooling is unexpected, especially since he always said homeschooled kids were shy and awkward. Then again, with Scott, all bets are off when it comes to his kids. Obviously, nothing is off the table.

I release an enormous sigh and glance out the window again. "This sounds like an awful lot of work for me."

"You're right, it will be. But no one can pull this off better than you. And you will have my help. I can promise you that. Think about it, I've always been the math guy. I can help with math, and I will still read with her at night. That won't change. I can even maybe take an afternoon off one day a week, to give you a break. And just think how much she will relax, knowing she won't have to come here"—he points to the old school building in front of us—"and stare at animal-printed walls all day."

His point is valid; Mallory needs someone to focus on her needs specifically. And no one knows her better than me. I could customize her learning. We could do her schoolwork during the time of the day that works for her.

And truthfully, my job has grown stagnant. I've been unhappy at the hospital for a while now and have considered looking elsewhere. This could give me the push I need to move forward and regroup. Figure out what I want to do professionally. All the while helping my daughter thrive and learn.

Could this work? I can feel the fire of purpose and hope burning within me. I turn to Scott, gently biting my lip.

I must have zoned out for a while because the excitement on Scott's face vanishes. He runs his fingers through his hair and sinks into his seat. "I shouldn't have suggested this, huh?"

"No. Honey, that's not it. Just thinking."

"And what do you think?"

I smile and squeeze his hand twice.

"Let's do this."

18

THE NEXT DAY

Jake

"You can't be serious right now?"

I glance between my mom and dad, my eyes darting back and forth. They are sitting on the ottoman facing me, and I'm on the couch. It's late on a Friday night, and I'm home with my parents, getting this crappy news. Mallory is in her room, probably playing with her dumb dolls.

My dad lets out a long breath. "We are serious, Jake. Mallory is struggling."

"Yeah, right," I huff out as I roll my eyes, throwing myself back onto the couch cushions and crossing my arms over my chest.

My dad's face gets serious, his eyes narrowing as he points at me. "*Do not* roll your eyes at me. You know better."

He's right; I do know better. But when my parents told me that Mallory was going to be homeschooled, I saw red.

Because, of course, they are.

You know that one *saying ... Marcia, Marcia, Marcia.*

Well, I have no idea where it's from, but I know what it means. And that's how it is in this family. It's always ... *Mallory, Mallory, Mallory.*

And look, I know my sister has issues, and it's not her fault. She's not "normal." She thinks differently. She gets upset and cries a lot, and for God's sake, don't touch her. Don't know what that is all about. I know it has to do with her autism, I think, but I stopped asking questions a long time ago, if I'm being honest.

When I say that this entire house revolves around Mallory and her autism, I'm not playing.

Her sensitivity to sound: "Don't talk too loud, Jake," or "Turn down the TV, Jake. You know Mallory doesn't like the noise."

How she doesn't like certain clothes: "I know you need to be at your friend's house in ten minutes, but we need to stop at one more store to get the socks that don't bother your sister."

All her therapy appointments: "We will go to Game Stop next week, bud, I promise. I have to drop Mallory off at therapy, or we will be late."

Mallory is always the center of attention, and I'm so tired of it.

Do you even know how hard it is to have a sibling with autism? Well, I'm here to tell you it sucks. And sometimes I show that. By rolling my eyes at my dad.

"Sorry, Dad," I lower my eyes and mumble back. I direct my next question to my mom. "Do I get to be homeschooled too? Or just Mallory?"

Because, let's face it, being homeschooled sounds pretty sweet. And I want in on this. Sleeping in, staying in my pajamas all day. How awesome does that sound?

My mom shifts her position on the ottoman. "Just Mallory, sweetie."

I can't help myself, and I know I will get in trouble, but I shoot off the couch anyway. "Why does Mallory get everything she wants?" I shout, which I know will be a mistake.

My parents' eyes follow me. My mom's voice sounds full of hurt as she answers me. "Jake, that's not true, and you know it."

"It is true!" I yell, throwing my hands in the air.

"Hey!" my dad yells back as he stands up. He's towering over me right now. "You are walking on thin ice. Do not yell at your mother."

"And lower your voice, Jake," my mom follows, "you know how Mallory doesn't like—"

"Loud noises," I put my hands on my hips. "Yeah, I know all about it. You guys say it every single day." I'm crossing my arms over my chest again. I'm a glutton for punishment, I guess.

My dad takes a step toward me, and he's breathing heavily.

Crap. I'm in trouble. Goodbye, world. It's been a fun thirteen years. Nice knowing ya.

"That's it. I'm done. Go to your room!" My dad yells as he points to the steps. "You are grounded!"

"Dad!"

"Go right now. Don't make me say it again. I will be up to talk about your punishment shortly."

I turn on my heels and take off toward the steps.

"And, Jake," my dad calls to me. I stop dead and turn around. When I do, I see my mom with her face buried in her hands. Now, I feel really bad. I've hurt my mom. "I better not see you playing any video games, watching TV, or looking at your phone. Understood?"

"Fine," I say while I stomp up the steps. As I pass Mallory's room, I see her door ajar, and she's peeking out. She's the last person I want to see right now. I don't stop as I walk to my room and slam my door shut. I throw myself on my bed in a huff, and I wonder how long I have to lie here, staring at the ceiling, waiting for my dad to come in and yell at me.

And also to talk to me about my attitude toward my sister.

You know...

Because it's always *Mallory, Mallory, Mallory.*

I decide to grab a book. I mean, Dad didn't say I couldn't read, and I've been sitting here in my room for an hour waiting on him to come in.

Longest hour of my life.

I'm trying hard to get into *The Lord of the Rings*, but I can't. My head is spinning, and I know I was a brat. I need to apologize to my dad and mom. And I will, I swear. But I have no clue what to say to them.

I need to tell them how I feel insignificant in this family. I need to tell them how they don't hear or care about my feelings. But I know that I have to tread lightly. I mean, my favorite racing game comes out in a few weeks. I can't risk getting grounded longer than Dad already intends.

Sitting my book down on the bed, I stare at the textured ceiling. My head turns to the door at the sound of my dad's footsteps coming up the stairs. I have no idea what's going to happen next.

Is he going to yell at me?

How grounded am I going to be?

How will he react when I tell him what I've been feeling?

My hands feel sweaty, and my head feels hot waiting for the knock on the door. I swear it feels like time is standing still.

Why is he taking the steps so slowly?

Knock, knock, knock.

Normally, he waits for me to answer.

Not tonight.

The door opens with a swoosh as he walks in and grabs the chair from my desk. He turns it toward my bed in one swift motion, like it weighs next to nothing. He sits, and I feel him staring at me. I can hear him breathing as I stare at the ceiling, hoping it opens up and lifts me out of here.

"Jake, sit up, turn around, and look at me," he commands in a low, stern voice.

I don't want to get into any more trouble, so I turn and sit cross-legged on my bed, facing him.

"You know better than to act the way you did downstairs just now." I lower my gaze and nod in agreement.

"Your mom and I were talking, and we feel you should spend the next two days with no electronics. As long as you apologize to us for your behavior."

I'll take it! Two days is nothing.

I keep my head down. "I'm sorry, Dad."

He opens his mouth, ready to say something, but then closes it again. He takes a deep breath before he continues as he sits his hand on my knee. "We were also talking, and that outburst was out of character for you, and I want to give you the chance to explain yourself. You're not a kid anymore."

This catches my attention. I snap my head up to look him in the eye.

"So, let's talk ... man to man. Is there anything bothering you?"

His voice is softer now, which makes it easier to say what I want to say to him.

I shift my weight some out of nervousness. He's right, though. I'm not a little kid anymore. Granted, I'm only thirteen, but still, I am a teenager now. I'm not a toddler. I need to tell him how I feel.

"I am really sorry for how I acted downstairs, Dad, but..." I swallow hard before I continue.

"It's okay," my dad says. He's furrowing his brow and appearing sad. Like what I am about to say will hurt his feelings. Maybe it will.

"I meant what I said. I feel like this whole house revolves around Mallory. And I mean everything. We can't even cheer when we watch football or baseball because it may hurt Mallory's ears. We can't go to the movies because it's too much for her. She can't get overwhelmed, like ever, which means she gets to be homeschooled now. I feel like I walk on eggshells all the time, and sometimes, I just want a normal sister. Why can't she be normal? And I know she can't be. I know that none of this is her fault. But still, it's hard." Tears well up in my eyes, and I pause and look at my hands. "I'm sorry if that hurts your feelings. But it's how I feel."

My dad lets out a long exhaling breath, and the only sound in the room is the air kicking on. "Are you mad at me?" *Because that is the last thing I want.*

"No, Jake. I'm not mad at you. Thank you for being honest with me. I respect you for that. I just wish we could have talked like this downstairs. How long have you felt this way?"

"For as long as I can remember," I whisper.

My dad purses his lips and turns his head away from me. He wrings his hands together, and I can tell he doesn't know what to say. "Well, I wish you would have come to us sooner."

It's quiet again. Neither of us talking. This whole thing feels awkward. My dad breaks the silence first. "I know this has to be hard on you, buddy. It's hard on all of us. Your mom especially."

"I know."

"Just hang in there, okay? Your mom and I are trying our best. We really are."

"I know."

The long, awkward silence returns. "Well, okay then," my dad finally says as he slaps me on the leg. "I'm glad we got to talk about this." He stands and puts the chair back. "Thank you for telling me how you feel. Your punishment still stands, however."

He quietly shuts the door, not even looking back in my direction as he left.

That's it? I mean, that can't be it. Can it?

I throw myself on my bed because I can't believe it. I told him my feelings, and all I got was, 'Hang in there, buddy.' Geez. A wave of guilt consumes me. I should have never said what I said about Mallory. Now, I think my dad is mad at me, and he is going to tell Mom what I said, and her feelings will get hurt.

Great. It hurts me more than anything to make my mom sad. She is sad all the time now already.

I grab my book and open it to start to read again. But I can't, so I throw it across the room and watch as it slams against the wall with a loud thud. I'm so mad at myself right now.

I am a terrible son, and I know one thing for sure.

I hate autism.

19

THE NEXT MORNING

Scott

"Welcome to Starbucks. How can I help you?"

"Yeah, can I get a venti black coffee and a..." I pull up the coffee order Johnny texted me last night. "Blonde Latte with an extra shot of espresso, sweet cream, extra foam, and sugar-free vanilla?"

Stinking Johnny and his fancy drinks. I can't believe I said, 'extra foam.' Why in the world does he need that?

I'm feeling especially annoyed and touchy today. I can't stop thinking about Jake and what he said to me in his bedroom. He caught me off guard, and I'm pretty sure I didn't handle it well. I had no clue that he felt the way he did.

I could have done better.

I *should* have done better.

The sadness in Laura's voice when I told her and her heartbroken expression was unforgettable. We didn't talk about it after. My heart feels heavy, and I don't know how to remedy the situation. I mean, Mallory is Mallory. We can't change our circumstances. Parenting an atypical and a neurotypical child at the same time is no walk in the park.

And now I sit in a drive-through, waiting for coffee, thinking that I need to go to my voice of reason in life.

My cousin Johnny. The biggest goofball who gives the best advice.

I pay for his over-priced coffee and drive to the job with the sound of the wind blowing through the open window. It's Saturday, but we have a few things to check out on the current job site. I hate leaving the family on a Saturday morning, especially after last night. But Johnny and I like to inspect things without our crew present.

As I drive, I can't stop replaying some things Jake said in my head.

The whole house revolves around Mallory.

I have to walk on eggshells all the time.

I just want a normal sister.

That last one hit me hard. I've been there before, but I don't feel the same way now, so I understand his frustration. But how do I fix this?

I hear the gravel crunching under my truck tires as I pull onto the makeshift driveway of the house we are here to check on. I've always loved the sound of gravel underneath my tires. It's a soothing noise that gets me in the right frame of mind for a workday. I can't help it. The love of construction runs deep in me.

I pull my truck into its usual spot on this job, listening to the birds chirping as I take a sip of my coffee while I wait for Johnny. The cool breeze coming in through the window feels refreshing. And although I hate to admit it, the vanilla coming from Johnny's coffee smells good.

Glancing out my window, I see Johnny's truck headlights. I turn off my engine, grab his coffee, and get out of my truck. I lean up against my driver's door, waiting for him, his weird drink in hand. He steps out, his clothes rumpled, his hair disheveled, and he hasn't shaven. To make it even weirder, he has sunglasses on. The sun isn't even up yet. Johnny, who is usually so concerned about his appearance, looks like he has just rolled out of bed. He may be the biggest jokester, but he wants to look good telling those jokes. Even on the job site. That means a clean-shaven face, gelled hair, freshly applied after-shave, and ironed work clothes. But not today. I have no clue who is standing in front of me right now.

"Hey," he says, his voice low and horse.

I hand him his drink. "Well, don't you sound and look delightful this morning?"

He takes a deep, slow sip of his steaming hot coffee, savoring the flavor before exhaling a content sigh. "Wow ... that tastes amazing." He takes another long sip, gulping this hot coffee down like it's a bottle of ice water after a long run.

"You alright, man?" I ask, raising an eyebrow.

He doesn't answer. His throat bobs with each gulp as I stand and watch in awe because the drink must be hot. After a few more seconds, he downs the whole cup. He wipes his mouth with the back of his hand and tosses the empty cup into the truck bed. I watch it glide through the air and clunk as it lands.

He leans against his truck, facing me as he crosses his arms over his chest. He peers down at the ground and kicks some of the gravel with his feet. After a few seconds, he removes his sunglasses and meets my gaze, and I can see his bloodshot eyes. He lets out a long breath, then says, "Rachel broke up with me last night."

If it wasn't weird, I would pull him in for a hug right now. I know Johnny liked Rachel a lot. He couldn't take his eyes off her when she was in the room. They have been dating for about six months now, and going by how Johnny talked about the relationship, I assumed it was serious. He would light up anytime he talked about her in a way that he never had with any other woman. They would chat on the phone pretty much every day. Laura and I even went out with them a few times, and Rachel seemed to be into him. They appeared happy. I wonder now if it was all one-sided.

I place my hand on his shoulder, hoping it brings some measure of comfort. "I'm so sorry, man. Did she say why?"

He nods. "Just that she felt we were moving too fast and the age thing." He shrugs as he looks away.

Rachel is fifteen years younger than Johnny. It never seemed to be an issue. For him, at least.

"You want to talk about it?"

"Nope," he says, popping the p. He shoves his hands into his pockets.

We stand there, not talking, as Johnny continues to kick the gravel, and the sound of passing traffic fills the air. Johnny is a talker. Sometimes to the point of being obnoxious. His silence on the matter speaks volumes, and it's clear that he's hurting.

"Well, do you feel up to shelling out some of your Johnny wisdom, because I could use some?" I'm hoping the subject change will provide a much-needed distraction.

He sniffles as he wipes his thumb along his cheek.

Wait. Is he crying? Impossible. I've never seen Johnny cry. Ever.

"Lay it on me. I need to think about something else. Anything else." We both turn and move toward the job, the sight of half-finished work looming before us. I fill him in on everything. How we decided to homeschool Mallory, telling Jake, and then Jake's reaction. Johnny nods along, taking in my every word. By the time I'm done, we are in the almost complete kitchen, leaning up against the new stone countertop.

"Okay, so let me get this straight," he starts, "my little dude mans up and spills his guts to you, and all you say to him is 'hang in there.'

"God, it sounds so bad when you say it out loud."

"Because it is bad, man. Did you take a second to stop and think about what he was really saying to you?"

"I was there, Johnny. I know what he said."

"I don't mean the actual words. I'm talking about the meaning behind those words."

I pause, my eyes widening as I take in what he said.

"Dear Lord. Do I have to spell it out for you?" he expresses, rolling his eyes. "Little man is lonely."

"No, he's not. We are together as a family all the time," I retort, raising my voice defensively.

"And that's the problem," he says, poking me in the chest. "Mallory is always there when you are all together. And Jake's right, Mallory needs extra attention, extra help. And there's nothing wrong with that. But he's not wrong when he says that everything revolves around her. Maybe it's time that something revolves around him."

That last sentence was a punch in the gut. I run my hands down my face. "Ugh. You're right."

"Always." I cast him a sideways glance and sigh with exaggeration. "I'm serious, though. You and Laura are Mallory's parents. It's your sole job to help her in any way that you can. But that's not Jake's job. You need to spend some time with Jake *without* Mallory around. He needs some attention from you and Laura that isn't attached to Mallory or her autism." His eyes dart around the kitchen in confusion. "Where's my coffee?"

"You chugged it down outside. Remember?"

He snaps his finger, the sound echoing in the empty room. "That's right." He sighs, regretting the decision. "Anyway"—he waves his hand in the air—"when was the last time you spent time with Jake? Just you and Jake? Or just Jake and Laura?"

I take a minute to contemplate that one. Other than him and I watching football together on Sundays or baseball in the summer, we rarely spend time together outside of the usual family activities. And I'm not sure Laura and Jake have ever done anything, just the two of them.

"It's been a while," I say in a whisper. God, I'm so embarrassed. We have been so preoccupied with Mallory that we have almost forgotten that we need to raise another child. "Any suggestions on what I can do with him? I'm desperate, man."

"You must be if you came to me for advice." He smiles, which is nice to see, considering the current state of his personal life. "I have an idea if you're interested."

"Sure, lay it on me."

"I have four tickets to the Pittsburgh/Chicago game tomorrow. Rachel and I were supposed to go with her brother and sister-in-law. Great seats. Right behind home plate."

"Dang. How did you snag those?"

He shrugs. "Connections. Anyway, Rachel's a huge Pittsburgh fan. So is her brother. I bought them for her."

"Ha! I bet he's gonna be mad," I say with a chuckle.

"Oh, I'm sure. But he can take that up with her. Anyway, why don't you see if Mallory can hang out with Shay and Kyle, then you, me, Laura, and Jake go to the game? And if I'm being honest, I hope she watches the game and sees me on TV, behind home plate, having fun without her." A sly smirk crosses his lips.

I'm truly touched by Johnny's offer. "You serious, man?"

"Yep. You know Jake would love it. And I could use the distraction."

He's right, Jake would love it. And this would be good for Johnny as well. "Alright. Sounds like a plan." I lift my hand to give Johnny a high-five as a thank you. He smacks my hand, grabs it, and pulls me in for a hug, slapping me on the back, his strong arms embracing me tightly. It catches me off guard.

Because I'm pretty sure that hug is for him and not me.

I'm standing at the bottom of the stairs, holding onto the banister. "Jake? Can you come downstairs, please?" I shout.

"I'll be right there," his muffled reply comes from behind his bedroom door.

I re-enter the kitchen and meet Laura at the island. She's sitting on a barstool, her foot tapping nervously against the floor. I slide onto the stool next to her and squeeze her leg, trying to calm her nerves. After my conversation with Johnny, and when I got home from work, Laura and I talked. We both agreed that we had let our time with Jake go by the wayside. We also came up with a plan to fix it. But first, we need to talk to Jake, apologize, and make sure he knows he is a valued part of this family.

I hear Jake's steps as he comes barreling down the stairs. He rounds the corner, passes the living room, and stops dead in his tracks when he sees us both sitting with our hands clasped together. Staring at him.

"I did nothing wrong." The words spill out of his mouth.

A chuckle bubbles up within me, and I can't help but laugh. "No, Jake, you didn't. We did."

He cocks his head to the side. "Huh? I'm confused."

"Take a seat, and we will explain," Laura says, gesturing to a barstool.

Jake scraps the barstool across the floor as he pulls it out, sitting to face us. He lifts his eyes and surveys the house. "Wait. Where's Mal?"

"She's with your Uncle Kyle and Aunt Shay. She's going to spend the day with them and their new puppy," Laura explains.

"Oh," he murmurs, his voice barely above a whisper, as he lowers his head. His shoulders slump low as he nervously fiddles with the hem of his shirt. "That sounds like fun."

Now that I know how Jake feels about everything, I understand the hurt in his voice, and his body language is speaking volumes. He thinks we sent Mallory off to have fun with his aunt and uncle and forgot about him.

"Jake, we owe you an apology," I start.

He shoots his head up. "Me? Why do you owe me an apology?"

"We haven't been very fair to you when it comes to Mallory." His eyes grow wide as he looks between Laura and me, not knowing what to make of the situation. I continue. "Jake, you opened up to me the other night, which was very mature of you, by the way." I see him straighten up as he shifts his weight in the chair. "What you said surprised me. Your mom and I did not know you felt that way. And we should have. And for that, we are very sorry."

He nods in agreement. "It's okay. I know Mallory needs a lot of your attention. I understand."

"No, Jake, it's not okay," Laura says. "It's true that Mallory needs extra help and time from us." She reaches across the island and grabs Jake's hand. "But so do you. You are our child, just as much as Mallory is, and you deserve our one-on-one attention as well. And your dad and I plan to fix that."

I see a small smile come across his face as he anticipates what's coming. "How?"

"Well, for starters, we are going to make sure that you get some time alone with both of us. Without Mallory present," I say. "Also, on game day, Mallory and your mom will make themselves scarce, so that we can be as loud as we want when Pittsburgh scores all those touchdowns and hits all of those home runs."

"Yeah! Let's hope so. Last football season was a bust." He chuckles, but then his face softens and turns serious. "I would love that."

"Also, I thought it would be kinda nice if I started taking you to school in the morning. It's not a lot, but it would give us a chance to be together."

His grin widens, and his face lights up. "So, I don't have to take the bus anymore?" Jake hates the bus. With a passion.

Laura shakes her head. "No more bus. You know what that means, right?"

"I can sleep in an extra forty-five minutes! This is incredible! Plus, I love your truck, Dad. I will look like a boss rolling up in that thing."

Laura and I snort out in laughter. Oh, to be thirteen again.

Jake fixes his gaze on Laura with remorse. "Mom, I'm sorry if what I told Dad hurt your feelings."

God, this kid. How did I get so lucky in the offspring department?

Laura steps down from the barstool and rounds the island, the kitchen lights reflecting off its glossy surface. She wraps her arms around Jake and hugs him tightly. "Jake, what you said didn't hurt my feelings. I hurt myself because what you said made me realize how I've been neglecting you." She pulls away and looks him in the eye. "That ends today."

"It does? Since Mallory isn't here, do you guys have plans for us? Please say yes!" The kid is jumping out of the stool with excitement.

I take the baseball tickets out of my back pocket and toss them on the island. They slide across the smooth granite as Jake grabs them and studies them. His eyes light up. "NO. WAY."

I chuckle. "Yes, way."

He leaps off the barstool, pointing at the tickets in his hand. "Dude, these are for today!"

"They sure are. And did you see where the seats are? Right behind home plate."

He frantically looks at the tickets again. "Oh, my God! This just keeps getting better and better!" He pulls Laura into a tight embrace before running around doing the same to me. "Thank you so much! Thank you, thank you, thank you!" He glances at the tickets, then takes a moment to consider something. "Wait, there are four tickets. Who else is going?" Jake asks us as he raises his eyebrows.

Even though we just got done telling him we plan on spending more time with him without Mallory, he's still concerned that she's coming with us.

"Cousin Johnny should be here any minute."

Jake pumps his fist in the air. "YES! He is so much fun!"

Laura ruffles Jake's hair. "Now go upstairs and get ready to go. Your Pittsburgh shirt is clean in your dresser drawer, and your hat is in the hall closet."

"This is going to be epic!" Jake flies out of the kitchen, the excitement of the news still on his face.

"Hey, Jake," I say with a wave of my hand as he swivels around and returns. "We love you, buddy. Always remember that, okay."

He rolls his eyes with an exaggerated sigh. "Love you guys, too. But no more mushy talk."

I watch him as he turns and runs up the stairs. His steps, lighter than they have been for a while.

20

THREE YEARS LATER

Laura

"**M**allory honey, you have to get out of bed to start your schoolwork," I demand as I smack her leg that's hanging over the edge of her bed, uncovered.

Mallory grunts and pulls the blankets over her head. "Can I just have five more minutes, please?" she muffles into the pillow.

And so starts my Monday morning. Or should I say every single morning if it's Monday through Friday? I bend down to scoop up the dirty clothes off the floor and drop them into the hamper while I wait for her to move. She doesn't.

Mallory's room is now her teenage haven. Gone are the American Girl dolls and their beds (putting those away was a sad day for me), as well as all the pink. Two years ago, she asked Scott if he would paint it a soft green. They painted it that weekend. She decorated the room with flowers and plants. They covered the ceiling in plastic vines purchased from Amazon. The entire room has an enchanted, dreamy feel to it; something a fourteen-year-old girl would adore. And she does.

Her desk is covered twenty-four-seven in art supplies and unfinished drawings. Every time she picks up a pencil or a paintbrush, her art improves. Her talent is amazing. If she isn't doing schoolwork or spending time with us as a family, you can find her with a pencil in her hand and a sketchpad in her lap.

"You have five minutes, then I want you at the table for breakfast. Got it?" I stand in the doorway with a hand resting on my hip.

Another grunt comes from under the covers.

Homeschooling Mallory for only a year, like Scott and I decided in his truck, has turned into three years of this same morning routine. Now, don't get me wrong, homeschooling Mallory was the best decision for her, hands down. Between Scott and me, we had our daughter reading and handling basic math in just one year. Take that, Liberty Elementary!

It didn't take long for us to understand that the comfort of being home with me was what she needed. We now had more time for her therapies. She could concentrate and learn in a quiet environment and, well ... thrive.

Now Mallory is fourteen and finishing up eighth grade, which means next year is high school. Spending time at home was a great opportunity to get back on track, but now that she's older, we know she can handle more. Scott and I both agree that she needs to be in a school to suit her needs. And that school is on the campus of the Autism Global Institute. It's a school whose sole purpose is to teach autistic kids. We feel it's time for her to return to the classroom, and we plan on bringing it up to her after dinner tonight.

I make my way downstairs and see Scott in his usual spot in the morning, sitting at the island with his laptop open. He peaks at me over his reading glasses perched on his nose. "Five more minutes, huh?" he smirks.

"Yep. Any bets on how much longer it will be?"

Jake comes from upstairs and enters the kitchen. "I say fifteen at the minimum," he wagers as he grabs a banana from the fruit basket and peels it. He shakes his head and takes a bite as the sound of chewing fills the room. "She's so lazy," he mumbles with a mouth full of banana.

"Hey!" I turn from the sink, hand on my hip, to glare at him. I get a tad bit defensive when he says this about his sister.

"Jake, leave your sister alone," Scott counters as he closes his laptop.

Jake rolls his eyes, "Whatever. I mean, she is."

Scott points to the garage. "That's enough. We are leaving in five minutes. Go get your stuff."

Jake scoffs off in a huff up the stairs, taking them two at a time. Scott pours his OJ into the sink and leans in to kiss me on the cheek. "What are you guys working on today?"

"I'm going to keep it pretty simple. Maybe just an hour of book work, then a trip to the science center. I want to keep her calm since we are approaching her about putting her back in school."

That's the other new thing these past few years. Anxiety and depression. With that has come mild panic attacks, sleeping too much, and a generalized worry about everything and anything. She also has a Sunday through Saturday pill bottle that houses all her meds. The ones that keep her level when they work right. This new challenge we faced threw a wrench into our lives that we weren't expecting. My daughter has changed, and it scares me some days.

Scott comes around me and grabs my waist, pulling me closer to him. "I think it sounds like a great idea." His lips tenderly graze my forehead. "It's going to be fine later, I promise. Her reaction to it might surprise us. You never know."

"I honestly don't know what to expect. She has been doing so well on her meds. I don't want this to set her back, ya know?" I rest my forehead on his chest, taking in the comforting smell of his sporty deodorant.

He lifts my head with his finger under my chin, forcing me to stare into his brown eyes. I can feel myself relax as I peer into his confident gaze. He kisses me as Jake comes around the corner.

"Oh, GOD! Ew ... that's so gross, you guys." He shields his eyes with his hand. "I'll be in the truck, Dad," he says as he heads out the garage door.

Scott and I laugh, our shoulders bouncing with each chuckle. He pulls me in closer. "Good, now we are alone. I can give you a proper goodbye kiss." With his hands around my waist, he pulls me in tighter and kisses me deeper.

"GROSS! Why do you guys kiss so much?" Mallory says as she enters the kitchen. She whirls around and scurries away. "I'm going to go get dressed!" she calls out as I hear her feet pounding on the stairs on the way back to her bedroom.

Caught making out with my husband twice this morning by both of my teenagers.

Outstanding.

Scott rolls his eyes and sighs. "I swear finding time to be alone was easier when they were little."

I snicker and give him a pat on the shoulder. "Have a great day, honey." He grabs his lunch box from the counter and kisses me on the cheek.

"Come on, Dad!" Jake slams his hand on the truck horn, the loud noise reverberating off the garage walls. "I can't be late. I have a math test first period!" Jake calls from the passenger seat of the truck. His voice is deep at sixteen, like his father's. The entire neighborhood probably heard him.

"Coming, bud!" Scott calls out.

I stand in the garage, watching as my son waves from the car window, and they drive away. I head back into the house and see the sun streaming through the windows, illuminating the dining room table as I set it up for another school day, wondering how many more of these I have left.

Mallory

Knock. Knock. Knock.

"Come on in!" I yell out over Taylor Swift singing from my phone. I know my parents are on the other side of that door. All night long, they were acting strange, stealing concerned glances at one another at dinner every time I spoke. And this can mean only one thing. They want to talk to me about something.

Great.

My parents walk on eggshells around me lately. And I know it's because of the anxiety I have been experiencing. The attacks started out of nowhere around a year ago, and they take on a life of their own. I hate that I have no control over my mind. The medicine I take helps, but sometimes, that doesn't feel like enough. I worry about absolutely everything. Like, all the time. It's exhausting, which causes me to sleep a lot.

If I'm being honest, I have no idea who I am as a person. The only thing that makes me feel alive is my art. So, I'm happy that I'm working on something when I hear the knock on my door. I'm currently drawing a picture of a girl holding an umbrella in the rain. I'm in a groove, so I really don't want to stop, but I kinda have to.

I hear the creak of my door opening, but I don't take my eyes off of my drawing to greet them. I hate eye contact. "Hey, sweetie," my dad starts, "do you mind turning down the music? Your mom and I need to talk to you."

I pause, sigh, and pop a Smartie in my mouth from the half-eaten package. My black, soot-covered finger from my charcoal pencil hits the pause button on my phone. I turn toward Mom and Dad, who are sitting on my perfectly made bed. My eyes zero in on the wrinkles in the comforter their weight creates, causing me to cringe.

God, now I'm going to have to remake my bed once they leave.

"I knew something was up. You guys were acting strange all dinner long." I plop my pencil in my flamingo-shaped pencil holder. It makes a soft thud as it hits. The Smartie bag crunches as I grab another pink disc and pop it in my mouth. I'm super nervous because I have no clue what this could be about, so I need to chew on something.

Mom starts. "Well, sweetie, your dad and I want to start by saying how proud we are of you."

Dad shakes his head in agreement. "Yes, so proud."

Mom continues. "You work hard on your schoolwork. Seldom complaining, even though I know how hard the struggle is for you."

They pause and are both studying me, I think, expecting me to say something. But is that it? Did they come up here and mess up my bed just to tell me that? I'm so confused. "Um, thanks, I guess. Is that it?" I question in an uncertain tone.

"No, that's not it," Dad keeps going. "So, your mom and I have given this a lot of thought, and we wanted to talk to you about it before we decided since it involves you." *Oh, God.* "We wanted to see what you think about it."

No sooner have I taken in what they said than my leg begins twitching uncontrollably, and my fingers start tapping on it. My mom and dad got me a fidget ring last year. It's on my right thumb, so I roll the balls to help calm my nerves. "Mm-hm," I murmur, keeping my eyes focused on my ring.

Dad starts again, "So, the Global Autism Institute has a school. A school specially designed for kids with autism. To help them with their learning and to give them the tools to succeed. And since you are getting older and will start high school this fall, your mom and I thought maybe it would be a good idea for you to attend the school."

Okay, I was not expecting that. Going back to school sounds ... scary. Yet, for some reason, it doesn't. I need a few minutes to process this, so I say nothing as I continue to study and play with my fidget ring.

What would all of this mean?

I wonder if the other kids would like me.

Would the school be loud and bright?

Are the teachers nice?

I'm taking too long to say anything because out of the corner of my eye, I see Mom shift her weight on my bed, messing up the comforter even more. Dad is just sitting still like a statue. My silence is making them nervous, or maybe they think I didn't hear them. This happens sometimes because I tend to get in my own head a lot and zone out, which causes me to not hear what's going on around me. Finally, my mom speaks up. "You're awful quiet, honey."

"Yeah, I know. I'm thinking. You said you wanted to see what I think about it. So, I'm thinking," I explain, deciding to state the obvious.

So, we all sit here while I think. Not talking. Just sitting, breathing, and thinking. *This is so awkward.* But my head is whirling from all the uncertainty, and I need some time to process it all. After minutes of unbearable silence, Dad finally speaks up.

"Do you have any questions? Or concerns? Does this worry you at all?"

My hands have a mind of their own and clamp over my ears. "That's too many questions at once, Dad." Something I cannot handle is questions thrown at me in rapid-fire succession. It's overwhelming, and my brain can't handle it. I don't know if it's because of my autism or my anxiety. Or maybe both. Who knows? But one thing is for sure: one task or question at a time. Always. My parents forget sometimes.

"You're right, sweetie. Sorry about that." Dad lowers his head in regret.

I lower my hands and finally decide that I want details. "So, will the kids that I have group therapy with be there?" A familiar face might be nice.

"Yes, honey, they will be. I asked your therapist, and it turns out your whole group therapy class attends the school. The class sizes are tiny, so you will see them more."

"That's cool. But that means Travis will be there. I hate that kid." I start chewing on my fingernail because I cannot stand Travis. He's loud and obnoxious. Two things I can't handle. But at least my other friends will be at the school.

The more I think about this, the more I'm liking the idea. Not that I don't like being homeschooled. My parents made the right choice three years ago. But I have been feeling lonely. I need friends. Even though making friends and being social is very difficult for me.

It's more than difficult. It's downright brutal. I feel an endless tug-of-war going on inside me. That's the best way to describe it. I *need* friends. I *want* friends. It's something I crave. But when it comes time to talk to an actual person, I freeze up. I run in the opposite direction, sometimes literally.

What this all boils down to is, my only friend for the past few years has been my mom. And I love my mom. I really do. She is my rock. But being with kids my own age, kids that can relate to me, might not be that bad.

I think I can do this.

"So, honey, we don't need an answer right away," my mom says. "We can think about it."

"Nah, I don't need to think about it anymore." Time to blow my parents' minds.

Mom and Dad turn to each other, anticipation written on their faces as my decision hangs in the air.

"I want to go. It might be fun." With that, I turn around in my chair, grab the pencil from the flamingo cup, and go back to my umbrella picture. This sounds like it could be fun. But I don't want to think about this anymore. All this decision-making has made me tired, and the only thing I can think about is fixing my bed.

Of course, my mom is nervous about the whole thing, which was her idea to begin with. "Are you sure honey, because—"

"Now, babe," my dad says, placing his hand on my mom's knee, "if Mallory says she wants to go, then that's that." He stands and kisses me on the top of my head. It's one touch I don't mind receiving from my parents. "I'm proud of you for being so mature about this, sweetie."

"Thanks, Dad," I mutter, my eyes glued to my drawing because I just want this to be over with. "Can I go back to my picture now?"

"Of course," my mom says. I don't look to watch them leave, but I turn around when I don't hear my door close all the way. Ugh. There's nothing that bothers me more than when something is left unfinished. So, I stand up, walk to the door to shut it, and that's when I hear my mom and dad talking in the hallway. I mean, of course, I'm going to eavesdrop. I stand as still as possible.

"Wow," Dad says. "That was surprisingly—"

"Easy."

"Yep. What a relief. I told you she might surprise us," my dad says. I hear them make their way down the hall toward their bedroom.

Hoping my door doesn't creak, I slowly open it and see them entering their bedroom as I hear my mom say, "But was that too easy?" They disappear.

My shoulders slump in defeat. Why don't my parents have any faith in me? They always assume I'm going to freak out or have a breakdown. They baby me and are so overprotective, and sometimes, I get so sick of it. Like right now.

With determined steps, I walk back to my desk and hit the play button. Taylor Swift starts singing to me again as I tear my bed apart to fix it.

I'm going to show them and everyone else that Mallory Givens can do anything she puts her mind to.

I got this.

21

THREE MONTHS LATER

Mallory

What was I thinking?

I'm standing outside the building of my new school. The Global Autism Institute School for Learning. The campus isn't big. It consists of two small brick buildings, each only two stories tall. One is for grades K-6, and the other is for grades 7-12. They are across the street from where my doctor's office is.

This is going to be my freshman year. Not gonna lie, it floored me when my mom and dad approached me about coming here. I was so determined that day, but as more time passed, the more nervous I got.

I turn so that I can see my mom one last time as I watch her drive down the street. She beeps and waves at me, flashing a smile. I can tell she is trying to be brave, but I see the sadness in her eyes. If I know my mom — and I'm pretty sure I do — she will break down in tears at the next intersection. My mom wanted to walk me into the school, but I refused. I'm trying to look cool, calm, and collected here. I wanted to feel brave and independent, so over breakfast this morning, I told her.

"Mom, I don't need you to hold my hand as I walk through the doors," I said as I kept my head down while taking a bite of my oatmeal. Every morning, I have oatmeal with almond milk, cinnamon, and a sprinkling of brown sugar. If

I don't eat oatmeal in the morning, then my day is ruined. I know it may sound weird, but for me, it feels like life or death.

"I know, honey, but do you remember everything you learned at orientation?" she asked as she poured herself a cup of coffee.

She came with me to freshman orientation last week. They gave the new students a tour of the entire school. We got our class schedules, and they even showed us the directions we needed to go from class to class, along with a map. We got to see the lunchroom, the gym, the library, and the outside commons. There was even a girl there that said hi to me. I froze, of course, and all I could muster was a wave. But it felt like a big deal to me. With all that still fresh in my mind, I was feeling pretty confident.

Kinda.

"Yes, Mom. It's not that much to remember," I said as I sighed heavily, trying hard not to roll my eyes.

Even though I wasn't worried, I have to admit my short-term memory is crap.

My dad looked from his laptop. "Laura, babe. Mal will be fine. Give her some credit." He winked at me. I smiled and nudged his leg under the table. My dad and I have a special relationship. He is always there to pick me up and show me what I can do, no matter how scared I am. He does this in words mostly, but also, he knows how to push me. I love him for it. And not that my mom doesn't. But with my dad, it's different somehow. I think my mom harbors all the worry, while my dad harbors all the hope.

"No, no, you're both right," she said as she held her coffee mug in both her hands, drumming her fingers on the warm mug, unsure in her own words.

See, worry.

Then, my brother chimed in. Because, well, he's my brother, and he can't control himself. "Now, Mal, you know you will need to actually do work, right?" he says as he shovels cereal into his pie hole and continues with a mouth full of Fruit Loops. "No more laziness and whining because you don't understand something. You may be at a different school, but I have a reputation to uphold. I can't be known as the dude with the crybaby sister."

I smacked him on the shoulder. "Shut up, you jerk!"

He laughed, unfazed, as he took his bowl to the sink.

"Hey!" my dad exclaimed. "Jake, be nice to your sister." My dad is also the first to come to my defense.

Jake rolled his eyes as he walked out of the kitchen. "Whatever."

Then, he stopped and turned back around. "Hey, Mal." I twisted my neck to look at him. "Remember what I said last night?" I gave him a slight nod as I watched him walk away.

I had a lump in my throat, and my heart raced as I forced down the rest of my breakfast. I don't think I ever felt that nervous before. My whole life was about to change, and it was a change that I wanted.

As I watch my mom's car drive away, I'm regretting my decision, and I can feel my heart sink as I stand outside the school entrance.

Why did I agree with this?

I try to shake the uneasiness I'm feeling. And besides, I need to walk in there to show off my killer outfit, my new green Chucks, and my awesome backpack.

As I stand here staring at the elaborate brick entryway, I keep hearing my dad in my ear.

"Mal Pal, you are the bravest person I know. You can do this!"

I also hear my brother's words from last night.

"Mal, walk in there like you own the place. Because you do."

I hear Cousin Johnny.

"Mal, you are fierce." I like that one.

I hear Aunt Shay and Uncle Kyle.

"Don't let anyone tell you that you can't do something."

And, of course, I hear my mom.

"No matter what, Mallory, always remember, I love you. I believe in you."

These amazing people believe in me. They may doubt me at times, but at the end of the day, they are always in my corner, cheering me on. So why can't I believe in myself? Maybe one day, that confidence will come. I don't know.

I know I need to take the first few steps and walk through those doors. It is necessary for me to be brave and show my family that what they believe about me is true. A sudden, unearned feeling of confidence propels me forward. I open the doors to what is going to be my new life.

Once I'm inside, I take a minute to adjust to the change in light. The hallways here are darker than in most schools. The lighting is dim, which is intentional since some kids here have a sensitivity to light. Me included. I play with my fidget ring without even realizing it. As I make my way down the hall to my assigned locker, the smell of fresh paint and schoolbooks hits my nose. All the kids crowd the hallway, so I curl into myself, pulling my arms close to my body to avoid any physical contact. Some have noise-canceling headphones on. Some are walking, turning their attention to the floor, holding some kind of fidget toy and using it. Some are staring straight ahead as they walk, trying to avoid all eye contact.

Can't blame them there.

As I take in my new surrounding, I see a girl approaching me, and she has a huge smile on her face. I recognize her as the same girl from orientation.

Gosh, what was her name? Layla, I think.

I notice her glance down at my shoes. "Hey, nice Chucks. I love the green," she says as she walks past me.

I only nod at her to say thank you because conversing with these students will take some time for me. I find my locker and stop, happy that I have something to concentrate on other than my nerves and all these new, unfamiliar smells and faces. The number 102 is staring at me. I realize this is my bedroom of sorts until May of next year. Rummaging through my backpack, I fish out the combination to the lock. I wheel the nob back and forth until I hear a click and it opens. As I unload my backpack, I think of how nice that girl was to me. Not once, but twice. I grin, proud of myself because I realize I didn't run away. Instead, I took her compliment, and I kept moving forward.

Who knows ... maybe I will make a friend or two. Or better yet, maybe I'll even meet a boy.

Maybe. You never know.

THE LATER YEARS

22

ele

TWO YEARS LATER

Mallory

"Welcome to French Street Cafe and Coffeehouse. How can I help you?"

My mom and dad are standing at the counter of their favorite coffee house in front of their favorite barista in her black smock.

Me.

That's right, I got a job!

It's been two years since I started at the autism school, and I feel like I am doing so much better both socially and academically. Wait ... I *know* I'm doing better. So much so that I was brave enough to want to get a job. My parents jumped on the idea.

And there is no better place for me to work than The French Street Coffeehouse. Their sole mission is to hire kids with special needs, help them learn life skills, and set them on a path of success. So, when I turned sixteen and my school recommended it to my parents, we jumped on it!

I've been working here for a few months now, and it's been amazing. My parents come in every Sunday to have coffee, and I know it's because they love to see me being independent. And I love to show them that I am.

Now, my dad is in front of me, acting like a dad as he orders. "Let's see, what do I want," he pauses, tapping his index finger to his chin as he pretends to study the menu hanging above my head. "What do I want?"

"So, that's one large black coffee and a blueberry muffin," I say as I tap his usual order into the touch screen. When I'm done, I stick my tongue out because he loves to tease me, so of course, I love to dish it right back. He gives me a sly smile as I turn to look at my mom. "Do you want your usual, Mom?" I ask as I'm already tapping in her order of a Flat White and a piece of coffee cake.

"Of course, sweetie," she says with her classic warm smile.

My parents always order the same thing. And let's be honest, no one likes blueberry muffins and coffee cake that much. I know the real reason they never change their orders. They don't want me to get flustered, so they order the same thing every single Sunday. Honestly, I wish they would switch it up. I want them to see that I can handle this.

The owners here make it super simple. They've designed the POS system so that it's mostly pictures of the desserts and coffee drinks. And if an employee has a hard time with reading (like yours truly), then the system can read out loud the names of the desserts and drinks. Honestly, it's foolproof. But of course, they are always trying to help and protect me.

The delicious smells of coffee and pastries waft through the air as I tap away at the register. "Okay, that will be ..." I pause as I look down at the total, and something's off. I know by now how much this costs my parents. It's the same every Sunday. $15.75. But for some reason, the total is higher. Much higher. $105.75.

CRAP! What did I do wrong?

My mom notices my hesitation about giving them the total. I'm sure she thinks that I can't read the numbers right because of my dyslexia, so she decides to step in and try to save the day.

"Mallory, do you need help?" she asks as she cocks her head to the side. I don't answer right away. My stomach is in knots, and I bite my lower lip. Because I know what I need to do to fix this problem.

I need to get Caleb.

And I *do not* want my parents to meet Caleb. He's the owner's son and my new mentor. French Street assigns a mentor to each shift. A neurotypical individual who helps guide the employees and assists them with any concerns. I told my parents that I was getting a new mentor, but I may have left out a few details.

And I have a confession ... I like him. Like, I like him, like him. A lot. And he is so cute! I mean, he's gorgeous. He's taller than me, but not as tall as my dad. His hair is the perfect shade of almost black, and his skin is olive-toned. And did I mention his eyes? He has amazing blue eyes. They are the prettiest eyes I have ever seen. In short ... he's close to perfect.

We exchanged phone numbers when I started four months ago, and we have been texting more and more these last few weeks. Lately, though, I've had a feeling that he might like me. I've caught him stealing glances in my direction from time to time. I didn't want to ask my mom about it because ... embarrassing. So, I asked my friend Layla from school. She is an expert on relationships since she has a boyfriend. Layla thinks he likes me, so I'm going with that.

My parents know everyone that works here. Mostly because I talk about my day non-stop when they pick me up from work. But I never talk about Caleb. I've managed to keep him all to myself since he never works on Sundays. But unfortunately, today we had a call-off, so Caleb is filling in. And Sunday is the only day my parents come in. My dad and Johnny prefer Starbucks during the week. *Whatever.* But now ... it's about to get interesting.

"Um ... no, it's okay," I say, peeking toward the back where I know Caleb is, then to the register, then toward the back again. I'm nervous and stalling since this whole turn of events is throwing me for a loop. "I'll just, um, go get Caleb." I take off in a flurry, tapping my fingers on my leg as I go.

Before I round the corner that leads into the stockroom, I glance back at my parents. Confused expressions are etched all over their faces. I overhear my dad asking my mom, "Who is Caleb?" I heave a heavy sigh because I know I will get asked twenty questions when I get home. And I hate getting bombarded with questions. It's overwhelming and exhausting.

I walk into the stockroom, and Caleb's arms are stretched over his head as he's lifting a box onto the top shelf. His biceps are flexing, and his shirt is stretching across his back. I avert my eyes for a second and take a deep breath in because I need to get myself together since my parents are only fifty feet away.

I clear my throat. "Hey, Caleb." He places the box on the shelf, turns around, and flashes me the same smile he always gives me. The same one that melts my heart and turns my insides to goo.

"Hey, Mal. Is everything okay?" he asks because I know he can sense my nervousness. We've only known each other for a few months, and he can read me like a book. He abandons stocking, approaches me, and almost immediately, I feel more relaxed and at ease. Because I know he will help me. He always helps me.

"Yeah, I think I messed up somehow on the register and charged my pare—" I stop myself, "—the customer too much. I'm going to need you to fix it."

"Wait, did you say your parents?" he asks, almost giddy. "Are they here? I'd love to meet them."

Crap.

We walk back to the front of the café. I can feel Caleb walking behind me, and I can't help but smile. Because that is what his presence does for me. There are a few people who I feel relaxed around. My family being at the top of that list, and my friend Layla. And now, this gorgeous boy that is standing behind me, helping me, smelling like sandalwood. I hate feeling crowded by someone. But not with him.

Caleb works his magic, and it turns out there was an actual issue (I didn't screw it up, thank God), and Caleb solves it with a wave of his badge. A couple of boop-boops, along with entering a manager's code, and all is okay. Caleb leans his head down; his nose brushes my earlobe, and he whispers. "What's it called when you steal someone's coffee?"

Another coffee joke. He has a million of them. "What?" I giggle.

"A mugging." I snort out a laugh and focus on his incredible blue eyes, and a satisfied grin crosses his lips.

Suddenly, the loudest throat clearing I have ever heard echoes throughout the whole café. It's my dad. I was so caught up in my Caleb haze that I completely forgot about my parents. *Not smart.* My head snaps to attention, which is what my dad wanted. I straighten up and look my dad right in the eye. The throat clearing gets Caleb's attention as well. He takes a step backward.

"Oh, yeah, that will be $15.75," I say.

My dad gets out his wallet—a little too aggressively—and pulls out his credit card. All his playful banter is gone. My mom is standing closer to my dad now, resting her hand on his arm, like she always does when she is trying to calm him down. The whistle of the espresso machine and patron chatter are all I hear. He taps his card on the card reader.

Boop.

"Mallory, don't you want to introduce us to your workmate?" he asks, trying to sound calm yet failing while he puts his wallet away. He keeps missing his back pocket.

I bite my bottom lip as my nervous gaze darts between my mom and dad. I am not eager to introduce Caleb to my parents. He is my little secret crush that I want to keep all to myself without my parents worrying or questioning his motives. Or mine.

Caleb must sense my hesitation because he takes it upon himself to help and speak for me. Which I love. He clears his throat, takes a bold step forward, and offers his hand to my dad. "Hi! You must be Mr. and Mrs. Givens. I'm Caleb Horvath." My dad takes Caleb's hand, and as his grip tightens, I can see his knuckles turn white from the pressure. Caleb releases a burst of nervous laughter. "Oh, wow, that's some grip you have there, sir." My dad lets go, and Caleb flips his hand a few times.

Gosh, Dad, how hard did you squeeze?

Caleb then turns to my mom and shakes her hand. "It's so nice to meet you both at last. Mallory has told me so much about you."

My dad speaks up. "Funny, Mallory has never mentioned you." He glares at me and raises an eyebrow.

"Yes, I did," my voice cracks slightly. "Remember, Dad. I told you guys at dinner last week that there was a new mentor." I know this answer won't satisfy him, but I had to say something. Plus, I'm pretty sure he can tell I like Caleb. My dad is a smart man, and he knows me really well. He's showing his overprotective side, which, honestly, can be exhausting.

"Mm-hm," he murmurs under his breath.

My mom decides to diffuse the situation and speaks up. "Caleb, you look so young to have a position like this." My mom is smart as well. She's trying to figure out how old is this boy standing close to her daughter.

Caleb chuckles. "I know. I get that a lot. But my dad and mom own this place. I've been working here and helping since I was a kid. I'm seventeen now, and this is my first time being a mentor." He fixes his gaze on me and smiles. "I'm enjoying it so far." I catch his smile and turn my head downward because I don't want my parents to see my cheeks turning a soft shade of pink.

Too late. My dad notices my reaction because his body tenses, and I hear a sharp intake of breath as he grapples with this new reality. Caleb and I like each other.

My mom turns around and takes in that a line has formed behind them. Which I'm grateful for. "Okay, well, we better let you two get back to work. I'll be here at six to pick you up," she proclaims. My dad walks away, which gives me the confidence to ask what I want to ask. And what Caleb and I talked about a few days ago.

"Um ... actually," I pause before I continue, and I tap the side of my leg. "Caleb offered to give me a ride home today. If that's okay."

"It's no trouble at all," Caleb interjects. "It's on my way home."

Before I know it, my dad is back at the counter. *I thought he was out of earshot!* "Mallory," he says curtly as he jabs his finger onto the counter, "your mom will be here at six to pick you up."

My eyes grow wide because I can tell he means business. I shake my head. "Okay."

Well, there goes that. Thanks, Dad.

I watch Caleb turn and walk to the espresso machine to assemble my parents' drinks, the whistle from the milk steamer filling the air. I think he wants to be as far away from my dad as possible.

Me too, Caleb. Me too.

23

ele

Mallory

"Mallory, I'm going to take you off the register now," Caleb says with a wide grin and a brief gleam in his eye.

I'm as eager as he is. And not just because I've been looking forward to this all day. But also because I hate being on the register. There is always an issue (like earlier) that frazzles me. But it helps sharpen my math skills. And I hate math ... with a passion.

But now it's time to learn how to make lattes, mochas, and my mom's favorite, Flat Whites. I told my mom on the way to work that I was going to be learning the espresso machine. She was happy for me and proud that I was going to be learning some new skills. I tried hard to mask my over-enthusiasm about it all because it meant that I get Caleb's full attention for the rest of my shift. I get to spend the next four hours with him, standing beside me, behind me, all around me. My stomach erupts into butterflies just thinking about it.

Which is a strange feeling for me. I have a hard time conveying my feelings because of my autism. I do with my parents, of course, and my brother. But that's about it. Sometimes people call me a robot, which is rude and completely untrue. I have feelings. I just don't know how to *show* those feelings.

But with Caleb, it's different. I feel a sense of calm and assurance when I'm with him. I have anxiety, and the panic is always there, ready to explode. It's as if it's a resting dormant volcano waiting to erupt without warning. But when I'm with him, those feelings disappear. I feel....

Normal.

And don't get me wrong, my parents make me feel special, and I appreciate that. But it can be hard. They hover. A lot.

Speaking of which, where are my parents? I look at their usual table, and I don't see them. Did they leave? I shake the thought of my mom and dad out of my head.

Back to Caleb.

He takes me over to the huge espresso machine, which is big and scary-looking. For the first time, I get a chance to study it, and I'm immediately overwhelmed by the number of buttons, lights, and levers.

Gosh, I hope I don't mess this up. I tap my fingers on my leg.

"Okay, are you ready for me to impress you with my mad coffee-making skills?" he asks, being cute as always.

I let out a snort. "You think an awful lot about yourself, don't you?"

He exhales deeply, his eyes full of worry as he examines me. "I can tell you're nervous." He's right, I am. *How could he tell?*

"You can? How?"

"You're tapping your leg." He points down to my leg, my fingers tapping away, and he shrugs.

I *was* tapping. I tap my leg out of pure habit. It excites me, though, that he notices these things about me.

There go the butterflies again.

Caleb calmly rests his hands on mine and then places them on the counter. A jolt of electricity pierces through me. His warm touch feels good and calming in a way that no one person's touch ever has. And that's because I hate it when people touch me. It's a sensory thing for me. I normally flinch when anyone other than my parents or those on the Hug List touches me. And sometimes, even then.

And while we are on the topic, I don't understand people's fascination with touching. Why does everyone feel the need to hug every time they see each other?

Or worse yet, kiss you on the cheek. For example, why do we always have to shake hands? Maybe the first time we meet someone, okay. But every time you see that person, you shake hands? Shouldn't that be a once-and-done type of scenario? Makes no sense to me. I'll never understand it. All of it feels like a special kind of torture. And that's why I have the Hug List. I only touch or hug those that are on it.

Speaking of which, I think I want Caleb on the Hug List.

But this soft touch of his hands on mine feels different. When I'm around him, I *want* him to touch me. Which is an odd feeling for me. To *desire* someone's touch ... well, it's a whole new experience. Him putting his hand on mine surprises me so much that before I know it, my head jerks up in shock. He quickly pulls his hands away.

Nice going, Mallory.

"Oh, I'm sorry. I know you don't like to be touched," he says as he squeezes his eyes tight with regret.

"You have nothing to be sorry for," I say to reassure him. "I appreciate you trying to help me relax. It just took me by surprise, that's all." I flash a comforting smile, my skin still burning from his touch.

The sight of his gentle smile makes my heart flutter with joy. Before I know it, our eyes are locked on each other.

That's the other thing. Holding eye contact with him, well, it's easy. Normally, I have a hard time looking people in the eye. But I guess if they all had Caleb's blue eyes, it would be easier.

He clears his throat and glances down, breaking up our small moment. "Okay then," he says as he claps his hands together, "let's make some coffee." He pulls out some bags from the cabinet under the counter and sets them with a thud. "I'm going to make you the best barista that French Street has ever seen!"

"Yeah, okay. I thought that was you?"

He pauses, tapping his finger on his chin while he looks at the ceiling. The same way my dad does when he's teasing. "Yep, you're right. My bad."

I let out a laugh and, on impulse, flip my hair back. *I guess I'm flirting now. Cool.*

He brews the perfect cup of espresso in no time, the aroma of freshly ground beans assaulting my nose. As he does, he tells me the steps (which I will forget). I'm trying to listen ... I am, I swear. But it's hard because he's cute and smells so good. When I concentrate on something hard, I stick my tongue out. I catch myself doing it. Did Caleb notice? I hope so.

"Okay, now it's your turn," he says. I let out a huge nervous breath that shakes a little on exhale. He places his hand on the small of my back.

Another touch that I don't mind.

"You got this," he says with conviction. He lowers his hand, the warmth lingering on my skin. It is a sweet gesture that doesn't last long enough and one that gives me enough confidence to do this.

I put the coffee grinds into the portafilter and press them down with the tamper. "Like this?" I ask.

"Yep. You're doing great!" he exclaims, his head bobbing up and down.

Now I have to put the portafilter into the machine. I attempt to do it the way Caleb showed me, but I can't seem to get it right. His gentle touch rests on my hand as he guides it into the machine with me. "See, just like that."

"Thank you," I say as I press the button to get the brew started. I wipe my hands on my apron, nervous because I suck at conversation, and I don't want any awkward silences while the coffee brews.

But Caleb doesn't.

"So, your dad. He's ... intense," he inquires. He nods over in the table's direction closest to the counter. "He's been over there staring at us. I'm pretty sure he wants to kill me."

Glancing over, I see them, and sure enough, Mom and Dad are sitting right at the table in full view of me and Caleb. I was so engrossed with making coffee (and Caleb's presence) that I didn't even see them sitting this close. Normally, their usual booth is clear on the other side of the café. It's pretty obvious they are keeping an eye on us. They are talking to each other, and they look... I don't know, sad maybe. I sigh and place my hand on my hip. "Sorry. Yeah, he is very protective of me. He is having a hard time, I think, with me getting older and more independent. I love that he cares so much, though."

"That's sweet. But yeah, he's so big. Like a gigantic man. He squeezed my hand so hard," he chuckles, "I swear he was going to go green on me."

"Wait, did you say, 'go green?'" I ask, confused.

"You know, like The Hulk."

I suddenly picture my dad turning green and ripping his shirt off like The Hulk in The Avengers, and I can't stop myself from bursting into hysterical laughter. My head flies back, along with my howling.

Gosh, Caleb is hilarious.

Out of nowhere, I hear a thud and see my dad take off like he's being chased. He grabs his coffee, and he's out the door in five seconds flat, his chair lying on the floor. He doesn't even say bye.

That was weird.

Mom gathers up their plates and places them on the dirty dishes end of the counter. She makes her way over to Caleb and me. "Is Dad okay?" I ask with a knot in my stomach, my head racing with worrisome thoughts. I hope nothing bad happened.

"Um..." she hesitates to answer as she looks out of the window. Tracking her eyes, I see my dad sitting in his truck. "He's just having a moment, I guess." A sense of relief washes over me. She turns her attention back to me and Caleb. "So, I will be here at six to get you."

"Okay," I reluctantly agree, "sounds good. I hope Dad's alright."

She throws her purse strap on her shoulder. "He will be, honey." She then acknowledges Caleb. "It was very nice to meet you today."

"You too, Mrs. Givens. Have a good rest of your day," he says as he waves, and my mom walks out the door. I watch her as she gets in the passenger seat of the truck. My dad glances one last time at the café before they drive away.

I can't worry about my dad. I'm sure he's fine. Besides, I need to learn how to make espresso from the cutest barista at French Street.

24

Caleb

I implored my mom to listen to me.

It was last week when she, my dad, and I were going over who of the new staff was ready to learn the espresso machine. I immediately voted for Mallory. I knew she was still struggling with the register and counting back the change, which is why Mom thought it was a bad idea. Navigating the espresso machine's knobs and buttons can be confusing.

But I also knew that I would be the one to teach her, which meant I got to be close to her. My mom was right. Mallory was struggling with the register. At the same time, I had faith in her. It made sense to me that if you gave her more responsibility, it would boost her self-esteem, which would give her more confidence. Plus, there was also the minor detail of me wanting to be closer to her.

I've been working at French Street since I was a kid. I'm seventeen now, and I have never been attracted to an employee. But the day that Mallory came in to interview, my stomach did a flip I didn't know it could. I've dated girls in the past, and I've had a few girlfriends. They were cool but never lasted beyond a few months. But there is something about Mallory. She is so stunning with her tall, lean frame and long, wavy hair that sways to her every movement. She only wears her hair down when she arrives at work, then she pulls it up into a ponytail before her shift starts. So, I always make sure to see her when she gets here. Her eyes are big and brown, and she has the cutest button nose. Also, she smells amazing ... like grapefruit and peaches combined.

It's weird because I feel a need to protect her. We've been texting a lot lately. And I know she deals with some sort of anxiety, or maybe it's depression. She hasn't told me directly, but something's up. Since French Street employs teens and adults with special needs, we have a separate space called The Quiet Room. Our employees can take a few moments of calm in this peaceful place to take a deep breath and relax. Mallory is in there a lot with her Smarties in hand. I always check on her if I see she's in there. Honestly, all I want to do is make her feel better ... like all the time.

That's why when I saw her get anxious about showing her the espresso machine (she was tapping), I touched her. Her hands were butter-soft. It was an impulse that I regretted as soon as I saw her reaction since I know she doesn't like to be touched. She looked at me with shock in her eyes, so I jerked my hands away with regret. But then she reassured me and told me that she appreciated my help. Which means she was okay with my touch.

So from there, the touches just kept coming. My hand on her lower back. Yep, that happened. My hand was on hers to help her with the portafilter. I mean, she was struggling. What was I supposed to do? I was training her.

Then there were her lips. I couldn't stop staring at them. They are full, pink, and shaped perfectly. Plus, she does the cutest thing when she concentrates. She sticks her tongue out ever so slightly. It's the best, and I had to keep checking myself since I was gawking.

After that, flirting. And not from me ... it was all Mallory. Hair was being tossed, and her giggles filled the air. Which unfortunately, her dad noticed because, in record time, he flew out of the café and jumped into the biggest truck I have ever seen. Of course, his truck is as intimidating as him. I've never seen a man move that fast.

I'm not dumb. I know that Mr. Givens had a hard time seeing me with Mallory, which is why he was so against me taking her home from work. Honestly, I expected that reaction when Mallory and I talked about it. I'm sure they are very protective of her. As they should be. But all I wanted to do was spend some time with her outside of work. Can they blame me? I mean, I'm sure they know how wonderful their daughter is.

But it's cool. I have another idea.

"Yeah, Mom, it's super slow. We haven't had a customer in the past"—I glance at my watch—"forty-five minutes." I'm nervously pacing in the break room, my shoes squeaking against the linoleum floor as I wait for her to take the bait. And I'm not lying. It has been dead in here today.

"So do you think we should maybe close early?" she wonders as I hear dishes clanking together in the background while she cooks dinner.

YES! It's working!

"I think we should. I mean, I don't see it getting any busier in the next hour and a half." It's a Sunday, and the café is always slow after three o'clock. I knew if I called my mom and told her this, she would suggest closing early. Which means I get to send everyone home ... except for Mallory. Which *also* means I can get some alone time with her. I hope that after we do our end-of-the-day cleaning, she and I can hang out and talk until her mom gets here. Man, I hope she's up for it.

My mom sighs in defeat. "Okay. Sure. Send everyone home and clean up. This can save us on payroll, anyway. And try to be home close to six for dinner." I pump my fist into the air and say a silent *'Yes!'* to myself.

"Alright, sounds good, Mom." I try not to sound too excited. "I'll see ya at home soon." I hang up the phone and make my way to every employee to tell them they can get the heck out of here. Then I ask Mallory if she would like to stay and help me clean up. Her exact words are, "You betcha!" Gosh, she's so cute!

After we finish cleaning up the café, we hang up our smocks, and I notice the time. Five o'clock. She looks at her watch, then outside, and I wonder what's going on in that pretty head of hers. She knows her mom isn't coming for another hour. I clear my throat to speak up.

"So, I was thinking..." I try to steady my voice. "Maybe we could just hang out here for a little while. You know, until your mom comes to get you." I put my hands up in mock surrender because I don't want her to think I'm pressuring her. "I mean, only if you want to, of course."

Please say yes, PLEASE say yes.

"Sure. That sounds nice." I feel a tingle of happiness as a small smile graces her face.

"Okay, great. I'll go to the cooler and get us some sodas. What do you want?" I walk over to the drink cooler that sits next to the side of the counter where you place your order. I feel like I'm floating as I walk over to it and open the door.

"Just water is fine," she says as I see her make her way to one of the high-top tables at the back of the café. I grab water for her and a Dr. Pepper for me and shut the door. It suctions shut, the noise echoing throughout the empty café.

"One water coming right up!" God, I sound ridiculous.

Calm down! Just be yourself. I try to give myself an inner pep talk because I don't want to screw this up. I get an entire hour with her. Alone.

I make my way over to the table and feel a bead of sweat roll down my forehead as I hand her the water. Our fingers brush for only a second, and it feels like heaven. Her hands are incredibly soft and delicate. Why does such a small touch feel so amazing?

Touch number four, by the way, if anyone's keeping count. Because I sure am.

I smile at her, hoping that the brief brush of our fingers felt as good for her as it did for me. Her soft eyes tell me it did.

The next hour flies by. We talk about everything. My school (Liberty High School, I hate it), what classes I'm taking (all the AP junior courses. They're so hard, and I feel dumb when I'm there, but I don't tell her that), my plans for the future (my dad wants me to go to Stanford and major in business), and so much more.

But enough about me. I want to know all about Mallory.

She finally opens up and starts talking about herself. She tells me about her struggles with anxiety and depression (my heart aches for her even though I already figured as much), her autism school and how it has helped her, and then all about her art.

"I would love to see some of your art sometime," I suggest. "I bet it's beautiful." I've seen some of her doodles on napkins around the café. They are incredible.

"It's okay," she says as she plays with the label on her water. I can tell she is putting a wall up about this. I know creative people can be private about their work. So, I press, just a little.

"Oh, come on," I say as I wave my hand, trying to dismiss her modesty. "I'm sure your drawings are amazing. Have you ever entered them in any art shows?"

"What! No way!" She exclaims with shock that I even suggested such a great idea.

"Come on. Why not?"

She shrugs and thinks about this. The once-reserved face she had is fading. "Maybe I could," she says, pondering the thought. "It's just ... I don't know." She looks out the window onto the street at passing cars. "I always wonder if they are good enough or pretty enough."

She cannot be serious right now. If her pictures at home are anything like her doodles, I bet they are spectacular. All I want to do is reassure her and boost her confidence. So, I reach across the table, grab her hand, and lace our fingers together; they are a perfect fit.

Touch number five. *I can't believe I am doing this right now.*

"Is it okay if I hold your hand?" I ask. I need to make sure this doesn't make her uncomfortable. Much to my happiness, she nods, and her big brown eyes are staring right at me.

"Mallory, you will always be good enough and pretty enough."

And she is ... so pretty. The prettiest girl I have ever seen.

My compliment makes her blush, and I can't stop staring at her. With our eyes locked together, time seems to stand still. I can die a happy seventeen-year-old tonight after this last hour.

Much to my disappointment, I decide to release her hand since our time together is almost up. I glance down at my watch. Her mom will be here in five minutes. "We better lock up and head out. Your mom is going to be here soon." "Okay, sure." She lets out a heavy sigh. I can hear it in her voice. She's reluctant to say goodbye.

We toss our drinks in the trash and march to the front of the store. I hold the door open for her as she heads out first. I set the alarm, then I walk out, take the keys out of my pocket, and lock the door. We are standing shoulder to shoulder with the café and the workday behind us.

"Alright then, I guess I will see you next week," she says, her voice trembling.

Does she think I am going to let her stand out here by herself while I leave? Is she serious?

"Okay, I'm not going to let you stand out here all alone. No way. I'll wait with you until your mom comes."

She's visibly relieved as a soft, audible sigh escapes her lips. "Thank you," she says. "I was feeling nervous that maybe I would have to stand here all by myself."

I turn toward her, and I feel a need to look at her brown eyes again. "Mallory, I would never do that to you."

I have no control over the words coming out of my mouth right now. I need to act on all this newfound bravery and confidence and go for it before I chicken out. "Also, I was hoping I wouldn't have to wait till work next week to see you again."

"Oh?" she says. I step forward, hearing her breathe as I hold her hands in mine.

Touch number six.

"Um ... yeah." God, I'm so nervous as I glance at our hands because I can't watch her while I ask this. "I was wondering if you would like to maybe hang out next weekend." I'm suddenly compelled to look at her. So, I do, then I continue. "I know you don't like big crowds. We could go to the park or the mall or whatever you want. I just want to see you again. Soon."

I can't believe I'm doing this. I mean, I've dated other girls, and asking them on dates was easy. Whether or not they said yes wasn't a deal breaker. But this.

This is different. I feel a magnetic pull toward Mallory, and I can't explain it. It's like nothing I have ever felt before. And her reply feels huge.

She finally answers me.

"Yeah. I would like that. A lot, actually," she says with a smile and a sparkle in her eye.

THANK GOD! I let out a long breath that I had been holding until she answered me.

"Okay, good! So, I will text you about it tomorrow." I can feel my heart racing with excitement.

"Sure. But I will have to ask my parents, of course. I've never been on a date before."

I hadn't thought of this one. *Dangit.* She has to ask her parents. Talk about bursting my bubble. I can only hope that I made a good impression on them.

"Oh, yeah. For sure." I let out a nervous laugh and let go of her hands because my hands are sweating thinking about her dad. And he's not even here. I run my hand over the back of my neck, trying to play it cool. "I'm sure your dad will love that conversation."

Just then, I see, and hear, a big intimidating truck coming toward us, and I realize quickly. It's not Mallory's mom picking her up.

It's her dad.

Fantastic.

25

Scott

I round the corner to pull onto the street of the café, and my eyes widen at the scene in front of me. Mallory and Caleb are standing outside of the café, alone. Way too close to one another.

What is happening in my life right now?

Today did not go as planned. Every Sunday, Laura and I come here to French Street to have coffee and see Mallory. We love it. For two reasons. One, we get to see Mallory working and being independent. Every week, she improves more and more. And second, it's our weekly coffee date, and there's nothing I enjoy more than spending time with my wife.

But what I wasn't expecting was to meet Caleb. A tall, skinny kid with pimples on his face, making googly eyes at my daughter. And her returning those looks. The poor kid had so many strikes against him from the get-go. He was standing entirely too close to my daughter; he whispered in her ear (right in front of us, I might add) and made her giggle. Not good.

From the moment he made his entrance, my primary goal was to make him nervous and get under his skin. And when I noticed his quivering hand and cracking voice as he handed Laura and me our drinks and pastries, it confirmed my success.

And there was no way I was going to sit in our usual booth, which was all the way over on the other side of the café. No way. I needed to be in full view of those two. But I quickly realized, after Laura and I ate our treats and stalked them, that it was a mistake.

Watching Mallory flirt with Caleb ... well, I didn't handle it well. While teaching her how to make coffee, he must have said something to make her laugh because when her head flew back into a fit of giggles, I had to get out of there. I ran out of that café as if it was on fire. Not even saying goodbye to my daughter.

Yeah, not my finest moment.

Here's the thing: I knew Mallory would eventually grow up, date, meet someone, and fall in love. As a parent and a father, you know this. But I was not expecting to experience this wave of ... I didn't know what this emotion was. It wasn't anger. It wasn't jealousy. Watching my daughter permit Caleb to touch her, I realized what was happening to me.

It was fear.

I'm afraid this kid is going to take my Mallory away from me. Or worse, take advantage of her.

As my truck roars onward and I approach the café, I push these feelings aside. I take a quick scan of the area. *Where are the rest of the employees?*

On a normal night, when Laura or I pick up Mallory from work, all the employees are streaming out all at once. Something's fishy. But I can't react, not with it being just Mallory and me. Laura gave me a lecture when I insisted on picking up Mallory.

"Scott, please don't grill her about this kid as soon as she gets in the truck. You know she will get upset and shut down," Laura pleaded with me as I was grabbing my keys to walk out the door. As soon as I ran out of that café like my life was in danger, I knew I was picking her up today.

"Yes, babe. I know. Give me some credit," I interjected as I stood at the doorway that led to the garage, swinging my keys in my hand. I paused before I walked out the door. "I don't know why, but suddenly, I have this need to spend time with her. She's slipping away. I can feel it." Swallowing hard, I turned my gaze to the floor. "I can see it." On impulse, I grabbed the door handle to leave, not wanting to open up like this because I hate sharing my feelings. Sometimes even with Laura. As I turned the knob, I felt Laura's warm touch on my hand, stopping me from leaving. Her arms wrapped around me and pulled me to her as I closed my eyes and listened to the sound of her breath. How after all these years she knows what I need when I need it is never lost on me.

Laura let go of our embrace first, looked at me with warmth in her eyes, and placed her hand on my cheek, rubbing her thumb over my day-old stubble.

"Mallory will always be our baby. Always. Remember that, okay." I shook my head, grabbed her hand from my cheek, and lightly kissed her palm.

"I'll be back soon."

Now, I'm pulling down the street, and I see my daughter making googly eyes at this boy.

Keep your cool. Keep your cool.

As I get closer, they both turn to look at me. Mallory cocks her head to the side in confusion, clearly expecting Laura. Caleb, on the other hand, his eyes grow wider and wider the closer I get to them.

I mean, I don't want to freak the kid out. But it's pretty obvious he likes my daughter. And isn't that the job of a girl's dad? To scare the living daylights out of any boy that so much looks at his daughter?

Yep. It sure is. A sly, almost evil smile comes across my lips.

I approach them and pull the truck over to the curb right in front of them. I roll down the window and prop my arm up on the door, flexing ... just a little.

"Hey, Dad," Mallory greets me. "Where's Mom?"

"I'm picking you up tonight, sweetie. Mom got busy," I lie. She's more than likely reading a book on the couch.

She hesitates. "Oh ... Um. Okay." She glances back at Caleb, not sure what to do. It's obvious I interrupted them.

And trust me, I'm noticing that she isn't getting in the truck yet. I also want to know where the other employees are. "So, where is everyone else?" I ask, scanning the area as if some of the other employees are going to materialize magically.

The little twerp speaks up. "Hi, Mr. Givens," he says as he waves at me. I glare at him. He slowly lowers his hand. "Um ... so we closed early tonight. That's why everyone else is gone."

Interesting.

"Mm-hm." I pause. "Mallory, you could have called us. We would have picked you—"

"It was okay. We only closed a few minutes early." *Boy, she interrupted me quickly.* Mallory is rocking on her feet, and her hands are in her pockets. This is something she does when she doesn't want to talk anymore. OR she's hiding something.

Caleb speaks up again. "I didn't want her waiting alone since everyone else left. I figured I would stay until she got picked up."

Well ... huh. That was nice of him. *Crap, don't make me like you, kid.*

"Well, thank you, Caleb. That was very nice of you." I have to give this kid some credit, I guess. He refers to me as Mr. Givens. He took the initiative and shook my hand when he met me and with a proper greeting. He's well-dressed and articulate. And he waited to make sure my daughter was safe.

He's okay, I guess.

"Mallory, we need to get going, honey." We really don't. We don't have a dang thing planned in the Givens' home tonight.

"Okay, Dad." She turns to Caleb, and they exchange a few muted sentences that they obviously don't want me to hear. She waves at him and rounds the truck to the passenger side. I wait until I hear her seatbelt click into place. I turn to Caleb, and he's watching her ... with intent in his eyes as he looks past me to get a clearer view of my daughter. She leans forward so she can see him through my window, and they wave at each other for another stinking time.

I pivot forward to obstruct his view and give him a sharp wave. He clears his throat. "Good night, sir."

I nod my head, put on my sunglasses, and drive off. I peek in the rearview mirror. He's still standing in the same spot, watching us drive away.

Then I glance at Mallory. She's doing the same. Watching Caleb getting smaller and smaller, with a shy smile on her lips.

On the ride home from the café, the only sound is the hum of the truck engine, a far cry from the norm. Mallory is quite the chatterbox when we pick her up from work. She tells us all about her day, what kids from school may have popped in to see her, and if she learned anything new. And that's why the silence is deafening. Mallory was taught how to use the espresso machine today. Laura said she was excited about it, so I'm sure this all has to do with Caleb. Talking about a boy you like is something you don't want to do with your dad. So, instead of talking my ear off, she's staring at her hands, picking her nails, and her leg is bouncing as she's tapping on it.

She's anxious and stimming.

"So, how was my Mal Pal's day at work?" I finally ask, looking over at her with my left hand hanging off the steering wheel.

"Um ... it was good, I guess," she replies as she turns to face the passenger door window, avoiding eye contact with me.

"Mom said that you learned how to work the espresso machine." She nods as the corner of her mouth turns up. "How did that go?"

"Yeah. That went great. Caleb said that I caught on really quick, and he's hoping that I should be able to run it on my own in maybe a couple of weeks. They wrote all the specialty drink recipes for me on cards using the Dyslexia font. They laminated them and will keep them at the machine. That should be helpful. And my reading has gotten a lot better these past few years. Caleb was an outstanding teacher. He's really smart."

I nod along as I listen to her. I love that she feels like she can accomplish things on her own. But I don't like that she thinks Caleb is "really smart."

He's seventeen. How smart can he be?

"A couple of weeks, huh?" She nods. "That's amazing! So maybe if you work even harder, you can be on your own in a week."

As soon as I see her tense up slightly, I regret the words as they leave my mouth. It may sound like I'm encouraging my kid to try harder, to live up to her potential. But that's not how things work with Mallory. I've now made her feel like her dad *expects* her to do this in a week, and I won't be happy if she doesn't live up to *my* expectations. I've added extra pressure to my anxiety-ridden teenager.

Ugh! Why did I say that? I need to fix this.

I gently squeeze her knee and give it a slight shake. I'm relieved she doesn't flinch at my touch. "But it's okay, sweetie. You will learn it at your own pace. And you'll be great at it!"

She shakes her head in agreement. "Oh, I know, and it's okay. Caleb thinks I can learn it a week also if I really work hard at it."

Oh, well, if Caleb says so.

I clam up, refusing to listen to anything more about Caleb. I need to end the conversation, so I turn on the radio and sit in silence while my daughter sits beside me, daydreaming about a tall, skinny kid with pimples.

After we left the café, Laura and I agreed we should talk to Mallory about Caleb as soon as she got home. As I pull the truck into the driveway, my heart pounds with nervousness, not knowing what to expect from the conversation. Like with all things Mallory, we have to tread lightly and speak with calm and ease.

Mallory walks into the house, and I trail behind, my hand on the door handle as I shut it behind us. She takes off her jacket and places it in the coat closet. Same spot, same hanger. Every single time. Then she takes off her Chucks and places them on the floor of the closet. Same spot, every time. I watch her as she places them down, stands up, and notices they aren't quite straight. So, she kneels, shifts the left Chuck an inch to the right, then stands satisfied with the placement. Inside, I chuckle because I love her little quirks so much.

I see Laura sitting on the couch with a book in her lap. She hears us come in and looks over the back of the couch.

"Hey, Mal! How was work?" she asks hesitantly, her voice trembling.

"It went well." She pauses and glances over at me, then back at Laura. Then back at me. She opens her mouth to say something, then stops. She starts to tap her leg, and Laura senses her anxiety.

"Mallory, is everything okay?" she asks as she takes the blanket off her legs, tosses her book, and walks over to where Mallory is standing in the kitchen.

"Yeah. Everything's fine," she says as she looks at the ground. "I'm going to put my purse upstairs, and then can I talk to you and Dad for a minute? It's kinda important."

"Of course, honey," Laura says, her voice is full of empathy, but she's biting her lip.

"I'll be right back!" Mallory exclaims as she rushes up the stairs.

"What do you think this is about?" I ask, thinking back on our conversation in the car.

"I have no clue. You were just with her. Did she say anything in the car, or was she acting strange?"

We make our way to the couch to settle in. I rest my ankle on my knee, my foot bobbing. "Well, she was really quiet."

"She's always so talkative when we pick her up." Laura pauses, and I can sense her concern. "She didn't talk about learning how to make coffee?"

"Only because I asked her about it."

"That's so odd and unlike her."

Mallory makes her way back down the stairs and sits right across from Laura and me on the ottoman. No one says anything. She's playing with the hem of her shirt.

"So, Mom and Dad, Caleb asked me out on a date today after work. And I want to go. But I told him I had to ask you guys first."

My brain is short-circuiting as my body becomes rigid. I'm dumbfounded. I turn to Laura and see the same expression of disbelief on her face. Neither of us was expecting this.

"Can I go? Please," Mallory finally pleads.

Laura speaks first because my mind can't form a sentence. "Um ... well." She pauses and looks at me, then back at Mallory. "Mallory, honey, we don't know him that well."

"So, I can't?" she asks, her shoulders slumping over in defeat, and her leg shakes.

"Well, like I said, we don't—"

"He's really nice, Mom," she interrupts. "He's kind to me and really cool. At work, he always makes sure that I'm comfortable and checks on me when I have to go to the Quiet Room. He even stayed with me tonight while I waited for you to pick me up."

"Wait, where was everyone else?" Laura asks.

I clear my throat because now I know what's going on. "They closed early today."

"Ah," Laura says. "I see." We get it now. At this point, who knows how early they closed? But one thing we both know for sure. Caleb made his move while they were alone.

"Mallory, did he..." I pause because the thought is too much, but I have to ask. "Did he try to kiss you tonight or touch you in any way?"

"What!" Mallory's head shoots up, drawing back in shock at my question. "No! Of course not. We talked a little, and then he asked me. That's all. Geez, Dad." I notice her hands are clenching the ottoman.

"I'm sorry, honey, I had to ask." Why I felt the need to ask, I have no idea. I do like her answer, though.

Everyone is quiet for a minute.

Although I don't like the situation, it's important that she understands we are here to help her, and we aren't against her. "Mallory, I'm proud of you for asking us first. That shows maturity on your part."

"Thank you," she whispers.

Laura speaks up. "Mallory, your dad and I were going to talk to you tonight anyway." Mallory's eyes widen. "We could tell at the café this afternoon that you kinda liked this boy."

"You could?"

Laura shakes her head. "We could." She grabs Mallory's hand, and Mallory lets her. "Your dad and I just want to make sure that he is as nice as you say he is. So, if it's okay with your dad"—I look over at Laura because I have no clue what she is going to suggest—"maybe Caleb could come over here for dinner first. We could get to know him more. Then, after, the four of us could go somewhere together."

"That sounds like a double date to me," she says as she lets go of Laura's hand and crosses her arms over her chest.

I mean, the kid's not wrong.

Even though I don't like Caleb, and only because he likes my Mallory, I have a sense that he cares for her and is trustworthy. I pride myself on being an excellent judge of character. And so is Mallory. She has always been able to tell the good eggs from the bad ones. Taking a leap of faith, I'm going to trust her.

"I agree with your mom, Mallory. Caleb should come here first. We can have dinner and ask him some questions. However, I think it would be okay if he took you out alone."

Her body language shifts, her shoulders straightening and her chin lifting. Her eyes widen, as well as her smile. "Really?"

Laura's eyes meet mine, and she reaches out to touch my knee. "Are you sure about this, honey?"

I pause and observe Mallory closely. I can see the plea in her eyes. "Yes, I'm sure." Mallory squeals and jumps with excitement, and I can't help but smile. "But this is the only way that you can go out on a date with him. So, if he doesn't want to come and get to know us first, then you can't go out with him. Deal?"

She shoots off the ottoman. "Yes! Deal!" She runs over and hugs me, then Laura. "Thank you! Thank you! Thank you!" She heads over to the stairs and pauses as she glances back at us. "I'm going to text him right now!"

Mallory flies up the stairs, her feet barely touching each step.

Laura's face twists into a smug grin as she looks at me. "What?" I scoff.

"Nothing. I'm just wondering who this man is sitting next to me. Because it's not the same man at the café. Remember him? The one who looked like he wanted to choke Caleb."

I chuckled. "Yeah. That guy was fearful."

"Oh, yeah," she says. "And what is this guy?" she asks as she waves her hand over me.

"This guy"—I look towards the stairs—"this guy loves and trusts his daughter more than his fear of losing her."

Laura stands, and her lips brush my cheek.

"I like this guy."

26

Mallory

I run up the stairs like someone is chasing me.

I launch myself onto the bed, the mattress bouncing beneath me, and bury my face in my pillow.

"AAAHHH!" I scream as I shake my arms and legs like a lunatic because I can't help it. Excitement is coursing through my veins! I can't believe Mom and Dad said it was okay for me to go on a date with Caleb.

I need to text him!

I jump off my bed, run to my purse, and grab my phone. My purse shifts from its usual spot on my dresser, so I place it back. Then I head to my bed and straighten out the comforter and pillows I just messed up. My bed is nestled in the far corner of the room. I climb onto it and arrange myself in a comfortable position, crossing my legs and resting my back against the wall. I open my phone and hit the message button. A burst of nerves erupts inside me as my fingers fly over the keyboard, and I text Caleb.

Me: Guess what?

I hold my phone and stare at it, waiting for those three magical dots to appear. I'm so nervous that I pull my big fuzzy pillow into my lap, and I fidget with the long strings because I need to keep my hands busy. Finally, the dots appear.

Caleb: Um.... you're going to take up scuba diving lessons?

Me: Haha. Nope, guess again.

Caleb: You are going to shave off your hair and get a buzz cut.

Me: WHAT! I shudder at the thought.

Caleb: Good, because I love your hair long.

I place my hand on my cheek because I can feel them getting hot.

Me: Well don't worry. It's not going anywhere.

Caleb: How many guesses do I get?

Me: Three.

Caleb: Man, I better get this next one right then.

Caleb: You asked your parents?

Me: Ding! Ding! Ding!

Caleb: Seriously??!! What did they say?

Me: They said it was okay. They just want for you to come over for dinner first. So they can get to know you better. Then we can do whatever we decide.

Caleb: Well, that makes me nervous.

Me: Why?

Caleb: I don't think your dad likes me very much.

Me: Actually, it was my dad that suggested we go alone on the date. My mom wanted them to come with us.

Caleb: What, like a double date????

Me: LOL! That's what I said!

Caleb: Great minds think alike.

Me: So, what do you think? Is
that OK? To come over and have
dinner before the date?

I bite the skin on my nails as I wait for his reply. Is he going to say yes? Does
he *want* to say yes? I can't go on the date unless Caleb agrees.

Caleb: If it means getting to
spend even more time with you,
then I'm in.

After I read those last words, I clutch the phone to my chest and rest my head
on the wall. I seriously cannot believe this is happening to me. Being autistic, I
thought no one would ever like me that way. Especially not someone like Caleb.

Me: I'm really excited.

Caleb: Me too! I'll think about
something fun we can do, and
I'll text you tomorrow with some
ideas. Sound good?

Me: Sounds awesome!

Caleb: And how about we go out
this Friday night? Maybe we can

meet for dinner at your parents
at six?

Me: I'll ask them but I'm sure that
will be okay.

Caleb: So I know you don't like
crowds or anything really loud.
Does that mean a movie is out?

Me: No, not necessarily. I have
noise canceling headphones I
could wear. But I wouldn't want
to wear them around you.

Caleb: Why not?

Me: They look stupid and I feel
so dumb wearing them.

Caleb: Who cares? I wouldn't
care either way. I just want you
to feel comfortable.

We never go to the movies as a family since they are always so loud and crowded. I had a complete meltdown when we went once when I was younger, and I can still feel the tightness in my chest when I think about it. We left before it even started. It was a Marvel movie, and Jake was so upset. Since we were going for him, he and my dad stayed to watch the movie while my mom and I went home. It was horrible.

My parents always want me to feel comfortable. They have said those same words to me over and over. But for some reason, seeing these words from Caleb means something different. It feels different. Like, maybe I shouldn't care what people think when I wear my headphones. A movie with Caleb sounds doable. I mean, what happened at the Marvel movie was a long time ago. I'm older now and more mature. Thinking about going with Caleb is making me feel brave and bold, and like maybe I can do this.

And besides ... maybe he will try to hold my hand again.

> **Caleb**: No pressure! There are a
> lot of other things that we can
> do together.

I took too long to respond, so he must think I'm nervous about this idea. I hesitate for a brief second, my fingers hovering over the keyboard of my phone. Caleb makes me want to get outside of my comfort zone and try new things. Plus, I want to look like the other girls he dated. I can do this, right? Besides ... it's just a movie. What's the worst that could happen? I type my reply.

> **Me**: No. A movie sounds like a
> great idea. Let's try it.

> **Caleb**: Awesome! Are you sure? I
> don't want to push you.

Me: Yep. I'm sure!

Caleb: Maybe we could get some ice cream after. I know you love ice cream.

Me: I never told you I liked ice cream. How did you know?

Caleb: I heard you telling Kaitlyn at work one day. You guys were talking about your favorite flavors.

Me: What's mine?

Caleb: Vanilla.

Me: Boring, huh?

Caleb: Never.

27

THE NEXT DAY

Scott

I'm leaning against my truck, waiting for Johnny to pull up, and I am exhausted. I slept like garbage last night since I was awake thinking and worrying about Mallory and how, apparently, she's dating now.

Great, now I have a knot in my stomach *and* a caffeine headache. I glance at my watch. Where in the world is he? He's fifteen minutes late.

I need my coffee!

Just then, I see his headlights pull onto the dirt driveway of our most recent job. He comes to a stop right next to my truck. He rolls down his window and hands me my Starbucks.

"Who peed in your cornflakes this morning?" he asks with amusement.

"Morning to you, too," I say as I take a sip.

God, this tastes good.

Johnny extends his arm through the window of his truck and opens the door from the outside. He gets out, stands next to me, and flashes me a mischievous grin.

I give him a side glance. "You're awful smiley," I quip because his chipper demeanor is annoying. He's so dang happy every morning, but today, he looks downright giddy.

"That's because I had a date last night," he smirks before he takes a drink of his coffee that has a straw and chocolate drizzled on the inside of the cup.

"Mm ... fun. What's her name?" I ask, genuinely interested because I am really rooting for Johnny to find someone.

"Rachel," he says and waggles his eyebrows.

I choke on my next sip of coffee as a coughing fit ensues. Johnny is laughing as I try to get myself under control. I wipe my mouth with the back of my hand and clear my throat. "Wait, you mean Rachel, Rachel?" I demand through a hoarse voice from the coughing. "The one that broke your heart, Rachel? The one that said you were too old for her, Rachel. That Rachel?"

"One and the same," he replies with a sly smile.

"How did this come about? Because you're older now than when she dumped you. She knows that, right? Like, she can do math?"

"Haha. Yes, she knows that, you idiot." He rounds his truck and reaches into the bed to grab his tool belt. He turns, looks at me, and shrugs while he smacks me on the shoulder. "I guess she missed me, or maybe I'm sexier in my old age," he says with that same smirk.

"Good Lord, your ego knows no bounds." I hear him chuckle as I grab my belt, and we walk toward the small plaza being built. "Seriously, how did you reconnect?"

"I ran into her at the grocery store, of all places. We started talking in the dairy aisle, and I found out she wasn't seeing anyone, so I thought 'why not?' and I asked her out to dinner. Thankfully, she agreed, and it went well." He pauses before we enter the first store of the plaza. "Really, really well." He swings the door open.

I can't help but smile because he's so hopeful. "I'm happy for you, man. I hope it works out this time."

"Did I mention how good she looked?" he asks, our voices echoing in the huge empty space.

"You didn't, and I'll assume good since you're mentioning it," I say with a laugh.

"I'll spare my married cousin the details. Just take my word for it."

"Roger that," I say with a chuckle.

I take out my flashlight and begin inspecting the ductwork on the ceiling that was installed yesterday. I decide to open up and tell him about Mallory and Caleb. "You're not the only one dating these days."

"Who? Jake? I thought he had a girlfriend?" he questions as he studies the ceiling on the other side of the space.

"Nope. I mean, yes, he has a girlfriend. But guess again."

He lowers his flashlight and shines it on me as he walks in my direction. "Mal Pal?!" he exclaims, his voice dripping in equal parts shock and concern.

"Geez, that thing's bright," I say as I shield my eyes. He's close enough to me now, so I smack it away.

"Mallory has a boyfriend. Are you serious right now?" He grins as he rests his hand on his hip.

"No, not a boyfriend. But yes, she has a date. With a boy ... who is a friend."

"So, a boyfriend?"

I take a step closer, the smell of his aftershave filling my nostrils. "So help me God if you say boyfriend one more time."

"Alright, alright," he says, laughing and putting his hands up in surrender. "Tell me more about this non-boyfriend." We both go back to inspect the ceiling.

"Well, she works with him at the coffee shop. He's tall, dorky, and has pimples, which apparently, she digs because he asked her out, and she said yes. Laura and I want to get to know him first, so he is coming over for dinner Friday night before their date."

"Is he nice to her?" I love that he asks this question. It's a simple one, but the meaning and love for my daughter behind it is there.

"Well, they closed early yesterday, and he was nice enough to stay with her until I came to pick her up. You know, so she wasn't alone."

"That was decent of him," he says. I can feel his eyes on me as I continue to unload on him and inspect the ceiling.

"Although I suspect he closed early on purpose to spend some time with her alone. Pretty sure that was when he made his move and asked her out. When I pulled up, they were standing a tad bit too close to each other for my liking."

I hear him chuckle and turn his attention back to the ceiling. "Nice move. Smart kid. I like him already."

I give him some major side eye before we continue our inspection in silence for a few more minutes.

"It sucks, Johnny," I admit out loud, placing my hand on the back of my neck. He lowers his flashlight and walks over to me. "When Jake started dating, I felt none of this worry. We talked about the usual stuff. You know, being respectful, opening doors for your date, treating her the way a woman deserves to be treated. But this ... I mean ... this is *my* daughter. My *special needs* daughter. I'm worried, man. I mean, this kid seems nice enough, but I know nothing about him. People take advantage of those with special needs all the time. Just thinking about that being a possibility already makes me hate the kid, and I don't even know him."

"Well, that's kinda unfair, don't you think? Jake can have your trust when it comes to dating, but Mallory can't?"

I lower my gaze to the ground. He's not wrong. I am being unfair to Pimple Face.

"You're right." He always is. *Stinking Johnny.*

"You better believe I'm right. Get used to it." I give him a disbelieving glare. He continues. "Seriously though, this is more about you not wanting to let go. Yes, Mallory has special needs, but you guys have always encouraged her to be independent and shown her she can make it in this life on her own. Am I right?"

I begrudgingly shake my head in agreement.

"It's time you show her you trust her judgment. And embrace the possibility that this kid could become a more permanent feature in her life." He shines his flashlight back in my face. "If you like it or not."

I slap his hand out of the way again.

"God, I hate you," I say with a chuckle.

"Nah. You love me and my pearls of wisdom." He puts his hand on my shoulder. "Seriously, give Mallory a chance."

"Understood," I answer, giving him a sharp salute.

He turns and trudges away, taking a sip of his disgusting coffee drink. "However, if he breaks her heart, I'll be your backup." He peers over his shoulder and winks at me. "And alibi."

28

FIVE DAYS LATER

Laura

Knock, knock, knock.

That sound can only mean one thing. Caleb is here for dinner and his date with Mallory. I swear, I have never seen Mallory this happy before. As a young girl, when she was anticipating something, her bubbling excitement was evident in the rapid-fire questions she asked. No matter the event or what was happening, the sheer volume of questions was mind-numbing. She would hyper-focus on it, and that was that. Nothing else mattered. Now that she is older, she has replaced the questions geared to us with her own questions, statements, or actions to herself.

"Only three more sleeps," she mumbled to herself at dinner on Tuesday.

"Maybe I should wear that red shirt," she said as she dug through her closet for the hundredth time this week.

"No, he likes my hair down," she said in the mirror yesterday as she let her hair out of the French braid she had it in. I've never seen her hair in so many styles in less than a week.

"I bet he won't like me anymore once he spends time with me," I heard her whisper under her breath at breakfast this morning.

Her words sent a chill down my spine. Something that autism and anxiety do to a person is tell them they aren't good enough. Pretty enough. Smart enough.

And it doesn't matter how often we tell her differently. Sometimes, those small voices in her head can be louder than the truth.

I'm standing at the stove, pulling the roasted potatoes out of the oven, when I hear Mallory barreling down the steps. "He's here!"

I take the oven mitts off, wipe my hands on a dish towel, then weed it through the oven door handle. Scott is in the living room watching TV. He stands and turns it off as I grab his hand, and we walk over to the door with Mallory to greet our dinner guest. Scott is tense, so I rub his forearm. "Relax, babe."

"I can't," he whispers under gritted teeth, along with the fake smile he's wearing for the sake of his daughter.

Mallory is now at the base of the stairs, facing the door, wearing the red shirt that hugs her body and buttons down the front. She's wearing her black denim, which surprises me because Mallory hates jeans. She always said that the waist of jeans around her stomach felt too tight for her and exacerbated her sensory issues. Funny how all that goes right out the door for Caleb. Her hair hangs over her shoulders in loose waves. Hold on—*is she wearing mascara?*

My thoughts abruptly come to an end as Mallory swings the door open. "Hey, Caleb!" Mallory exclaims.

Caleb is standing at the threshold holding two bouquets of flowers. I take a quick second to scan him up and down. He's wearing dark denim, a pair of gray Vans, a white button-down shirt with the sleeves rolled up, perfectly gelled hair, and the most nervous smile I have ever seen on anyone. Ever. And I'm pretty sure I see some beads of sweat on his forehead.

He's a nervous wreck. Poor kid.

"Hey, Mallory," he smiles and takes a quick scan up and then back down her body. "You look really"—he clears his throat—"nice. Um ... you look really nice."

Mallory tucks a piece of hair behind her ear and turns her gaze to the floor. "Thank you."

Now that I see the side of her face, I also see her cheeks change into a pink hue. *Or is she wearing blush?*

We are standing behind her, and I feel Scott squeeze my hand twice. He clears his throat.

"Oh yeah," Mallory says, "come on in." We all take a step back, and Caleb strides into our home as Mallory shuts the door. Caleb then turns his attention to Scott and me. He extends his hand to Scott, and Scott takes it.

"Mr. Givens, it's nice to see you again, sir." Scott shakes his hand and—good Lord—he gives him an extra tight squeeze. Again.

"You too, Caleb," Scott says in his fake, nice work voice that I've heard him use over the phone a million times. Right before he hangs up and says, 'What a jerk.' I nudge him lightly on the ribs. He turns to me and mouths, '*What?*'

Caleb then turns his attention to me. He extends the beautiful bouquet wrapped in brown paper he has in his hand. "Mrs. Givens, these are for you. Thank you both so much for having me over for dinner." I take the flowers from his hand, the paper crinkling under my grasp.

"Thank you, Caleb. These are beautiful," I say with a genuine smile because they are gorgeous. I lean in to sniff one rose in the bouquet, and it smells heavenly. You can tell that he didn't purchase these flowers out of a black bin at a grocery store. He took the time to visit a floral shop for these.

One thing is glaringly clear ... his parents raised him with manners. He always refers to us as 'Mr. and Mrs. Givens,' he waited with Mallory for Scott to come and pick her up from work last week, and he didn't come to a dinner invitation empty-handed. He seems like the type that, when he turns twenty-one, he will come with a bottle of wine instead of flowers. I like him already.

He turns to face Mallory. "And these are for you," he says as he hands her the other bouquet.

Mallory's face lights up like a Christmas tree. "Daisies!" She grabs the flowers and looks at him as if he is the most important person in the entire world. At this point in her life, he probably is. "Thank you. I love them!"

Yep, he brought her favorite flowers. There is no mistaking it. This kid likes my daughter. A lot.

"I know they are your favorite," he says as he reaches to touch her arm but realizes the company he is in and retracts his hand. He looks over at me as he puts his hands in his pocket. "Dinner smells amazing, Mrs. Givens."

"Thank you, Caleb. The chicken piccata should be done shortly. Why don't you and Mallory take a seat in the living room?" I take Mallory's flowers from her. "And Scott and I will put these flowers in some water."

Mallory and Caleb make their way to the living room as Scott follows me to the kitchen. I'm keenly aware of Scott's noticeable lack of conversation. He sits on one of the island bar stools as I grab two vases from the top of the refrigerator. Scott's hanging his head and is playing with the button on his shirt cuff.

"This was very nice of him. To bring the flowers." I focus on filling the vases with water while stealing glances at Scott, wondering what he's thinking.

"Mm-hm." He peers over his shoulder at Mallory and Caleb, laughing and talking on the couch. He huffs out a breath. "This is harder than I thought it was going to be."

I lay my hands on his as he looks up at me with a pained expression on his face. I see a man who is worried he is not only going to lose his baby girl to a boy, but also he is going to lose the role of hero. Autism or not, that is a huge pill to swallow.

I unwrap the flowers and arrange them in their vases, the sweet, floral scent filling the air. "I understand. This is hard for me also, but we really need to go into this with a good and accepting attitude. For Mallory's sake. And to be honest"—I point in Caleb's direction—"he seems like a very nice young man."

"Well, I'm not willing to go that far just yet." I let out a small chuckle as he squeezes my hand. "But you're right. We need to send a message to Mallory that we like this kid and that we trust her." He then leans across the island, and I meet his lips for a small peck. He smiles, and his eyes are softer. "I'm going to set the table."

—ell—

"Mrs. Givens, this chicken is delicious!" Caleb exclaims as he takes another bite.

"Well, thank you. It's Mallory's favorite." I glance at Mallory. I can see her wide, beaming smile. Scott and I are sitting side by side at the dining room table. Mallory and Caleb, on the other. Jake isn't here since he is working.

Scott gets the conversation moving. "So, Caleb, tell us a little about yourself."

"What would you like to know, sir? I am an open book." I can tell that he is pulling out all the stops to make a good impression.

"Anything, really. Let's start with your family life and maybe goals for the future," my husband says with a sly smile as he pops a few potatoes in his mouth. Scott has always said that if you want to get to know someone, get them talking about their family and their future plans. That way, you get a piece of their past, present, and future life. I mean, he isn't wrong.

"Well," he glances over at Mallory before he starts with a knowing smile. I'm pretty sure she is already privy to the information he is about to give us. "I am an only child. My mom's name is Vanessa, and my dad is Frank. As you know already, they own the café. I've been around the café since I was a kid and practically grew up there. When I was about fourteen, my dad started teaching and training me in pretty much everything. And because of him, I started to really get interested in the business side of things. You know, the inner workings of all of it. I'm fascinated by it, actually. So much so, that after I graduate with my bachelor's and then eventually my MBA, I want to take over the café and expand it."

Well, color me impressed.

I can tell Scott is, as well. He nods his head in agreement. "Wow. That's pretty impressive, I gotta say." I notice Scott glancing over at Mallory, who is looking at Caleb. She shifts in her seat and smiles, pleased Caleb gave an answer that Scott likes. "I know Mallory really enjoys working at the café. It has really helped her."

Mallory shakes her head in agreement. "I love it," she says as she grabs a roll from the breadbasket.

Caleb eyes her expression. "Yep. She is one of the hardest workers we have ever had there." Mallory's cheeks turn a soft shade of pink as she butters her roll. He turns his attention back to Scott and me. "And even though I love the café and the business end of things, my favorite part has been meeting all the atypical people that have worked there. Some of the most caring and hard-working individuals I have ever met."

We all nod in agreement. But a hushed silence falls over the table as we wait for someone to talk. The only noise is the clinking and clanking of forks hitting plates. Scott continues his grilling.

"So, Caleb, you are starting your senior year this year, correct?" Scott asks.

"Yes, sir," Caleb replies as he takes a bite of salad.

"Have you decided on a college you would like to attend? Since you have such a clear-cut goal in mind for your future."

Thanks, babe. You took the question right out of my mouth.

I wonder if Scott is thinking the same thing as I am. Is this kid, in less than a year, going to break my daughter's heart when he leaves for college?

I immediately notice Caleb's shoulders tighten up some. He turns his glance to his plate and sighs before he answers.

This must be a sore subject.

"Well, that one is harder to answer." He pauses. I can tell he is trying to come up with the right reply and tread lightly. "My grandfather and my dad both are Stanford alumni."

"Wow! Stanford. That's impressive," Scott says. "Mallory has told us how smart you are. I'm beginning to think she may have been right."

"I told you he was smart, Dad. I wasn't kidding. Caleb is more than likely going to be valedictorian next year," Mallory says. Her eyes soften into a lovesick gaze, conveying her feelings for him. "He's the smartest guy I know."

Oh, boy. I peer over at Scott because Mallory says that about him all the time. Scott stabs a few potatoes into his fork. I rest my hand on his forearm as Caleb continues.

"Yes, sir, you're right. Stanford is an impressive school. It has the highest-rated MBA program in the country. So, my father is dead set on my attending there."

I can hear the hesitation in Caleb's voice. You can feel it. Stanford is his father's dream for him. Based on his body language, I'm just not sure it's what Caleb wants.

"It sounds like maybe, though, you aren't so sure?" I ask as I focus on Mallory. I can tell that she is waiting patiently for his answer. She's holding her breath, and her leg is bouncing under the table.

"Well, I haven't talked to him about it yet. But I really would like to explore other schools as well. Maybe some closer to home. I don't really know if I want to move clear across the country." He looks over at Mallory. "I have so many reasons to want to stay here."

Scott clears his throat and wipes his mouth with his napkin. "Well, you have time. I'm sure you will make the best decision. One for you and only you. And I'm speaking from experience here ... This is your future on the line and no one else's. Remember that."

Scott has found some common ground with this kid. His mother pressured him to go to college and get an education, but he refused. He always said that college wasn't in his DNA. His brother, on the other hand, got his degree, and Scott's mom never let him forget it. It wasn't until Scott built his construction business from the ground up that she saw the value in his decision.

"Yes, sir, thank you for that." Caleb and Scott nod in agreement, a sense of mutual understanding passing between them.

After some more small talk, dinner is over, and Caleb offers to help me clear the table, which I appreciate. Mallory and Scott are sitting on the couch in the living room, their voices low and serious.

"Mallory and her dad seem pretty close," Caleb says as he rinses the dishes before handing them to me to place in the dishwasher. I glance over at my husband and daughter.

"Yes, they are." I pause before I continue. "You know he struggled with accepting her autism diagnosis." He stops mid-rinse and does a double take.

"Really?" He looks over at them. "I would have never thought that, seeing how attentive and protective he seems to be of her."

I decide to ask what I have been wanting to ask Caleb since I saw them together at the café.

I have to ask.

I need to ask.

"It's true. He struggled with not being able to protect her from this lifelong struggle. So, he ignored it for a while. It was hard on him. And that's why we are very protective of her now." I shut the dishwasher door and turn to this boy who is about to take my daughter on her first date. "We don't want to see her hurt, Caleb. Ever. I need to ask you this. Is this just a casual thing for you? Because I see the way she looks at you, and trust me when I say that this isn't casual for her. She likes you. A lot. So, if this is just you messing around—"

"No! Never, Mrs. Givens!" he says as he interrupts me, jerking his head back in shock at my question. "I like Mallory so much." He steals a quick glance back at her in the living room. "She is special. And it's not just about how she looks. She's beautiful, of course, but I just really want to get to know her better. I care about her and would never intentionally hurt her." He turns his head to face me and makes eye contact. "I swear to you."

An involuntary smile crosses my lips. His answer gives me a sense of satisfaction, and I can hear the sincerity in his voice. But more than anything, I can tell he really likes my daughter. "Thank you for saying that, Caleb. And it's not that I thought ill of you. But as her mom, I had to know."

"I understand. I would be concerned if you hadn't asked," he says. I give him a quick nod, pleased that this part of the evening is over.

This kid seems like the real deal.

Caleb and I make our way into the living room, and I ease into the spot next to Scott on the couch. "So, Caleb, where are you taking our Mal Pal tonight?" Scott asks.

"DAD!" Mallory exclaims in horror at the use of her nickname in front of Caleb.

"What? I can't call you Mal Pal in front of Caleb?" Scott asks as he lets out a laugh.

Caleb snickers. "I like it, Mallory."

"So embarrassing, Dad." Mallory rolls her eyes as she gets off the couch and stands next to Caleb.

"To answer your question, sir," Caleb says as he glances at Scott, "we thought about going to see the new Tom Hanks movie and then maybe some ice cream." He casts a look in Mallory's direction, and she nods in agreement.

Scott and I exchange uneasy glances at this information before turning to Mallory. The sights, sounds, and smells of crowded places can easily fluster her. And nothing is louder, darker, and more crowded than a movie theater. Which is why, after the Marvel movie debacle, we haven't gone back.

Was this Caleb's idea? Did Mallory know that's what they were doing before he came here tonight? Is she actually okay with this?

Scott voices his thoughts, which I'm pretty sure are the same as mine. "Mallory, are you alright with this?"

"Of course, Dad. I'll be fine with Caleb there." She looks at him adoringly.

"Oh well, then ... if Caleb is going to be there," Scott mutters under his breath. I nudge him on the shoulder.

Mallory heads to the coat closet to take out her shoes. Chucks, of course.

Caleb, being a good kid again, turns his attention to Scott, "What time would you like to have Mallory home, sir?"

Scott sits a little straighter with this question. I can see the surprise on his face as he looks at me, clearly impressed. "What do you think, honey? Ten-thirty?"

I give a quick nod in agreement. "I think that seems reasonable."

With that, Caleb and Mallory say their goodbyes. Scott and I stand on the porch as we watch Caleb open the car door for Mallory, make his way over to the driver's side, start the car, reverse out of the driveway, honk, wave, and then drive away.

The whole thing seems to take place in slow motion.

We both sigh in relief as if we are letting go of an hour's worth of tension. I make my way over to the doorway and stop when I notice Scott has sat on the porch swing. He signals me to join him by tapping the empty spot next to him. "C'mon, sit with me," he says, smiling.

I plop down next to him, and he wraps his arm around me, giving me a gentle squeeze as he pulls me closer.

"So, how do you think it went?" I ask as Scott slowly rocks us back and forth, the swing's chains creaking.

He lets out an exhausted sigh. "Good. Great, actually. He's a nice kid. Which irritates the crap out of me."

I can't help but giggle as I stare at him. "Why does that irritate you?"

"It really doesn't. Or maybe it does." He pauses. "The nicer he is, the more likely she is going to fall for him. Hard."

"Oh, I think we are already there."

"You know what I mean. I don't want to see her get her heart broken."

We both sit in silence for a minute as we ponder this possibility, knowing what it could do to her moods and her depression. I shudder to think what could happen.

I raise my eyes to his. "I mean, that could happen. He could hurt her. *Or* she could hurt him. You never know. But whatever happens, we just have to be there for her."

He gives me a kiss on the top of my head as I settle into him, resting on his shoulder while we continue to swing.

After a few minutes, Jake's car creaks to a stop as it pulls into the driveway. He slams the car door shut behind him and sprints up the porch steps, holding his Home Depot smock (like father, like son), his shoes pounding on the wooden boards as he whizzes past us.

"Hey, son! You're not going to even acknowledge your parents? What's the rush?"

Jake stops in his tracks. "Sorry, Dad. I gotta run. I have a date tonight, and work kept me over." He runs into the house and shuts the door behind him. It opens again seconds later, and he pops his head back out. "Hi, Mom!" He shuts the door and disappears.

Scott turns to me. "Seriously, is this my life now?"

I stand and kiss his forehead. "Afraid so, honey." I walk to the door but stop because I notice Scott isn't getting up. "You're not coming inside?"

"Nah, it's beautiful out. I think I'm going to chill here for a while."

I let out a small laugh. "For how long?"

His eyes dart to his watch. "Oh, I don't know. Till about ten-thirty."

29

Caleb

I honk the horn as Mallory and I wave at her parents, who are standing on the porch and watching us drive away. A sense of relief washes over me as I release a long, deep breath. The dinner went well, don't get me wrong. I feel like I made a good impression on them.

At least, I hope I did.

But my brain needs a break. For over an hour, I was on my best behavior, trying my hardest to say the right thing and not do anything stupid. Impressing Mallory's parents, other than impressing Mallory, was my sole mission in life tonight. Quite frankly, I'm exhausted, and our date hasn't even started yet.

I glance over at Mallory and notice her hands are fidgeting in her lap as she picks at her cuticles. Turning my attention back to the street, I watch the houses pass us by, one by one.

This silence is maddening. We have talked each other's ears off for months at the café. We text every day, sometimes all day. But as soon as you attach the word "date" to our time together, we get all weird and awkward. I'm usually a pretty calm and collected kinda guy. But right now, I feel like I want to crawl out of my skin.

"So, I hope your parents liked me," I ask, giving the conversation a go.

"Don't worry, they did. You would have known if they didn't. Especially my dad. He gets quiet when he doesn't like someone, and he talked to you. So, you're good." She pauses. "Just wait till you meet my dad's cousin, Johnny. He's just like my dad. Maybe even a little worse. He's also very protective of me."

Oh, geez! There's two of them!

She's wearing a big smirk as if she is already playing out the "meet Cousin Johnny" scenario in her head. I will put that family meeting off as much as possible. Thank you very much. The Givens men are intimidating, to say the least.

After that lame attempt at conversation, we both get quiet again. I turn onto the highway, and all you can hear is Imagine Dragons and Mallory's breathing. *God, why is this so hard all of a sudden?* I need to address the elephant in the room. Or ... car.

"Okay. Let's be honest here, Mal." Her eyebrows raise in concern. "Are you as nervous as me? Because my stomach is in knots, and I feel like I'm going to throw up your mom's delicious dinner."

Her gorgeous face breaks into a curious smile, and she sighs in relief. "You're nervous?"

I glance at her knowingly. "Yes. Very." I turn my attention back to the road.

A nervous giggle escapes her lips. "Me too."

"I mean, this is ridiculous. We have talked and become so close over the last few months. Why does this feel different?"

I know why it does for me. Because, over these last few months, Mallory has become way more to me than just a friend.

She taps her leg nervously and avoids looking at me by staring out the passenger window. Eye contact is hard for her, especially when she wants to say something important. "I like you, Caleb. And I'm afraid that you'll spend time with me outside of the café, and you may see things you don't like. I can be kind of ... well, people have called me weird. I don't want you to see me that way."

This admission is baffling to me. I could and never would see her that way. Mallory is Mallory. And I like her just the way she is. I open my mouth because I want to say this out loud, but I decide maybe to keep it to myself until the end of the date. That way, she will see that I do really like her. Even after spending time with her. So instead of saying it, I'm going to show her.

"Mallory?" She averts her eyes from the world outside and focuses on me. "Can I hold your hand?"

A broad smile comes across her face as she moves her left hand in my direction. I slowly take my hand off the steering wheel, and our hands meet in the middle. With a feather-light touch, our fingers brush, then before I know it, we interlace together our fingers and rest our hands on the middle console. Her touch feels like fire. She stares at our hands as I rub my thumb in circles on her silky-soft skin.

"Is this okay? I know you don't like touch all that much," I ask, praying that she doesn't let go.

"I've never held hands with a guy before," she says, still studying our hands.

"What?! Yes, you have. I held your hand outside of the café on Sunday. Both of them, actually."

She giggles. "I know. But this…" she trails off and doesn't finish her sentence. "This what?"

She sighs heavily. "Does this feel weird? Like, my hand? Does my hand feel weird? Okay, that was a dumb question. I don't know what I'm trying to say." She shakes her head before she continues. "So, you like this?" she asks, pulling our hands up and placing them back down again. "You actually like holding *my* hand?"

I can feel the lack of self-confidence oozing out of her. Is she convinced no guy would ever like her? Or want to touch her? Because that's the vibe she's giving off here. And it totally confuses me. Any guy that wouldn't fall for Mallory is an idiot.

I need to put her mind at ease.

"Yes, I do. Very much." She grins slyly. "And Mallory?" She can't seem to take her eyes off our interlocked hands. "You or your touch could never be weird. Not to me."

She gazes at me after finally looking away from our hands. I see the reflection of the sunlight in her eyes, and all I can see is hope. "Thank you."

Mallory

OH, MY GOD! OH, MY GOD!

I'm holding Caleb's hand. And he wants to. Like, he actually said it.

And not just in the car either, where no one can see us. No, no, no, my friends. He also held my hand while we walked into the movie theater and while we stood in line to get popcorn. Unfortunately, we had to break apart to hold our popcorn and drinks. Nothing's even happened yet, and so far, this is the best date ever.

Not that I have anything to compare it to.

When someone touches me, my skin crawls as if thousands of tiny needles are stabbing it. I can't explain it any other way. Hugs feel like I'm being rubbed with scratchy sandpaper. Kisses feel like … I don't even know. Not that I've kissed a ton of people. I hate it when I see a family member whom I haven't seen in, like, forever, and they kiss me on the cheek. Ugh. Lips are supposed to be soft. But to me, they feel almost slimy.

I wonder if Caleb's are slimy. I hope not.

However, when Caleb took my hands on Sunday outside of the café and then just now in the car, there were no needles. Just warmth. And when he started rubbing his thumb on my hand, I was worried again about feeling needles. Instead, it felt soothing and nice. I couldn't stop looking at our fingers laced together. It felt so right, and safe.

And normal. I felt … normal.

There were no needles, no sandpaper. Just warm human touch.

Once we broke the ice in the car, we chatted up a storm the rest of the way to the movie theater. Just like we do at the café when we are together. I struggle with conversation, sometimes even with my parents. But with Caleb, it feels so easy. I can open up with him, and I feel comfortable in my skin.

This is probably how it feels to be a regular teenager. *I love it.*

Caleb takes my popcorn and drinks. "I can carry it," I offer because I have no clue how he is going to juggle it all.

"Nope. I got it," he says as he balances the popcorn containers on top of each other and somehow holds two drinks all together in both hands. After he gets settled, he turns to me and grins. He's impressed with himself and looks so cute right now, trying to be a gentleman. "Are you ready?"

I smile and nod as we head down the hallway to the theaters. We turn left toward theaters 6-10. Our movie is in theater 10, which is clear down the end of the hallway. As we walk, my chest tightens with anxiety, knowing what awaits me in that theater.

Caleb is talking about ... something; I have no idea what because a million things are crowding my mind. All I can think about is how to keep my already panicky thoughts at bay.

We locate theater 10, and he holds the door open for me. I miss how he must have juggled our drinks and popcorn in one hand because he's holding it all like a pro. I'm two steps in, and *BAM!* I'm enveloped in a thick, inky darkness, and I stop dead, my legs refusing to move. Caleb stops behind me, practically running into me. My breathing is getting heavier, and I can feel my heart starting to race. I squeeze my eyes shut, then open them multiple times, straining to make out shapes in the darkness.

No. Not now. Please, not now.

I can't have an anxiety attack on our first date.

"Mallory?" I hear Caleb say my name. But I'm frozen.

"Excuse me." A woman says as she brushes past my shoulder to get around me, causing my shirt to brush against my skin ... like sandpaper. I wince at the sensation, still not moving.

Out of nowhere, I feel Caleb's hand on the small of my back. With his one touch, I suddenly feel like I can move, and he leads me to the far wall.

"Hey, are you okay?" he whispers softly in my ear. He's standing behind me, and his hand is still on my back. Which feels nice, warm, and calming.

The sound of rustling clothing and chattering voices fills the theater hallway as people walk past us. Groups, couples, families—more and more people.

Sheesh. Tom Hanks really knows how to draw a crowd.

I stay silent. More than anything, I want to go into the theater and show Caleb how I can be like the other girls.

"I'm okay," I finally say, trying to sound confident. "I just needed a minute for ... um ... my eyes to adjust to the light change."

I turn my gaze over my shoulder and smile at him, trying my hardest to not appear fearful.

With a sigh of relief, he buys into my fib. I take steps forward, inching my way deeper into the darkness with his hand never leaving my back. We round the corner, and *BAM!* I'm smacked in the face with nothing but a sea of people. My fingers dig into the plush carpet of the sloped wall as I grasp for something to help me through the sensory wave that is hitting me. My nose crinkles up because the air smells musty, coupled with the scent of stale popcorn. The combination is rank, and I can't figure out why it doesn't seem to bother anyone else. I scan the theater, and my vision blurs. There are so many faces and people. Looking for seats, talking to each other, looking at their phones, looking at the theater screen, looking at their watches. A Sprite commercial telling everyone to silence their phones during the movie is blaring from the screen. I squeeze my eyes shut. Maybe if I don't see them, they won't be there.

I open them.

Nope. Still there.

"Man, this place is packed," Caleb says, oblivious to my inner freak-out. He takes in our limited seating options. "We should have gotten here earlier."

I notice that there are some seats clear in the back row. Nope. Won't work. Then I can see everyone. Like, the entire room. Then I glance at the dreaded front of the theater, and there is a pair of seats in the first row. God, no! Then the screen is right in your face. All the actors, larger than life. I feel like I have to make your eyes bigger to even take it all in. No, thank you.

"How about right over there?" Caleb points to two seats about halfway up to the left, clear up against the wall.

"Okay," I say with fake confidence again. "That could work." We head in that direction when I realize ... CRAP! I will need to walk past an entire row of people, brushing up against them as we walk to our seats. I take a deep breath in and hold my stomach because I suddenly feel nauseous. Both from nervousness and the nasty smell of this theater.

You got this, Mallory. You can do this.

We walk up the few steps and stop in front of our row with Caleb in front of me. I'm standing against his back as a couple passes me up the stairs, and the woman's shoulder touches my elbow. I feel like I'm being stabbed.

"Excuse me." Caleb taps on the shoulder the guy who is in the aisle seat. "Are those seats taken?" He points to the two empty seats.

"Nope. All yours, man," the guy replies as he stands and nudges the woman beside him. She stands, and then it's like a domino effect. One person after the other stands as we make our way to our seats, shuffling my feet as I go.

In these types of situations, what do you do? There's no room. Do you shimmy down the aisle facing them? Which is weird. Or do you not face them, which is weirder because if they don't stand—like the fourth guy in, who just shifts his legs to the left—then your butt is in their face. It's awkward all around. I'm brushing up against people, and the sandpaper feeling returns. It feels like my skin is being rubbed off my body. God, I hate this. Plus, I'm wearing jeans. I hate jeans. Huge mistake.

Why did I wear these things? Right, because Layla said they make my butt look good. And I wanted to look normal.

To make this even worse, I step on someone's foot. "Sorry," I mutter to whoever it is, my eyes glued to my shoes, not wanting to make eye contact with these strangers.

Caleb lets me have the seat closest to the wall. Thank God I won't be sitting next to anyone. We finally sit, and Caleb hands me my popcorn and places my drink in the cup holder. We are situated finally, and I feel all amped up. That was by far one of the most stressful experiences of my whole life. And the movie hasn't even started yet. I feel hot, my body is tense, and my senses are in overdrive. And to top it all off, my jeans feel like they are cutting off my circulation while digging into my stomach.

"Hey," Caleb says, as he rests his hand on my knee, "what's wrong? Are you sure you're alright?" I must be wearing my distress all over my face for him to notice.

After taking a deep breath, I rest my head on his shoulder, taking in the warmth of his touch. I can't keep up the charade any longer. "I just need a minute. That was a lot."

He rubs his thumb on my knee. "We can go," he whispers, "if this is too much for you. I would totally understand."

And he would. I know he would. Caleb has never judged me for who I am. But I *need* to be someone different tonight. I don't want to be autistic, anxiety-ridden Mallory. I *want* to be like the other girls. Fun, free, and full of life.

I move my head from his shoulder and feel his warm breath as I search his eyes. He leans in closer, and I can sense his concern in the intensity of his gaze. I wish I could see the flecks of green that I know are in there, but it's too dark.

"No, I'm okay," I reply, trying to convince myself more than him.

"I wondered if this would be hard for you, so I brought something. I hope it helps," Caleb whispers. He places his popcorn on the seat in between his legs and leans forward. He reaches behind his back and pulls something out of his back pocket. In the dark, I can't make out what it is. He takes my hand and places two Smartie packs into my palm.

Oh, my God.

"You brought me Smarties?" I can't stop staring at the two sleeves of candy. Not only did this amazing boy want to go on a date with me, but he also brought me my favorite candy. "How did you know?"

"I see you eating them when you are in the Quiet Room. So, I assumed that they help you relax." He shrugs. "I took a chance."

My mind moves my head without even realizing it because before I know it, I turn my gaze to look at him. "Thank you." He nods, and a small smile creeps on his lips. We stare at each other longer than makes me feel comfortable, so I turn away.

I place my hand over his, and we lock our fingers together again. I lay my head back on his shoulder, squeeze the Smarties in my other hand, close my eyes, and settle into my seat as we talk for the next ten minutes before the previews start. Closing my eyes and feeling Caleb's comforting touch helps me to center myself. It feels like no one is in the theater. The voices fade, the smells recede, my stomach settles.

But then the lights dim even more, and the previews blare, assaulting my ears. And I feel like I'm about to die.

30

Caleb

The theater goes dark, sending a hush of anticipation through the audience as my favorite part of the movie experience begins.

The previews. Or trailers. Whatever you want to call them. I love it all.

Mallory removes her head from my shoulder, and I pray that the dimming lights will settle her nerves. I know she said that she was cool with a movie, but I had my doubts. But she seemed okay when we got here and when we were getting snacks, so I thought we were in the clear.

We had barely taken two steps into the theater before she froze in her tracks, overwhelmed by what, I had no clue. She stood in the middle of the theater entrance like a statue. Right now, she's not saying anything, but I think she is trying hard to put on a brave face. After I gave her some Smarties (proud of myself for that one), we talked for the last ten minutes with her eyes closed and her head on my shoulder. I cracked a few coffee jokes to make her laugh, and it worked. I could feel the tension leaving her shoulders, and her breathing steadied. At this point, I just have to hope for the best.

After a few commercials, the trailers start. I steal a glance at Mallory, and I notice her eyeing her popcorn. Not eating it, just staring at it as she spins the Smartie packs in her hand. As I look at her to study her breathing, I become acutely aware of the curve of her chest, and I find myself gawking. I quickly glance away because, well, it's her chest. I don't want to make her feel awkward.

Gosh, I hope she didn't notice me staring like a pervert. Taking another quick glance at her (I admit, and her chest again), she seems okay.

And sitting this close to her feels fantastic. Our shoulders are touching, and I can smell her body spray. I love it when her hair hangs in loose waves. It felt so soft on my cheek when I leaned in to ask her if she was okay in the entryway. When she casually laid her head on my shoulder, I swore my heart stopped, and my brain shut off. I know she did it to make herself feel better, but still. I loved it. And I never want to let go of her hand. Ever.

The second trailer is underway, and it's for the new Jim Carrey movie. My favorite comedian of all time. The dude cracks me up.

Jim says something hilarious. I mean, of course, he does, and the theater explodes in laughter. I feel Mallory flinch beside me, so I lay our hands on my knee to comfort her. She's still eyeing her popcorn. Come to think of it, she hasn't looked at the screen. Not once.

My man Jim runs in a scene and trips comically over some garbage cans while making one of his signature funny faces. More explosive laughter erupts from the packed theater. This time, she jumps, lets go of my hand, and covers her ears. Her popcorn spills out all over the floor, with the smell of butter coating the air in the dark theater. I can tell the noise is bothering her.

"Did you bring your noise-canceling headphones?" I lean to whisper in her ear, concerned about her but also not wanting to take my eyes off the screen.

Jim runs right into a glass door, and it shatters. Another outburst of laughter. She jumps again, her hair swaying around her face as she shakes her head no.

"I'm okay," she whispers. But I doubt that's true. I decide to sit back and let her work through this on her own. She takes her hands off her ears once the trailer is over. She looks around at her feet at the spilled popcorn.

I gently shake her leg. "Hey." She looks up at me. "Don't worry about the popcorn. It's no big deal." She gives me a small, pursed smile before turning her attention to the screen. I muster up some bravery as I put my arm around her shoulder and squeeze. She leans into me, and I can feel her relax some. Hopefully, the worst is over, and she is adjusting. Because I do not want this to end.

Next one up is for the new Transformers movie. Sweet! Optimus Prime's deep voice narrates the trailer. I watch with anticipation and shift in my seat with excitement because I am a guy, after all, and what guy doesn't love Transformers?

I watch Optimus and Bumble Bee transform on the screen, running from what looks like a bunch of black window-tinted SUVs. Suddenly, there is an enormous explosion behind them. The SUVs are blown to high heaven in a ball of flames. The sound is so loud that I feel the vibration of it in my theater seat. Mallory and I both jump, and I watch as she springs to her feet, the seat whipping back and rocking from the sudden jolt.

The look of panic on her face is so intense that I feel a chill run down my spine. She stares at me with wide, tear-filled eyes. She's shaking so much that her clenched fists are trembling at her sides. "I gotta get out of here," she yells at me.

I reach out for her arm with a gentle grip as I try to guide her back into her seat, but she violently yanks away. I stare at her in shock because I don't know what to do, but I feel like I have to comfort her somehow. "It's okay," I say reassuringly. "There are only a few more trailers, and then the movie will start," I whisper, trying to put her at ease with my words.

Another explosion, this time with screaming people running from ... I don't even know what because I am so worried about my date. My seat vibrates again. Her eyes flick to the screen, then back to me with her face tense. "I SAID I GOTTA GET OUT OF HERE!" she screams.

Oh, no. This isn't good.

In an instant, three hundred eyes are no longer watching Optimus Prime fight Megatron. Instead, they are staring at my panic-stricken date. She's the only person standing in a theater full of people. Her outburst draws everyone's attention away from transforming robots and straight to her. She pauses for a second, then bulldozes her way out of the aisle. "Excuse me, excuse me," she says over and over as she crawls over the six people in her way.

"Geez, lady. What the heck?" one of them says with irritation. It's the dude that wouldn't stand when we walked past the first time.

"Mallory, wait!" I yell out as I stand to get to her. The sound of popcorn spilling hits my ears as my tub falls on the floor. I glance down quickly at the pool of buttery popcorn now at my feet. I turn my attention back to the task at hand (I can't be concerned with two buckets of spilled popcorn), trying to make my way past the same people. There's another explosion on the screen, causing Mallory to move even faster. "Sorry, excuse me," I say to the row of people I'm trying to get past. "Mallory!" I yell out to her. They are all standing now, well, except the jerk, who I'm pretty sure I heard say, "God, that girl's a freak." If I wasn't so worried about Mallory, I would have knocked that word out of his mouth. With my fist.

She's out of the aisle now, faster than I can get to her, and is running. Like a full-on sprint, down the steps, past the other theatergoers. Her hair is bouncing as she turns and disappears out of the theater.

God, she's fast! And these people need to stand and get out of my way!

I'm out of the aisle slower than I wanted to be and run after her as Optimus tells us that the new movie is being released on Memorial Day next year. I hear people murmuring under their breaths. There are a few 'What is going on?' and 'I hope she's okay.'

I barrel out of the theater so fast the door hits the wall as I'm rushing out into the hallway. Frantically searching for her, I stop and quickly look left and right. She's up against the wall, crouched on the floor, knees pulled up to her chest, and head buried into her hands. "Mallory!" I call to her as I run. At the sound of my cry, she looks up at me with tears in her bloodshot eyes, mascara running down her cheeks. I collapse onto the tacky theater carpet and wrap my arms around her. She's sobbing now. "Shh … it's okay." I speak in a gentle whisper, allowing the calmness of the hallway to wrap around her.

She breaks our embrace, and her eyes meet mine. They are full of regret. "I'm so sorry, Caleb. God, I'm so embarrassed."

"It's okay," I reassure her as I brush the hair away from her face. It's wet with her tears. She rests her head on my shoulder, and her legs fall out straight in front of her. Since we were in the last theater in the hallway, we are all alone. Just two kids sitting on the floor of a movie theater, hugging each other. No big deal.

After a few minutes, I pull away from her and take hold of her chin, making eye contact. She stares at me, her big, brown eyes wide and unblinking. I take a second and brush my thumb over the mascara tracks. "You wanna get out of here?" She shakes her head in agreement. I stand up first and wipe off the back of my jeans.

I extend both of my hands to her, and she takes them. After I pull her to her feet, she wipes her jeans off as well. I wrap my arm around her shoulder and lead her out of the theater.

I don't think we will ever go back to the movies.

ele

Mallory

Caleb will never want to go on a date with me ever again.

I can't believe I freaked out like that. But, my God, was that theater over the top? Maybe not for the average person, but for me, it was sensory overload central. The crowd, the darkness, the smell, the sounds ... all of it.

And a Transformers trailer. Like, really? Those movies are so obnoxious.

I tried; I did. The Jim Carrey trailer was alright. I worked through it. But as soon as I heard that first explosion, and my seat vibrated, I knew I was done. A surge of energy pulsed through my body. I was sweating, and I could hear the blood pumping in my head. Flight-or-fight took over.

I don't even remember what I screamed, but I yelled something. Everyone, and I mean the whole theater, turned and stared at me. I raced out of the aisle, crawling and stepping on people as I fled. I thought maybe I heard someone say 'freak,' but I'm not sure. Next thing I knew, I was running. I slammed through the door and ran down the hallway. I stood with my back against the wall, feeling my heart throbbing as I clasped my stomach and tried to regulate my breathing. Then the tears started. I slid down the wall until I was sitting on the floor, pulling my knees to my chest and burying my head in shame.

I hate myself. I actually hate myself.

And Caleb is more than likely done with me now.

But just as fast as I was out of the theater and on the floor, Caleb was at my side. Comforting me. Soothing me. Wiping away my tears.

Now we are back in his car. He's probably taking me home because why wouldn't he? We haven't said a word since we left the theater. I'm staring out the passenger window, watching the businesses of Rt 26 fly past us. One by one. Caleb makes the turn for the bypass.

"Are you taking me home?" I whisper, my fingertips brushing away another tear that has escaped. My heart is sinking in shame.

"What?" His head snaps toward me in surprise, then refocuses on the road ahead. "No. Of course not. Unless you want me to."

I shake my head. "No, I don't. I just thought after what happened, you might want—"

"All I want to do is get ice cream with you, Mallory," he says with reassurance. I look over at him. "Really?"

"Yes, really." He slides his hand over to the middle console and faces his palm up. A small smile curves my lips up, and I feel a fluttering in my chest as our fingers intertwine again.

Maybe he wants to be with me after all.

We are sitting on top of the picnic table in a park, the wooden bench feeling slightly warm from the sun as we eat our ice cream. Vanilla for me, of course, and mint chocolate chip for him. It's a gorgeous night. The sun is setting, and the air is still warm with a hint of a chill. We've barely said anything since we left the theater. I think he knows I need my space to process what happened, and he is being respectful. When I'm in the Quiet Room at work, he only glances in to check on me, giving me the privacy I need. This feels like the same thing.

He takes the last bite of his ice cream and turns to face me. "You wanna talk about it?"

I take a bite of mine, pondering my answer. Plus, I swear this vanilla ice cream is the best around. I savor the taste of the ice cream as it melts in my mouth, the coldness being a calming sensation. I sigh as I use the spoon to play with what's left in my bowl. "I thought I could do it, Caleb."

"Do what?"

"The movies."

"Have you ever gone to one before?" he inquires as he throws away his empty bowl in the trash. His bowl and spoon hit the bottom of the steel drum with a thud.

I take another bite, letting it melt in my mouth before I answer. I'm trying to decide if I want him to know the whole truth about me. "We went to one as a family when I was younger. I had a meltdown. My dad and Jake stayed. Mom and I went home."

"What movie was it?"

"A Marvel movie."

"Ah. I get it. A loud one." He clasps his hands together as he leans forward, his arms resting on his knees.

I bob my head in silent acknowledgment.

"We didn't have to go, you know. I would have understood."

"I know. But Caleb..." I stop myself.

"What Mallory? You can tell me anything." He takes my empty bowl and throws it in the trash for me.

"I just wanted this to be a normal date. Sometimes, it feels like everything is difficult for me. No matter where I go, I have to think about how the atmosphere will affect me. Will it be too loud, too crowded, too cramped? And it drives me bonkers. I wanted to feel like every other girl you have dated." I sigh before I continue. "I didn't want you to see me freak out and then never want to go on a date with me again. And that's exactly what happened."

He turns to face me and tucks a piece of my hair behind my ear. "Mallory, yes, it's true you freaked out, but I *want* to go on another date with you. Hopefully, more than one."

I look into his eyes, and I can see flecks of dark blue around his irises coupled with the green that I know is already there. "Seriously?"

"Yes, seriously. And no, you aren't like the other girls I have dated. You are better. So much better."

Those words are all I need to hear. All doubt that I had about how he felt about me melts like the ice cream that was left in my cup.

Caleb reaches up and cups my cheek in his hand. "Mallory, may I kiss you?"

Is this really happening right now?

A wave of nervousness washes over me, and I feel my stomach do a somersault. "Y-yes," is all I can bring myself to say. And it comes out all broken and nervous-sounding. Which makes sense since this is my first kiss. He stares at me for another second before moving his face closer to mine. His warm breath tickles my skin as it hovers close to my face. I try to take in and memorize this whole moment. The chill and cool breeze in the air, the feel of his hand on my face, the way he smells earthy, like sandalwood. I close my eyes, and he leans into me, tilting his head until I feel the warmth of his lips on mine.

Yep, this is a soft kiss. His lips don't feel slimy at all. *I knew it!*

He rests his other hand on my hip as he pulls me closer to him. On instinct, I wrap my hands around his neck, and I feel like I'm floating. His lips move over mine with ease, and I can tell he's done this before. And it feels good. So good. My whole body is alive with a humming sensation, as if it's being charged from the inside out. I'm always in tune with my senses, and this is like nothing I've ever experienced or felt before. And I hope to feel it again.

We break apart and rest our foreheads together. His breath is hot on my skin as he exhales. And, of course, my awkward self comes to life, and I say the first thing I'm thinking.

"Your lips didn't feel slimy."

What in the heck am I saying right now? Way to break the mood, Mallory.

Our foreheads are linked together like magnets, and the softness of our skin creates a perfect seal. Caleb chuckles. We are so close right now that I feel his chest vibrate. "Thanks, I guess."

With a laugh, I break our embrace and glance at him. "Sorry. It's just, I meant
... what I meant was ... kisses are hard for me, just like all other forms of touch."

He lifts one of his eyebrows. "You've been kissed a lot?"

I let out a sigh as I shake my head, and my arms fall to my side. "No. Gosh, this
is coming out all wrong. That was my first kiss, actually. But anytime a family
member has kissed me on the cheek, I hated the way it felt."

"It felt slimy?"

I can't help but chuckle. "Yes, they felt slimy. I know that it sounds ridiculous."

"It doesn't sound ridiculous at all. How did mine feel?" he whispers as he
puts his hand on my cheek again.

"Soft," I say. "But maybe we should try again. You know, just to make sure."

"Just to make sure."

And I got the second kiss that I hoped for.

After we kiss a little longer—okay, a lot longer—we take a walk. Since we didn't
make the movie, we have some time to kill. We stroll through the park, our
fingers linked, talking each other's ears off. I tell him more about my anxiety
and depression. He confides in me about his strained relationship with his dad.
We lay it all out on the table. Our deepest fears (mine, never being able to live a
somewhat normal life. Him, never making his dad proud). What makes us the
happiest in life (mine is my family. Him, his love of learning new things). By the
time we make it back to his car, I feel like I've known him for years, the warmth
of his hand still in mine.

I wrap my arms around my body, and I shiver. The sun has set, and the
temperature drop has made it colder than when we got here.

"Are you cold?" Caleb asks, his tone laced with concern.

"I am. I should have brought a light jacket."

He holds up a finger. "Stay here." He rounds his car and, with a boop from his
key fob, the trunk opens. He pulls out a red hoodie and hands it to me. "Here,

try this. It's really warm." I take it and pull it over my head, removing my hair out of the back. It's so soft, and it smells like him. I immediately feel warmer, in more ways than one.

"Thank you," I say. He walks over to me and starts rubbing his hands up and down my arms. "I'll give it back when we get to my house."

"Nope. I don't want it back. I want my girlfriend to wear it."

My eyes shoot up to his. "Your girlfriend?" *Is that seriously what he just said?*

"I mean, if that's alright with you?" he asks, his voice shaking.

I wrap my hands around his waist. "Yes, that's what I want. More than anything."

"Phew ... Good." His body relaxes, and he kisses me on the forehead. "So, I was thinking I better kiss my girlfriend good night here. It might not be a good idea to do it when I drop you off at your house."

I chuckle. "You're right. I guarantee my dad will be waiting on the porch when I get home."

He places his hands on my cheeks and kisses me for the last time tonight.

Best. Date. Ever.

31

TEN MONTHS LATER

Caleb

It's been three hundred days of love and laughter with Mallory as my girl-friend.

Being with Mallory for the last ten months has taught me more than I ever thought possible. I'm a different person now. When we aren't together, which is almost never, we are texting or talking on the phone. She fills my world with light.

I know that's a lot of sappy talk for a guy who is only eighteen, but it's all true. And I've also realized something else these last few months. I don't know when it happened, honestly. It could have been the night I kissed her for the first time. Maybe it was the day we went sled riding, and her infectious laugh billowed through the air every time we went down the hill. Or maybe it was the night we stayed up and talked till four in the morning on the phone about our futures. Maybe it was gradual. But I know one thing for sure—I am in love with Mallory Givens.

And I'm going to tell her tomorrow. We are going out for dinner, then a walk in the park so Mallory can feel the grass beneath her feet. Simple and easy. Just like Mallory.

But right now, I'm feeling the weight of a critical choice. I'm sitting on my bed, staring at five different acceptance letters from different colleges. All are wonderful. But not all of them are within miles of my girlfriend.

Before I met Mallory, I had my sights set on Stanford because it was my dad's dream school for me. One problem—it's not *my* dream. I've always wanted to keep my options open. My ultimate goal was to get my MBA, take over the café from my dad, and then expand it. But Stanford is clear across the country. I would only see Mallory when I came home at Christmas and then in the summer. I can't do that to her or to us.

So, I folded the Stanford letter and placed it in my desk drawer. I know it's my dad's alma mater, but it's not like I won't get a superior education at the other schools. University of Chicago, University of Pennsylvania, Northwestern, University of Michigan, and Carnegie Mellon. These are within striking distance of home. I could live on campus during the week, drive home (or take a quick flight), and spend the weekends with Mallory. It wouldn't be ideal, but it's worth it. Now it's just trying to decide which one.

And I've got another challenge to tackle. My dad.

He has his heart set on Stanford. It's a whole generational thing. My grandfather and great-grandfather went there also, and my dad met my mom there. When I handed him the acceptance letter, his face lit up with pride.

"Fantastic, son! I knew you wouldn't let me down," he said as he brought me in for a hug. He was beaming. I was dying inside. He has talked this school up since I started kindergarten. Every other school was 'trash' and not up for debate. He's clueless that I even considered other schools; I can only imagine his disappointment if, or I should say when, he discovers the truth.

The only person I've talked to about this is Mallory. She encouraged me to apply to other colleges and not just because she didn't want me to leave, but because she knew Stanford wasn't what I wanted.

"So, have you picked a school yet?" she asked as we walked hand in hand through the zoo last weekend. Mallory adores animals, so this is one of our favorite places. We stopped at the tiger enclosure and leaned against the railing, listening to the deep, throaty roars of the tigers that echoed throughout the area.

"Not yet. It's so hard. All five of them are elite schools." I chewed my lower lip as I wrestled with this huge decision. "I'm really leaning toward Carnegie Mellon."

"Oh, yeah? Why?" she asked, curious and waiting for my answer, while I watched the tigers lounge around.

I turned to face her. "Because it's closer to you." Carnegie Mellon would only be an hour and a half drive from home.

Her gaze remained fixed on the ground, and her fingers continuously twisted and turned her ring. "Caleb, I want you to pick the best school for you. Please don't pick one just for me."

I grabbed her hands. "Mallory, look at me, please." She was anxious, I could tell. When I need her to look at me, I face her and hold her hands. She has told me it makes her feel like she is in a safe bubble and it's only the two of us.

Mallory turned her gaze to me. Her eyes were glassy, and she was breathing heavier. Which she does when she struggles. I could see the panic building in her eyes. I needed to calm her down. This has been happening more and more lately, so I pressed one of my hands on her cheek, brushing it with my thumb. "Carnegie is a fantastic school. I will get a superior education, and I will get to be closer to you." She nodded. She closed her eyes and took a deep, calming breath. I could feel the tension leaving her body with each exhale. I wrapped my arms around her waist and pulled her closer to me. "Maybe after you graduate, you could come back with me on Sundays and spend the week with me."

She threw her head back and let out a billowing laugh. "Oh, come on. As if my dad would allow that."

I knew that would make her laugh.

"A guy can dream, right?" I brushed my lips softly against hers before pulling her in for a tight hug. We reluctantly separated and walked toward the elephants.

"But what about your dad? Have you told him yet? That Stanford is out," she asked.

I shook my head. "Not yet." She squeezed my hand and laid her head on my shoulder as we walked in silence.

I shake off the memory and take in the five letters spread across my blue and black comforter. A pamphlet for the schools is tucked under each one. I pick them up individually and study them. All of them have the same goal: trying to woo future students. Deep down, though, I know what I want to do. I want to take care of Mallory.

And things are not the same as they used to be. Anxiety has completely taken over her mind. I can tell she needs quiet, so we have been spending time in places that are calming to her (like the zoo because of the animals). Her panic attacks, though small, have been coming on more frequently, and it can take her a few days to recover. I love to take care of her, though, as I try to make her feel better and calm her down. She is struggling in silence and is doing her best to hide it from her parents. And I know she isn't being one hundred percent honest with me. Something is off. She seems so sad.

I see it.

I feel it.

But I can't bring myself to ask her. I've been confiding in my mom about it. I need a sounding board, and she has been wonderful with advice since she has worked with atypical individuals for years. Her suggestions on how to help have been invaluable. Whatever happens, I know one thing for sure.

I want to go to Carnegie Mellon. I want to be closer to Mallory.

Now, I just need to break the news to my dad.

Me: I'm going to tell my Dad tonight after dinner.

Mallory: REALLY?! Wow. Okay, well I'm sure it will go better than you think.

Me: I hope so. Mom is making his favorite for dinner so he will at least be in somewhat of a good mood.

Mallory: Well your mom's Chicken Parm is top notch.

I chuckle to myself. Mallory always lightens my mood.

Mallory: Call me when you can and tell me how it went.

Me: I will. Can't wait to hear your voice.

Mallory: <heart emoji>

I set my phone down on the bed before padding silently down the stairs. The air smells like fried breaded chicken and garlic. I make it to the dining room table right as my mom is serving up her specialty.

Dinner is uneventful. As my mom and dad make small talk, I focus on staying composed and level-headed. My palms are clammy, and my appetite is non-existent since I'm so nervous. I barely touch my food. My mom, who knows me better than anyone, picks up on my unease.

"Caleb, are you alright? You've been quiet tonight, and you've hardly touched your dinner," she asks as I pick at the half-eaten piece of chicken on my plate.

I sit my fork down and wipe my hands down my pants. "Actually ... um ... Mom, Dad, I need to talk to you about something."

"Well, this sounds serious," my dad says with a slight chuckle in his tone.

"It is, Dad," I deadpan.

"Oh." He wipes his face with his napkin when he realizes I mean business. He sits it down next to his plate. "What's on your mind, son?"

I swallow down my nerves. *Here goes nothing.* I watch my dad intently as he spears the chicken with his fork.

"Dad. I don't want to go to Stanford. I've decided to attend Carnegie Mellon instead."

My dad drops his fork mid-bite as it hits his plate, sending a clang through the room. I've obviously surprised him.

He puts his elbows on the table and laces his fingers together as he studies his half-eaten dinner. My mom sits in stunned silence while she puts her hands under her thighs, bracing herself for the inevitable fallout.

"I see." My dad clicks his tongue, his anger growing as he glares at me. "I had no idea you applied to other schools."

"Yes, eight others, actually. I got into Chicago, University of PA, Carnegie, Michigan, and Northwestern."

"Those are elite business schools."

"Yes, they are, and—"

"But they aren't Stanford," he says as he slowly raises his chin. He pauses, raising an eyebrow and pursing his lips together.

He's mad, I can tell. My dad rarely yells. He's cool as a cucumber, and he knows how to get his point across with just a look. Everyone always says that he is very intimidating, and his piercing gaze backs up that sentiment. Plus, he has a vein that pops on his forehead when he's furious. The vein has entered the conversation.

My mom busies herself with clearing up the table. She knows that this is between my dad and me. Unwavering support has always come from my mom. It's my dad that has always felt Stanford was a non-issue. Turns out it was only an issue for me.

"No, they aren't. But, Dad, Carnegie has a top-notch business program. One of the best in the country. My goal is still the same. Get my MBA and take over the business. I will also be closer to home."

"Ah," he says as he claps his hands together and then points to me. "There it is. This is about that girl, isn't it?"

"Her name is Mallory," I say, my teeth clench together in anger.

My dad has never been keen on my dating Mallory. He says it's because she is an employee, but deep down, I know the real reason. It's because she has autism. What my dad does at the café is amazing. Giving atypical individuals a purpose, teaching them life skills, which gives them self-confidence. I've seen it time and time again. I've seen it with Mallory.

But don't date one.

It's a disgusting double standard, and I think he knows how I feel.

"You've never liked me dating her. Admit it." I do not know where this courage is coming from. Wait, yes, I do. It's love. And that love is making me bold.

My dad retorts. "Caleb, come on. It's not that I don't like her. She is a lovely girl. It's just that—"

"What?"

He takes a deep breath in. "If you decide to continue this relationship with her, your life will be so much more difficult. Do you realize that? Are you willing to throw away Stanford for an autistic girl?"

Whoa. I can feel the rage starting to build inside of me.

Title

I

Body

The

"First, she isn't an 'autistic girl,'" I say as I use air quotes, "she is a girl *with* autism. It's two different things. You, of all people, should know that and respect the difference."

My dad throws his hands up and slams them down on the table. Dishes clank against silverware. "Jesus Christ!" He scoots his chair out and throws his napkin on the table.

He heads toward the living room, and I am hot on his tail. "And yes, I want to go to Carnegie to be closer to her. I LOVE HER, DAD!" This outburst makes him stop. He's standing with his back to me. "Stanford has always been your dream for me! I've never wanted to go there. EVER!" I shout this louder than I mean to. I've never raised my voice to my father before. I'm breathing heavily, and it feels good to get that off my chest finally.

He turns slowly and takes two steps toward me, and we are inches apart. We are so close that I can see the gray hair on his temples. He points his finger at me. "*Do not* raise your voice when speaking to me, young man. This is your one and only warning."

I put my hands in my pocket and lower my gaze to the floor. He's right; I was out of line. With those two sentences, I'm back to being eight and not eighteen. "Yes, sir," I whisper.

He lowers his hand and backs away, crossing his arms over his chest. He knows he has the upper hand as we stand squaring off in the middle of the living room. "Now, if you decide to go to Carnegie and continue to date Mallory, that is your choice."

I jerk my head upward in shock. *Is he actually going to support me on this?*

"Seriously? Dad, thanks—"

He raises his palm to me. "Let me finish."

"Yes, sir." My mom has now appeared from the kitchen holding a dish towel and is leaning against the door frame.

"If you make this decision, you will not get any money from your college savings to pay for schooling."

"WHAT?!" I'm stunned. I can't believe what I'm hearing.

"Frank!" my mom exclaims from the doorway.

My dad is essentially bribing me. I knew he was ruthless in his business dealings. He's always told me he had to be in order to be successful. But that ruthlessness never bled into the family. Until now.

He raises his finger and points it at both of us as his eyes travel between my mother and me. "You both heard me. If you go to Stanford, I will give you every red cent of your college fund, and you will be financially set for your education and far beyond. But if you go to Carnegie and continue dating Mallory, then you will have to apply for student loans. You will get no help from me."

And there it is. The invisible line in the sand.

My mom speaks up to plead with my dad. "Frank, do you realize what you would do to your son? It would take him years to pay those loans back... decades even."

My dad doesn't even look at my mom. He's not fazed by any of this. He just nods and doesn't take his eyes off me because he wants me to realize what my mom just said. "This is his choice to make, Vanessa."

"What if I went to Stanford and also continued to date Mallory?" I press, seeking the truth of what this is really about—Stanford or my relationship with Mallory.

"Come on, son? Do you really think you and Mallory are going to last? Especially when you are at school?"

"Yes, I do," I reply with firm belief in my words. *Without a doubt.*

He takes a step closer to me and chuckles under his breath in amusement. "Mallory isn't the girl for you. You'll see. You are young and in love. I get it. I was eighteen once, too. But you need to ask yourself ... can you really give her the life that she needs and deserves? She will always need some kind of special care. How are you going to concentrate on your classes if you are always worried about her? And I know she has been struggling lately." My mom catches my eye, and I realize in an instant she has told him everything. I shoot her an angry look as she lowers her head in shame.

He places his hands on my shoulders and tightens his grip. "If you love her like you say you do, and I have no doubt that you do ... let her go. Go to Stanford. Give her time to grow, mature, and become an adult." He drops his arms and puts his hands in his pockets. "Now, those are my terms. I'll give you till tomorrow to let me know your decision." With that, he turns on his heels and heads to his study.

I turn and stare at my mom ... in shock. She has tears streaming down her cheeks. "I can't believe you told him," I say, deeply hurt by her betrayal. She doesn't reply and heads back to the kitchen and starts loading the dishwasher. I hang my head down and make the slow ascent up the stairs. My legs feel heavy with each step I take. Just like my heart.

I push open my bedroom door, the creaking of the hinges echoing in the room, and I step inside. I place my head on the back of the door. Slowly, anger builds in my chest.

Anger at my dad.

Anger at myself.

Anger at what my life has become.

Anger at the autism, anxiety, and depression that control the girl I love.

I slam my head against the door and walk over to my bed. I pause and look down at all the pamphlets and letters as the anger continues to build inside of me. Using my arm, I swoop them off my comforter onto the floor. I heave myself onto my bed and cover my face with my hands.

Is he right?

I tug on my hair and internally scream as I slam my hands on the mattress. Questions are swirling around in my head. *Am* I good enough for her? Would she be better off without me? Can I give her what she needs? Mallory needs a routine. Is Dad right? Maybe Mallory needs time to mature. I love her so much, and I want her to grow and learn. Plus, she will be a senior this year. She should spend it with friends. Having fun. Not constantly worrying when she will see me or talk to me. After my dad's revelation, I doubt if I went to Carnegie, I could come home on the weekends like I planned. Dad said he won't pay for anything. Which means student loans and me finding a job ... probably working most weekends. Our relationship would suffer.

On the other hand, could we make it work? I mean, long-distance relationships aren't that hard, right? I could go to Stanford. Granted, I wouldn't see her on weekends, but I would at winter and spring break, and of course, we would have the summers. We would video chat most nights. And we could hide our relationship from my dad. It's not ideal, but I will do anything to be with her. I would be careful and make sure he never finds out.

Could this work?

My head is racing with a million and one thoughts.

I head over to my desk and pull out *the* acceptance letter. The bold Stanford letterhead is staring at me.

My phone buzzes.

> **Mallory**: Hey, how did it go? Can
> you talk?

I can't have this conversation over the phone. I unfold the letter and place it on my bed.

> **Me**: Hey. It didn't go well. I'll tell
> you about it tomorrow. Too much
> to text. Plus I'm exhausted.

> **Mallory**: Oh.

> **Mallory**: Okay. I understand. I'll
> see you tomorrow then I guess.
> <kissy face emoji>

I know she's disappointed. God, I hate this. I sit my phone down on the bed next to the letter. A picture of Mallory kissing me on the cheek, my wallpaper, stares back at me. My eyes move from the letter to my phone, then back to the letter again.

The line in the sand is going straight down my heart.

32

ele

THE NEXT DAY

Mallory

C aleb said he'd be here in an hour, and I've been listening for his car, every
second feeling like an eternity. Why couldn't he tell me on the phone
last night how the conversation went with his dad? He said it didn't go well, but
what does that mean?

I'm sitting in my room, the pencil in my hand scratching against the paper as
I draw, hoping this will help me pass the time. My knee is restless and won't stay
still, shaking incessantly. I find myself struggling to stay focused, which seems
to be happening more often. It's like I'm walking on eggshells as if something
is about to happen to me, and I'm not sure what it is. I've had a few mild panic
attacks that left me feeling dizzy and breathless. My sadness is so strong it feels
like a physical weight. The happiness I once had is leaving me. My mom and dad
don't know because, somehow, I've gotten great at hiding this from them. I'm
almost positive Caleb knows something's wrong because he's been asking me
more and more about how I'm feeling.

I lie and say I'm fine.

Sometimes, my anxiety and depression shift. There's no reason for it. It
comes in waves. Or maybe like a rollercoaster. Up and down. I've been more
down. I imagine lifting my gaze up to the next hill. The one that leads to
happiness, and it's too high and difficult to climb. So, I don't.

We have filled these past ten months with so much joy that it makes no sense that I wouldn't feel happy. Being with Caleb has given me a peace I never knew I could have. He's kind, caring, and in tune with my feelings. He always makes sure I'm happy and cared for. Everything is perfect.

So why am I so sad?

Now, he's graduating and heading off to college, the feeling of change is in the air. And I hate change.

With a passion.

My life needs order, routine, and structure. I see or talk to Caleb every day. He is a constant in my life. Even though he's only going to Carnegie, and I will get to see him on the weekends, it won't be the same without his presence and our conversations.

The familiar feeling of doubt and self-loathing creeps into my mind, making my heart heavy.

Is he going to pick Stanford?

Does he want to be with me?

Am I good enough for him?

Caleb deserves better.

These thoughts are present and accounted for as I wait for him. I abandon my drawing, unable to stay still as I pace my room. My fidget ring feels cool against my fingers as I play with it, and I tap my leg. All of which is doing a poor job of calming my racing mind. I look at my watch, since he should be here any minute. We are going to my favorite park. Being outside and having my feet in the grass always ground me. I need that now more than ever.

The doorbell rings.

He's here!

I grab my backpack and phone, throw on my shoes, and head toward the stairs. I hear my mom answer the door.

"Hey, Caleb. Mallory should be down in a second. Would you like something to drink?"

"Um ... no, thank you, Mrs. Givens. I'm fine," Caleb replies, and there's an edge to his voice. He's nervous, maybe.

When he locks eyes with me, there's an awkward tension as I come down the stairs, and his smile seems forced. *He is nervous.* I have a feeling this will not be good. I roll the balls on my ring. Back and forth, back and forth.

"Bye, Mom! Bye, Dad!" I say hastily as I grasp his hand, and we race out the door.

I'm leading the way as we walk down the front steps and head toward Caleb's car. He stops walking and tugs my hand, causing me to turn and face him. He furrows his brows. "Mallory, can we talk before we go?"

"Yeah, sure." My voice cracks as I say it.

He leads me to the front porch steps. We sit down. He turns to face me and grabs my hands. He's rubbing his thumb on my skin.

"I need to say this now before more time passes and it gets harder," he begins. *Oh, God.*

"So, I talked to my dad last night." He pauses and turns his head away. "He wants me to go to Stanford."

I can feel the blood drain from my head. Everything feels instantly hot.

"Um ... okay. So, what did he say when you told him that you aren't going to Stanford?" I ask as I hold my breath. I wait for him to answer.

When he turns to look at me, there are tears pulling in his eyes. I take a sharp breath. I let go of his hands. "You're going, aren't you?"

"Yes," he whispers.

I stand up. I pace.

Oh, my God. I walk to the cars.

Oh, my God. I walk back to the porch.

Oh, my God. I walk back to the cars.

I head back to Caleb and stop. He's watching me intently. I turn around. I don't want to see him watching me. I close my eyes. I take a deep breath in. I let it out slowly. I need to center myself. I wrap my arms around my body.

Think, Mallory! Think! My thoughts are becoming choppy in my head.

This might not be too bad. We can make this work. We can totally do this.

I feel his hand touch my shoulder. I turn and open my eyes. He's standing in front of me. I ask the question. I don't want to know the answer.

"So, what does this mean for us?"

Please say we can make this work.

A tear runs down his cheek. He looks at me. He opens his mouth. He closes it. He pauses. Looks down, then back at me again.

Why is this happening in slow motion?

"Mallory ... I don't think ... it's just going to be so hard ... maybe it would be easier if—"

"Are you breaking up with me?" I ask. I take a step back.

"NO! Mallory, it's complicated. Let me—" He grabs for my hand. I yank it away.

My vision blurs.

"No." I shake my head. "Why are you..." I try to take a deep breath.

I can't breathe.

I can't breathe.

Why can't I breathe?

I place my hand on my stomach. I need to steady myself.

Caleb again. "Mallory, I want to explain. I have an idea—"

I shake my head. "No."

I put my hand on my heart. It feels like it's going to explode.

I need to sit down.

My legs aren't working.

The ground is moving.

There's a ringing in my ears. I cover my ears.

I'm walking backward. I need to get away from him.

I hit the step. I grab the railing.

I'm falling backward. I am. I'm falling.

I fall. I hit the porch step.

Thud.

I hit my head. I gather myself up. I sit on the step.

I draw my legs up. I wrap my arms around them.

OMG. I'm having a panic attack. Or an anxiety attack. I don't know.

What's happening?

This feels different.

Does it matter?

He's leaving.

He's breaking up with me.

I'm a loser.

I'm not good for him.

I still can't breathe.

My breath is short.

"I ... can ... brea—"

"Mallory!" Caleb calls my name. I'm in a fog.

"Are you okay?" he asks, panic-stricken. "Mallory, look at me!" he pleads.

He steps toward me. He reaches to touch my arm.

"DON'T TOUCH ME! Sta ... away fro ... me ..." I swat his hand away. Still can't breathe.

What is happening to me? I can't think.

I hear my dad's muffled voice from inside the house. "What is going on out there?"

I'm rocking. My hands now back over my ears. I can hear the blood rushing through my head.

Humming. I need to hum.

No. Not helping. My head hurts.

It's so loud.

I hear Caleb. He's breathing heavily.

He's near me. But I don't know where.

I feel like I'm in a tunnel.

This isn't happening.

"No, no, no, no, no, no, no, no..." I say in a low voice. Rocking.

"Mrs. Givens!" Caleb screams.

Stop yelling!! The noise. Glass breaking in my head.

Mom and Dad run out the door.

Why are they stomping? So loud.

"What happened?" My mom. She rushes to me. She's at my side.

"OH, MY GOD!" My dad. "What did you do?!" I open my eyes. Dad rushes past me. Down the stairs. Toward Caleb.

My mom is crouching next to me. She's rubbing my back. It helps. Not enough.

"I'm sorry, Mr. Givens." Caleb is stumbling backward. My dad's walking toward him. Caleb's scared.

His eyes are open wide.

"Did you hurt her?! I heard her scream 'Don't touch me!'" Dad points at me. He's yelling now. He's standing in front of Caleb.

"God, no!" Caleb shakes his head. He lowers it. "I told her I'm leaving. I'm going to—"

"What the ... ?" Dad turns to me. "You said he was going to Carnegie." He spins toward Caleb. "You did this to her?" Dad pauses. "Get out of here! NOW!" My dad. Pointing to the street. Screaming again.

Caleb looks past my dad. At me. He's crying. "Mallory, please let me explain!" He's pleading. He's reaching for me. "I said LEAVE!" Dad again. Still screaming.

So. Much. Screaming.

Caleb spins around. He runs to his car.

He turns. His eyes meet mine. He looks sad. I close my eyes.

I'm rocking and humming again.

I don't want to see him leave.

Tears are forming. The sobs are sitting on my chest. They need to come out.

Great. Now I'm crying.

His engine starts.

He drives away.

I don't hear it anymore.

He's gone.

Everything's fuzzy.

I'm seeing spots. Or are they stars?

I'm shaking now.

I'm so cold.

"Shh," I feel my mom's breath in my hair. She's stroking it.

She is rocking me.

It's quieter now.

More humming.

Make this stop. Why is this happening to me?

"Let's take her inside," my dad whispers.

I feel powerful arms under my knees. Around my back.

My strong dad. He's carrying me.

"I got you, baby girl. I got you."

Mom's crying.

We are in the house. Going up the stairs.

My body feels heavy.

Am I floating?

I want my bed.

My dad sits me on my bed. I scooch to the back of the wall. I pull my knees to my chest. I hug them. I bury my face in my knees.

I'm so scared. I'm shaking. I'm cold.

Humming again.

My mom grabs my face.

"Mallory, I need you to open your eyes and look at me."

I do. I look at my mom's big brown eyes. Eyes like mine.

"Breathe with me, sweetie." I nod my head.

"Deep breath in." I fill my lungs with air.

"Let it out slowly." I blow the air out.

We do this eight times. My dad is pacing the room. I'm feeling better.

"Scott, can you please get some water?"

My dad leaves the room.

"Are you feeling better?" my mom whispers.

The room is quiet. But no. Not better.

"Y... yes."

I lie.

My mom wraps me in her arms. I sob on her shirt.

"I'm so sorry, Mom. I'm so sorry." I'm crying so hard. I can't talk anymore. I grab her shirt.

My mom. My lifeline.

"Shh ..." She strokes my hair, and she's slowly rocking me in her arms again. "It's okay, sweetie. Don't apologize."

My dad's back. My mom lets go. "Here, Mal." My dad hands me the water.

I break away from my mom, and I drink. I rest my head on the wall. Close my eyes. I can breathe better.

The room is quiet. So quiet.

I don't feel my heart in my chest anymore.

My dad crouches in front of me and puts his hand on my knee. "Do you want to talk about it, sweetie?"

"No," I say, emotionless. I hand my mom the water as I move to lie down. I hear her sit the glass on my nightstand. I want under my blankets. My mom helps. She covers me. "I want to sleep."

"Okay, honey." My mom swipes my hair off my face. She kisses my cheek. "I love you."

My dad kisses my cheek. "I love you, Mal Pal," he whispers. Something wet hits my skin. They leave. The room fades to black.

I wake up to a silent, pitch-black room. I'm exhausted. I'm sad.

My watch tells me it's past nine-thirty. No wonder it's dark outside. I must have slept for about three hours. I'm hungry, and I have to pee, so I get out of bed. Plus, I need to find Mom and Dad.

I take care of business, go back to my room, and get my phone. I glance at it. Twelve text messages, four missed calls, and a voicemail. All from Caleb.

I can't deal with it right now, so I turn my phone over and head downstairs. Mom, Dad, and Jake are all sitting in the living room. They perk up when they see me. Jake gets up first and heads over to me.

"Can I give you a hug?" he asks. I nod. He pulls me in for one of his big brother hugs. "I'm so sorry, Mallory," he says.

Jake releases me, and I head over to the living room and plop down on the couch next to Dad. He puts his arm around me. I place my head on his shoulder, and he kisses me on the head. "You wanna talk about it?"

I shrug my shoulders. "Nothing to talk about. Caleb is going to Stanford, and he's leaving. I guess we kinda broke up. I don't know, honestly." I glance at my mom, who is sitting on the ottoman, and I can feel the warmth of her presence. Jake is on the love seat.

"I thought you said he was going to Carnegie?" my mom asks.

"That's what he told me. He was supposed to talk to his dad about it last night. I don't know what changed his mind."

I see Jake stand, his body tall like my dad's. He's pacing back and forth, a scowl on his face. His hands in tight fists. "He's a coward. Probably wants to just go there and party. You're better off, Mal. I swear if I see him—"

"You're not helping Jake," my dad says.

Is Jake right? Maybe that's what this is about. A girl back home would just tie him down. He probably just wants to party. I'm sure those California girls are gorgeous. Why stay with me, a girl with autism and an obvious head case, when he can have hot sorority girls throwing themselves at his feet?

I'm not good.

I'm ugly.

He's better off.

I really just want to be alone. Maybe coming down here was a bad idea. "I'm going to go back upstairs and lie down. Mom, can you make me a sandwich, please? I'm starving."

She shoots off the ottoman. "Of course, sweetie. I'll bring it right up."

"Are you sure you don't want to stay and watch a movie or something, Mal?" Dad asks. "We can all hang out together and just chill."

I stand up. My legs still feel weak. "No, thanks, Dad. I just want my bed."

"Okay, honey. If you change your mind, just let us know."

With a slight nod of my head, I walk past Jake. His eyes are full of sadness as he watches me pass him. I head up the stairs. My legs feel like lead weights. Time seems to have slowed down. It feels like the journey up the stairs takes an hour.

I go into my room and shut the door. I turn on the desk light, and my bulletin board slaps me in the face with all the pictures pinned to it.

Caleb and I at the park.

Caleb and I at work, sticking our tongues out at the camera.

Me kissing Caleb on the cheek. The picture he has as his wallpaper on his phone.

Caleb and me. Caleb and me. Caleb and me.

One after another after another.

My anger is so intense that I can feel my face getting hot. I grab my garbage can and rip the pictures off one by one, tearing them off the pegs that are holding them in place. I throw them all in the garbage. His hoodie is resting on the back of my desk chair, catching my attention.

I yank it off the chair. Slam! In the garbage. I take out the liner, tie it shut, and heave it. It lands on the back of the closet floor, then I throw the door shut.

Slamming the door on Caleb. On us.

As I turn my head, my eyes land on my phone. I pick it up and unlock it as I walk over and sit on my bed. My usual spot. Back against the wall, legs crossed. I open the first message.

Caleb: Mallory are you okay?

Caleb: Please call me. I need to explain.

Caleb: Mallory, I'm scared. Call me please, I'm begging you.

Caleb: I'm worried about you.

Text after text, just like these.

I hit the voice mail button, then the speaker. Caleb's voice fills the air.

"Mallory, please call me. I'm so scared. I've seen you have a panic attack before, but that was different. Or maybe it was an anxiety attack. I don't know. I just want to make sure you're okay. (He pauses. I hear him sniff.) *I really just want to explain to you what's going on. But not over a voice mail.* (Another pause. He sighs.) *I'm leaving in a few weeks, and I would like to see you before I go. I don't want to leave until I know you're alright.* (Another pause.) *Please call me, okay. Please. I'll stop texting and calling till I hear from you."*

The line goes dead. I rest my head back on the wall as I hold the phone in my hand.

He deserves better.

Set him free.

I decide to send him a text.

Me: Caleb, I need time. Please stop calling and texting. Good luck at school.

I hit send.

Then, I let my finger hover over the three dots in the upper right-hand corner. *Do I want to do this?* He's leaving. Yes, I do.

I tap the three little dots. Then I hit the one word I never thought I would think when it came to Caleb Horvath.

BLOCK.

I let out a frustrated yell as I hurl my phone across the room.

33

Caleb

Mallory: Caleb, I need time.
Please stop calling and texting.
Good luck at school.

I feel a rush of heat as I slam my phone onto my bed and muffle a groan into my palms.

I can't believe I screwed this up so badly. Why did I let my dad do this to me? And I can't go back now. I'm committed to Stanford. I've already accepted their offer of submission.

It's done. I'm off to Stanford, and I've lost Mallory.

Mallory has been wearing a constant look of worry and fatigue lately. She was sleeping more and not talking as much. I couldn't tell if my looming college decision had anything to do with it or if it was just a part of her usual up and down moods. Regardless of the reason, I feel so guilty, and my stomach is in knots. Seeing her rocking back and forth, with her hands over her ears, humming on that porch was the worst experience of my life. I felt helpless and out of control. And when I reached out to touch her ... hearing her scream for me *not* to touch her made my heart drop. If I had known that the last time I held her hand would be the last, I would have memorized the softness of her skin.

Her dad heard her scream as well as the commotion from inside the house and was wondering what was happening. Hearing that and then seeing Mallory on the porch in the condition she was in, I could tell her dad thought I had hurt her, but I would never have been so cruel.

The way it all played out surprised me. I figured I would explain to her the situation and that maybe we could date in secret and hide it from my dad. I thought she would go along with it … especially when I told her I loved her. Which I never got to do.

God, I'm so stupid.

I know she said not to contact her, but I can't help but try to reach out one more time. If anything, I need to know she is okay. Her text sounded so … final. I pick up my phone and find her name in my favorites. I swipe right. Immediately, Mallory's perfect voice fills my ear.

"Hello! You have reached Mallory's voice mail. Sorry I missed your call—"

I tap the red X, feeling a slight vibration in my finger. It went straight to voice mail, which can only mean one thing.

She's blocked me.

No. She wouldn't. Would she? Maybe she just has her phone turned off.

I try again. Straight to voicemail.

I feel my pulse quickening and my heart thudding in my chest with anticipation. I scramble my brain, thinking of another way to contact her. *Instagram!* Frantically, I go straight to the app on my phone and open it. My fingers fly over the keyboard as I search for her username.

Nothing.

I scroll through my followers, my finger swiping up on the screen as I scan through my small list. I reach the end.

She's not listed.

It's over. She's officially cut me out of her life.

I need to let out all this frustration and sadness. As I slam my head against my pillow, my body instinctively releases a grunted, primal scream. I can feel the vibrations reverberate throughout the room. Seconds later, there's a knock on my bedroom door.

"Caleb. Son?" It's my dad. Quite possibly the last human being I want to see right now. Shoot, I would spend an evening with Mallory's dad, risking death, than spend one second with my father.

When he opens the door, I can feel his intense gaze from across the room. I suppose he wants an explanation for the outburst.

"I'm fine, Dad," I retort, not even glancing in his direction. I'm lying on my bed with my forearm across my face.

"Well, you don't sound fine. You just ... screamed. What the heck is going on?" He steps into my room. Okay, if he wants to know what's going on, I'll clue him in. I sit up and swing my legs off the side of the bed.

"Well, I went to Mallory's tonight and told her I'm going to Stanford, *per your demand*. Then I broke her heart, *per your demand*. So there. That's why I screamed."

He smirks and lets out a small snort. "A little dramatic, don't you think? This won't be your first breakup, kid. Trust me." His dismissive tone is only fueling my anger. God, I'm so mad right now my hands are trembling.

"Dad, she had a complete anxiety attack, or maybe it was a panic attack. I don't know." I stand up to face him. "Her parents came storming out of the house; her dad kicked me out. I didn't even get to tell her the reason. Or what was going on. It was horrible." I'm begging him to show some empathy for Mallory.

"She had an anxiety attack because you're leaving. What a whack job." I'm stunned. I can't do anything but stare with my jaw on the ground. "Sounds like I was right. You're better off. You don't need to be worrying about her mental state while you are away." He walks away. "Anyway, just wanted to make sure you were alright." I dart past him and beat him to the door.

"Dad, don't you get it. I'm already worried! I feel so guilty because I practically put her in that condition. So, no, your plan didn't work. I'm going to be leaving in a few weeks, and all I will think about is HER!" *Great, now I've yelled at my dad two days in a row.*

Despite my outburst, he stays unfazed, his hand landing on my shoulder with a firm slap. "Pull yourself together. You'll be fine." He shoves past me with a dismissive wave of his arm. I stand there, watching as my dad's feet softly pad down the hall while he disappears into his and my mom's bedroom, whistling as he goes.

Speaking of my mom ... where is she in all of this? She has always been my confidant. Even though I'm still seething at the thought of her telling my dad what was happening with Mallory, I need her support right now. Why didn't she come and check on me when I got home? She knew I was going over there to talk to Mallory. God, I feel so alone.

So utterly alone.

I slam my door shut and return to my bed. I pull up the photo gallery on my phone and scroll through my pictures of Mallory. We were so happy.

But now, in the blink of an eye, we are nothing.

Mallory is already an hour late for her Sunday shift at work. And she's never late. I'm working the register; the sound of the espresso machine and the smell of coffee are everywhere as I stare at the door, hoping the next ding of the bell will be her. Normally, we give the employees a warning when they are late. But I will make sure this one slides.

My hope is that once she gets here, we can sit down, and I can tell her what happened and clear the air. I'll explain my plan to her and apologize for provoking her already fragile mind and causing her to spiral. This desire I have to see her is strong. I need her.

I'm bundling up the trash in the back room when I hear the bell ring for the door. My whole body jolts up. Then I hear a familiar voice.

"Is Caleb working?" It's Mallory's mom.

I drop the trash and come out from the back. "Mrs. Givens?"

"Hi, Caleb," she says with warmth in her voice. "Are you able to step away for a minute?"

"Yes, of course," I say as I wipe my hands on my apron. "Phyllis, can you hold down the fort for a second?" Phyllis is our newest mentor that I'm training to take over when I'm gone.

"Sure, Caleb. Take your time," she says with a warm smile.

I walk around the counter and usher Mrs. Givens to the back of the café. This amazing woman felt like family to me only a few days ago. But now, the tension is like a wall between us, making it feel like I'm getting ready to talk to a stranger. Once we are out of earshot of the other customers, I wave my hand over the chair across from me and offer her to sit. She shakes her head and declines. "This isn't going to take long." My stomach sinks to the floor.

I ask the one question I am desperate to know the answer to. "Is Mallory okay?"

She takes a deep breath, then pauses, collecting her thoughts before she answers me. "She's not doing well, Caleb. But she is home, safe and recovering."

I grab onto the back of the seat closest to me for support and fall into it. I run my hand down my face. "Mrs. Givens, I am so sorry. This is all my fault." I pause, my mind taking me back to Friday night and Mallory's front porch. "I feel so sick to my stomach."

She's standing over me now, her hands clasped together in front of her. She nods. Desperate and pleading, I lift my gaze to meet hers. "Can I see her? Please, Mrs. Givens. I just want to explain what's going on."

"Well, I thought you might ask that. Scott and I talked last night, and we both agree that should be Mallory's decision." She slowly unzips her purse, reaches in, and hands me two crisp envelopes. One says *French Street Cafe Management*, and the other is addressed to me. "She wrote this letter to you this morning. The other is her official resignation. She explains it all in her letter to you."

I take the letters into my hand, my fingers shaking as I stare at her handwriting and ponder how I got myself into this mess. "Good luck at Stanford, Caleb." I barely look up before she's already halfway out the door of the café.

I glance down at my letter and tear it open.

Dear Caleb,

My mom and dad left it up to me if I wanted to see you again. I don't think I can right now. I'm not in a good place mentally, Caleb. And that's not all your fault. I've been struggling a lot lately, and I've kept that to myself. Even though I am so mad at you, the other night wasn't entirely on you. It was just a trigger for what was brewing deep inside.

Please don't contact me. I need to be alone. I need to heal and get some help. Maybe it's better you're leaving. Maybe you breaking up with me is for the best. I don't know anything at this point. I know, however, that you have made me very happy for these last ten months. You were my first boyfriend. Any other boyfriends after you will have a lot to live up to. If there ever will be another one.

And obviously I can't work at the café anymore. Seeing you there would be a special kind of torture. Then when you leave ... too many memories. Plus, I just need some time. Alone. Please give my resignation letter to your mom.

I wish you all the best at Stanford. I know you will go far. Try to forget about me and have fun.

Love always,

Mallory

P.S. I got really mad and threw away your hoodie. I'm not going to apologize.

Lowering the letter, I peer out the window, watching the cars drive past. I'm sitting here, motionless and lost in thought. My body feels numb, and I'm completely heartbroken. When I went there yesterday, I knew telling her I was leaving would be upsetting, but I also wanted to come up with a solution. Instead—I look at the letter—I got this. She doesn't want to see me or talk to me. And worse yet, she thinks I broke up with her. I could never.

The weather decides to match my mood, and it begins to rain. The raindrops pound the window when it hits me: I won't see her at work anymore. I won't ever kiss her again. I won't be able to say goodbye. My time with Mallory is over.

"Hey, Caleb," Phyllis approaches me, breaking up my miserable thoughts. "I have a question about the cup order."

I quickly wipe away the stray tear that has escaped my eye as I glance over at her. "Yep, I'll be right there." I fold up the letter and put it in my apron pocket.

All I can do now is pray that for the next four years, there will never be "any other boyfriends."

Because I am waiting for Mallory Givens.

34

ONE MONTH LATER

Scott

D*ing dong.*

I jump in surprise as the loud, shrill sound of my doorbell echoes through the house.

Who in the world is that?

I let out a huff as I drag myself off the couch and away from watching Sports Center. It's a Wednesday evening at six-thirty; the house feels still and empty since I have it all to myself. Laura has taken Mallory to therapy, Jake is out with his friends, and I had the kind of workday that makes you want to never go back. This glass of bourbon and hearing how screwed up the general manager for Cleveland is are what I need.

But now I'm being rudely interrupted by the sound of my doorbell ringing on a Wednesday evening. By whom, I don't know. I sit my glass down with a thud, the amber-colored liquid splashing out. I head toward the front door, outstretching my hand to grab the handle.

I swear if it's old Mrs. Kuhn coming to complain about how bright our outdoor garage light is, I'm going to—

I turn the knob, open the door with an aggressive yank, and I'm not met with old cranky Mrs. Kuhn.

It's Caleb.

The last time I saw Pimple Face (I'm back to calling him that again), I was so enraged I could feel heat radiating off my body as I shouted at him to get off my property while my daughter was having an emotional breakdown. The type of breakdown that I think we should have taken her to the ER for. But for whatever reason, we didn't.

"Caleb." It's all I can muster.

"Hello, Mr. Givens." His eyes are wide with fear. Which makes me feel kinda bad. I'm not going to hurt him, of course. But I don't think I can ever view him the same way again.

"Mallory isn't here. And besides, she doesn't want to see you." I put my hands in my pockets.

"Yes, I know, sir. And I will respect her wishes, of course."

What is this twerp doing here then?

"I'm here to talk to you"—he lowers his gaze to the floor and swallows—"sir."

I stop and think for a second because I have no clue what this kid could say to me. However, my daughter is mad crazy about him. I don't want her to discover that he was here, and I was cold and unfriendly to him. I need to approach this cautiously since she's in a fragile state.

"Okay. Let's step outside." He takes a step back as I close the door behind me. I sit on the porch step as I watch him slowly approach the space next to me, filled with hesitation. I know exactly what he is thinking as he peers down at the step. This is the spot where Mallory became unhinged. "You okay?"

"Um…" He searches around frantically as if there is any other place for him to go. There isn't, so he finally sits. "Yeah. Just nervous."

A few minutes pass, neither of us talking, our breathing and the occasional passing car the only sound. The sky is overcast and gray, and there is a breeze in the air. He's looking out at the street, wringing his hands together, occasionally wiping them on his pant leg. His palms must be sweating.

"So, did you come over just to stare out at my street or…."

"No." He glances over at me, his eyebrows knit together in worry. "Mr. Givens, I just wanted you to know that I never laid a hand on Mallory that day. I never hurt her."

I have to turn away from him as thoughts of my daughter rocking back and forth, humming to herself, and her hands cupping her ears come flooding back to my mind.

"Oh, you hurt her, alright."

"I did." He sighs audibly, his breath shaking upon exhale. "I know how it must have looked from your perspective. Mallory screaming for me not to touch her." He turns again to look at me. His eyes brimming with sorrow. "You have to believe me, though, sir; I never laid a hand on her. I was just reaching out to her because I was so scared. I just wanted to comfort her in any way I could at that moment. But she was too far gone at that point."

This confession brings me some sense of relief. I know Mallory swore up and down that Caleb didn't hurt her physically, but as a father, I still had my doubts. I make a subtle nod of understanding. "Good, I'm glad to hear that." I feel a desire to ask the next question, though. "Why did you do it? Did you cheat on her?"

"NO! God, no, I would never do that to Mallory!" His answer is instant and somewhat explosive as he realizes he raised his voice and recoils some. "Sorry, I didn't mean to yell at you."

"It's okay. I just needed to know." I pause. "But you didn't answer my first question. Why did you do it?"

He hesitates, his breath catching in his throat before he answers. Then, he says the same thing he said to Mallory. "It's complicated."

The kid's voice is flat and emotionless, and it's obvious he isn't interested in discussing it. I'm fine with that.

"I can see that you don't want to talk about it, and I can respect that. But, Caleb, I think it is a good idea that you don't contact Mallory for a while. She needs time to heal. She's not in a good place right now... mentally."

He cringes slightly when he hears that. "It's all my fault. I did this to her."

Out of nowhere, I feel a sense of empathy for this kid. He feels guilty, and he's afraid he broke his girlfriend with the choice he made. And it's not on him. Mallory confessed to us she had been struggling for a few months and was keeping it to herself. How Laura and I didn't pick up on it, I have no clue. And trust me, the guilt that we carry is a constant, weighty reminder of that mistake. The only thing I can think of is that she has become an expert at masking her depression. Unfortunately, what happened was just the trigger of something that was simmering.

But none of this is anyone's fault. No one is to blame.

Wait, I can blame one thing.

Mental illness. Autism. Anxiety. Depression. All of it.

I'm learning more and more how anxiety, particularly, is a quiet and silent monster that sneaks up on you when you're doing great and feeling your best. And it steals that happiness like it owns it and you. It's the worst kind of monster.

I look over at Caleb and wrap my arm around his shoulder. "Come on, Caleb. You know that's not true. Mallory told us that this has been brewing for a while now. It's not your fault."

"That's what she said in the letter she wrote me."

I knew she had written him a letter. But she didn't share with us what it said. She only told us that she didn't want to see him and that she was letting him go. My soul ached for my daughter's first broken heart.

He continues. "But if I would have just stood up to my..." He trails off and stops himself short of what seems like a confession, and then suddenly jolts up. "Anyway, I just wanted to come over and tell you that. Your opinion of me means a lot. I didn't want to leave tomorrow and have you and Mrs. Givens think I physically harmed Mallory."

I stand, follow him down the last few steps, and face him.

"Well, I appreciate and respect that of you, Caleb. And I do feel it's better if you and Mallory take a break from each other. Like I said, she needs help and time to heal mentally."

"Well, that won't be a problem. She's blocked me. My number and from Instagram."

Oh. I didn't know that. Interesting. A small smile crosses my lips. My girl may be fragile right now, but she knows what she needs. I feel a deep sense of pride in my daughter because that must have been hard for her.

"Well, okay then." I extend my hand. "Good luck at Stanford, Caleb. I wish you all the best." He takes my hand and shakes it. It's a firm handshake as always, but this time, I don't squeeze as hard as I once did.

"Thank you, Mr. Givens. Please give my best to Mrs. Givens."

With that, he turns on his heels and heads toward his car, the sound of his shoes echoing off the pavement as he goes. I watch as he drives away, wondering if I will ever see Caleb Horvath again.

I doubt it.

After about an hour, I hear the garage door grind open. I'm back on the couch; the TV is dark, and the air feels heavy and still. I'm running my fingers along the smooth surface of my bourbon glass, swirling the brown alcohol around, letting it coat the inside edges. For some reason, I can't bring myself to drink it. I've been debating internally whether I should share with Mallory that Caleb stopped by.

Mostly, though, I can't shake something Caleb said. 'But if only I would have stood up to my...'

My what? What did he mean by that? I mean, he is his own person. An adult in the eyes of the law. But was there an outside source influencing him or telling him what to do? I know firsthand the weight of expectations that can come from those who care about you when it comes to making choices about your future.

I have no clue what happened, but honestly, I can't think about it anymore because Laura and Mallory are going to be walking in the door any second, and I need to decide whether I tell her Caleb stopped by. This is that moment.

I give myself a quick inner pep talk. *Act natural. Act natural.* I stand and sit my glass down when I hear them come in. Laura is talking. "Well, it sounds like it was a good session, then."

"I guess so." Mallory shrugs as she picks at her cuticles while staring at the kitchen floor.

"Hey, hey! So, how are my all-time favorite girls?!" I say with over-the-top enthusiasm as I walk over to Mallory. Laura gives me a puzzled look because I never greet them this way.

Way to act cool, Scott.

I move to wrap my arm around Mallory, but she recoils and pulls away. This has been happening more and more. Her breakdown was a month ago, and it feels like there hasn't been much progress.

"I'm okay, I guess. Therapy was good," she says with zero emotion. I decide to tell her because, at this point, no time is a good time. And honesty is better than lying by omission.

"Mallory, honey, I didn't know you blocked Caleb's number."

Her head snaps at the mention of his name, her eyes wide and wild. "How did you know that?"

"He told me." I take a deep breath. "He was here. About an hour ago."

"What!" she yells out as she takes a step backward. "Why? I told him I didn't want to see him. Why would he come here?" She's pacing now and flapping her hands.

Laura shoots me a glare loaded with meaning. She didn't even know Caleb came over, but it's obvious she doesn't want me bringing up Pimple Face's name. But I can't worry about Laura right now. I need to stop my daughter from teetering over the edge.

"Mallory, honey. He came to see me."

"Oh." She stops pacing. "Why did he want to see you?" Her brow furrows with concern. "You weren't mean to him, were you?"

"No, honey, I wasn't. He came to tell me he never physically hurt you that day."

"He didn't! I told you that."

"Yes, I know, and I believe you. But I think Caleb needed to tell me personally. Man to man. He didn't want to leave without me knowing that. He said that my opinion meant a lot to him."

"It does." She pauses. "I mean, it *did*." She comes closer and looks at me with sad eyes that have lost their spark. "So, are you still mad at him?"

I'm having difficulty coming up with an answer to that question. I pause for a brief second. "Not completely mad, no. I don't think throwing all my anger at Caleb does anyone any good right now. Plus, he's leaving."

"Did he say when?"

I feel a lump in my throat as my fear builds, wondering how my answer will affect her. "Tomorrow."

She stands still and rigid, Laura and I both watching her intently. After a few seconds, she turns abruptly and opens the refrigerator to get water. She twists open the cap and takes a drink, then pauses. I can sense her desire to ask more about my and Caleb's conversation. But she doesn't. "If it's okay, Mom, I want to go upstairs and lie down."

"Sure, sweetie," Laura says. "Of course."

Mallory heads to the stairs and takes them two at a time as she makes her way to her bedroom. I hear her door shut, followed seconds by muffled music.

SMACK!

"Ow!" Laura smacks me on the head. I gingerly rub the spot where her slap still stings. "What was that for?"

"Why would you tell her he came over?" she whispers through gritted teeth.

"Because I wanted to be honest with her. Hiding things, anything, isn't what this family needs right now. And I figured this way, she would know I wasn't mad at him, and that might give her some peace of mind. At least about something."

Laura glances upstairs and sighs. "No, you're right." She pauses. "Sorry, I smacked you."

"It's fine." I touch her arm and continue, "I feel like there is something else to his situation."

She glances back at me. "Really? Like what?"

I shrug. "No clue. But I could tell he was holding something back. I didn't pry, but there is more to this story. I have a gut feeling someone pressured him into ending the relationship or maybe forced him to go to Stanford."

"Seriously? I bet it was his dad. Remember, we had dinner with them a few months back. Most condescending man I have ever met."

"Longest dinner of my life. His wife was cool, though."

"Very."

As I take a few steps toward Laura, I hear her exhale with relief when I wrap my arms around her. We haven't had a moment alone to ourselves since that night, everything around us feeling chaotic and overwhelming.

"You feel good," she says with a soft moan. I kiss her on the head.

"We'll get through this," I say. "As a family, we will get through this."

35

THE NEXT DAY

Mallory

Caleb left today.

I can't help it, but I'm consumed by thoughts of him and what he could be doing right now. Is he on a plane heading across the country? Or maybe he is there, checking into his dorm? He's probably already making friends. Caleb exudes a magnetic energy that has an instant appeal to anyone he meets.

Well, except my dad.

I wonder if some of his new friends will be girls. California girls. All blonde, tall, tan, and pretty.

I curl up into a ball in my bed, my hands tightly gripping my stomach as I think about it.

My bed.

I haven't left it since yesterday when I came home from therapy and heard my dad mention Caleb. My mom has been hovering around me, making sure I'm alright. I think she can feel something is not right. She keeps trying to get me to eat, to join her, Dad, and Jake while they watch a movie, or offer to take me to the art supply store. But all I want to do is stay in bed.

To be fair, over the last few weeks, I've mostly stayed cooped up in my room. I've shrouded it in darkness by keeping my curtains drawn. Not that it matters at the moment since it's the middle of the night. The feel of my fuzzy blankets on my skin always gives me a sense of safety and security. And yet, I still feel sad. When I think, my mind keeps going straight to him. Everything that happened, our relationship, how much I love him, and never got to tell him. All of it has only added to my depression.

Depression.

That's what my therapist says I have. Clinical Depression. And I believe her one hundred percent. I'm on meds, but they aren't helping. It feels like nothing is helping. Even if Caleb barged through my bedroom door right now, declaring his love and telling me he was staying—even then, I would still feel this way. I know it.

The heavy weight of depression doesn't just come from Caleb leaving. I was feeling this way even when I was with him. If it's possible, I was happy and sad at the same time, which are weird emotions to experience together. Caleb was my happiness when we were together, but recently, that happy feeling was fake. I was dying inside. Even he couldn't take away this deep loathing for myself that has developed over time. I have lost my desire to do anything.

I don't want to get out of bed. *Too much work.*

I don't want to draw or paint. *Too much creativity is needed.*

I don't want to get dressed. *Why bother since I'm not leaving my house again.*

I don't want to see or talk to anyone. *Conversations are hard.*

My mind feels ... empty. Of everything. All thoughts, all desires, all motivation.

I don't even want Smarties. That's how you know it's bad.

All I want to do is sleep. Sleeping is better than lying here and feeling sad all the time. At least it turns my mind off. My tears have dried up, and I can't even find the strength to cry. Not one tear.

Long story short, my mind is a mess right now, and it has been playing tricks on me. It tells me things about myself that I know aren't true. Yet, I choose to believe them.

You are ugly.

You are selfish.

You aren't good enough.

You're stupid and dumb.

Who would ever want to marry you someday?

No one likes you.

Your family would be better off without you.

You should just die.

Those last two are new. Well, not really.

I have to be honest; I've been having those last two thoughts for a little while now. But lately, they are the loudest.

And I believe them.

I'm keenly aware of the strain my needs put on my parents. All the therapy appointments, all the needless worry. Without me complicating things, everything would be much simpler for them. Mom doesn't know I know this, but one day, I overheard her and my dad talking. She said that I was an accident. Well, she corrected herself and said 'surprise,' but I knew what she meant. I know she loves me, of course. What parent doesn't love their child? But they never told me I wasn't planned. In other words, from the very beginning, I have been a burden to my parents.

And I can't help but wonder if the voices in my head are right.

I roll over and stare up at all the vines that are hung up on the ceiling. Lightly, I rub the scabs and scars that are over my arm. There are about a dozen of them. All perfect straight lines running up my arm.

Yep … I've been cutting myself. It started that night a month ago.

It sounds strange, but the physical pain that the cutting causes masks the emotional pain I feel. Even if it's for a moment. The scars left behind are raised and smooth, and I enjoy running my fingers over them when I get anxious. It's only a few, but I have used a knife that I have hidden in my mattress to cut myself. Mom and Dad don't know, and I haven't even told my therapist. Because if I do, then she tells my parents, and then they take away the knife. One day last week, I almost told Jake. I felt the burden of my secret, the heaviness of it in my chest, and I had to tell someone. I was so close but couldn't bring myself to utter the words, knowing how disappointed he would be in me.

When I'm at my therapy appointment, the therapist asks the same question.

Have you thought of harming yourself since your last visit? No. I lie. I always lie.

Then, on the way home, my mom or dad asks the same question.

So, how did therapy go today? Great. Another lie.

I know cutting is wrong and not a healthy coping skill. I don't need a therapist or my parents to tell me that. For whatever reason, though, the cutting feels worth it.

I roll over onto my hands and knees and crawl over to the corner of my bed. I lift the corner of the fitted sheet and trace my finger along the side of the mattress until I feel the roughness of the slit I had cut. Since I've hidden it here, I've made sure that when my mom washes the sheets on the weekends, I put mine back on my bed. She can't find the knife. I need it.

I slide my fingers into the hole, feeling the texture of the plastic handle beneath my fingertips. It slides right out, a motion I have done a hundred times in the last few weeks. The knife isn't big. I mean, a butcher knife is kinda dramatic and large. I needed something that was easy to hide. It's only a paring knife, but I know it's sharp. I've seen my mom use it on cherry tomatoes. It slices right through those suckers like butter. Just like my skin.

I lie back down on my bed, my heart thudding in my chest as I slowly turn the knife with my hand. The steel feels cool to the touch, and I like it. I'll do this sometimes, just lie here and stare up at the vine, turning the icy blade in my hand. Over and over. Wondering what I will do with it. If anything.

The thought of cutting myself isn't even appealing right now. Nothing feels right anymore. Which leads me to my next thought.

If I have nothing to look forward to in life, should I just give up? I mean, do I want to? It's a sobering thought and one that I can't believe I am thinking about.

How far gone am I?

I look at the small knife, then I turn my hand and study the inside of my wrist, my veins blue under my skin. Would it hurt? I mean, of course it would, but how long would the pain last? How long before the silence took over? Or for my inner turmoil to be gone and darkness to settle in?

God, this is all so depressing. It feels right and wrong all at the same time. I know one thing ... I don't want to be in pain anymore. I don't want to be sad anymore. I'm done. I'm over it.

The longer I lie here and think about this, the more doable it feels. But can I? Will I?

Suddenly, my mind is racing, and my thoughts are all over the place. Everything is in overdrive. More than it has been in weeks. My heart races, and my hands feel sweaty. I'm full of adrenaline and terrified.

There is one thought that keeps taking hold. My parents.

If I follow through with this, how would that be for them? What would they see when they found me? I can imagine the scene in my head.

Mom, calling me for breakfast tomorrow morning.

Her, walking up the stairs because I hadn't answered.

Her, expecting to find me sleeping.

Her, opening the door to my dark room.

Her, turning on the light and seeing me lying there ... lifeless. Gone.

Her, screaming for my dad.

Him, running into my room.

Him, seeing me, then trying to help me.

Jake, being woken up from the commotion.

Jake, running into my room and seeing his sister ... dead.

In one swift movement, I jerk upright in my bed, and the knife I was holding flies across the room. I need it out of my hand. I crawl over to my favorite spot and lean up against the wall, pulling my knees to my chest and wrapping my arms around them. For the first time since my breakdown on the front porch, tears well up in my eyes.

I turn my gaze toward the closed door, and then my eyes roam over every inch of my room. This space feels like it's closing in on me. The darkness that once felt comforting now feels unfamiliar and uneasy. A wave of nausea washes over me. And before I can stop it...

I scream.

36

ele

Laura

"MOOOOOOM!!!!"

I spring upright in my bed, my heart pounding at the sound of my daughter's blood-curdling scream coming from her bedroom. The room is dark and quiet, with just the streetlights streaming in through the windows illuminating the space. I glance over at Scott. He's lying on his stomach, his face smashed into his pillow, snoring and sound asleep. I glance at my watch. One fifteen in the morning. I rub my eyes and shake the cobwebs out of my head.

Did I dream that?

"MOOOOOOM!!"

Now, that was real. I fling the comforter off my legs so quickly that it makes a whooshing sound, slapping Scott in the face. "Babe?" he questions in a tired stupor. I leap from the bed, the fabric of my pajama pants rustling as I tug them on and race out the door before I can answer him. When I'm in the hallway, I hear him calling. "Laura, what is going on?"

I have no idea what could be happening. Why on earth is my daughter screaming for me at the top of her lungs in the middle of the night? I run to her door, the five seconds it takes to get there feeling like an eternity, my head filled with different scenarios.

Did someone break in, and she is being attacked?

Is there a spider?

Is she having a nightmare?

I can hear Scott shuffling around in the bedroom, digging through his drawers to find his pants.

I throw open Mallory's door, my hasty entrance echoing in the room as I search for answers. As I cross the threshold, I hear her sobs, loud and heavy in the air. The darkness of the room wraps around me, but I can still smell her body wash. I push open the door all the way till it touches the wall. Something glimmering on the floor immediately catches my eye. The small object glows in the hallway light that is reflecting off it. I narrow my sleepy gaze, trying to focus on the object. It's a knife. My paring knife I thought I had lost.

Where did she get that? And why is it in her room?

My heart racing, I quickly scan the room for Mallory. I find her. She is lying in a ball on her bed, her comforter muffling the sound of her muted sobs. Racing to her, I snatch the paring knife off the floor and place it on her dresser. I crawl onto her bed with her, the mattress sinking in. I stroke her hair, and as soon as my fingers touch her head, her sobs become louder.

"Mallory, honey, what's wrong?"

More crying.

I try to coax her into a sitting position by placing my hands on her shoulders and nudging her up. She shifts slightly and raises up, resting on her elbow. She gradually lifts her head, her gaze meeting mine.

I take a sharp inward breath because the person in front of me is a mere shadow of the daughter I know. Her eyes are red, bloodshot, and hollow. Is that from crying or lack of sleep? I can't be sure. I can see where the tears have dried on her cheeks, and her hair is a disheveled mess. The bright light she carries is gone. Flushed out. Now, I only see darkness. And it scares me to death.

"Mom," she whispers through a sob.

I use my thumbs to clear the tears from her cheeks, and my fingers whisk her hair from her face. "Sweetie, what happened?"

"Mom, I'm not okay," she says as she shakes her head. "I need help."

Before I have time to process what she said, Scott barrels through the door. Without missing a beat, he rushes over to the bed and sits on the edge of her mattress, his weight causing it to sink even more. His eyes are wide as he looks at me, then turns his attention to our daughter. "Mallory, honey, what's wrong?" Scott asks. I can hear the quiver in his voice.

"Daddy," she implores as she rushes over to him, throws her arms around his neck, and sobs again. Scott's eyes shoot over to me, full of worry and panic as he rubs her back. "Shh ... it's okay, baby girl."

We all three sit in silence for a minute. Mallory's sobs fill the nighttime silence.

"Mom?" I turn to the sound of Jake's voice. He's standing in the doorway, his eyes blinking rapidly. "What's going on? I heard Mallory scream." He rubs his eyes with the palms of his hands.

"I don't know, buddy." I turn back to Scott, as he is still holding Mallory. Jake lingers in the doorway, a hesitant look on his face.

Scott continues to rub Mallory's back for a few more seconds. "Mallory, honey," he whispers. "I need you to look at me." He pulls back and places his gigantic hands on either side of Mallory's head. He gazes at her, seeing what I saw in her eyes just moments ago. His eyes flick to me, full of worry, then back to Mallory. "What happened? What's wrong?"

She shakes her head. "I can't say," she whispers.

Jake takes a few steps into the room. "What did she say?" I wave my hand behind me, signaling to Jake to be quiet. He takes a few more steps into the room until he is standing in front of her dresser. I glance over my shoulder, and he is reaching for the knife. He gingerly picks it up, his eyes lingering on Mallory, then on me, then on Scott. His face grows pale, and his eyes grow wide as he looks back at the knife. Realization flashes over his face. "Mallory, why is there a knife in your room?"

Her head snaps out of Scott's grasp and turns to Jake. She opens her mouth as if to say something, then closes it again. She gazes at her hands and picks away at her cuticles. I hear her take a quick breath. "I ... I ... was going to hurt myself with it."

My hand flies to my mouth as I let out an involuntary gasp. I glance at Scott, and he hasn't budged from his spot, his gaze still fixated on Mallory.

She wants to hurt herself. How?

As if Jake can hear my inner thoughts, he speaks up.

"Mallory," he says, his voice deep and stern. Jake pauses and gives her a chance to look at him. She tears her eyes away from her hands and raises her head to look at her brother. "Were you thinking of killing yourself?" he questions.

"What?!" I snap. "What kind of question is that?"

"Jake, that's ridiculous," Scott says in anger. "Stop jumping to conclu—"

"Yes," Mallory whispers her answer.

Scott

A glorified prison cell.

It's the only way I can think of to describe the room we are in. We are waiting in the psychiatric wing of Atwood Children's Hospital ER, the fluorescent bulbs overhead casting a harsh light on the white-padded walls. They told us four hours ago the doctor should be in any minute.

After Mallory's confession of wanting to take her life and cutting herself, Laura immediately called the mental health help line at the hospital. While she talked to an intake specialist and Mallory fell asleep on the couch, I pulled Jake aside.

How did he know Mallory was thinking of suicide?

"Jake, did Mallory tell you she was cutting herself?" I asked him in a hushed voice, not wanting to wake Mallory. Jake and I were in the kitchen, sitting at the island.

"She didn't," he said, shaking his head and fidgeting with his hands.

"I feel a 'but' coming on," I said.

He glanced over his shoulder at Mallory before continuing. "Last week, I saw she had two slice marks on her forearm. They looked fresh, like maybe they had just stopped bleeding."

"Wait," I said, shaking my head in disbelief. "What day was this?"

"Last Tuesday. You were working late, and Mom went to the grocery store. Mallory was in her room, and I was playing video games in the living room. She came downstairs and sat on the couch, so I asked her if she wanted to play, and she said no. It shocked me she even left her room."

I watched him recall the story and could tell he was struggling. He studied his hands with a frown, lost in thought. Before he continued, he took a sip of water, then he sat the glass down, clutching it tightly with his hands.

He looked straight ahead and sighed before he continued. "Then she said that she was hot, and she took off her sweatshirt. She balled it up in her lap and was playing with the drawstring of the hood. She just sat there in her pajamas, legs criss-crossed, staring at the TV screen. It scared me, Dad. She looked so distant. Like she wasn't even present in reality. I could sense that there was something on her mind when she turned her attention to me. That's when I noticed her arms and saw the cuts."

"Did you ask her about them?" I questioned, trying to sound like I wasn't accusing him. So, I rested my hand on his arm. His pain was obvious, and I felt the need to reassure him he had done nothing wrong.

"No. And I should have. When she didn't say anything, I just went back to playing. She sat there for a while, then she stood, and I swear I heard her say under her breath, 'You would be better off without me, and I wish I was dead.' So I asked her as she headed up the steps what she said because I wasn't sure if I heard her correctly. I mean, come on, that's unbelievable, right? She just muttered 'nothing' under her breath and went back to her room. But then tonight, when I saw the knife on her desk and saw her with you on her bed, I just knew."

He buried his face in his hands. "God, Dad, I'm so sorry. I should have told you and Mom. Honestly, I didn't think I heard her right or thought that the cuts were just accidents, maybe. I feel like this is all my fault."

I wrapped my arm lovingly around his shoulder. "Jake, none of this is your fault. You hear me? None of it."

Tears welled up in his eyes as he looked at me. "But if I just would have said someth—"

"Stop it," I said in a soft yet firm voice to get his attention. "Now look, more than likely, we are going to be headed to the hospital with your sister tonight. If you had told us this, the outcome would have been the same. We still would have taken her to the hospital. Do you hear me? Don't beat yourself up over this. You saw and recognized something tonight that your mom and I missed. I should thank you."

With that, I pulled him in for a hug. He buried his face into my shoulder, and I heard a soft sob come from his throat. Jake has matured, not just in age, into a full-fledged man. But as I held him, comforted him, and let him release his guilt, he felt like my little boy.

At that point, Laura informed us the hospital recommended that Mallory be taken to the ER for a psych eval. We all agreed it was the best choice. Even Mallory.

"I want to go. I need to go," were her exact words.

We drove Jake to Johnny's since he didn't want to be alone. Johnny met us outside his house. He said nothing as he hugged us all. But when he approached Mallory for a hug, she shook her head and took a step backward. "It's okay, kiddo." I saw a tear fall from his cheek. "I love you so much." The one and only tear I ever saw him shed was for my daughter. It's decided ... Johnny is getting a lifelong supply of his fancy drinks from me.

The two in the morning drive to the hospital seemed to drag on endlessly, the fifty minutes feeling like a lifetime. Mallory slept in the back seat while I filled Laura in on what Jake told me. For the rest of the drive, I held Laura's hand, never letting go. The only sound was the hum of the car's engine. Every now and then, she would squeeze it. I wondered what she could have been thinking to make her need to anchor herself to me. Probably the same as me. Our daughter is suicidal.

The intake specialist alerted the ER that we would be arriving, so when we got there, they immediately ushered us back.

And as if the whole situation wasn't surreal enough, this is when it got real.

They brought us back to a special wing of the ER. Once we arrived, I quickly scanned the area and took stock of my surroundings. I counted seven patient rooms. All with imposing doors, complete with large hinges and a window, shuttered with a mini blind. There was a restroom down at the end of the wing with a sink outside of it and no trashcan. Only a brown paper bag to dispose of the paper towels used to dry your hands. We stood at the nurse's station, which was small and uncluttered. I noticed a surveillance monitor that was manned by a police officer, his gun holster placed firmly on his hip, his torso covered in a bullet-proof vest. Footage from eight cameras was on display. I saw a black and white grainy image of my family on the camera feed labeled number one. I looked up at the ceiling and saw the black dome. A chill went up my spine.

What kind of stuff happens here?

And in the middle of it all stood my daughter. Her long hair cascaded around her face, her eyes fixed on the floor. She was crying silently. There was no life in her. And I couldn't help but wonder if she would ever get it back.

They handed us a brown paper bag similar to the ones you get at the grocery store, crinkling softly as they passed it to us. "Please deposit all your belongings in here," the nurse instructed us. Our phones, our keys, Laura's purse, anything that wasn't our clothes or our shoes, we placed in the bag. The nurse headed to a locker with a number 4 on it and placed our bag inside. She pulled a key out of her scrub pocket and twisted it in the lock, the loud click the only sound in the silent atmosphere.

The silence in the wing was deafening. Granted, it was three in the morning, but this place was eerie. Nothing about it felt friendly or comforting. But maybe that was the point. They didn't want people to come back.

After locking up everything that we brought with us, they handed Mallory a bag similar to the one now secured in locker number 4. Inside was a pair of standard blue hospital scrubs.

"Mallory, I need you to change into these scrubs. If your bra has an underwire in it, you will need to remove that as well, but keep your underwear on. There is a pair of slippers in there also," the nurse explained in a tender yet soft voice.

"The restroom is right over there. Put your street clothes in the bag and meet us back right here, okay?"

Mallory nodded in understanding, took the bag, and walked to the restroom, head down, zombie-like. While we waited, the nurse explained to us what was going to happen. We would be placed in room number 4. They would take Mallory's vitals, and then we would wait to see a doctor. The doctor will talk to us together, then to all of us separately.

And that's where we are ... waiting. I glance across the empty room at my wife and daughter. Laura is lying on the uncomfortable hard rubber couch, the smell of its synthetic material strong in the air. Mallory is lying on her back, and her head is resting on Laura's legs. She's wide awake.

I glance around the room, wondering if I can find something different to look at. There's nothing. I'm sitting across the room on an equally hard rubber chair. There's another chair in front of me, my long legs resting on it. There is a TV on the wall, encased in hard plastic, that's bolted to the wall. They installed a heavy-duty steel mini blind to cover the window so it can't be opened or tampered with. All of this protects these kids who are a danger to themselves. There is not one thing in this room that can be used as a weapon to either harm others or themselves.

And honestly, if you weren't feeling mentally unstable when you came in here, sitting and waiting in this room would make you go insane. There is nothing but time and your thoughts.

I glance over at Mallory again. She hasn't moved, her body's involuntary mechanism of breathing keeping her alive. There is a tight sadness that fills my chest, and my mind is in overdrive.

How did we get here?

Will she ever recover?

Am I going to lose my daughter?

I close my eyes tightly and press my fingers against my nose as the fatigue and stress have given me a pounding headache. I turn my head and take in Mallory's face. "Mal Pal?" I whisper to her, not wanting to wake up Laura. Mallory's eyes lock with mine as she turns. They are shallow and void of life. "Are you hungry or thirsty?" I ask her. It's a simple question, but I feel like I need to help her somehow. Any way possible.

She shakes her head slowly and turns her attention back to the ceiling. "Mal, when was the last time that you ate?" I had noticed in the last few weeks she was looking frail.

She shrugs her shoulders. "I don't remember." She moves away from me, her body shifting as she turns her back to me. I hear her scrubs rub against the rubber of the couch. "I don't want to talk, Dad." Normally, we do not tolerate this kind of dismissive response from our kids. However, today, exceptions are made.

Just as Mallory shifts her body to get comfortable, there is a soft knock on the door. All three of us jolt up. A doctor in black scrubs and a white coat, holding a clipboard in his hand, enters the room.

"Hello, I'm Dr. Perry. I'm the psychiatrist on duty tonight," he says in a polite tone. We exchange a few more pleasantries as he shakes my hand and Laura's, then greets Mallory. I move the chair that was once housing my legs so the doctor can face us. He sits down in the chair, crosses his ankle over the opposite knee, and clicks his pen.

"Alright, let's begin."

37

THREE DAYS LATER

Laura

M allory has been in the hospital for three days.

And I've never left her side.

After meeting with the doctor in the ER and then with a PIRC specialist (Psychiatric Intake Response Center), it was decided that Mallory should be admitted to the hospital for further evaluation. Scott and I agreed.

So did Mallory.

They have filled these last two days with numerous visits from doctors, nurses, psychologists, psychiatrists, as well as a social worker. It's been exhausting.

But we have a plan in place to help Mallory going forward. We will fill our weeks with different therapy appointments and spend our nights taking turns sleeping with Mallory in her room. The doctors feel she shouldn't be alone in the evenings. Her medications have been changed and adjusted. Once they release her tomorrow, she will partake in a partial hospitalization program for two weeks. This way, she can remain in the comfort of her own home while receiving the same level of medical care at the hospital.

Also, we must lock away anything sharp. Knives, scissors, toenail clippers, my sewing box ... anything that Mallory might use to harm herself with. Cooking should be interesting.

I've come to accept that this is our new reality. One that we need to endure and embrace equally. For Mallory. For our family.

Scott isn't here today. He's working. One, to take his mind off everything, and two, because he was needed. Even though Johnny would take charge every day all day in a heartbeat, I could tell Scott was itching to check out the jobs. He will be back later tonight because, at the end of the day, nothing will keep him away from his daughter.

I glance at Mallory, and she is watching one of her favorite anime shows. I observe the slow rise and fall of her chest as her delicate fingers tap on her leg, which is covered in a thin, crisp hospital sheet. We were permitted to bring her favorite fuzzy blanket from home, and it lies neatly at the foot of the bed. A small smile crossed her lips when she saw it. It was the first smile she gave us in months.

I take a minute to survey the room; it's basic and plain, not so different from the ER. Some of the same protocols are in place as well. They told me not to bring flowers or cards, and I had to put all my belongings in a locker. Basically, it's her bed, a night table, a TV encased in plastic that hangs on the wall, and the chair that now has my permanent butt print in it.

She's sitting up in her bed, and her cheeks have a hint of pink back in them, likely because the hospital is making sure she's eating regularly. Her communication has improved as well. She also has a pack of Smarties resting on her lap. Every so often, she pops one in her mouth.

With a bit of hesitation, I decide to test the waters and see what would happen if I try to get her talking.

"So, how was art therapy this afternoon?" I ask her. Since being admitted, music and art therapy have been a part of her daily routine.

She shrugs and answers me without taking her eyes off the TV. "It was good, I guess. The art teacher is lame. But it felt nice to have a brush in my hand again."

I am overcome with an internal sense of joy, like a spark of hope. One that I hope will ignite and that passion she once had for art will spread through her like a fire once again.

"That's good to hear," I reply with a smile, trying to sound pleased but not overly enthusiastic. Scott and I were able to sit down with a therapist and discuss our feelings while we were here. They suggest containing our enthusiasm when Mallory expresses interest in her hobby for fear of putting too much pressure on her, which is how she would perceive it. They also advised us not to react if she asks us shocking questions or confides in us about something we may find distressing. Which she could interpret as judgment. Mallory needs to know that we are a safe space and a haven for her thoughts.

Mallory turns into her bed to face me. She rests her hands under her cheek and on her pillow.

"Hey, Mom," she says as she looks at me with those big brown eyes I love so much. "Would you, Dad, and Jake be sad if I died?"

Don't react. Don't react. Don't react.

To keep my composure, I tightly clutch the cold plastic of the chair, all my emotions funneling into my hands.

"Mallory, honey, I promise you, if you were to ever die, it would break open a hole in our lives that we could never fill. Ever."

I place a comforting hand on her leg and gently squeeze. She doesn't pull away. Another victory. I don't know if that was the right thing to say, but it's the truth.

She sighs and turns her attention back to her show. "So, you guys love me?"

At that moment, my heart is breaking so loudly that I'm sure the entire hospital hears it. "Mallory, we love you with all our hearts. More than you could ever know or even understand."

She nods slightly, her hair brushing against her shoulder, then she slowly turns to face me again.

"That's good to know because I love you guys too."

38

ONE MONTH LATER

Jake

I stare at my phone, trying to collect my thoughts before I type out my message to Emma.

> **Me:** Hey Em. I'm going to have to cancel our date tonight. I'm going to give my parents the night off and sleep in Mallory's room with her. I'm so sorry.

I sigh and hit send, shoving my phone in my back pocket as I descend the creaky basement steps to get the air mattress. Mallory has been out of the hospital for over a month now. Her therapist feels that she shouldn't be alone, especially at night, since this is when she would cut herself and think about—I shake my head to remove the images of that night. Mom has been sleeping with her ever since she got released from the hospital. Dad was supposed to switch nights with my mom and sleep on the floor. But Mom wouldn't leave her side.

And I can tell it's taking a toll on her.

She's utterly exhausted, her shoulders slumped in a constant state of worry. Dark circles have appeared under her eyes. This morning, she fell asleep with her chin resting in her hand while she sat at the kitchen island, her avocado toast and hot coffee in front of her, untouched. I knew then that she needed a break. So, I offered to bunk on the air mattress in Mallory's room for the weekend. This way, Mom can get some well-deserved rest, and she and Dad can enjoy a quiet evening together. They deserve it. Mom jumped at the opportunity, and Dad looked pretty stoked.

I head up the stairs, air mattress in hand, and open the linen closet to get a sheet, some blankets, and a pillow. After opening the door and going over my options, I decide we need to get some new backup sheets since my only two choices are Tinkerbell or Thomas the Train. I sigh and pull-out Thomas as my butt vibrates. Emma is probably texting back, and I hope she isn't too disappointed. I place everything down on the hallway floor and check my phone.

> **Emma:** It's okay! I totally under-
> stand. Your mom must be ex-
> hausted.

As I read her words, I feel my lips curl up in a smile.

Confession time.

I like this girl. A LOT. Like, a lot, a lot. I don't want to use the other 'L' word yet, but it's bubbling to the surface more and more. It also doesn't hurt that she is drop-dead gorgeous. Picture Natalie Portman's face with Gal Gadot's body, and you have my Emma. I am very, very lucky.

> **Me:** Thanks for understanding.
> <kissy face emoji>

Maybe I am in love. I just used an emoji.

Emma: Do you guys need anything?

Me: Nah. Thanks though. Rain
check on our date? Next Friday
maybe. I promise to make it up
to you. <heart emoji>

Yep, I'm gone.

Emma: I'll hold you to that!

Emma: Or better yet, how about
tomorrow I stop over and you,
me, and Mal can hang out? Get
pizza, watch a movie or something. Would she be up for that?

Me: I'll ask her tonight and let
you know. Thanks for the offer.

Emma: Sure. I just want to help
anyway I can. I really like your
sister. She's amazing and I want
her to get better.

Me: She really is amazing.
Thanks. Talk to you soon.

I stop myself short of another emoji. Because, well, I'm not a girl.

I gather up my makeshift bed and head to Mallory's room as I tap lightly on the ajar door. That's the other thing. She can't be alone in her room with the door shut. At least not right now.

"Mal, you up?" I ask.

She's sitting on her bed in her favorite spot. Legs crossed, sketch pad and charcoal pencil in her hand, her fingers covered in black soot. It's been nice seeing her take an interest in her art again. Even if it's just a little.

"Hey, Jake," she says as she sits her pad down on the bed beside her. I enter her room and drop all the bedding down on the floor. The air mattress hits the floor with a soft thud, followed by the slight smell of rubber. "What's going on?" she asks, her head tilts to the side.

"I'm bunking in here all weekend with you." She glances up at me, her eyes lingering on mine before dropping to the air mattress.

"Seriously? What about Mom?" I notice she fidgets with her ring, and her leg begins to bounce.

"I'm giving Mom the weekend off. She and Dad are going out tonight. So, it's just you and me," I inform her as I busy myself attempting and failing to get the air mattress out of the bag. I glance at Mallory, noticing the hush that has settled over her in the past few minutes. She's watching me with intent. "What?"

"You don't have to do this, Jake," she says flatly. "I know you have a date with Emma tonight." She quickly grabs her sketch pad and pencil and begins drawing, the sound of the lead scratching against the paper filling the room. She seems indifferent to this idea, and I can't figure out why.

"I canceled it. Emma understood."

"What did you tell her? That you had to babysit your crazy sister?" she asks without even looking at me.

My body sags in sadness that she would even think I could ever say that about her. "Mal, come on. You know I wouldn't say that." She keeps sketching. I walk over to her desk, pull out her chair, and whip it in front of her, facing the chair backward. I straddle it, resting my arms on the back. "Mal." I gently pull down on the sketch pad, forcing her to look at me. She glances up and starts twirling the end of her ponytail. "Mom needs a break. She is exhausted and needs to sleep in her own bed for a couple of nights. Plus, she and Dad need some alone time."

"Ew," she says as her nose crinkles. "I don't need that picture in my head. Thank you very much." I chuckle at that because she's right ... ew.

She immediately focuses back on her drawing once again. My eyes are drawn to the charcoal-covered paper, and I can make out the details of the sketch—a girl walking along the shoreline, her dress billowing in the breeze. It's incredible, and I'm mesmerized by her talent as I watch her fingers manipulate the pencil and paper to create a work of art. We both sit in silence for a little while, her creating, me observing. "That's really good, Mallory."

She never loses her focus, and the pencil keeps moving. "Thanks."

I yawn, stretching my arms before getting up to fill the air mattress. Mallory sits her pad back down on the bed and grabs her favorite fluffy pillow. I see her playing with it out of the corner of my eye. It feels like she wants to say something because she keeps looking at me, then back at her pillow. I plug in the pump and click the start button, and it hums to life as the mattress gets fatter and fatter. After a few minutes, she takes a deep breath, still concentrating on the pillow. "I feel so bad, ya know? Everyone's life has come to a screeching halt because of me. First Mom and Dad, and now you." Her eyes meet mine, and I can see the sadness and regret. "I feel really bad, so please tell Emma I'm sorry."

Mallory's chin dips to her chest, and her shoulders slump as she goes back to picking at her pillow. I can almost see the guilt radiating from her, and it triggers something within me. It never occurred to me that Mallory was struggling with feeling like a burden to us. And she isn't. There was once a time when I was younger that I was jealous of the extra attention she got from Mom and Dad. But now that I'm older, I get it. She needs them, and she needs help. Especially now.

I stop the pump. "Mal, she understands. Please don't worry about that, okay?"

"But I worry, Jake. Like, all the time. I feel like you guys all hate me because of how much things have changed around here. Now Emma probably hates me too." She bangs her head on the wall behind her, and tears well up in her eyes. "I get it. I hate myself for all of it."

I honestly have no clue what to say. No matter how often we tell Mallory how much we love her and want her around, this is something she needs to come to terms with herself. I hope that time comes soon because I hate seeing her like this. An idea pops into my head, so I take out my phone and pull up Emma's texts from just ten minutes ago. I hand it to Mallory. "Here, read this." Mallory takes my phone in her hand. "Does that sound like someone who doesn't like you or is mad at you?"

She reads the text thread and does something that I haven't seen her do in months. She laughs.

"What's so funny?" I'm confused as to what she could have found funny in the text exchange.

"You sent her a kissy face emoji *and* a heart emoji!" she exclaims as she extends her arm to show me the text thread.

Crap! Forgot about that.

I reach out my hand. "Give me my phone back."

She raises my phone high in the air to get it out of my reach. Laughing hysterically. "Are you in *looooooove?*"

I reach across the bed in a desperate attempt to get it back from her. "Mallory, come on."

She quickly maneuvers around me and off the bed, her feet barely touching the floor as she makes her way to the middle of her room. *Dear Lord, she's fast.* "What else have you guys said to each other?" she asks with a wide, evil grin on her face as she glares at my phone and scrolls. Giggling as she does.

Oh, heck no.

"Mallory, I swear to God. Give me back my phone." I bite back, extending out my hand. "Now." This whole idea took a turn I wasn't expecting.

"Fine." She hands it back to me, and I shove it back into my pocket. "I wasn't really going to read anything."

I kneel back down in a huff to the task at hand, the air mattress, as Mallory stands and watches me. "So, she really wants to hang out with me?"

I stop and turn around to face her. "Of course she does. She really likes you, Mal. You saw it, she said so in the text. She thinks you're awesome and is really worried about you. Just like the rest of us. I'm not joking when I say that she asks about you all the time."

She's chewing on her lower lip, and I can tell she is pondering this as she plays with the hem of her nightshirt. "That's nice to hear." She crawls back onto her bed. "Tell her I'm in and that tomorrow sounds like fun."

"I'll tell her," I say with a small, satisfied smile. "And, Mal?" She looks at me. "It was nice to hear you laugh."

Once we have the air mattress set up, and I change into my blue plaid sleeping pants and a white t-shirt, Mom and Dad come in to say bye. Now, we are lying here in uncomfortable silence. Me on my Thomas-covered rubber bed and Mallory in hers. I'm scrolling through Instagram, my heart pounding in my chest, when the urge to ask her the question I've been wanting to ask for a month overwhelms me. "Hey, Mal?"

"Yeah," she answers from above me.

"Would you have really gone through with it?" I don't elaborate because she knows what I mean. I hear her let out a sigh, and it's quiet for a minute or two. It's taking her so long to answer, I regret asking. "You know what ... never mind. I shouldn't have asked."

"No, it's okay," she reassures me. "I don't know ... if I'm being honest. I mean, obviously, I wasn't thinking clearly." From my position on the floor, I can't see much of her, so I listen as I stare up at her vine-covered ceiling. I notice she wraps her arms around her body. Almost like she is protecting herself from her own thoughts. "I told my therapist that it was an impulse thought. And it was. When

I was in that moment, I felt like if I was dead, all my emotional pain would be gone. Does that make sense?"

I ponder that thought for a second. And I can empathize with that, especially if she was in a lot of pain. I get a sense that she wants to be heard and understood. "Yeah, that makes sense. I can see where you are coming from."

"But then my therapist said that, if I get tempted again ... to think about how even though my pain would be gone, it would be projected onto you guys after the fact. I had never thought of it like that before."

I'm staring at the ceiling, listening to my sister talk about taking her own life along with the aftermath. My chest hurts thinking about how much she has gone through in her short seventeen years of life.

"Mallory, I'm sorry I wasn't there for you more." As she turns to her side, her eyes meet mine. She rests her chin on her hand as I turn my head to face her. "I should have been."

"Don't be ridiculous. None of this is your fault. But thank you for saying that."

"I promise to be there for you more from now on. You can count on me, okay. Whenever you get tempted to cut or to ... you know." She shakes her head in understanding. "Call me, text me, or knock on my door. Anytime, day or night. I'm serious." And I mean every word. I've not been the big brother that Mallory needs. I will always hold on to some guilt for not asking her what was wrong that day in the living room. But I plan to make it up to her by being the brother she deserves. Starting tonight.

"Thanks, Jake." She smiles and lies back again, staring at the ceiling.

"So, what do you want to do tonight?" I ask.

"Well, technically, this is a slumber party. So, we could paint each other's nails, or you could braid my hair. Personally, I would love to give you a makeover, but it's your call. Oh, wait ... a facial!" She giggles, and it sounds so wonderful. Because it's the sound of happiness brewing.

I sit up on my elbow and toss my Thomas pillow at her, laughing. "Fat chance! How about we go downstairs and have a Star Wars marathon?"

"Cool." She jumps out of bed, tossing me back my pillow. "As long as it's either the prequels or the originals. In my current mental state, episodes seven through nine are out of the question." She walks out of the bedroom.

I follow her with a satisfied smile on my face. "I'll make the popcorn."

39

FIVE MONTHS LATER

Laura

"Camelot Center. This is Donna. How can I help you?"

"Hi, Donna. My name is Laura Givens. I was calling for information on your riding lessons. It would be for my daughter, Mallory."

"Of course. I'd be happy to help. What would you like to know?"

That conversation was a week ago with Donna, the director of The Camelot Center. It's a facility that specializes in therapeutic horseback riding for those with both physical and mental disabilities. Mallory has always loved animals. Especially horses. It all started with her first American Girl doll, Saige, who is both an artist and rides horses. Her therapist thought maybe this could be a beneficial activity for her, so I did some research. It amazed me to find out that horses can calm those with autism, allowing them to focus and think clearer. It can ease anxiety, help with moods and depression, and even improve communication skills.

Well, sign us up!

So much has changed since that night. After they released her from the hospital, we removed Mallory from school. I started homeschooling her again to take some of the pressure off her life. Something else that has helped tremendously is Mallory teaching herself the basics of art by using YouTube videos. Every time she shows me another piece of art, I am in awe of her incredible talent. I fear that she's becoming isolated with all the time she spends alone. So, Scott and I, as well as her therapist, feel it's time for her to get some more social interaction. That's where The Camelot Center comes into play.

When I presented the idea to Mallory, she practically jumped out of her skin with excitement.

"You mean they will teach me how to ride a horse?!" she exclaimed.

"That's right. And the director said that you will learn how to take care of it as well. How to saddle it up, brush it. All the fun stuff. Then, over time, you can volunteer if you want."

"Um, yes, please! I want to. When do I start?" I couldn't help but smile at how excited she was. It's been six months, and she is improving with each passing day, each week, each month. My daughter is finally making her way back to me. And I love it.

"Well, we are going tomorrow to the barn to meet Donna and the horses," I explained. "She said that once you meet each horse, you can pick one that you feel connected to. There's some paperwork that you will need to fill out, and I can help you with that. From there, we can get you started this week, hopefully."

That was yesterday. Now, we are pulling onto a long gravel road. I can see the barn in the distance. I glance over at Mallory, and she is tapping her finger on her pants. "You okay, sweetie?"

"Yeah, just nervous. But it's a good nervous." She turns and smiles at me, something I will never tire of seeing from her.

As we approach, I see a woman who appears to be in her sixties, with short blonde hair peeking out from under her knit hat, wearing a Carhartt jacket, dirty jeans, and boots. It's winter, so she's also sporting work gloves. You can tell she's the type of woman that isn't afraid to get her hands dirty. It's ten in the morning, and she's probably already been here since dawn, working and doing whatever needs to be done to keep this place running. I can only assume this must be Donna. She waves to us as I pull in and park along the front of the barn.

Mallory and I get out of the car (more like Mallory leaps out). The stable door is open, and I'm immediately hit with a smell of sawdust mixed with manure. I quickly realize that Mallory and I are way overdressed for this place. Me in my white puffer coat and black heeled boots. Mallory in her dressy pea coat and white Chucks. Oops.

Note to self ... shop for barn-appropriate attire that can get dirty.

We walk over to Donna, and she removes her dirty work glove and extends her hand. "You must be Laura and Mallory Givens. I'm Donna. It's nice to put a face with the voice," she says warmly. I take her hand, warm from being protected from the elements, and shake it.

"It's great to meet you, Donna," I say with enthusiasm.

Donna then turns her attention to Mallory, who has made her way to my side, but she is focused on the barn entrance. The horses must be excited because we can hear them neighing and kicking their stalls in anticipation of new people. "And you must be Mallory?"

"Hi!" Mallory says, never taking her eyes off the stalls that lay just ahead.

"So, Mallory, can I shake your hand? Or does that make you uncomfortable?"

It says a lot that Donna has been kind enough to ask this question. I explained to her about Mallory's autism, her anxiety ... all of it. You can tell this isn't Donna's first time at the rodeo. She knows what she's doing and what questions to ask.

"Um ... no. I don't think so," Mallory says, turning her gaze away from the barn and to the gravel below her feet. "I'm sorry."

"Oh, it's fine, Mallory. I understand. One thing that we expect of our riders and volunteers is that they advocate for what they need and want. And also, to never apologize for how you're feeling. So, thank you for telling me."

With that one sentence, I see Mallory do something that I rarely see her do with someone she meets for the first time. She looks at Donna square in the eye ... and smiles. "Okay. I can do that."

"Alright, great!" Donna exclaims as she claps her hands together. "Now, how about we go meet some horses?"

Mallory bounces on her heels. "Yes, please!"

Donna leads the way into the barn. Stall after stall houses the most beautiful horses, all shades of black, brown, tan, and even some that look like they have paint spatters on them. Donna kindly introduces each horse to Mallory and tells us their story and how they made it to Camelot. She explains what type of horse they are, as well as their personalities. It's fascinating, and Mallory is hanging on to her every word. Other than her art, I haven't seen Mallory express interest in anything this past year. She is getting better, yes, but I have been trying to find something to break her out of the shell that she still hides in.

Today, I see her peeking out.

She's asking questions, listening intently to Donna's answers, and then follows up with another question. She hasn't even mounted one of these horses yet, and her communication is already improving.

I think the horses' names are my favorite part. Flash, Kai, Tucker, Levi, Kruzer, Mike, Storm, Fiona, Cash, Mandy, and finally, Tony the Pony. After getting a tour of the barn, it's off to see the arena that houses the lessons. It's a massive dome-like structure with a sand floor. It's attached to a small room that is used for viewing in case parents want to watch their kids ride. In the front of the arena is a ramp used for mounting the horses. Donna explains that it's used for beginners and for those who are in a wheelchair or use a walker. The thought of those with physical disabilities being afforded the opportunity to ride a horse makes my heart swell. What a gift this place provides for them.

Along the back wall is all the equipment for different games they play with the younger riders. Shelves on top of shelves of fun games. Next to that is the equipment needed for jumping. Stands, poles, fake brick walls, cones, and blocks for mounting the horses all lined up in perfect rows. Mallory zeroes in on all the stuff for jumping and points to it. "I'm going to be using those one day, Mom." Her voice carries so much assurance it's like I'm talking to a stranger.

I wink at her. "I have no doubt."

At the end of the tour, Donna shows us the pasture that the horses graze in, as well as the outside course they use for lessons during the warmer months. In short, this place is incredible. As soon as I stepped out of the car, I could feel the serene vibe this place gives off. It's an energy that sucks you in and settles into your bones. Once you're here, you don't want to leave.

I glance at Mallory as we make our way back to the stable. She's talking Donna's ear off, and I notice her shoulders are relaxed, her head is up as she walks, she isn't tapping her leg or fidgeting with her ring. She appears calm and peaceful. It's a look I don't think I have ever seen on her, and I like it very much.

We make our way back to where we started, the stable, as Donna asks, "Alright, Mallory, did you see a horse that you liked?"

"Yes, I did!" Mallory screeches out and marches straight over to Levi's stall. His coat is dark chocolate brown, his mane is black, and he has a white patch on his forehead. He's absolutely gorgeous. When she approaches his stall, he walks right up to the front. Mallory places her hand in between the steel poles and starts stroking Levi's neck with no fear or trembling in her hands. Levi leans into her touch.

"Hey, Levi," Mallory says in a whisper. "I think we are going to be best friends." It's like they've known each other for years and not mere seconds. When we met each horse, I looked for any sign that Mallory might like one over the other. There was nothing. She greeted each horse with the same wave and, 'Hi there, girl' or, 'Hi there, boy.' I was worried that maybe she wasn't connecting with any of them. Watching my daughter's face light up as she strokes the horse's mane, the tears in my eyes grow stronger.

"Would you like to give him a snack?" Donna asks as she grabs some carrots off a nearby shelf.

"I would love that!" Mallory observes as Donna shows how to properly offer the food to Levi. Mallory takes the carrots, and she holds out her palm, facing up, the carrot lying in her hand. Levi drops his mouth, and you can see his huge teeth rake along her palm as he takes the carrot. Mallory giggles. "That tickled. Can I give him some more?"

"You sure can," Donna says as she hands Mallory the rest of the carrots. "Just give him one at a time, okay. I'll be over here with your mom." Mallory only nods, never breaking concentration and eye contact with Levi.

Donna and I walk a few stalls over to a small counter. We set up a lesson time, and I sign a bunch of papers. I hand her a check that pays for six weeks' worth of lessons, although I'm pretty sure this will go way beyond that time frame.

We both stand there watching Mallory. "Donna, I honestly didn't think she connected with any of the horses. I'm so surprised."

"I'm not. Sometimes, there is an unspoken connection between a person and a horse. It only exists between them." She points to Mallory and Levi. "It's a beautiful thing."

"Are you connected to any of these horses?"

"Oh, I have a special bond with all of them. That happens when you see them day in and day out, feeding them and taking care of them. But there was a horse, Maggie." Donna's voice takes on a softer quality as soon as she says Maggie's name. "She was my everything. Our hearts were connected. They still are, even though she's been gone for a few years now. Not a day goes by that I don't think about her."

A small smile crosses my lips. "That's amazing. I hope Mallory finds that here. That connection," I say as I watch her talk to Levi.

Donna gives me a sly, knowing smile. "Oh, I'm pretty sure we are already there."

40

Six months later

Mallory

"So, do you have everything?" my mom asks for the hundredth time this morning.

"Yes, Mom. Why do you keep asking?" I internally roll my eyes.

"I'm just excited for you, that's all." I know she is, but I'm not lying when I say she's asked a million times.

We are making our weekly trip to Camelot. I've been riding now for six months, and it has completely changed my life. I will forever be grateful to my mom for introducing me to this place. These horses and the people here have been my lifeline. I call it my second home and would sleep on haystacks and stay here all night long if they would let me.

But starting today, I am taking my love of riding and horses to the next level. I am going to be a volunteer. Yep, I'm going to be scooping poop, brushing the horses, feeding them, and helping with lessons. I'm so excited I can't stand it. Being here gives me purpose, and it makes me feel important and wanted. Not that my family doesn't do that for me. But somehow, this is different. And I know it's because of the twelve beautiful souls that live here twenty-four/seven.

Levi is my horse. Well, technically, I don't own him, but when I'm here, he belongs to me, and I belong to him. I always arrive with treats in hand, and he greets me at his stable door, happy to see me. Levi took hold of my heart and never let go. Being with him brings me inner peace and a calm that I can't find anywhere else.

He has made me whole and put me back together again.

There is no other way to describe it. When I'm here with Levi and at this barn, sometimes it feels better than medicine. I mean, I will always have to be on medicine to control my anxiety and depression. But this barn, this place, is also my medicine and my therapy.

It's been a year since that awful time. After Caleb, I was left with an emptiness that made me consider ending it all. I am determined to never go back to that deep, dark place and feel that way again. And to do that, I need to put in the work. Which means taking my meds religiously, regular checkups with my doctors, going to my different therapies to help maintain my autism. As well as seeing a regular therapist to talk through my anxiety and depression. I've been diligent in my efforts, and it shows.

Because I have never felt better.

And Caleb? I haven't heard from him since that night. That's what happens when you block someone. However, he is never far from my thoughts because I think about him every day. I still miss him. But my therapist is helping me to move on. It's hard. I think some part of me will always miss Caleb and care about him. But he's my past. I have a future to worry about. And I am ready to tackle it head-on.

We make the turn to the barn, and the familiar sound of the gravel under our tires fills the silent space in the car. My mom pulls our car into a spot next to about a dozen other vehicles. Today is New Volunteer Orientation Day, so the place is packed. Suddenly, the familiar nerves fill my stomach. I can feel my head getting hotter. This feels like the first day of school all over again. Even though I know Donna, Kayla, and Erin—the ladies who will be showing us the ropes—very well, I'm still so nervous.

My mom places her warm hand on my knee. "Are you ready, sweetheart?" she asks me, her gentle touch calming me almost immediately. She is one of the few people that has the power to do that. Plus, my dad.

And Caleb.

He used to hold my hand or rest it on my knee, and then he would rub small circles with his thumb. No matter what I was going through, that small gesture would steady me.

But not anymore.

Pushing the memory of him out of my head, as I have done countless times before, I shift my gaze to my mom and give her a confident smile because I am. I know I can do this. "I'm ready, Mom."

I feel her smile radiating through me as I gather my things, ready to tackle this next phase of my life. In my hands, I juggle my helmet, work gloves, and lunch as I get out of the car, kicking it closed with my boot. I walk away toward the barn when I hear my mom roll down the window. "I'll be here at six to pick you up."

I blow her a kiss.

"I'm so proud of you, sweetie," she proclaims with a gleam in her eye.

"Thanks, Mom! Love ya." I turn on my heels and walk toward my new future.

Because I am pretty proud of myself, too.

As soon as we arrive, we sign in with Bridget, who is head of the volunteers. She explains to us some basic things like where to sign in and out before and after a shift and where we can take breaks, both physical and mental, if needed. After we are done, I place all my stuff in the locker they assigned each of us in the viewing area, and I join the rest of the new volunteers. I survey everyone, and we are nothing if not a mixed bag. There are a few who are my age, a woman who is maybe in her sixties, a few kids who are younger than me, and another woman who could be my mom's age. There is an excited energy in the room. Donna, Kayla, and Erin make their way to the front of the group.

"Welcome, everyone," Donna says in a booming voice. Standing next to her is Kayla, she's my riding instructor, and Erin, who is another instructor and the barn manager. They are all three PATH-certified therapeutic riding instructors.

Which means they can teach horseback riding to those with disabilities, and that's what I want to do. My goal in life is to be PATH certified and help those like me.

"We are so happy to have you all here with us today," Donna starts, raising her voice so everyone can hear. "The volunteers at Camelot keep this place running on all cylinders. So, thank you again for taking time out of your day to help these horses." I see her taking a quick head count. "Now, there are supposed to be twelve of you here, but one is running late." She turns to Erin and says in a low voice, "Do you think we should go ahead and get started?"

Erin nods, and Donna turns her attention back to us. "Alright, even though we are a man short, we are going to get started. Our plan is to divide you up into pairs. Three of our other seasoned volunteers are going to help us out as well." Peter, a volunteer regular, Bridget again, and someone I don't recognize join us. The close quarters of the viewing room becomes increasingly more uncomfortable as seventeen people fill the space. I can feel my anxiety increasing, but I'm learning to recognize what my triggers are. And being in a confined area, full of people I don't know, is one of them. I close my eyes and clench my fists as tight as I can. This helps to release any anxiety I have, and it forces it to become physical and not emotional. As soon as I do it, I can feel my body relaxing.

They give us our partners and assign us volunteers. From there, we rotate different jobs to learn the daily chores. Mucking out the stalls, brushing the horses, saddling them up, the proper way to enter and exit a horse's stall. We will follow those jobs up by explaining the tack room, feeding the horses, what needs cleaning, how to lead the horses during lessons. Needless to say, it's a lot, but I am loving every minute. Who knew learning how to scoop up poop can be fun and therapeutic?

Since we are a person short, I am alone with my instructor Kayla, and she is showing me the different brushes for the horses when I hear a voice. It's deep and masculine. "Hey, sorry I'm late," the voice says.

"Oh, it's no problem," Kayla says. "You must be Ben?" I see Kayla stretch out her right hand to this stranger. Fiona, the horse I'm brushing, obstructs my view, so I can't see his face completely.

"I am. Nice to meet you, ma'am," he says. I immediately like the tone of his voice. It's deep but soothing.

"Oh please, call me Kayla. My mom is a ma'am, not me," Kayla says with a chuckle and a wave of her hand.

"Well, okay then," the deep voice replies.

"You should probably meet your training partner for the day. Mallory, why don't you come around and meet Ben?" I drop the brush in the basket and walk around Fiona, making sure my hand never leaves her body so she knows where I am. When I glance up, I lock eyes with the most handsome boy I have ever seen. Well, since Caleb.

He extends his right hand. "Ben, nice to meet you," he says with a smile that flashes me perfectly straight white teeth. He's tall, very tall. Like, as tall as my dad. His shoulders are broad and all masculine. He has tanned skin, blond hair, and hazel eyes. In short, he's gorgeous. Suddenly, the butterflies are in my stomach again.

Where did those come from? My palms feel sweaty, too.

I look at his hand, which he's been holding out for a beat too long. "I don't like to touch people," I blurt out.

Oh, my God. What am I saying right now?

He retreats his hand and puts it back in his pocket. "Oh ... okay. Sorry. I didn't know," he says, embarrassed.

"Oh, it's okay. I'm autistic, and I don't like to touch people." Looking at the ground, I shake my head to clear my thoughts. "Sorry. I know it's weird."

"Hey," he says with reassurance that makes me look at him again. I see his lip tick up a little from the corner of my eye. "It's not weird. I get it. My brother has autism."

"How about an elbow bump?" I say as I extend out my elbow.

He chuckles as he shrugs. "Well, that works. I'll take it," he says as he bumps his elbow to mine and then nods. When he does, a piece of his blond hair falls into his eye, and he smooths it back with his hand.

How did he make that look so good?

"Hey, Kayla, can you come over here for a minute?" Erin calls out from the tack room.

"Sure! Be right there," Kayla yells back. She walks over to me and places a hand on my arm. "I'll be right back, Mallory. Do you think you will be okay with showing Ben what you learned so far?" Kayla knows that communication can be hard for me, and I love that she is checking with me first. Normally, I would *not* be okay explaining something like this to a stranger. But for some unknown reason, I kinda want to talk to Ben.

"Sure, no problem," I say.

"Attagirl," she says as she walks out of the stall. I watch her walk away, and I turn my attention back to Ben.

"I hope I didn't miss too much," he says.

"No, you didn't. We just started. This is our first station, then there are others after this one. We are going to rotate around, I guess, and learn everything." I explain.

"Cool, sounds like fun."

After showing Ben all the brushes and what to do, we go to work on Fiona.

"So, Mallory, pretty name, by the way," he says as he looks over Fiona's back at me. I glance up and give him a quick grin. "What brings you to Camelot?"

"Well, I already told you about my autism."

"Mm-hm," he murmurs as he brushes Fiona's side.

"Also, I deal with anxiety and depression." I pause, wondering how much I want to share with this boy who is a stranger to me. "I was in a dark place last year. My mom found out about Camelot and all the good it does for people like me. So, we signed up for lessons, like, six months ago. And now, I'm volunteering."

"Those dark places are scary. Trust me, I know," he says without missing a beat, brushing Fiona. He never looks at me when he says it.

This revelation catches my attention. "You deal with similar stuff?" I question, suddenly curious about his story.

"I deal with depression, anxiety, and possibly my doctor thinks I might be bipolar." He shrugs with the last part.

I take a moment to take this in and examine Ben. He looks to be about my age. Maybe older. I've never had a friend who has such similar issues as myself. Layla has autism but has never dealt with mental illness. I love her, but she can't relate. It might be nice to have someone to talk to about it all. Someone besides my parents and my therapist.

"I'm sorry to hear that. I understand. Well, not the bipolar side, but ... you know what I mean."

He's gazing at me now with razor-sharp focus. "How bad did it get for you?"

I pick up the next brush I need, not sure if I want to go there. I start on Fiona's mane and clear my throat before I answer. "Pretty bad. Nothing that I want to talk about, though."

"Sorry, I didn't mean to pry. It's just nice having someone who understands, ya know."

"No, it's okay. I get it." We brush Fiona in silence until Kayla comes back.

Much to my delight, we spent the rest of our training talking and even ate our lunch together. I found out that he takes lessons here as well but on a different day than mine. He has a girlfriend, and I was right, he's a year older than me. Nineteen years old.

Surprisingly, I find Ben easy to talk to. There aren't many people in my life that fit into that category. He's cute, really cute, and honestly, I could use a friend. He felt the same, and we exchanged numbers at the end of the day.

My mom picks me up, and I rehash the whole day to her. Well, minus the Ben part. I don't want her to think that I met a boy and I'll date him, and then go back to being a head case. The last thing I want to do is make her worry about nothing.

At the end of the day, as a heavy wave of exhaustion hits me and I lie in bed trying to sleep, I think of Ben. But for some reason, thinking of Ben makes me think of Caleb. More than anything, I want to call him and share how amazing this has all been for me. I know he would be happy, and I want him to know all about it.

And how much I still miss him.

41

TWO YEARS LATER

Caleb

M y dad died two weeks ago.

He had cancer. Pancreatic, to be exact. He received his diagnosis only three months ago and, like countless others who are unfortunate enough to get this type of cancer, they caught it too late.

They discovered my dad's *way* too late.

He and Mom tried treatments for a while, but those made him sicker, and eventually, they stopped working. I wanted to be home for it all, but Dad refused.

"Don't you dare leave Stanford for me. You stay and study and make me proud of you," he said to me just a month ago when I called home. The usual strength behind his voice was gone. He sounded weak and frail.

"But, Dad, I want to be there to help. Mom shouldn't be alone right now. Stanford isn't going anywhere. I can always come back," I pleaded with him.

"Don't be ridiculous. Your mom has her sisters. She's fine. What I need for you to do is stay at school and continue your education, not fuss over me. Are we understood?"

"Yes, sir."

Those were the last words we spoke to each other. By the time my mom called and said that I needed to get home—fast—he was unconscious and never woke up. My mom and I were at his bedside when he took his last breath. Before that sad day, I did get to spend some time with him alone. I told him all about school since that was the only thing he cared about when it came to me.

I'll never forget what I said to him. He was lying in his hospital bed, alive but barely. I decided, since he was unconscious, to tell him how I felt about everything. He was a lifeless man, lying in a hospital bed, a tube coming from his mouth, breathing for him, IV needles inserted into his flesh. His hair and skin grayer than when I left. Somehow, the man I knew as strong and, at times, scary now looked feeble. My dad used to think that nothing could touch him. Funny how he couldn't stop his own body from turning on him. I sat on the hard plastic chair next to his bed for the longest time, staring at him before I decided to talk.

Finally, I got the nerve.

"I know you're dying, but I am so mad at you," I said as a single tear ran down my cheek. I wiped it away. The hospital room was quiet, with only the beeping of the machines that were keeping him alive filling the air. A row of dying flowers sat on the window ledge, bent over and wilting. The room reeked of impending death.

"You would probably call me a coward for not saying this to your face, but I know that it would have been pointless." I paused to find the courage to say what I needed to say to him. I was actually nervous. Why, I didn't know because he couldn't talk back to me. "Dad, you knew I wanted to stay home three years ago. You knew I didn't want to go to Stanford. I think you always knew, and that's why you hyped it up all the time. You were trying to convince me." I stopped to collect my thoughts as they went straight to her. "And yes, I wanted to stay for Mallory, but it was more than that. Stanford was your dream, Dad. It was never mine. And yet, you kept pushing it on me. Your reputation meant more to you than your son's wants or needs. You wanted me to live *your* dream. I had no dream until I met Mallory. But you know how that story went. You took her from me. And I hate you for it. There, I said it."

God, it felt good to get that off my chest. I sniffed and pushed down the tears, then I continued. "You always pushed me. Probably too much. But despite it all,

I love you, Dad. It's strange to love and also have such anger for someone at the same time. But that's how I feel. You raised me to always be honest, so I'm just listening to your advice. You always hated irony." I chuckled as I took a deep breath and looked around the room because it felt strange talking to myself, which is what I was doing. I knew no one was there to hear my words. My dad was just a dying body at that point.

"I hope I made you proud. I really do. But you're leaving us, so now I'm leaving your dream. You can take it with you. And I know it will disappoint you to hear that I'm transferring to Ohio Northeastern for my senior year, but I don't care. You always despised that school. But I hate Stanford. I hate it. And Mom will need me. You instilled in me a sense of responsibility. Well, she is my responsibility now, and I promise to take good care of her." I leaned into him, hoping that maybe if I was closer, he could hear me.

"Stanford ruined my life. *You* ruined my life. But I forgive you. I have to, or I won't find peace. I hope being happy will make you proud. Because that is all I have ever wanted to be. Happy."

I stood from the hard plastic hospital chair and watched nothing happen. To be honest, I was half expecting him to spring up from his bed, rip out the breathing tube, and tear me a new one.

I mean ONEU ... the audacity! We are Horvath men. Stanford men.

Instead, he lay motionless.

After a few beats, I leaned down to kiss his forehead. "I love you, Dad." When I walked out of the room, I turned to look at my dying father again, feeling lighter than when I entered.

That day was almost therapeutic, in a way. Saying all the things I needed to say to him, even though I got no response, helped me to let go of all the anger I felt toward him.

Now, all I'm left with are memories.

Some of those wonderful memories come flooding back as my mom and I reminisce and pick through pictures scattered on the coffee table. Mom is sitting next to me on the couch, and we are laughing to the point of tears as we swap stories. Her laughter sounds incredible compared to all the tears I heard her shed these last few months. One picture buried in the corner of the pile catches my eye. I pull it out, and the day floods back into my mind.

"Oh, my gosh, Mom, remember this vacation?" I hand her the picture of her, my dad, and me in a tent when I was about twelve years old. I vividly remember my dad extending out the camera for a selfie of us.

She takes the picture from my hand. "Yes! That was when we went to that tiny beach town in Florida. What was the name of it?" She tilts her head to the ceiling, trying to remember.

"Flagler, wasn't it?"

"Yes, that was it!" She hits me on the arm and looks back at the picture.

"I remember our house rental was so bad. Do you remember the smell?"

"I do!" She is cackling at this point. "Then we found that dead mouse in the cabinet. Every surface had, like, a two-inch layer of dust on it. And I'm pretty sure the sheets in the main bedroom had bloodstains on them."

"And don't forget how nasty the bathroom was. Dad was furious!" Recalling how upset my dad was has me in hysterics. His face was beat red, and boy, did I learn a few four-letter words that day. It was one of the few times that I saw my dad lose it.

We looked for another place to stay, but all we kept hearing was 'fully booked.' My dad, one to never accept defeat, made the best of a bad situation. "I remember he marched straight to the nearest sporting goods store, and he bought this tent and everything we needed to camp in the backyard of that house. The tent was massive. Remember?" I glance over at my mom, and the laughter is gone. With a soft exhale, she gives a single nod, her eyes still locked on the photograph. She runs her finger over my dad's face. I know she misses him. And even though my dad and I had our differences, he was a good provider, and I know he loved me. And he was madly in love with my mom.

"That was the best vacation, wasn't it?" I ask solemnly.

She nods in agreement and sits the picture down on the massive pile as she gathers them all. A wave of sadness suddenly washes over her face. My mom has cried enough tears to last a lifetime these past few months. And with how she's wrapping up our conversation, I can sense that she's done revisiting the past and doesn't want to feel any more pain today. She turns and gives me a shy smile while tapping me on the knee. "Sweetie, can you get the mail for me while I start us some lunch?"

"Sure, Mom," I say as I give her a kiss on the cheek.

I grab the mail from the mailbox at the end of our driveway. After a quick chat with our neighbor, old Mr. Bates, about how amazing my dad was, I trudge back up the driveway with an enormous stack of mail in my hand. Most of the sympathy cards arrived last week, so now we only get a few here and there. Most of these are just long white envelopes, which means only one thing.

Bills.

My dad took care of the finances for the home and the business. My mom took on more of the management role, both at home and at French Street. Now that I'm home and my dad is, well ... gone, these white envelopes are my responsibility. Once I'm back in the house, I walk over to the small table in the entryway that houses three metal bins that sit neatly on a buffet table. Each bin has its own label: Personal, Junk, and Bills. My mom has always been an organizational wizard. Everything has a place, and everything is in its place.

Words she lives and breathes by.

I weed through the wad of mail in my hand, one envelope at a time, throwing them in their respective baskets. I finally make it to the last envelope in the pile, and my heart drops. My hands, unmoving, grip the envelope, and my head feels hot. It's green, and I'm pretty positive it's a sympathy card. We have received hundreds of these, as well as Get-Well cards, over the last months and weeks. But this one is different because I recognize the perfect penmanship right away. It's addressed to Vanessa and Caleb Horvath. I slowly turn it over in my hand to see the return address, even though I know who it's from. As I look down, my favorite name comes into focus.

Mallory Givens.

With amazing timing, my mom comes into the entryway, wiping her hands on a dishtowel. "Was there a lot of m..." She stops in her tracks, her words trailing off, and she fixates her gaze on me. "Honey, what's wrong? What is that? Another sympathy card?" she asks, looking at the green envelope.

I clear my throat. "Um ... yeah. I think ... I think it's another sympathy card."

She comes around behind me, and, with curiosity, she glances at the envelope. "Who's it fro—*oh*." She sees the name.

I walk into the living room and sit down on the couch, still holding the card, still staring at her name. My mom follows and sits down beside me. We sit in silence for a few moments, the only movement the slight tremble of my hand as we stare at the unopened card. Mom finally asks the million-dollar question. "Are you going to open it?"

I hand it to her. "Here. You can do it." She nods and takes the envelope in her hand, then grabs the letter opener from the table and slides it under the flap. *Zzzt*. The sound of paper tearing fills the room, echoing through the walls. I sit with my elbows on my knees, wringing my hands together. I haven't talked to or heard anything from Mallory in three years, but she never left my thoughts. Or my dreams.

Out of the corner of my eye, I see my mom pull the card out, and she gasps. I whip my head toward her. "What? What is it?"

"This is gorgeous. Caleb, look at this." I feel her hand brush against mine as she hands me the card. I take it, and I'm astonished at what I see; Mallory has hand-painted the front of the card. The picture is of a horse in a pasture with the sun setting behind him. I run my finger over the delicate brush strokes that are small and intricate. The raised and dried paint feels rough on my fingers. I can't imagine the time it must have taken her to do this.

"Wow," I whisper. "This is amazing."

My mom puts her arm around me. "Are you okay?" She knows how much Mallory meant to me. *Means* to me. When I left for school and was struggling through my first year, my mom was my rock. I confided in her, and she gave me the strength to keep going. And this time, she never told my dad.

I shake my head. "Yeah. I think so." I don't take my eyes off the card.

"Open it, sweetie," she says. With shaky fingers, I open the card and read.

Mrs. Horvath and Caleb,

I am so sorry about your loss. Please accept my deepest sympathies. I hope you are both able to find comfort during this difficult time. You are in my thoughts and prayers.

Love,

Mallory

"Well, that was very nice of her," my mom says. I nod in agreement. All I can picture is Mallory, sitting at her desk in her room, painting this, her tongue peeking out in concentration. Popping a Smartie in her mouth every few strokes. Then, once she's done, opening it and, with her perfect handwriting, writing to us. Writing to *me.*

I close the card and take another quick glance at the painting. Standing abruptly, I hand the card to my mom. I need to get as far away from it as possible. "You should put that on the mantle with the other ones. I'm going to go upstairs and get dressed and hit the gym. Do you need anything from the store? I can stop on my way home." The shaky words spill out of my mouth in rapid succession.

My mom's face twists into a painful expression as she takes the card out of my hand. "Caleb, honey, are you—"

"I'm fine, Mom," I interrupt her before she asks me a question that I'm not sure I can answer right now. Because if I'm being honest, no, I'm not fine. I glance down at the card in my mom's hands.

I gotta get out of here.

My mom nods in understanding. "Okay. I understand." She stands, places a hand on my shoulder, and kisses my cheek. "Well, if you're offering, we could use some milk and maybe some OJ and a bag of coffee for tomorrow. We are running low." She walks to the mantle over the fireplace and places the card from Mallory front and center. I stare at it as my mom walks past me. "If you need to talk, honey, I'm always here." With that, she disappears into the kitchen.

ele

I ran my fastest time ever on the treadmill that afternoon. Working out and having a good sweat session is by far the best stress reliever. I discovered this while I was away. There was a gym near my dorm, and I was such a mess my first year that I found working out helped me to weed through all my emotions. Eventually, it became a habit, and now I'm here at least five nights a week.

As I run to nowhere, my playlist blaring in my ear and my feet pounding on the rolling rubber, Mallory is front and center in my mind. It's not that I haven't thought about her every day for the last three years. But this is different. Seeing her card, reading what she wrote ... it feels like my dad has thrust her back into my life. My father is the reason she left, and now, he's the reason she is back. Again, with the irony. My dad would be furious.

Well, she's only kinda back. It was just a card. And she's not the one who returned. I am.

I'm the one who left her.

But she didn't need to send a card—she *wanted* to. I wonder if it was hard for her. Honestly, I wonder a lot of things about Mallory.

How is she doing?

Is she okay?

Did she get the help she needed?

Is she seeing anyone?

How does she look?

That last one is dumb because Mallory is and always will be gorgeous.

Something else stood out to me, and it's something I can't unsee. The return address. It was from her parents' house, which means she probably still lives at home. Which also means I am closer to her now, physically, than I have been in three years. The thought of that makes my heart rate increase even more than it already is as I run on the treadmill.

After the intense run, a stop at the store for my mom, a quick shower, and dinner, I'm back home sitting in my dad's chair that faces the fireplace. I have a cold beer in my hand while I stare at Mallory's card. It's taunting me. The glow from the fire that my mom started is the only light in the room. The crackling of the fire the only sound.

My mom rounds the corner and nearly jumps out of her skin. "Oh, my God!" she yells as she clutches her heart to her chest. I turn to look at her. "Caleb, I didn't know you were down here. Good grief, you scared me to death."

"Sorry, Mom. I know it's late. I didn't mean to startle you." She comes into the living room and sits on the couch.

She stares at me for a few seconds. I glance at her before taking a long swig of my cold beer, the bubbles tickling as it goes down. "What?"

"It's nothing..." She slowly shakes her head, her eyes avoiding contact as she looks away. "You look just like your father sitting here. Well, him, like twenty-five years ago. But yeah." She exhales a heavy sigh, and I can feel the air become thick with sadness as tears form in her eyes.

I reach my hand out to her, and she takes it. I can't imagine the grief she is experiencing. To lose the love of your life, your high school sweetheart, and the father of your child has to be brutal. "I'm so sorry, Mom."

"I'll be okay. It's you I'm worried about." She pauses, then points to the card. "That really threw you for a loop, huh?"

I take another swig of beer and swallow hard as I look back at the card. "I miss her so much."

"I know you do, honey. Your father and I fell in love as teenagers. I couldn't imagine losing him the way you lost Mallory. So abruptly like that."

"You would think after three years, it would have gotten easier. I dated a few girls in school in an attempt to get over her. I really did try."

"Oh, I remember that girl I met when your father and I came out to visit last fall. I have no idea what you saw in her. She was rude and couldn't tear her eyes away from her phone to engage in conversation with us. What was she trying to be again?"

"A fitness influencer." I chuckle because, thinking back, I have no clue what I saw in her. Other than her looks, obviously.

"Your father was not happy." My mom shakes her head and laughs. "I was thrilled to hear that didn't last."

I laugh as well. It's true. Over time, the pain of losing Mallory lessened. I started to open myself up to new possibilities. New relationships. But none of them stuck, and I know why. It wasn't them (well, except the influencer); it was all me. None of them were Mallory.

"Deep down, Mom, Mallory never went away. I loved her. I mean, I love her." I turn to my mom, her face illuminated by the warm light of the fire. "Maybe I should try to get in touch with her because I think that's part of the problem. I never got to talk to her and explain what happened. Maybe knowing that she is okay would make me feel better, ya know?" I'm longing, hoping that she will agree with me.

"Caleb, is this about knowing that she is okay, or more about finding out whether she still has feelings for you?"

Gosh, my mom is like a freaking mind reader. I turn away from her because I know she's right. I pick at the label on my beer. "You're right. It's both."

"Oh, I know I'm right." She lets out a light, tinkling laugh, and I join in, smiling at her. "But, Caleb, you just got back home." As she grabs my hand again, I turn to face her and see the intensity in her eyes. "I think you should take a little time. Maybe just a month or two. There is a lot being thrown at you right now without tossing unresolved feelings for Mallory into the mix. Wait a little while, then try to get in touch with her. You have to at least try. You still love her, and you can never move forward until you close this chapter of your life." She squeezes my hand. "But you need to prepare yourself. She may not feel the same way anymore, or she may have someone else. Or worse yet, she might not be in a good place mentally. But you won't know unless you try. Maybe just not right now."

She's right. I have a lot on my plate. These last few weeks, heck, these last few months, have been an emotional roller coaster. Before I even think about possibly contacting Mallory, I need to help my mom with some things and get my head straight.

"Thanks, Mom." I bring her hand up and kiss it. "You're the smartest woman I know."

She stands up and kisses me on the top of my head. "Now, you really do sound like your father."

I snicker because that is something my dad would have said. "Good night, Mom. Love you," I say as she goes to her bedroom, her footsteps echoing down the hallway before the door shuts with a muted click. I still don't know what she was coming in here for. Perhaps she forgot as well.

I take a minute to process what my mom said. Mallory might never want to see me again. She could be with someone else. The thought of that makes me take a huge swig of beer.

But I have to try.

I'll give it a few weeks or months, and I will formulate some kind of plan to get in touch with her. And you never know, maybe I will run into her before that. We are back in the same zip code, after all.

You never know.

42

ONE MONTH LATER

Mallory

I have so much to do today.

I'm attempting to not let myself become overwhelmed, something I can easily do. My therapist always reminds me to stay focused, to take on one task at a time. With that in mind, I'm off to tackle my day.

First stop, French Street Cafe and Bakery.

I dreaded the thought of ever coming back here. After everything went south when Caleb left, I quit and didn't step foot in the café for two years. Then I saw the manager, Phyllis, at Camelot. She started volunteering there and told me about the new program the coffee shop was starting. They give autistic kids the chance to display their art in the café, and if they're interested, they can put it up for sale. Thirty percent goes to the café, and the artist gets the other seventy, and you can sell one painting a month.

I jumped at the opportunity with no reservations. After my breakdown, I started painting again to keep my mind occupied. Now, I have an abundance of horse paintings I'm not sure what to do with. This was the perfect opportunity to showcase my work. Plus, I'm older now, twenty years old, to be exact, and I'm more mature. Coming here isn't such a dreaded thought anymore. Plus, with Caleb at school, I knew there was a slim chance of ever running into him.

So here I am, bringing in a new painting to sell. I've sold seven paintings since the program began but haven't brought in a new one in months because I have been working on a special one. It's of my horse Levi, and even though I don't want to part with it, I love supporting the café, so here I am. I'm wearing my riding clothes so I can go straight to the barn after I leave here. I need to hurry, though, because I'm going to be late for my lesson. I'm filled with anticipation as we take on the challenge of some new jumps today. And I hate to be late. I'm only late if I'm nervous or anxious about going somewhere. That hasn't happened lately. Which is great.

I park my car and grab the painting from the trunk.

God, I hope they aren't busy. I'm not sure I can handle a crowd today.

I walk into the familiar sound of the door chime, the smell of coffee and sugar, as well as coffee lovers enjoying each other's company. Phyllis is bustling behind the counter, and a few other employees are all keeping busy and doing their jobs. There's a new mentor training someone on the espresso machine. Instantly, I'm transported back to four years ago when Caleb was showing me the ropes. It's hard to think of him. You would think that three years apart and me no longer a swoony teenager in love would have helped lessen the pain of losing him. But it hurts. Even still.

"Oh, hey, Mallory," Phyllis says with her usual cheerfulness. "Have you brought us another painting?"

"I have," I say with a smile as I turn the canvas around with pride to show her.

"Oh, wow!" Her face lights up in a smile. "It's Levi! I think this one may be your best yet."

"Thanks. I love it. It's going to be hard to part with it." I hand it to her over the counter.

"Oh, I bet it will sell quickly. No doubt about it. Let me just go get a ticket for you to fill out and sign." She disappears in the back. While I wait, I busy myself admiring all the yummy treats in the display case.

I think maybe I'll get Dad a muffin and Mom her favorite coffee ca —

"Mallory?"

I'm quickly brought out of my thoughts by the voice that has been echoing in my head both during the day and in my dreams at night. My breath hitches as I rise up, and I'm met with my favorite piercing blue eyes on the other side of the counter.

Caleb.

What in the heck is he doing here? He's in a smock, so that means he's working. Why is he working? Why isn't he in California? My mind is suddenly racing with a million thoughts and questions.

I take a second to compose myself and clear my throat. "Hey, Caleb," I muster to say with an awkward wave. I haven't seen him or talked to him since that day my dad screamed at him and told him to leave while I sat in a panic-induced episode. "Um ... what are you doing here? Why aren't you at school?"

With ease and confidence, he comes around the counter as if he can't get closer to me fast enough. That one quick movement from him makes my heart race. But it's not because I'm anxious; it's because I'm standing in front of the only boy who has ever made my heart do that. I take a quick once-over of him, and he looks good. Very good.

"I moved back home. You know, because of dad. My mom needs me."

I give him a slight nod of understanding. "That's cool."

That's cool?? What am I even saying? Why can't I communicate like a normal person?

I swallow hard and try to regain my composure. "I was so sorry to hear about your dad." It was Phyllis who told me he had passed a couple of weeks after it happened. My heart broke for him and for his mother. All I wanted to do was race to his side. But instead, I sent a card. It felt so impersonal.

"I got your card, Mallory." He steps closer. "That painting on the front was gorgeous. Thank you. My mom loved it. It took her breath away ... literally. We packed away all the other cards, but she kept yours on the mantle."

My heart feels like it's glowing. "Good. I'm so glad." I give him a shy smile because this warms my heart. Plus, it makes me wonder if Caleb has held the card, read it repeatedly, thinking of me.

"I didn't know you were bringing paintings here to sell. Phyllis oversees the program, so I don't keep track of who brings in what."

"For the past year, but it's been a few months since I've brought a new one in. The program is great! Was it your mom's idea?"

His baby blue eyes are studying me as he stares. "No. It was mine." He takes a deep breath. "I ran it past my parents, and they loved the idea. It's been a huge success."

"What gave you the idea?" I ask, genuinely wanting to know because if this program has been good for me, I can only imagine how it's also helping others like me.

"You. And your love for drawing. I knew other atypical kids probably did, too. So why not help them?" he says with a shrug.

UGH! Stop it, heart! Now, it's melting as warmth pools in my chest at this revelation. He thought of me while he was away. I lay my hand on my stomach to try and steady myself. "That's awesome," is all I can muster because if I say more, I might launch myself at him and hug him. As a thank you, of course, for no other reason.

He casts a quick glance over me, and I feel my cheeks flush and my skin prickle with heat.

"You look"—he swallows hard—"great. Great, you look great. But I have to ask, are you going to a costume party as an equestrian?" He chuckles.

"Well, actually, I *am* an equestrian, thank you very much." I say it with pride, even puffing my chest out a little.

"Seriously? That's amazing! You've always loved horses. When did you start riding?" His voice is full of energy, and his eyes are wide with excitement. He was always there to cheer me on before, and I can feel that same warmth now as I did in the past.

"About six months after you left." He nods, his smile fading, and that twinkle in his eyes that was there just a second ago is gone as he lowers his gaze. The mention of that time makes the air in the room shift. It now feels thick with uneasiness, which is making me feel uncomfortable. "I ride and volunteer at The Camelot Center three days a week."

"That's great, Mal. I'm happy for you." He pauses and peers around me. "And is your mom here? I would love to say hi."

"I drove here."

"Wow! You got your license?" He knows that, at one time, the thought of driving a car terrified me. The rules of the road, coupled with the anxiety of taking the test and making lightning-fast decisions while driving if needed, all of it was frightening. With therapy, encouragement from my parents, and driving lessons from my Uncle Kyle (Mom and Dad couldn't handle the stress), I conquered the fear. Another victory on the road to mental recovery.

"Yep. I guess I'm full of surprises today. I got it about a year ago. *And* a car." I point to my teal Mini Cooper in the parking lot.

"*That* little thing?" he teases.

"Hey! I love my car! Her name is Camille, and she's exceptional."

He bursts out in a deep, rumbling laugh. "That's not a car, Mal. That's ... I don't know what that is, actually."

"Ha ha." I smack him playfully on his arm, just like I used to. He freezes. *Why did I just do that?* God, I'm so awkward.

Our eyes lock, neither of us saying a word, the usual coffee house chatter in the background. I look away first because seeing him is making my head and heart think and feel things I'm not sure I can handle right now. Out of the corner of my eye, I glance at him for a second to study his appearance. He's older now, his chest is broader, his arms are more muscular, and he has styled his hair differently. It's longer, and I think I like it better.

Talking to him feels so good, easy, and comfortable. But also, it feels like we've hit a wall because neither of us is saying anything. Caleb opens his mouth to say something, then closes it again. He averts his eyes and nervously shuffles his feet, gazing downward. It's as if he is trying to build the courage to say something. He looks back up and takes a step toward me.

"Mallory, before you go, I just wanted to say—"

"Here ya go, Mallory." Phyllis suddenly appears and, thankfully, interrupts Caleb. He takes a step back, his lips curling into a gentle smile as he looks at

Phyllis, the words he was about to say hovering in the air. She hands me the ticket for my artwork.

I'm grateful for the interruption because I don't think I want to talk about what I'm pretty sure he was going to bring up. Which is that day three years ago. I was unprepared for this experience, my mind reeling and my palms sweating. We both know that things need to be said, but the air feels thick and full of unspoken words.

"Thanks, Phyllis. I'll fill it out and bring it in soon." I glance at Caleb. He's watching me intently. "Or I can give it to you at Camelot."

"Whatever works for you. No problem, sweetie. No rush." As she turns to leave, she gives me a gentle smile.

I turn back to Caleb. "I gotta go," I say, gesturing behind me. "My lesson starts in, like"—I look at my watch—"thirty minutes."

"Okay. Yeah, sure." His eyes flick from the floor to mine, and I feel a chill run through me. "It was nice to see you."

"You too, Caleb. Take care."

With my heart pounding out of my chest at this surprise encounter, I turn on my heels and walk to the door. I'm walking so fast that when I open the door to leave, I run right into it. I fumble with the door handle, feeling the cool metal beneath my touch, until I'm finally out of the café. Now, I'm rummaging through my purse, feeling around for my keys. Once I find them, my fingers are so shaky that my keys clatter, fall from my grasp, and hit the pavement. I quickly pick them up and unlock the door. I get in the car, shut the door, and put a hand on my stomach, letting the stillness of the car envelop me. So many thoughts flood my mind, and I'm trying to make sense of them.

There was no preparing for that.

Is he back here to stay?

Why does he still make me feel this way?

He looked soooo good.

My breathing is getting more labored, which means I have to get it under control. I ball my fingers in both hands into a fist and squeeze, and then I start my four/seven/eight breathing technique. I take a deep breath to center myself.

Inhale four counts. I close my eyes. I hold my breath, and I can feel my heart rate begin to slow.

Hold seven counts. I try to center my thoughts around my horses.

Exhale eight counts. I open my eyes and let out the air in my lungs slowly.

I do these two more times, and I already feel better and more relaxed. My therapist always says that these types of triggers are just an event. Don't let the event control me; I need to control it and how I react.

I got this.

I pull down the visor mirror and give myself a small smile. Then, I say my daily affirmations to myself. The ones I always recite when I feel stressed.

You can do this.

You are strong.

You can handle anything.

You are worthy.

I always find it hard to accept that last idea when I think about myself. What can I say, I'm still a work in progress. However, I am proud of how I can handle these types of situations and triggers.

I take one last quick glance in the mirror at my makeup to make sure it's presentable, knowing Ben will be at the barn today.

I'm already feeling calmer, so I flip up the visor and start the car because I need to get going, or I'll be late.

That's when I hear him.

"MALLORY!"

Then I see him.

I look in the rearview mirror, and he's running toward my car. I get out.

"Caleb, what in the world are you doing?"

"Mallory, I can't let you leave without saying this." He's not even breathless from sprinting to my car. "I've missed you," he says through steady breaths, "so much. I thought about you every day. Every. Single. Day. For three years." He stops. More than likely waiting for me to say something back. But I'm so stunned I can't speak. I grab onto my car door to ground myself from the shock.

"Please say something. Please tell me you missed me, too." He looks so cute with desperation as he squints from the sunlight in his eyes. But something holds me back from telling him what he wants to hear. What I need to say to him. And it's that day. The day that my life changed because he left me. The day he ripped my heart out of my chest. Out of nowhere, I feel guarded, and it's like a protective shield is in front of me. I can't do this.

So, I lie.

"Caleb. I missed you. I did ... at first." His shoulders droop in dejection. "But not lately. I've moved on. I'm sorry."

He slowly nods, his gaze distant, and he looks ... crushed. I've hurt him.

I gotta get out of here. I can't deal with this.

"I have to go. I'm sorry." With intent, I turn away from him. He steps away from the car. I get in and drive away. Leaving him hurt and broken.

Just like he did to me.

My ride was horrible today.

Levi and I weren't in tune with each other, and we didn't even try the new jumps. And it wasn't his fault. It was mine. My head wasn't in the game, and I knew Levi was feeding off the energy I was putting out. My instructor Kayla noticed as well and cut the lesson short. I went home with my tail between my legs.

All I can think about is running into Caleb at the café.

How he looked.

How he looked at me.

How I missed that look.

How his shoulders are broader and his face more chiseled. *Does he work out now?*

How I felt when I was with him.

And I liked it. Which is why I feel like a head case today. To be honest, I have thought of Caleb every single day since I last saw him drive away from my house. I've wondered how he was doing in college (probably on the Dean's list), how many parties he was going to (you know, those fun drunken parties you see in movies), how many girls he's dated (all gorgeous, no doubt. I mean, it's California). And worst of all, how many he has kissed (and I bet none of them were autistic or mental like me).

Seeing him made my heart skip a beat, and my head felt foggy and confused. Then, those all too familiar self-loathing questions boil to the surface, and they stir up my anxiety.

I'm not good enough for him.

Why would he want to be with someone like me?

I'm such a loser.

When I'm feeling overwhelmed, I take a moment to focus on five things I can see, four things I can touch, three things I can hear, two things I can smell, and one thing I can taste. I'm brushing Levi after my lesson, and I know I need to do this to calm down my fears.

Five things I can see: Levi, his food, the barn stall latch, his beautiful mane, Tucker in the next stall.

Four things I can touch: Levi's bridle, my feet on the ground, the brush in my hand, my scratchy socks.

Three things I can hear: the birds outside, country music playing, Ben's laugh.

Two things I can smell: Manure (always), my body spray.

One thing I can taste: my mint gum.

I feel the stress evaporate from my body.

Then, to top it off, Ben was being extra sweet today, only confusing me more. Just last week, he told me he broke up with his girlfriend. The same one he's had for two years. When I asked him what happened, the only thing he said was, "I just realized she wasn't the one for me. Plus, I met someone else."

I didn't pry, but after that day, he has been extra attentive to me. Flirty even. Which is strange because we have never been that way with each other. However, what is even more bizarre for me is I think I kinda like the attention from him.

At one point today, when we were putting saddles away in the tack room, he noticed I had an eyelash on my face. After I had hoisted my saddle up onto the rack and turned around, I could hear the silence between us as his eyes met mine, as if we were the only two people at the barn. The desire in his eyes made me feel warm and needed. But since I can't look anyone in the eye for longer than a few seconds (well, except the boy that I saw a few hours ago), I turned my head away.

"Mallory," he implored because he wanted me to look at him again. My eyes trailed up to meet his, and I noticed the intensity in his stare. "You have an eyelash on your cheek." He moved his finger in the direction of my face but stopped right before he touched me. "May I?" he asked.

I nodded. With a featherlight touch, he swiped the eyelash off my cheek. I closed my eyes and felt a tightness in my chest. I don't want to allow myself to be drawn to Ben. But when I'm with him, I get confused. Because I think I like him. Even if it's a little.

He held the eyelash out on his index finger. "Blow on it and make a wish," he whispered. I closed my eyes and blew away the eyelash. He brushed a piece of hair off my face and tucked it behind my ear. His touch didn't feel foreign or unwanted. It did feel different and strange. He took a step closer. "What did you wish for?"

"I can't tell you, or it won't come true," I whispered back. We were standing so close that if he wanted to, he could have kissed me, and I would have let him. Being that close to him felt good. Having someone look at me the way he did made me want to be closer to him.

Do I want him to touch me again?

Do I want him to kiss me?

As Ben leaned his face toward mine, Caleb's face flashed in my head, and I took a couple of steps backward. Having my body react like this for Ben felt like I was doing something wrong. And I was not. Caleb and I haven't dated in over three years. Yet, he's there. He's always there. I grabbed my helmet off the chair where I'd sat it in the tack room. "I'll see you next week, Ben."

I needed to remove myself from that situation. And besides, my wish will never come true.

I wished Caleb would have never left me three years ago.

I came home and showered, and now I'm in my favorite spot on my bed. Back up against the wall, legs crossed. I'm resting my head on the cool wall, my eyes glued to the ceiling as I turn my phone in my hand, trying to decide if I should text Caleb.

I know I blocked him that night, but I have a different number now and a new phone. However, I still have his number memorized.

Is that even his phone number anymore?

I have to be truthful with both me and him, so I swipe and unlock my phone and quickly type in his number before I lose my nerve. I hit the message button, then type out my text.

Me: I lied to you.

I stare at my text with my thumb lingering over the send button. *Do I really want to do this?*

Yes, yes, I do. I want to clear the air with him and be honest. Plus, I have questions, and I need him to know that I'm okay. And if I ever decide to pursue a relationship with Ben (because I am about ninety-nine percent sure he likes me), I need to close this Caleb chapter of my life once and for all.

Send. *There, it's done.*

I clumsily throw my phone onto the bed as if it's scalding my hand, and I fiddle with the hem of my shirt while my finger taps a fast beat on my leg. I've either opened Pandora's box or just texted a complete stranger.

Ping.

Oh, God. He, or someone, has texted back.

I grab my phone and turn it over.

Unknown Number: Who is this?

Well, I've contacted somebody. Let's see if it's Caleb or some random smelly guy living in his mom's basement. A small smile crosses my lips, and I feel a tiny jolt of excitement course through me with anticipation. I guess I'm doing this.

> **Me**: You guys changed the smocks at the café. I forgot to tell you I liked them.

Unknown Number: Mallory?

Phew. It's Caleb. Not smelly basement guy.

> **Me**: Yeah. It's me.

I add him to my contacts.

> **Caleb**: Sorry, you changed your number. I didn't know it was you.

> **Me**: It's okay. I was hoping you didn't change yours.

Caleb: You realize you could have just texted some random old lady named Pearl.

Me: Or a smelly guy living in his mom's basement. I took a chance. I was nervous.

Caleb: You remembered my number.

Me: I blocked you, but I never forgot.

Oh, God. Was that too flirty? Scale it back, Mallory.

Caleb: So I'm super curious. What did you lie about?

Alright, here goes nothing. I exhale and take my time pressing the keys of the keyboard to type out what I need him to know.

Me: I lied. I do miss you. Then and now. Every day.

I hold my phone in my hand and change positions, rolling onto my stomach, resting on my elbows. His reply takes a few more minutes than I expect. I see the three dots appear, then disappear, then reappear again. The suspense is killing me.

> **Caleb**: Can we meet? Like not a date or anything. Just at the café. I have so much I need to say to you.

I need to see him again.

> **Me**: That sounds good. I have a lot to say as well.

> **Caleb**: Okay, great. How about tomorrow? Say eleven? Does that work?

> **Me**: That works. I'll see you then!

> **Caleb**: Looking forward to it.

I decide to leave it at that. I don't want to engage any more than necessary. Not until I see him.

I sit my phone down and rest my head on my hands. I lie there, wondering what tomorrow will bring. What does he have to say to me? How is this conversation going to go? What is it going to feel like spending time with him again?

I slide off my bed, the soft carpet under my toes as I walk to my closet. I open it and search in the back. And there, under a pile of sweaters and shoes, is a garbage bag tied up tight. I never had it in me to throw it away. I use all my strength to pry open the plastic, and when I do, I'm met with the familiar sight of Caleb's red hoodie. Pulling it up to my nose, I inhale deeply. It doesn't smell like him anymore, but it feels like him. I pull the pictures out one by one and study them, warm memories filling my mind. We look so young.

We *were* so young.

I'm flipping through the pictures, feeling nostalgic when...

Ping.

I turn my phone over, and it's a text from Ben. *Talk about timing.*

> **Ben:** How about a trail ride tomorrow?

UGH! Why? Why tomorrow?

I let out a deep, heavy sigh, feeling my stomach twist with anxiety at the thought of disappointing him.

> **Me:** Can't tomorrow. I have an appointment. I'll see you next week, though.

> **Ben:** Counting down the days.

Okay. It's pretty obvious at this point. He likes me. We've gone on trail rides together in the past. But only as friends. Somehow, though, this request feels different.

What do I do about all of this? It's all too much too soon, and I feel confused and scared.

I walk across the room, set the pictures on my desk, and lay the hoodie on my bed.

I need to talk to my mom and dad.

43

Laura

"Do you know how hard it is to figure out dinners every week? It's exhausting."

I'm sitting cross-legged on the couch, scrolling through Pinterest on my phone, searching for a different way to prepare chicken. Resting on my lap, I have a pen and notebook and scrolled on the top it says *This Week's Menu.*

Mallory always laughs at me when she sees me using, as she calls them, old-fashioned methods. As if a pen and paper are old-fashioned. 'There is an app for everything, Mom.' It must be my age showing because those apps annoy the crap out of me.

Well, except Pinterest.

Scott and I are sitting side by side in comfortable silence, enjoying the evening. Our usual 'old people routine,' as Jake always says. Growing kids can make you feel you've aged overnight, a reminder that your twenties and thirties are long gone.

Scott takes a sip of his bourbon. "Anything you make will be great, honey." He replies, half-listening, while he mindlessly watches TV.

I'm interrupted from my chicken recipe search when I hear Mallory's bedroom door creak open and then her feet padding down the stairs. She strolls over and stands right in front of Scott and me, her hair still damp from her shower. "Mom and Dad, I need to talk to you."

Ever since her meltdown, I'm always aware of the signs that she might be heading toward another one. And honestly, there isn't a reason to worry because Mallory is doing so great. Better than I could have ever hoped. So, when she says this to us, looking nervous and uncertain, I, in turn, feel nervous and uncertain.

Scott shoots me a quick, concerned glance, raising his eyebrows in worry. "Sure, honey." He grabs the remote and turns off the TV. "What's going on?" he asks as he sets his glass on the coffee table beside him. I turn my phone off and place it beside me on the couch. She has our rapt attention.

Mallory sits down on the ottoman in front of us. She has her eyes drawn to her fidget ring while she plays with it ... rolling the ball back and forth, back and forth, not saying anything. Scott and I glance at each other.

"You okay, sweetie?" I ask, gently touching her knee.

"Um ... yeah." She pauses and stops fidgeting as she collects her thoughts. "So, I saw Caleb today."

Oh. Was not expecting that.

Scott's body goes rigid beside me at the mention of Caleb's name, and I can tell by his tense jaw he doesn't like this news.

"So, how did that make you feel?" I question. A knot forms in my stomach, scared of her answer.

Mallory rolls her eyes. "Oh, my God, Mom, you sound like my therapist."

She's right, I do. "Sorry, honey. I know that this is the first time you've seen him since—"

"Since I lost my mind." Her gaze drifts off to the side, and she lets out a sigh as she rests her hands beside her.

Hearing her say that about herself makes me wince. I rest my hand on hers, feeling the softness of her skin against mine. "Don't say that, sweetie."

"I know. I'm sorry." She stops as I notice the gentle rise and fall of her chest and the sound of her exhale. "Well, to answer your question, seeing him felt ... confusing."

"What do you mean, Mal?" Scott presses, his question laced with concern as he leans a little closer to her.

"If I'm being honest with myself, it felt good." She pauses. "It felt nice and familiar but also sad. Mostly, it was just shocking, I guess."

I keep my hand firmly in hers, letting her know she can use me as a source of security. "I bet it was confusing. But what is he doing here? His dad's funeral was over a month ago. I thought maybe he would be back in California by now?" I glance over at Scott, and it's not lost on me that he's barely said a word yet. He grabs his bourbon again and rolls it in his hands, peering down at the brown liquid as it swirls around the glass. I wish I could read his thoughts.

"He's staying here."

Scott's eyes shoot up. "Permanently?"

Mallory nods. "Yeah. I think so. But I'm not sure, really."

Scott continues, "Where did you see him?" Now she has his attention because Caleb being in the same city as his daughter is not sitting well with him, I can tell.

"The café. He's back working there. I didn't get into any details with him. He said that he came back home because he could tell his mom needed him close after his dad passed. I didn't ask, but maybe she is struggling."

Scott and I both nod in unison, our eyes fixing on her as she speaks. "There's something else," she says with hesitation as she bites the inside of her cheek.

"Oh, God," Scott mumbles under his breath. I nudge his leg.

"He said that he misses me and that he's missed me every single day. He asked me if I missed him, too."

I'm on the edge of my seat, my heart pounding from the suspense. Suddenly, dinner planning for next week is the furthest thing from my mind. I swallow hard. "What did you say?"

She clears her throat. "I said that I missed him at first. But not anymore." I glance over at Scott, and a sly smile crosses his face. "But I lied."

The smile disappears.

"I *have* missed him, you guys," Mallory pleads. "I miss him so much it hurts some days. So, I texted him and told him that."

Scott scratches the scruff on his face. He doesn't like this one bit. "I thought you blocked his number," he says with tension in his voice.

"I did. But I remembered it."

Of course, she did.

She continues, "So he wants to meet me ... tomorrow. He said that there is a lot that he wants to say to me."

"I don't think that's a good idea," Scott interjects with finality in his voice.

Holding her chin high, she looks over at Scott with a piercing stare. "I'm going, Dad," she declares with determination. "I have things to say to him as well. And there's another reason I need to see him."

I have no clue what this could be.

"There's a guy at the barn. Ben. He likes me, and I think I might like him too."

Scott jumps up from the couch, his eyes scanning the room as he paces. "Oh, my God. I did not pour enough bourbon to handle this tonight."

"Scott, honey, sit down, please. You're going to make her nervous."

Mallory looks at him, pleading, "Please, Dad. Mom's right, you are making me nervous."

Scott reaches the couch and sits without hesitation as he composes himself. "Sorry, honey." He pauses. "This is just ... a lot. You didn't tell us about this Ben kid, and now Caleb is back in the picture. We don't want to see you overwhelmed. This is a lot of emotions being thrown at you all at once. I'm worried. That's all."

Mallory's shoulders relax some. "I know. And actually, I don't feel over-whelmed. Just confused. I kinda like Ben. He's sweet and nice to me." She shrugs her shoulders. "And cute. But seeing Caleb today ... Mom, Dad"—her eyes dart between us both—"I need to meet him and talk to him again. I feel like there is so much that was left unsaid between us. I need to know why he left me. And I have to know if there are feelings still there. It would be unfair for me to maybe date Ben if I left Caleb unresolved, ya know."

Wow!

I'm left speechless. The girl sitting in front of us isn't a girl anymore. She is a woman. A mature woman making mature decisions. If you have just met her, you would never know she has autism or deals with any kind of mental illness. That's how far she has come. And I couldn't be prouder of her.

Scott must be experiencing the same feelings. "Mallory, honey, I am so proud of you," he says softly. She can't keep the corners of her mouth from stretching into a huge grin. "Now, I'm going to be honest here. You seeing Caleb again makes me nervous. I don't want you spending time with him to trigger any kind of episode again. Because I can't"—he catches the quick intake in his breath—"I can't ever see you like that again. I can't."

I remove my hand from Mallory's and rest it on my husband's knee, squeezing gently to offer the comfort he needs right now. "I agree with your dad, Mallory," I say. "I'm just scared that this might get you upset again. Maybe seeing him right away isn't the best."

"I get where you guys are coming from, I do," she says undeterred. "But I need to talk to him. And I won't jump into dating him again. Don't worry about that. I'm not ready for that. Even with Ben."

"Thank God," Scott mumbles under his breath again.

"But it would be nice to be his friend again." She shifts her weight. "But then, I think about letting him back in, and it makes me nervous. I'm also going to talk to my therapist about it at my appointment tomorrow morning. Get her thoughts."

I sense she needs our approval and our support, so that's what we are going to give her. "Mallory, your dad and I trust you. And I think that talking to your therapist is a good idea as well. But ultimately, you know if this is what you need. So, if you feel that meeting with Caleb will help, then we support you."

Scott nods in agreement. "Yes, sweetie, we do. One hundred percent."

She stands and wraps her arms around us both, giving us a warm hug. "Thanks, guys. I think I'm going to go watch TV for a little while. I need to think about ... nothing." She snickers as she trudges up the stairs, her fingers trailing along the railing.

Once she is out of earshot, Scott looks over at me. "Wow. I was not prepared for that conversation tonight."

"Me neither. I mean, where did all of this come from? Caleb's back. Now there's another boy."

"And for the first time in a long time, she seems so together and happy." Scott lifts his gaze to the top of the stairs. "God, it feels good to see her working through this all. And talking to us about it as well."

"I'm shocked. Like, my word, when did our daughter—"

Scott hushes me as he hears her footsteps coming back down the stairs. She whizzes past us in her PJs, and she's wearing something else. A red hoodie. I remember that hoodie very well because it was Caleb's. And I haven't seen it in three years. I assumed she got rid of it when he left.

We watch her as she opens the fridge. "Do you need something, honey?" I ask while both of us watch her every move.

She shuts the fridge and heads back toward the stairs. "Nope. Just want water. Good night, guys. Love ya." A few seconds later, her bedroom door shuts.

"Was that Caleb's hoodie she had on?" Scott asks.

"Yep."

"The one she didn't take off for practically the whole time they were together?"

"One and the same."

Scott chuckles. He takes a sip of his bourbon as he settles back into the couch, grabs the remote, and turns the TV back on. "Poor Ben. Kid never stood a chance."

44

THE NEXT DAY

Caleb

I 'm sitting at our favorite high-top table at the café.

Usually, it's Mallory's leg that shakes all the time. Today, it's mine. I'm so nervous that I didn't eat any breakfast. Or, perhaps the reason my leg is trembling is because of the obscene amounts of coffee I drank this morning as I stayed up all night waiting for this moment.

Heck, I've waited for this for three years now.

I'm rubbing my hands on my thighs, staring out the window, waiting for her teal Mini Cooper to pull up. I check my phone again. She's ten minutes late, and Mallory is never late.

She's probably not coming.

"Get yourself together," I say under my breath.

Yesterday, when I saw her in the café, I was so stunned because I never thought she would step foot in here after what happened. I mean, I knew eventually I would see her again. But, if I'm truthful with myself, I guess I was never truly ready.

And, dear Lord, did she look beautiful. She wore tan riding pants, which made her legs look a mile long, black riding boots, and a tucked-in navy shirt with a belt. Who knew I had a thing for equestrians? I guess now I do. More than anything, she appeared happy, healthy, and more mature. Mallory is a woman now, and it's a look I like very much.

And it's a vast change from the last time I saw her. Curled up in a ball on her front porch step, rocking back and forth, her voice in between humming and crying. It's an image that is burned into my brain for all eternity. Seeing her yesterday made me so happy that even if nothing comes out of this meeting, I know she's healthy now.

As I watched her walk out of the café, there was an ache in my chest. It felt like I was losing her all over again. She got in her car and lingered there for a while. I couldn't see what she was doing, but it bought me the time I needed to get out of my head and run out to tell her I missed her. I couldn't let her leave without her knowing. And when she said she didn't miss me and she's moved on, my entire world crashed around me for a second time ... because of Mallory Givens.

Then, out of nowhere, she texted me last night, and it floored me. When she said that she lied and that she missed me, a little voice in my head told me not to get too eager.

I didn't listen to it.

It filled me with so much hope that I couldn't help but ask if she would see me. To get to spend time with her again is a gift I never thought I would get. So here I am, ready to bear it all out to her.

A flash of teal blue catches my eye, and I see her car waiting at the light. I watch in earnest as she pulls into the parking lot and into a space close to the door. It's taking her a while to get out of the car, and I can't help but wonder if she's nervous, too. She finally does, and I can't take my eyes off her because—OH, MY GOD—she looks incredible. Her hair, which is shorter now, is curled in loose waves. She has on big black sunglasses and a tan T-shirt with a silhouette of a horse on it. It's tucked in the front of dark jeans, and, of course, she's wearing her signature Chucks. Red ones. It's simple, it's Mallory, and I love it.

I'd like to point out that red is my favorite color. Just saying.

I hear the door chime. Her eyes immediately scan the room and rest at our table, and she waves. She pulls the sunglasses up in one quick motion onto the top of her head, which makes her face even prettier because now her hair is out of the way. Mallory has never been one for makeup. But today, I notice right away that she's wearing mascara and lip gloss, which makes her lips stand out. My heart flips. Has she just matured, or did she do that for me?

Me, definitely me.

God, I think I'm going to be sick.

She walks over to me, biting her lip in nervousness. I fumble up from my seat to greet her. "Hey," she says in a soft voice. She pulls her seat out right away, the feet skidding across the floor as she sits down in the chair. More than likely to avoid any kind of hug or physical contact. That's okay. Being with her is enough for me right now.

She adjusts her chair and flings her purse on the back of it. She takes her sunglasses off her head and puts them in her purse, and her hair falls around her cheek. With her face turned away from me, all I see is a cascade of her brown, silky hair curled in soft waves. It takes every ounce of strength to not reach across this table and run my hands through it the way I used to. She pulls something from her purse and zips it shut. I hear the clink of metal from her strap hitting the chair as she finally turns around. I'm mesmerized by her. Always have and always will be.

She places her Smartie pack on the table and pulls on the plastic ends. I know why she pulled these out. She's nervous. *Me too, Mallory.* It crinkles as the candy pack twists around in a circle. She takes out a light purple disc and stops before placing it in her mouth. "What?" she asks, glancing around in confusion. I realize I'm sitting here gawking at her. I snap myself out of my Mallory trance.

"Oh, sorry," I say as I shake my head. "Hey." I can't help but smile. "I was just noticing your hair. You cut it. I was going to say something yesterday, but I was just so shocked to see you." Mallory's hair used to go all the way down her back. Now, it hits her collarbone.

She pops the candy in her mouth and runs her hand down her hair. "Oh, yeah. I cut it about a year ago, maybe. It's just easier with riding and all. I know you always liked it longer, though."

"I do like it long. But this suits you as well."

She bites her lip, allowing a shy smile to play across her face, turning her cheeks a subtle shade of pink. She glances at the bottled water. "Thanks for the water."

"Of course. I've never known you to drink anything else."

"Well, actually, you will be shocked to know that I have an iced coffee here and there," she says jokingly, showing that she is feeling more at ease.

"Really?" I say, raising my eyebrows. "I am shocked."

She shifts in her seat and clears her throat. "There's a lot about me that has changed," she says with an edge to her voice. The comment is pointed and sharp. As if she realized she was allowing herself to relax around me for a second, so she checked herself. I watch as she opens her water and takes a sip, then eats another Smartie.

We sit in an awkward silence, neither of us sure of what to say next. The noise of the plastic candy wrapper sounding louder than it should.

"So, you're working here again? What about your senior year? At *Stanford*." She says the word 'Stanford' with contempt like it's her most hated word in the English language. I know it's mine. Stanford ruined my life.

"Like I told you yesterday, I'm back home now."

"Permanently?" she asks with a little inflection in her voice. Is that a tiny bit of hope I hear? Or is that my imagination?

"Um ... yes, actually. So, when Dad died, I realized pretty quick that my mom needed me. I transferred to Ohio Northeastern for my senior year. I manage the café now, and I have school. After I graduate, I plan on taking over the business."

"Wow, that's a lot." She eats a white disc this time.

"It is. It keeps me busy. Plus, with my dad gone, he can't *force* me to stay at Stanford. The way he *forced* me to go." And there it is. What I have wanted to tell Mallory for three years. The real reason I left her.

"Wait." She shakes her head in disbelief as she runs her hands through the air. "What do you mean? Your dad *forced* you to go to Stanford? I don't understand." She's confused, obviously.

"Mallory, that's why I wanted to talk to you today. The day before ... *that* day"—she winces at the thought—"I talked to Dad. I told him I wanted to go to Carnegie and that I had never wanted to go to Stanford. He didn't take it very well."

"What happened?" Two candies fly in her mouth as she taps the table.

"He told me if I went to Carnegie, he wouldn't pay for my schooling. I had to choose. Stanford, or Carnegie and you."

She lets out a sharp breath and, in a huff, crosses her arms over her chest. "So, you chose money over us?"

"I know it sounds that way."

"It doesn't *sound* that way, Caleb. That's what you did." She sneers at me with disdain. She's mad, and I can't blame her because I'm mad at myself.

"My plan was to give my dad what he wanted. But when I went to see you, I was going to tell you I wanted to keep dating you. I could go to Stanford and make my dad happy, *and* we could still see each other, but in secret, and I could make you happy."

"That was a dumb plan. It never would have worked."

"I know. I know," I say as I stare at my hands, failing to compose myself. I'm trying to make this sound better because I am not coming across all that great right now. "Mallory, I felt so torn. I wanted to make you happy, and I knew deep down something was going on with you. But also, I felt the burden to make my dad happy and proud. A whole lifetime of pressure was coming down on me. He was so adamant about Stanford. And even if I went to Carnegie, I would have been working nights and weekends to pay for student loans. I would never have got to see you, anyway. Then, my dad put it in my head that maybe we should be apart for a while. That you needed time to mature. I should have stood up to him. My head was all over the place, and I was a coward."

She locks her gaze on me, and I hear her breath as she watches me, staring and taking it all in. I continue. "It was awful, Mallory. I was going to explain it to you that day, but then—"

"I flipped out."

"Yeah. And I'm not blaming you at all. I'm not. But when you broke down, nothing mattered to me in that moment but you. Nothing. Not Stanford or Carnegie. Just you. I would have traded places with you in a second. I would have given up anything to help you."

She's silent as she wipes a tear from her cheek and turns away from me. "It was so scary," she whispers. "I should have let you explain that day. But there was no controlling what was happening to me. That panic attack consumed me. I wasn't prepared for it and didn't know what to do or how to handle it."

I can hear the pain in her voice when she says this, and it makes me feel awful because I am making her relive it. She continues. "But it wasn't the scariest moment of my life."

"It wasn't?" *It sure was for me.*

She stares into my eyes, her gaze burning with intensity. "That was when I was lying in my bed a month later, the day you left for school, and I thought about taking my own life."

I whip back in my chair, and my mouth drops open. I'm shocked beyond belief because she just knocked the wind out of me with that bomb, and it feels like it detonated in my head.

Did she just say that she thought of ... suicide?

This world almost didn't have Mallory in it.

And it's all my fault. *I did that to her.*

"Mallory ... I ...okay, wow." I'm at a loss for words. "I need a second." I pause and place my hands over my face, trying to think of what to say next but also to shield my shame. As I remove my hands, I look at her, and an overwhelming tightness in my chest makes it hard to breathe. Her breath catches as she waits for me to say something, so I say the only thing I can think of. "I'm so sorry."

Tears well up in my eyes, and I choke out my next question. "What stopped you?"

She clears her throat and shifts in her seat. "The thought of my mom and dad finding me."

Coming here today, I never imagined the conversation going this way. I'm having a hard time processing everything she told me as I run my hands over my face. When people say that they are 'speechless,' this is what it feels like because my brain isn't able to form any words.

I have nothing.

Mallory senses my distress and continues. "It's a long story and something I'm not too keen on reliving, but I wanted you to know."

"Why? Why did you want me to know?" *Does she want me to feel bad? Mission accomplished.*

"I don't know." She shrugs. "Not to punish you, of course." She waves her hand in reassurance. "I just want to be honest, I guess. Plus, you're the one person I used to tell everything to." She places her arms on the table. "Old habits, I guess." A small smile crosses her lips. "It took everything in me to not call you when it happened. I needed you."

I wish she would have. I really, really wish.

"What happened after? I mean, you seem to be doing so well for yourself. You look beautiful, happy, and confident. How did you get better?" I'm crawling out of my skin, dying to know the entire story. I've missed so much of her life, and I am so mad that I wasn't there for her during this dark time.

"My mom and dad rushed me to the ER the night it happened. I was in the hospital for a few days. They adjusted my medications, and I started some pretty extensive therapy. The therapy taught me healthy coping skills, and it all really helped. But the best thing to come out of it was my riding and the horses. My mom took me to Camelot a few months after that night. I connected with my horse, Levi, and I've never looked back. Sometimes, it helps more than the medicine, I think. Plus, I paint"—she points to her painting adorning the wall—"as you already know."

"What about school?" My head is swirling with questions.

"My parents pulled me. I couldn't be in any kind of stressful environment, so I went back to homeschooling and graduated last year. I ended up getting behind, so it took me longer to finish." She shrugs.

"That doesn't matter. You finished, and you're better, plus I'm so glad the horses helped." It physically pains me to hear all of this. While I was off studying, lying on the beach in my free time, and dating so-called influencers, Mallory was suffering. I feel like I want to throw up.

She glances at her hands, and she's playing with her fidget ring. "You know, my parents and my therapist think that me coming to see you was a bad idea."

Crap.

"Why's that?" I'm hesitant to find out what the answer to this question could be, and I can almost taste the fear on my tongue.

"They think it may trigger something in me. Maybe cause me to spiral out of control or something."

"Oh, God, Mallory. I don't want that." The thought of me causing another breakdown is something I can't bear. "I can go. Really." I start to get out of my chair.

She looks up at me, her voice fills with emotion as the words spill out of her mouth. "I don't want you to leave."

Oh. I sit back down.

"After I saw you yesterday, it felt strange. It took me by surprise because I thought you had gone back to California. But then, seeing you ... I don't know what I expected. But the way everyone talks, they think I'm just going to flip out. So, when I didn't, I knew I had to talk to you. We needed to clear the air. Maybe get some closure."

Closure. That means final. I cringe.

"Sitting here with you, even though we are talking about painful things, makes me feel safe and comfortable. Not scared or anxious."

A wave of relief washes over me. "So, I guess that's a good thing, right?"

"Yeah. My therapist will be happy." She chuckles.

"Mallory, I'm so sorry. About everything." Her hands are resting on the table, and all I can think about is taking them into mine the way I used to. But I won't. I can't. Because we aren't together. And her guard is up.

"I know. And thanks for explaining everything." She pauses for a minute, grabbing her water bottle again, picking at the label, and popping a yellow disc. "I shouldn't have gotten upset when you mentioned what your dad did. That had to have been hard on you. All of it. Your dad pressuring you, seeing me that way, then *my* dad yelling at you, and him sending you away, not knowing whether I was okay." She pauses. "I should have made sure you knew I was alright. I wrote that letter because I thought you wanted to be away from me. So, I told you not to contact me. It was stupid of me to do that, but you have to understand, I wasn't thinking clearly. And my parents were only worried about me getting better. Thinking back, it was all such a mess." She stops and chews on the inside of her bottom lip. "Also, maybe me having a boyfriend wasn't such a good idea. I was young, *we* were young. Those emotions were raw and so real. I don't think I had the maturity to handle them."

"Having you as my girlfriend was everything to me, Mal. I should have proven that to you by staying. And you're right, we were young. I let my dad control me, which was stupid." I pause, taking a deep breath and centering myself. "Leaving was the biggest mistake of my life. It was a messy time. All of it."

She nods in agreement.

"You know I almost dropped out my first year?" Yep, I should bear it all.

"Seriously?" She cocks her head to one side, confused by this.

I take a sip of my coffee, its warmth radiating throughout my body and helping me to find the words to tell her what I want to say. "Yep. I was so worried about you, I pretty much almost flunked out of my first semester. I had a hard time concentrating. All I could do was think about you. I wanted to reach out to you every single day. But you blocked me, and I knew I had to respect your wishes, which made it even harder. Eventually, though, I had to find a way to cope, so I buried myself in schoolwork. I took extra classes and assignments. I worked out like crazy. Anything to keep my mind busy. I didn't even come home for winter break that year."

I shift my gaze to her, and she doesn't utter a word, her eyes wide with shock. "What?" I ask.

"Wow. You're kidding me?" She purses her lips together into a small smile. "Huh. I guess I always thought you were over there living the college life, partying in the California sun, surrounded by tall tan blondes with big boobs, having the time of your life."

I burst into uncontrollable laughter at the absurdity of this, and she soon joins in. Once we get ourselves under control, I need to explain. "That couldn't be further from the truth. None of those girls held a candle to you," I say as I stare at her, unable to turn away because what I said is the truth. Not one girl out there compared to the one sitting in front of me. None of them.

We are both locked in each other's gaze, and I feel my breathing increase. Hers too. She breaks the intense eye contact by reaching for her water and taking a sip. "So, did you date anyone? During those three years?" she questions sheepishly as she continues to stare at her water, tucking a piece of hair behind her ear before grabbing her last Smartie.

"I dated a few girls, yes." Her head snaps in my direction. "But nothing serious. I was so busy with my school load that I didn't have a lot of free time. My dad expected nothing but perfection, so I was studying constantly. After that first year, I started feeling like myself again. So, I went on a date that was forced on me by my roommate at the time. It was a double date, but *my* date"—I pause and chuckle at the memory—"got so hammered that she ended up barfing in my car. I had to get my car detailed twice to get the puke smell out. That girl was a hot mess, let me tell you."

She throws her head back, and her laughter echoes through the room. *Gosh, I've missed her laugh.* "Oh, my God, that's hilarious! Was she tall, tan, and blonde?"

Now, I'm laughing because her laugh is so contagious. "No! Short with dark hair. She was tan, though." We both are in a giggling fit and can't stop. Tears form in our eyes from the laughter. It feels good to be this way with her again.

After we calm down some, she pushes some more. "How about now? Are you seeing anyone? Do you have a girlfriend?"

"No. I don't have a girlfriend." Relief washes over her face. But now it's my turn. "Are you in a relationship with anyone?"

Please say no. Please say no. For the love of God, PLEASE. SAY. NO.

She shakes her head. "No. I'm not seeing anyone."

THANK GOODNESS!

"But there is this guy at the barn, Ben. We've worked together there for the last two years. He always had a girlfriend, but they just broke up. And we have a lot in common." She shrugs. "So ... I don't know."

I hate Ben.

"I think he might like me," She says as a small smile crosses her lips.

Why is she smiling??

I sit back in my chair, trying to gain my composure. Mallory isn't my girlfriend, and I have no right to be jealous. As much as I loathe the thought of someone else touching her or spending time with her, she deserves happiness. And I mean, in all fairness, I've touched and kissed other girls these last few years.

"Well, he sounds like a smart guy. What's not to like?" She grins, her cheeks rosy as she glances away.

I want her to be happy, but that doesn't mean I won't fight for her. I have competition now, so I need to be bold. As I lean forward in my chair, my arms rest heavily on the cool table, bracing myself to ask the difficult question, scared of her answer.

"Mallory, can I see you again? Please. I've missed this." I wave my finger back and forth between us.

She continues to stare out the window. "Me too." She takes a deep breath, composing herself. "I don't know, though." She lets out an exhausted sigh and glances back at me. "I don't know if I'm ready to spend a lot of time with you yet."

Ouch.

She pauses. "Can we maybe just text? You know, as friends do? I think that's what I need from you right now. To be my friend."

I'll take it.

"Sure. We can do that. I could use a texting buddy. I don't have many friends myself right now. Well, none since being back, honestly."

We both chuckle at that because here we are, just a couple of twenty-somethings who used to date having coffee.

We sit in silence for a few seconds, neither of us knowing if or when this should end. I know I'm not going to get up first. I could sit here all day in silence if that was what she needed or wanted from me. But if I'm being honest, the silence is killing me. I need to know more about this loser, *Ben*. How did they meet? How old is he? Is he kind to her? I need ... something.

"So, this Ben, how old—"

"I think I better get going," she blurts out as she grabs her purse and stands. *Okay. I guess we are done.*

"It was nice seeing you, Caleb. I'm glad we met and could air everything out."

She sounds so formal all of a sudden. I wonder if the mention of Ben has something to do with it. Or she's confused about her feelings and wants to end this before she feels anything else.

"It was nice to see you too," I say as I get out of my chair. The thought of Ben makes me feel jealous and bold again. "Can I give you a hug?" I know how she feels about touch, but I need to know if she removed me from the Hug List.

She takes a step backward.

Well, there's my answer. *Red line through Caleb.*

"I don't think so. I'm not ready for that yet."

"Okay, I understand," I say as I put my hands in my pockets. A tense silence hangs between us as we stand still. *God, why did I ask her that?* Now, I made it awkward.

She finally speaks first and breaks the tension. "I'm going to go. I'll be in touch."

With that, she turns around and walks away, leaving behind the smell of grapefruit and her empty Smartie package. I never take my eyes off her as I watch her get in her car. She backs out, looks at me through the window, and waves before she puts it in drive. Then I watch her leave the way she came.

Two things stand out in my mind.

One, she said, 'yet.' She wasn't ready for a hug 'yet.' *I'll take it.*

And two....

If I find out Ben has made the Hug List, I may go back to Stanford.

45

Caleb & Mallory

Later the same day

Caleb: I know I've already said this, but it was so nice seeing you again.

Caleb: And I'm glad we cleared the air.

Mallory: Me too. Have a good rest of your day.

The next day

Caleb: So I have a new hire here that I'm pretty sure caught onto the espresso machine faster than you did.

Mallory: Careful, those are fighting words.

Mallory: Will they take the French Street Best Barista title?

Caleb: Nope, that will always belong to me.

Mallory: So modest.

The following week

Mallory: I'm trying my hand at cooking.

Caleb: WHAT? Does your mom know? Have you burned the house down yet?

Mallory: Ha Ha.

Mallory: I was thinking of trying Chicken Parm next week. Do you think your mom would be willing to share her recipe?

Caleb: Well, she is pretty secretive about it. So probably not.

Mallory: <sad face emoji> Okay. No biggie. I'll just Google one.

Caleb: However, I know where the recipe card is. I'll take a picture of it and send it to you.

Mallory: Awesome thanks!

And the week after that

        Caleb: You didn't tell me. How was the Chicken Parm?

        Mallory: Utter disaster. I need to stay out of the kitchen.

        Mallory: Whoever my husband ends up being, well, he better like takeout.

        Caleb: If it means being married to you, he better.

One month later

        Mallory: I finally was able to ride Shoes today.

Caleb: That sentence makes no sense.

Mallory: LOL! I guess I should explain. Shoes is a horse at the barn. He doesn't like to be ridden because he was abused. We have been working on him for months now. It wasn't a long ride. But it was progress.

Caleb: That's awesome! How did it feel?

Mallory: Wonderful! He's an amazing horse.

Caleb: I would love to see you ride someday.

Mallory: Maybe. Yeah ... maybe someday.

Another month later

Caleb: I got accepted into the masters program I wanted!

Mallory: That's awesome! Is it....

Mallory: Never mind.

Caleb: Is it what?

Mallory: Is it close to home?

Caleb: It's all online.

Mallory: Good! Great!

Mallory: I mean for your mom. Of course.

Caleb: Of course.

A week later

Caleb: Hey! I have great news!

Mallory: Color me intrigued. What is it?

Caleb: That painting you brought in sold today!

Mallory: Awesome!

Caleb: How do you want me to get the money to you?

Caleb: I can drop off a check if you would like?

Mallory: Um...

Caleb: Or I can Venmo you.

Mallory: Yeah. That sounds good.

Caleb: Your artwork is phenom-
enal, Mal.

Mallory: Thanks <heart emoji>

Caleb: Will you bring in another
piece to sell?

Mallory: Soon.

Another week later

Mallory: I think I have to tell you something.

Caleb: Okay. This sounds ... weird.

Mallory: It is weird.

Mallory: Ben, from the barn. The one I told you about.

Caleb: What about him?

Mallory: He asked me out finally.

Caleb: Okay.

Caleb: What did you say?

Mallory: I told him I would have to think about it.

Caleb: Oh boy. That probably was a knife to the heart.

Mallory: Yeah.

The very next day

Caleb: Mallory, I need to know something.

Mallory: Need to know?

Caleb: yes

Mallory: Why do you need to know?

Caleb: You don't even know what I'm going to ask!

Caleb: You're teasing me.

Mallory: I am.

Caleb: Why?

Mallory: Because it's fun.

Caleb: UGH! Seriously, I have a question...

Mallory: Okay fine! But if you need whatever this information is ... I NEED to know why I should cough it up.

Caleb: So that I can sleep tonight.

Mallory: You didn't sleep last night NOT knowing this phantom information?

Caleb: Hardly a wink. Work was brutal today.

Mallory: I would hate to deprive you of sleep. What is so important?

Caleb: Why didn't you say yes right away to a date with Ben?

Only two hours later

Caleb: Mallory, are you still there?

Mallory: Yes

Caleb: You don't have to answer me if you don't want to. I would understand.

Caleb: Whether or not you go out with Ben is really none of my business. I shouldn't have asked. I'm sorry.

Mallory: It's okay.

Mallory: I didn't say yes because I'm trying to figure something out.

Caleb: What?

Mallory: Don't worry. I'll let you know when I do.

Caleb: I'll wait.

Caleb: Forever if I have to.

A long week later

Caleb: I saw you today.

Mallory: You did? Where?

Caleb: The grocery store. I was picking up milk and eggs for my mom. You were looking at ice cream. Studying what flavor to buy.

Caleb: Not sure why because I know you got Vanilla.

Mallory: I'm a creature of habit, what can I say.

Caleb: You looked pretty. Your hair is getting longer.

Mallory: I'm letting it grow out.

The next day

Mallory: Confession time.

Caleb: Hit me.

Mallory: I wish you would have talked to me in the store.

Caleb: I didn't want to push you. Or make you feel uncomfortable.

Mallory: That's sweet.

Caleb: I can be sweet when I want to be

Mallory: That seems to be all the time.

Three hours later

Mallory: Caleb?

Caleb: Yeah?

Mallory: Would you like to go on a trail ride with me?

Caleb: I would love to! I should warn you. Rip from Yellowstone I am not.

Mallory: LOL! It's Okay. I'll teach you. And it's just a trail ride. It's easy.

Mallory: Plus I LOVE that show!

Caleb: Okay. Tell me when and where and I will be there.

Mallory: The barn. Tomorrow at 6. Is that a good time?

Caleb: Even if it wasn't, I would make sure that it was.

Mallory: I'll see you then. <heart eye emoji>

46

TOMORROW AT SIX

Caleb

"Y ou have arrived at your destination."

The navigation system's robotic cheerful voice declares I'm at Camelot. The GPS lady with the British accent has no clue how much this destination means to me today. Because for the first time in three years, I am about to spend some quality time with Mallory. Is it a date?

Don't know, don't care. I'm just thrilled she asked.

The excitement coursing through my veins was too much to ignore, and I found myself wide awake at six this morning. When I rolled over and grabbed my phone to check the time, I realized I had twelve hours to fill. I attempted to fall back asleep to make the day go even faster. I was unsuccessful. So, I tried my best to keep busy.

Did some yard work for my mom.

Cleaned the house.

Worked out.

Payroll for French Street.

All the while checking my watch every ten minutes. Every second crawled by, making this one of the longest days of my life.

After three months of texting, hoping, wishing ... Mallory finally wants to get together. When my phone pinged, and I saw the text about a trail ride, I read it multiple times with a huge smile on my face. I have no clue what she has in store for us, and the anticipation is overwhelming. She wants to go for a trail ride—great—but I still don't know if she went on that date with Ben. I hope that this isn't a date to let me know she's moved on. Take me on a nice relaxing trail ride before she stomps on my heart.

Okay. I need to stop. That's not fair. I was the one who stomped on her heart by leaving. The one who sent her into a nervous breakdown that led to her thinking about ending her life. Me. I did that. So, if Mallory is officially going to friend zone me today, I have no one to blame but myself.

But on the other hand, this could end up ranking as one of the best days of my life. Maybe she wants to date again. And if she wants to take things slow, fine. So be it.

This is all about her.

She is calling the shots.

I'm following her lead.

The last thing I want to do is pressure her. And my hope is … if everything goes well, and if the opportunity presents itself, I'm telling Mallory that I love her. Because I do. I don't think I ever stopped. And besides, you know what they say.

Go big or go home.

Those three little words that I had planned to say to her haunt me every day since I broke her heart. Before everything went to crap, and I turned my life upside down. And in turn, crushed Mallory's spirit and put her in the darkest of dark places.

As I flip on my blinker and make the turn, I roll my shoulders to prepare myself. Passing a sign that reads The Camelot Center, I slowly drive down the narrow road that leads to the barn. I can see it in the distance, and the farther I drive, the faster my heart races. I clench my fists around the steering wheel, trying to steady my shaking hands. The barn comes into view, and I have to focus to help me process what I'm seeing. Because there's Mallory hugging whom I can assume is only one person.

Ben.

What in the actual heck?

They are standing in between two horses. The road turns into gravel, and the sound of my tires crunching on rocks startles them and forces them to break apart. I can't be upset or jealous. I have no right or claim to her. What I need to do is get the image of me punching Ben square in the mouth out of my brain and get myself together. For Mallory.

Mallory

Ben was kind enough to help me saddle Flash and Levi for the trail ride today, which I am thankful for. A few months ago, this offer of help from Ben would have made me giddy ... excited even.

But being with him feels different now.

I developed feelings for him, and the thought of a relationship seemed possible. But if I'm being honest, I liked the attention. Ben made me feel pretty and special for the first time since Caleb. Then I saw Caleb at the café, and everything that I thought I may have felt for Ben became muddy. Talking to Caleb and texting him for these last few months, it became clear what decision I needed to make.

Nothing would make me happier than being with Caleb.

It has always been Caleb. And it always will be.

But right now, I need to tell Ben that I can't go out on a date with him. When he initially asked me, I told him I needed time to think about it. He understood and has kindly given me the space I asked for.

Then, I avoided him at every turn.

When he arrived at the barn, I would make myself scarce. When it was time for lunch, I made sure to eat with my instructor, Kayla. When he texted me, my replies were short and sweet. It sounds awful; I know. My lack of communication is rearing its ugly head in this situation. Because, if I'm being honest, Ben is my friend. A friend I trust and care about. And because of that, I can't bear the thought of hurting him.

To prepare for this upcoming conversation, I practiced my breathing exercises to center myself. The horses follow us silently, the only sounds being the jingling of their harnesses. Then, to top it off, I haven't told him who this trail ride is with. Only that it's "one of my closest friends."

I mean, it's not a lie.

"You've been awfully quiet this morning, Mallory. Everything okay?" Ben asks with genuine concern in his voice as we walk to the trailhead, the horse's hooves crunching the gravel below our feet.

"Um ... yeah, fine. I'm fine. Everything's fine—fine—yep, I'm fine." *God, I'm such a loser.*

He chuckles. "That's a lot of ... fines." As we arrive at the start of the trail, Ben turns to me, his eyes tight with nerves. "Look, Mallory, I don't want to pressure you since you said that you needed time, but have you given any thought to my offer of a date?"

I knew this was coming. My eyes shift toward my boots, and I kick the gravel beneath them. And, of course, my anxiety gets the best of me as I pick my cuticles. "Ben"—I tilt my chin up and try to look him in the eye—"I think you're great, and I love hanging out with you here at the barn, but—"

"Oh, boy ... the dreaded 'but,'" he says as he puts his hands in his pockets and peers off into the distance, squinting as the sun illuminates his face.

"*But* I think it would be better if we were just friends." I peer back down at the gravel because I can't stomach it to see the hurt in his eyes. "I'm so sorry."

A heavy sigh filled with frustration escapes from his lips. "Don't be sorry, Mallory. Never say you're sorry for being honest and telling someone how you feel." He immediately turns his attention to Flash's already-in-place bridle. Seeing the hurt in his eyes is making me feel awful.

"I really do want to be friends," I add, resting my hand on his so he'll focus on me and not Flash, hoping to make him feel better. Even though I know this is the last thing you want to hear from someone you like. I mean, I've watched movies and TV shows. No one wants this.

He stops messing with the bridle and turns to look at me, a small smile crossing his lips. Lips I came so close to kissing. "Well, if that's all I can get, I'll take it."

"Can I give you a hug?" I request, shocking myself. Hugs these days don't unnerve me like they once did. My Hug List still exists, and Ben's not on it, but I want him to understand that there are no hard feelings.

"Of course." My hand is still resting on his as he wraps his fingers around mine and pulls me in for a hug. His muscular arms encase my waist, and he holds me for a few seconds. The hug doesn't feel awkward or uncomfortable. But it doesn't feel *right* either. "I just want you to be happy, Mallory," he whispers in my ear. "Find your peace."

"Thank you. And I have."

The sound of tires on gravel interrupts the uneasy feeling of Ben's arms around me, and I take the opportunity to break away. I look over toward the approaching car ... and it's Caleb.

CRAP! Did he see me hugging Ben? *CRAP! CRAP! CRAP!* I'm sure he did.

We stand in between Flash and Levi and watch Caleb park his car. "So, is this who you're riding with today?" Ben asks as Caleb gets out of the car, and I give him a slight nod in agreement. And Caleb—WOW—he looks amazing. He's wearing jeans, boots, and a long-sleeved navy-blue Henley, which makes his eyes pop as they gaze at me. He styled his hair to perfection because that's what he is: perfect.

My face lights up with a grin as soon as I lay eyes on him, even though I'm anxious about the hug he witnessed, hoping he didn't get the wrong idea.

"Is he your peace?" Ben asks as he turns to peer at me, his expression full of pain.

"Yes. He is a part of it ... Yes," I answer, smiling like a fool and not taking my eyes off Caleb.

Ben nods in understanding.

I know it sounds baffling, but Caleb leaving took away all the peace I had in my life. But having him back, texting him as a friend, made me realize how much I need him. I got my peace back. And I can't wait to tell him. But before I do, I need to make sure of a few things first. I'm looking forward to our conversation, to say the least.

Caleb strides over to us, exuding confidence as if he's in some kind of professional photo shoot. He hasn't taken his eyes off me, nor I from his. He stops in front of me. "Hey, Mal," he says with a smile. That smile ... the one that causes my insides to explode with excitement.

"Hey, Caleb."

A sudden and strange tension fills the air. Ben observes us both intently as we lock eyes with each other. He clears his throat. "Hey, man." He extends his hand to Caleb. "Ben. Nice to meet you."

Caleb breaks his glance from me and reaches for Ben's hand. "Caleb."

That's it. That's all he says. *He definitely saw us hugging.* Caleb's lips tense together, his knuckles turning white as he grips Ben's hand. Ben doesn't back down and returns the grip, his jaw clenching. *Dear Lord, boys.* I need to break up this testosterone-filled power trip. Pronto.

"Caleb, are you ready for this?" I interject with an extra dose of cheerfulness. He lets go of Ben's hand, faces me, and pivots away from Ben.

"You better believe it. Which one of these beauties is mine?"

"This is Flash," Ben says since he's holding Flash's lead. "Don't let his name fool you, though. He's quite the gentle giant." He turns his attention to Flash, rubbing and patting his neck. "Aren't you, buddy?"

Caleb ignores Ben and directs his focus to my best friend. "Then, this must be Levi?" Caleb touches Levi's neck and runs his hand down his coat.

"Yep! This is my baby. Isn't he gorgeous?" I declare with pride because Levi has been my savior. He pulled me from a very dark place that I never plan to revisit. Our bond is strong.

"He really is," Caleb answers, his hand stroking Levi's coat again and again.

The same awkward silence returns as we stand here, watching Caleb rub Levi's neck. I'm sure Ben wants to get away from Caleb as soon as possible, so he breaks the tension. "Caleb, have you ever ridden before?"

"No. Never. I warned Mallory. I mean, it can't be hard, right?" Ben and I both let out low chuckles since we both know how awkward and hard someone's first ride can be.

"Well, it can feel unnatural at first. But I'm sure you'll get it. I'm going to go get a block so you can mount. What do you think, Mal? Two or three steps?" Ben asks me with the smuggest of smug grins on his face.

Ben has the upper hand here at the barn, and he knows it. I sigh. I think he may be enjoying this a little too much.

Caleb

God, it annoys the crap out of me that these two share this horse thing.

And is he serious right now? I don't need a freaking step stool, like a toddler, to mount this horse. It's obvious he's getting a kick out of this at my expense. I saw him smirk at Mallory. He knows he can one-up me here.

"I don't need a step stool," I blurt out with cocky, unearned confidence.

"No, man. Trust me, you will. Especially if you've never—"

"I said I got it," I interrupt Ben's next words because I am sick of hearing his voice at this point. Honestly, I just want to mount this horse and get the heck away from cowboy Ben.

Ben puts his hands up in the air in surrender. "Okay, dude." He takes a step back and extends his arm out. "Knock yourself out."

"Caleb, are you sure?" Mallory asks as concern etches on her face, and her eyebrows knit together. "It's not as easy—"

I turn to face Mallory and plead with her, desperation in my voice. "Please, just let me try."

Look, I understand I'm being totally unreasonable right now. This animal I'm standing next to could trample me and kill me without remorse. He's enormous, and I'm acting like I know what I'm doing. But I can't help myself.

My brain is short-circuiting on jealousy, and it's a power trip at this point. Plus, when I'm around Mallory, I throw all rational thoughts out the window.

Shoving past Ben, I move to stand beside Flash, and I grab onto the saddle. *I mean, how hard can this be, right?* My mom and I have watched Heartland, I love Yellowstone, and my dad loved old Westerns.

I totally got this. Easy peasy.

I see Mallory in my peripheral vision take steps in my direction. She reaches her hand out to stop me, but I'm already committed. "Caleb, stop…" she pleads.

Ben has his arms crossed over his chest with that same smirk on his face. This is comedy hour for him, and it's grating on my nerves.

I put my foot into the stirrup and study Flash's back. *Was he this big a few minutes ago?* Shaking the fear from my mind, I place my boot in the stirrup and hoist myself up while pulling down hard on the saddle for leverage.

Big mistake.

I may have been okay with this display of masculinity. But Flash isn't. He jolts forward toward Ben as soon as I yank on his saddle to pull myself up. I hear Ben say, "Whoa, boy!" and before I know it, I'm jerked backward, thrown onto my back, staring at the blue sky. I land with such force it feels like I am a nail being hammered into the ground. *Are those stars?* Yep, I'm seeing stars. My back, head, and tailbone are yelling at me.

I am such an idiot. How do actors make that look so easy? Give them all the Emmys and Oscars.

Mallory's scream pierces through the air as she rushes to me, thrusting Levi's lead into Ben's hands.

"OH, MY GOD! Caleb, are you okay?"

Ben graciously extends his hand to help me up, which I take because the air that was once in my lungs is gone. I wipe the gravel dust off my jeans. "I'm fine." Well, physically, I'm fine. My ego, however, has taken a colossal hit. Humble pie is my dessert of choice today.

I can tell Ben is trying to suppress his laughter. "So … how about that block step?"

I nod, and Ben disappears into the barn, his shoulders shaking as he walks away.

WHAM!

"Ow!" I jolt and turn to face Mallory, who just punched me in the arm. "What was that for?"

"Caleb! You could have been hurt! What the heck were you thinking?"

She's right. I could have been. Well, hurt worse than I am. A sharp pain is radiating from my tailbone, and I think I might have a concussion, but I decide not to tell her that information.

"You're right, Mallory. I'm so sorry." I rub my temples to ease the instant headache I have. "It's just that..."

"Just what?"

With a sigh, I shift my attention to her. "I saw you hugging him, okay. And you two share this horse thing, and I mean, obviously, he likes you, or he wouldn't have asked you out. Plus, I'm not blind. I can see he's a good-looking dude and..." I lower my head because I am rambling on like a lunatic. "And I don't know ... I kinda lost my mind."

She takes a step toward me and rests her hand on my bicep.

She's touching me!!

"Caleb. Can you look at me, please?" As I feel her hand on my arm, I turn to look at her. The warmth of our first touch in three years feels overwhelming. *Her* asking me to make eye contact; the significance of that request is huge. It shows how far she has come. Not wanting this moment to end, I focus on the big brown eyes I love so much. There's a longing in her eyes, and I know that look. I remember it. And I love it. "You have nothing to worry about when it comes to Ben. Nothing."

Oh. Well, okay then.

"Right before you got here, I told him I just wanted to be friends. Nothing more."

My body feels lighter when I hear these words. The dull ache in my lower back from the fall ... gone. My headache? Cured.

"So, what are you saying?" I plead, dying to know what this means.

She opens her mouth to explain when you-know-who comes back with my block.

"Alright, cowboy," he says, still laughing as he places the block on the ground next to Flash.

I really, really don't like this guy.

"Let's show you how to do this."

Mallory and Ben help me mount Flash the proper way. Even with the block, it takes me a few attempts, but I'm finally able to sit on this animal's back. Mallory adjusts my stirrups, never tearing her eyes away from mine the whole time. She makes her way over to Levi and ... nope. No block needed for her. She hoists herself up and swings her leg around Levi so gracefully it's like she's doing ballet.

I am blown away by her. She is exuding grace and confidence in spades. This newfound independence looks very good on her.

The dynamic duo gives me a quick lesson on how to hold the reins, how to steer, how to use my legs to apply pressure to help steer, and finally, how to whoa.

Once we have mounted and are situated, she stops and glances over her shoulder at me. "You ready, cowboy?"

"That's forever going to be my nickname now, huh?"

"Yep. Afraid so." She giggles and makes some kind of clicking noise, and off Levi goes out ahead of me and Flash.

"Hey, man," Ben says to get my attention. I turn and look at him. He unclips the lead. "Take care of her, okay?" I nod, happy he understands he has no chance with her. He makes the same clicking noise and smacks Flash on the back.

And away we go.

Mallory

For the first twenty minutes of the ride, we stayed silent.

I keep stealing glances at Caleb, making sure he's alright. His eyes seem to follow me every time I turn my head in his direction.

I'm taking Caleb to a picturesque spot on the trail. We'll be able to see a waterfall spilling into a rocky stream and hear the soothing sound of the water. I always feel a sense of calm when I come to this place, and the sound of the water is like a lullaby that puts me at ease.

It's kind of a special location. I only know about it because my instructor Kayla took me here about a year after I started riding. Ben wanted to ride with me here, but I always said no. With Ben, this place always felt too intimate. This is where I can be alone and clear my head when needed. This is the only place where I can gather the courage to express my feelings to Caleb.

The sound of flowing water tells me that we are nearing the waterfall. The grunts and groans coming from the gorgeous rider behind me are increasing.

"You okay back there, cowboy?" I question him because I know how he feels. When you've never ridden a horse before, your first ride is, well, let's just say, uncomfortable. Especially when you are a man. I'll just leave it at that. Plus, adding in his fall ... I'm sure he's hurting.

I look back and see him shifting in his saddle. "Yeah, I think so. Are we going someplace in particular or just riding around?"

"I'm taking you to my favorite spot in the whole wide world. It's special to me."

"Wow." He pauses. "Have you ever taken anyone else here before?"

I know him ... he's trying to figure out if Ben and I have visited here together.

"Nope. You are the first." I meet his gaze, exchanging a smile.

When we make it to the clearing, the trail opens to a beautiful flat open rock outlook. It's not a massive area, and if you walk about fifty feet, you're met with a steep decline. The other side is almost identical, but it's covered in more trees, and flowing through the ravine is the river. And in the center of all this natural beauty is the waterfall. It's short and wide as it flows over smooth rocks, and it creates a mesmerizing pattern that catches the eye. The sound of rushing water grows louder as you follow the small pathway that leads to the waterfall. Flat rocks line the edge of the river, and if the wind is right, the spray from the waterfall will cool you on a hot summer day. In fall, the colors are stunning, and in the colder months, it's a winter wonderland, which honestly is my favorite.

"Unbelievable," Caleb breathes out as he takes it all in. "This place is amazing." I observe him as he scans his surroundings, absorbing the natural beauty. The sound of the waterfall and the flowing river is music to my ears. The cool breeze feels wonderful on my skin.

I'm in heaven.

"I know, isn't it? This is my happy place." I scan the scenery, taking it all in. Even though I have this place memorized, the view never gets old.

"Can we go explore? Because, honestly, I need to get off this horse," he chuckles as he shifts in the saddle. I decide to put him out of his misery and show him how to dismount. This time, he does it with ease.

"Okay, so getting off, a little easier than getting on." We share a laugh in relief, thankful that we didn't have a repeat of the mishap at the barn.

At the start of the clearing is a thick branch that hangs parallel to the ground, and it's a perfect place to tie up the horses.

"Come on, let's go to the waterfall," I say, leading the way to the path.

As he follows me for a few steps, his gaze lingers on the horses, and his body tenses up. "Wait," he says, stopping and rubbing his hand down his face as he peers at me. "Will they be okay here?" His genuine concern and affection for the horses are touching my heart, forcing me to love him even more.

I tilt my head in their direction as they graze on the nearby grass. "They'll be fine, trust me. I come here all the time."

He nods as his body relaxes, and we trudge to the small pathway that curves down to the waterfall. He offers to help me navigate the steep and rocky parts, and I accept his hand, even though I have made this descent hundreds of times. His hand feels the same as it did three years ago: familiar, comfortable, and warm.

Once we are in the ravine, we sit on a flat rock that acts as a perfect seat for both of us, our feet dangling over the edge. As it always was in the past with Caleb, we have no trouble easing into conversation. I blab on and on about the barn, how I learned to ride, and my paintings. He wants to know about my therapy, so I explain how it's taught me how to deal with my emotions. The topic changes to my family as I get him up to speed on Jake and his girlfriend, Emma.

"I think he might propose soon. He hasn't said yet for sure, but I have a feeling."

"Wow. I love that. And you like Emma?" he asks, his voice laced with genuine interest.

"I love her. She's like the sister I never had. She's amazing. You should meet her sometime."

His eyes widen at my suggestion. "Yeah, I would love that." His mouth ticks up into a small smile at the mention of a future beyond today and this ride.

"There is one thing that scares me. Something I've never told anyone." I can't believe I'm about to say this. Caleb's eyes narrow with concern as he looks at me. "I'm scared to become a wife and mom."

Now, his blue eyes open in shock. "Scared? Why on earth would you be scared?"

"I mean, what if I pass my mental illness onto my kids? What if y..." I clear my throat and stop myself from saying 'you.' "What if my future husband always sees me as fragile. I don't want that." I need to know that he won't forever view me as the broken girl on the steps.

He turns to face me. "You aren't fragile, Mallory. You are by far the strongest, most resilient woman I know. And any man that would treat you as fragile..." He pauses and scoffs. "Well, he wouldn't deserve you. Because I promise you are braver than he ever will be. Or could be." He stops for a beat and swallows before he continues. "And as far as being a mom. Well, no one could do it better. I know that. I *feel* that. And I hope to see it one day."

He's studying me, but I'm looking straight ahead, taking in what he just said to me and hoping that he's referring to himself and *our* future. Because that is exactly what I want. And he told me what I needed to hear. Caleb would love and respect me as the strong woman I have become. I crave that from him.

We let the sounds of nature fill the silence, allowing that heavy part of the conversation to seep in. Then, after a few minutes, he starts filling me in on his life. He tells me about his dad's death and how it changed his plans. His dad left his mom the business, but his mom is going to pass it to Caleb since he's running it now, anyway. The subject of Stanford comes up, and I can tell he doesn't like to talk about it much. But he lights up when he tells me about California, especially the Bay area.

"Half Moon Bay is just gorgeous. I swear there is nothing like the Pacific and the California sun. I know how much you love water, so you would love it there."

"Sounds amazing. We will have to go some time," I say as I lean back on my hands, looking out at the waterfall again.

Caleb is quiet for a minute, then bends his leg to rest on the rock as he turns to face me. His other leg hangs over the edge.

"Mallory, can I ask you something?" I nod, turning my head. "You've mentioned twice now about maybe us doing stuff together in the future. First me meeting Emma and just now, maybe you and I going to California someday. You also said earlier that there is nothing to worry about with Ben." He stops to gather his thoughts before he continues. "I have to ask; do you want a future with me? And if so, are we talking just friends or the way we used to be?"

He looks adorable right now, his vulnerability on full display. I turn and draw my leg up on the rock, mirroring his position with us now facing each other.

"Neither."

"Okay. Help me out here, Mal. I'm confused." Again, his cuteness is off the charts as he raises his eyebrows. I think it's time I let him off the hook and tell him what I know he wants to hear and what I have been dying to tell him.

I look at his hands that are resting on his leg, and I take them both in mine as I interlace our fingers together. This is the first time in three years that we hold hands, and it feels amazing. The warmth of his touch feels like hope. On impulse, he rubs circles on my skin with his thumb.

Gosh, I've missed that.

I see his chest rise and fall. He clears his throat and never takes his eyes off our hands. "Now, I may be wrong, but um ... this um ... is the third time you've touched me today."

With a nod of my head, I raise my eyes to meet his gaze. In seconds, his piercing blue eyes lock on mine.

"I don't want to just be your friend. I also don't want to go back to the way things were. We were young, and I was sick, even though I kept that to myself. We were together, but somehow, toward the end, we weren't because I wasn't one hundred percent there."

His eyes are softer, never breaking contact with mine. "Are you saying now it's different?"

"Yes, it is. We are older, I'm strong and healthy. I feel better than I ever have in my whole life. It's very different. So, what I want is to start now. Right now. Let's—"

"—be together?" He squeezes my hands and shifts closer to me on the rock. "Please tell me that's what you're saying. Because I want that more than anything. I've missed you so much, Mal."

We both lean forward, and our foreheads are touching. Nothing about how close we are feels foreign to me. "Yes. Let's start over. Let's be together. And I can't promise that I will be okay all the time. I'm still me. Autism, anxiety, depression, and all. And I might have another breakdown at some point in my life. I might—" Suddenly, all of my worries are bubbling to the surface.

He places his finger on my lips. "Mallory, I don't care. I mean, I care, of course. But you are so much stronger now. So, whatever happens, we will get through it together. Please, can I kiss you right now? I'm dying to kiss you."

I nod. He lets out a breath and smiles as he releases my hand and places his hand on my cheek, just like he did for our first kiss. I lean into his touch as he places his other hand on my knee. He takes a second to stare into my eyes as if he is studying me. And since it's Caleb, I don't turn away. With a light touch, he brushes his thumb on my jaw, and I can feel heat spreading through my whole body. He presses his lips against mine, and our first kiss in three years feels better than any kiss that came before it. His lips feel like velvet against mine, and, as before, it's effortless. This kiss feels fresh, full of hope and promise.

We break apart, and he continues to rub my jaw. "Mallory, I know that there may be times in our future that you will struggle. But I can promise you I will always be here for you. I will help you and protect you always. And I know you need things to be consistent and routine, so I will do everything in my power to make you feel comfortable and safe. Also, I can promise you one other thing."

"What's that?" I whisper.

"When you hear me say 'I love you,' whether I say it once a day or a thousand times, the words will always mean the same." I jerk back at his words. Those three little words. "Because I love you, Mallory. I never stopped."

It feels like everything has stopped moving as if time has stood still. The sound of the waterfall, the rustling of the trees, the chirping birds; all of it fades into the background. As I stare into the eyes of the boy from the café, there is only one thing left to say.

The truth.

It has always been Caleb.

I have loved him since I was sixteen. I can't imagine my life without him, and I need him to know that he's the one I want.

"I love you too."

With that, our lips crash into each other as his hands wrap around my waist and he pulls me closer to him, almost as if letting me go is the worst thing in the world. Because he did once, he let me go. But right now, he's telling me with his arms and lips that he won't make the same mistake twice. I wrap my arms around his neck, letting my hands get lost in the softness of his hair. The kiss brings back familiarity, and our hands trace the paths they've memorized. Caleb's touch is one that I have always craved. Minutes tick by as we sit on this rock in our passionate bubble. Never wanting it to end.

We pull apart, and Caleb kisses me with tenderness on my forehead and takes me in his arms. Holding him, I feel complete, like all the pieces of my life are finally falling into place. I breathe in deeply as I bury my head in his shoulder, taking in his familiar scent. His arms feel like my past and my future. He's my best friend. He's my love. He's my home.

"Mallory?" he whispers as I'm still encased in his arms.

"Yeah?"

He pulls away and tucks a piece of my hair around my ear. "Does this mean I'm back on the Hug List?"

I tell him another truth.

"You never left it."

47

THREE YEARS LATER

Laura

"Do you, Mallory Ann Givens, take thee Caleb James Horvath as your lawfully wedded husband?"

"I do."

Right before my eyes, with those two brief words, my daughter is now a married woman. Emotions flood my brain as I sit in a white folding chair, in front of a beautiful floral archway, on this warm June afternoon, watching my baby girl get married. I don't even notice that my draped one-shoulder jade-colored satin dress is scratching me, driving me nuts. Or that my Spanx is pinching me to where I can barely breathe. Or that Scott is shedding a tear or two.

Scott never cries. It's very rare, and it must be something pretty big to make him let it out. Turns out that big thing is his kids. I saw the single tear roll down his cheek as he walked past me, Mallory on his arm as he handed her over to Caleb. I watched as they walked down the aisle, passing our beaming friends and family. My parents and my brother Drew, Scott's mom, Kyle and Shay and their twin boys, Johnny and his wife, Rachel. Their three-year-old daughter, Piper, is the flower girl. When Piper and those boys entered Mallory's life, I saw the future mom she will become. She was ecstatic beyond words.

Jake is standing next to Caleb as his best man. Caleb's college roommate is up there as well. All three are looking sharp in their navy blue suits, white shirts, and blush-colored ties. Emma, my daughter-in-law, is Mallory's matron of honor. Layla, Mallory's best friend, is a bridesmaid. Both are wearing trumpet-style strapless dresses that match the boys' ties.

Mallory never tore her eyes off Caleb as they walked. Not once. Caleb wiped away a few tears as he watched her floating toward him. With a gentle kiss on his daughter's cheek, Scott handed her over to Caleb. He slyly tried to wipe away the tear as he sat next to me. I leaned over and whispered in his ear, "Busted." With his elbow, he gave me a slight nudge, then grabbed my hand and has held it in a vice grip ever since.

It's a surreal experience; watching your child get married. Looking at her and Caleb, I feel my heart racing in my chest. They are standing facing each other, holding hands, never taking their eyes off one another as the officiant talks about the sanctity of marriage. My daughter's smile never left her face. A smile that has been there every day since Caleb walked back into her life. The two of them are a complete match, bringing out the best in one another.

Mallory is a vision in her simple wedding dress, and let me tell you, finding a dress for her was interesting. All her sensory issues had to be taken into consideration. It needed to be comfortable; the fabric had to be soft to the touch, nothing too tight, no seams around the waist, nothing that scratched her skin, and it had to have pockets. A tall order in the world of wedding dress shopping. We shopped at bridal stores and browsed the internet for months. I was worried we would never find one. However, eventually, we struck gold at a small boutique bridal shop in Columbus ... three hours away. There, we found a white stretch crepe sheath dress, halter style, sleeveless, with a low back and a slight brush train. The dress was tailor-made for her, and of course, it had pockets. Her hair is down in long beach waves, swept to the side, and held in place with my grandmother's sapphire antique brooch. It's her something borrowed and blue. The only flowers she wanted were a small bouquet of wildflowers she picked herself at the barn. She was simple and elegant. Just like my Mallory.

Caleb proposed to her at their waterfall six months ago. Mallory described to us the picturesque scene as her oval-shaped emerald ring rested on her finger. They rode Flash and Levi to the waterfall through the trail that was covered in fresh snow from the day before. He got on one knee at their favorite rock as the sun glinted against the snow and declared his love and devotion. According to Caleb, she squealed and leaped into his arms before even answering him. He took Mallory by surprise, but we knew what was coming. Two weeks before, while Mallory was working, Caleb asked both Scott and me for our daughter's hand in marriage.

We agreed.

I sit in silence as I watch her exchange vows, place a ring on her husband's finger, and him sliding a beautiful diamond band on hers. The depth of my emotions right now is beyond words. It's a mixture of pride, joy, sadness. It's bittersweet. My daughter is forming a union with another human being right in front of me. My heart can only take so much. I look at my hands and blink hard to hold back the tears when I hear—

"I now pronounce you husband and wife," the officiant proclaims with a smile. "Caleb, you may now kiss your bride."

Caleb leans in, takes Mallory's face in his hands, and tenderly kisses her. I can feel Scott tense up next to me. But I'm sure for him, as a father, it's never easy to see your baby girl kiss her now husband in front of you.

Wedding kisses are the sweetest. But when it's your kid, they hit a bit differently.

"Ladies and gentlemen, it is my pleasure to present to you for the first time, Mr. and Mrs. Caleb and Mallory Horvath!"

Mallory and Caleb turn to face the crowd of well-wishers. Mallory raises her hand that's holding the bouquet in the air as everyone erupts into claps and cheers. She gives me and Scott a playful wink before beginning her walk up the aisle with her new husband.

The hard part is over. Now it's time to party.

As we roll into our driveway, I glance at the clock on the dashboard. One-fifteen in the morning. Scott pulls the SUV into the garage and kills the engine. We sit there in silence, both of us too exhausted to get out of the car.

He rests his head on the back of his seat. His bowtie hangs around his neck, undone, and his suit jacket sits neatly folded in his lap. He turns his head. "What in the world just happened?"

We both let out an enormous sigh and chuckle at the same time. This day that we have been planning for six months is over, and the whole thing was a blur. Visions of getting ready, smiling for endless pictures, eating cake, and dancing the night away swirl around in my head. My favorite part was Mallory and Caleb's first dance to You and Me by Lifehouse. They danced and swayed as if they were the only two people in the hall. The reception was dark, and the spotlight was only on them. With their foreheads touching, they held each other close, completely lost in the moment. It was beautiful.

"Well, I can tell you what *did* happen. You, the big, rough, and tough Scott Givens, cried not once"—I hold up one finger—"but twice." As I drag up my second finger, I shoot him a sly smile.

"Hey now," he says as he grabs my hand and pulls it down. "That is going to be our secret!"

"What?!?! You cried as you walked her down the aisle *and* during the fa-ther/daughter dance. Sorry, babe, I have about a hundred and fifty witnesses that will agree with me on this one."

He turns and looks at the ceiling of the car. "God, I'm never going to live this down, am I?"

"Nope. I may have slipped the photographer an extra fifty to make sure she captured those moments."

His head whips in my direction. "You didn't?"

"Nah. Just kidding. But for the amount of money we paid her, she better have."

"Johnny is going to tease me forever, isn't he?"

"Afraid so."

He takes my hand, brings it to his mouth, and tenderly kisses my knuckles. "Come on, babe. Let's go inside."

On tired legs and feet, we make our way into the house, our footsteps echoing throughout. It's quiet. Eerily quiet. Once I step foot into the bedroom, I peel my dress off and let it fall to the floor, not caring how much it costs. I throw on my pj's and see Scott has done the same thing. A rented tux sits in a heap on the carpet.

As Scott's brushing his teeth, I make my way to Mallory's room. I'm greeted with a hollow silence as I open the door, creaking on its hinges. The only thing that remains is her freshly made bed, her dresser and desk, both empty, and the fluffy pink rug. I scan the room, and I'm flooded with memories. I can still see her playing with Saige and her American Girl dolls in the corner of the room. My eyes land on her desk, and I can see her drawing horses. I peer at the other side of the door, where her riding helmet would hang, and boots would live. It's empty, too. She is present in every inch of this room and always will be.

I feel Scott come up behind me, and he rubs my arms, giving me goosebumps. "You okay?" he asks me as he kisses my shoulder, and I lean back on his chest.

"Yeah, I am. Just sad, I guess." We both stand there for a few seconds, letting the reality sink in. I reach out for the handle to shut the door, and the memories with it, as Scott stops me.

"Wait, babe." He pushes past me and steps into her room. He walks over to her bed, and that's when I see them. Two envelopes sitting on her comforter. One addressed to me, and one addressed to Scott. Our hands simultaneously reach for them, and we exchange a startled glance.

Did she write us ... letters?

We turn them over in our hands; written in her perfect handwriting on the back, they say the same thing...

PLEASE READ.

Without a second to think, we tear into our envelopes.

48

THE LETTERS

Dear Dad,

I hope this letter doesn't make you cry because I know you like to act tough and hate it. I have a feeling you cried at the wedding or when we danced the father/daughter dance. You're smiling right now because I'm right, huh? Mom's letter is going to make her cry, so give her a hug. Or two. She is going to need it. I think she is going to be sad for a little while without me at home. Make sure to take care of her. That was dumb to say, of course you will.

I wanted to write you this letter to say thank you. Thank you for being my dad. You are the best. People say that you can't pick your family. And that's true. But given the choice, I would have picked you as my father every day, all day. I mean that! Thank you for always believing in me. I know that sometimes I wasn't always happy. But you always tried to lift me up and make me see the better side of things. You always tried to make me laugh. Even though I've moved out, don't stop trying to make me laugh, okay?

Dad, I know you want me to be happy. Caleb makes me so happy. I promise you. He is a really good man. He loves and respects me so much. I know you trust me. So please, Dad, trust me when I say that I wouldn't marry Caleb if he wasn't going to take care of me and treasure me forever.

Anyway, I just wanted you to know those things. I mean, don't worry; you aren't getting rid of me that easily. I will be around visiting still. A lot, probably. I know I am going to miss you and Mom so much. I promise to call you all the time. I mean,

I know if I don't call, you will. And then probably yell at me for not checking in sooner. I won't take it personal. I might be moving out and getting married, but I will forever be Daddy's little girl.

Love,

Mallory

Dear Mom,

If you haven't already guessed, I'm writing this before I say I Do to Caleb. I hope the wedding went well. I know you put a lot of time and effort into planning it, so I really hope everything went off without a hitch. And I know you already know this, but I love Caleb so much, Mom. He is such a good man. He treasures me, grounds me, and takes such good care of me. And I hope that this doesn't offend you or make you sad, but he is number one on my hug list now. Sorry.

I know you know I'm not very big on communication. That's why I thought maybe I should write you a letter to say what I want to say. Don't worry, it's not bad.

Basically, I just wanted to say thank you. For a lot of stuff. First, for being my mom. You are the best mom I could have ever wanted or needed. I mean it! I also want to say thank you for giving me the help I needed. I know I didn't make things easy for you. My autism, anxiety, and depression sometimes have a mind of their own. But you never made me feel like I was less of a person because of them. Even though my depression was telling me I was worthless, your voice was also in my head telling me I was strong and worth it. Your voice saved me.

I also want to say thank you for taking me to the barn that day so that I could meet the horses. It changed my life. I love the horses, and they are a part of me. Is it weird that I have them on the Hug List? Honestly, I don't care if it is. I love them. I've been trying to think of different ways that I can pay you back for all that you have done. And honestly, even if I could do something, I know that you wouldn't accept it or that it would be enough. So, I just want you to know that I love you with all my heart and soul. I will try my best in life to always make you proud of me.

I have to admit, it's going to be weird waking up every morning and not seeing you. So, if it's okay, I want to come and visit a lot. I am going to miss you and Dad so much. But I want you to know that I am happy. So very happy. Everything you have done for me got me here. I am worthy.

Love,

Mallory

EPILOGUE

Laura

"Laura, honey, how many times are you going to fluff those pillows?"

"I can't help it. I just want everything to be perfect," I say as I grab one of the striped throw pillows and aggressively throw it on the couch, then karate chop the top of it. You know, the way they do on those redesign shows I love so much.

"Laura," Scott says softly as he grabs my shoulders and turns me around. There's tenderness in his gaze. "She grew up here. She knows what the house looks like. She and Caleb are here every single Sunday for dinner. Why are you so anxious today?"

The truth is, I am anxious about this visit. Scott's right, Caleb and Mallory come home every Sunday for family dinner. Jake and Emma join us as well. It's a tradition that started right after the wedding two years ago, and I live for those Sundays.

But this is different because it's a Tuesday. Mallory called yesterday afternoon and asked us if they could come over tonight to "talk to us about something important." How could I not be nervous? Neither of my kids call and asks if they can come over. Even though they are grown married adults, they still come and go as they please. And Scott and I love it.

"She called and asked to come over. I mean, isn't that strange? She wants to talk about something, and Jake and Emma are coming. It's just weird. I hope she's okay." I find myself staring at the freshly vacuumed floor instead of Scott, trying to avoid eye contact. Until the day I leave this earth, I will worry about her.

Scott cups my chin and pulls it up, so I'm looking at him again. The fine lines around his eyes are more prominent, the gray on his temples more visible. "She's fine, Laura. I'm sure this is a good thing. Please don't worry." I wrap my arms around him, and he pulls me into one of his enormous hugs that swallows me and always makes me see more clearly. I inhale his scent and settle into his embrace.

And he's right. Mallory is doing great. I mean, more than just great. She's doing *amazing*! As a woman with autism, she is truly excelling at life with her exceptional abilities. She's married and is still volunteering at The Camelot Center. Currently, she is working on getting certified to be a horse trainer. At times, she still struggles with her anxiety and depression, but this is being managed well with medication and therapy. Plus, she has Caleb, who grounds and centers her like no one can.

And speaking of Caleb. What a blessing he has been to her and to our family. He takes care of our daughter as if he's getting paid millions. He is so in tune with her he can detect her mood shifts before she even realizes them. More than anything, he loves her for exactly who she is ... one hundred and ten percent. When they got married, I gained another son.

Mallory and Caleb, Jake and Emma ... well, we call them the Fab Four. They are inseparable. I think secretly, though, Jake likes to keep a close eye on Mallory. He would never admit it, but he is fiercely protective of her.

Jake and Emma are killing it in the game of life as well. He works with Scott, learning the construction business, with plans of taking it over when Scott retires. Jake has a gift for building things, just like his father. Emma is still working at the hospital as a nurse with me. She is like a second daughter and adores my son. I have to say, we really struck gold in the in-law department.

I inhale deeply to compose myself and glance at Scott. He plants the softest kiss on my lips, then pulls away and rubs his hands on my arms. "Feel better?"

"I do. Thanks, honey." He bops me on the nose with his finger, causing me to giggle.

We both head into the kitchen, and after starting the coffee, I lay out some finger foods on the coffee table and fluff the pillows ... again.

"Alexa. Play my favorites list on Spotify," I command into the air. Just then, John Paul White's crooning voice fills the quiet space. I turn to survey the room I know like the back of my hand.

Yeah, this is ridiculous. It looks like I'm getting ready to show our home in an open house to some strangers. I'm trying too hard, and it shows.

The sound of the side door in the kitchen opening pulls me from my thoughts, and my daughter's sweet voice fills the air.

"Mom? Dad?" she calls out as she makes her way into the living room. Caleb is right behind her.

"Hey, sweetie," I say with way too much enthusiasm as I hug her. A hug she initiated. These are always my favorite.

"Hey, Mom." As she pulls away from the hug, she keeps her hands on my shoulders and studies my face with a raised eyebrow. "You sound weird. Why do you sound weird?" she questions. That's my Mallory, always brutally honest.

"I do?" I notice her scanning the room. Caleb takes her coat and hangs it up in the coat closet.

"You do. Why does everything look so fancy? The pillows are weirdly perfect, and you have out appetizers, for crying out loud." She giggles as she points to the perfect plate of cream cheese pinwheels. "And there's mood music."

"I know, I know," I say as I wave my hand over the room. "I just thought when you asked to come over that this sounded kinda important." Mallory gives me a sly, mischievous smile.

Well, that looks suspicious.

As usual, Caleb looks magazine-ready when he enters the living room. "Hey, Mom. The place looks great!" he says as he kisses me on the cheek. Wrapping his arms around Mallory's waist from behind, he rests his chin on her shoulder. "When are Jake and Emma getting here?"

"They should be here any minute, I hope," I say as I turn to glance at the clock on the wall. I turn back around at Mallory as she and Caleb are talking in low voices.

"...don't be nervous. They will be so excited," Caleb whispers in her ear. Mallory smiles in the way she always does when she's with Caleb and then notices that I'm staring.

"What?" she asks.

"Nothing. You two are being awful secretive, that's all."

"Are we?" Mallory asks with a hint of sarcasm in her voice as she glances back at Caleb.

"I don't have any secrets," Caleb shakes his head, and his lips tick upward.

"Alright, you two," I say, waving my finger between them because they are being brats now. "Whatever is happening, well, it better be good."

They laugh as we all walk into the kitchen, just as Scott is opening a bottle of wine. The bourbon and rock glasses are already out and ready. With a sudden burst of energy, the side door swings open. Jake and Emma have arrived.

"Sorry we're late," Emma explodes as she enters the kitchen frantically. Jake is right behind her. They are both breathless and whipping their coats off their arms in a frenzy. "Did we miss it?" Emma asks Mallory.

"Miss what?" I ask, bewildered, as I look around at everyone. The room falls silent and feels uncomfortable. Emma's eyes are wide as she looks mortified. I watch as she mouths 'I'm sorry' to Mallory, who then says a silent 'It's okay' in return. Jake shakes his head and lowers it. His shoulders bounce with silent laughter. Emma has a knack for putting her foot in her mouth. Caleb is snickering under his breath, and Scott is looking at me as he shrugs because he is just as confused as I am. "Okay, what is going on, you guys?" I demand as I smack my hand on the kitchen island, the sound reverberating through the space.

With a tender touch on my arm, Mallory's reassuring gaze meets mine. "Let's get some wine for you and Emma and some bourbon for the guys and go into the living room, and we will fill you in." How times have changed. Now, my daughter is the one trying to calm me down.

With alcohol in hand, we all make our way into the living room, which appears like it's ready to be photographed. As we come together, we take our regular spots around the space and get comfortable. Jake and Emma are on the love seat. Scott is in his chair. Mallory and Caleb are on the couch together. I'm in my chair, which sits right next to Scott's.

I zero in on Mallory's anxiety right away. Her leg is bouncing, and she's picking at her cuticles. Caleb covers her hands with a tender touch, which is his way of saying, 'Calm down. Relax.' And she does almost immediately. Mallory talks first.

"Mom. Dad," she says as she looks at us both. "I have a gift for you, guys."

She stands from the couch and retrieves her purse as she pulls out a white rectangle-shaped box that's tied neatly with a black satin bow. I take it in my hands and watch as she sits next to Caleb, and he puts his arm around her.

"What is this?" Scott asks as he gets up from his chair and stands behind mine. He places his hand on my shoulder.

"Like I said, it's a gift. Open it," Mallory pleads.

"Is it from all four of you?" I turn to Jake and Emma.

"Don't look at us," Jake says as he puts his hands up in surrender. "This is all these two." He waves between both Mallory and Caleb. I study the box, contemplating what could be inside. What on earth is inside this box that would merit a visit from my kids on a Tuesday evening?

"Oh, my God, Mom! Just open it!" Mallory exclaims. "You're killing me *here*!" The Fab Four snickers. Jake is rubbing his hands together. Emma's elbows are resting on her knees, and her chin is in her hands. The anxious foot bopping has taken over her now.

I pull at the satin black ribbon that feels cool to the touch. My eyes briefly meet Scott's before I open the box. Uncertain what could be inside, yet the anticipation is killing me. I glance at my daughter one last time. Her smile is reaching her eyes. A smile I love and longed to see during darker times. A smile that tells me she is happy, content, and fulfilled. And I know that whatever is in this box is putting that smile there.

I lift the lid and peer inside. A white stick stares at me that says...

PREGNANT

If you or someone you love is experiencing suicidal thoughts, self-harm tendencies, and/or battling anxiety and depression, please use the resources below. And remember, *you are worthy.*

Suicide and crisis lifeline

Text 988 — available 24/7

Self-harm crisis text line

Text 741741 — available 24/7

National mental health hotline

1-866-903-3787 — available 24/7

If you or someone you love has autism and you are seeking resources and/or support, reach out to the organizations below.

www.autismsociety.org

1-800-328-8476

www.autismspeaks.org

BECOMING MALLORY PLAYLIST

"Loved You Before" — **Natalie Taylor**

"Daughter" — **Sleeping At last**

"In Real Life" — **Mandy Moore**

"Better Place" — **Rachel Platten**

"Hate The Way You Love Me" — **John Paul White**

"Rainbow" — **Kacey Musgraves**

"Falling in Love at a Coffee Shop" — **Landon Pigg**

"Heaven" — **Niall Horan**

"Already Gone" — **Sleeping At Last**

"evermore" — **Taylor Swift (feat. Bon iver)**

"Please Don't" — **The Sweeplings**

"Breathe Again" — **Sarah Bareilles**

"This Town" — **Niall Horan**

"No Right To Love You" — **Rhys Lewis**

"I Was Made For Loving You" — **Tori Kelly (feat. Ed Sheeran)**

"Turning Page" — **Sleeping At Last**

"You and Me" — **Lifehouse**

"Next Thing You Know" — **Jordan Davis**

ACKNOWLEDGEMENTS

Growing up, I remember always having a pen in my hand, writing. I tucked stacks of notebooks filled with song lyrics, poems, and short stories under my bed. I plastered the poetry I had written all over my bedroom walls (yes; I wrote directly on them. Sorry, Mom). So, it would make sense that this love would bleed into adulthood, right? Well, life got in the way, and I abandoned my passion for writing. I never thought this desire would swell back up in my mid-forties. Yet here I am.

So, when I sat down at my laptop and wrote this book that was close to my heart, never did I think readers like you would read it, let alone buy it. First and foremost, I need to thank you, the reader, for allowing my thoughts and Mallory's world to become a part of yours. I can only hope she touched your heart the same way she touched mine.

Since this book is my debut novel, it wouldn't have been possible without the unwavering love and support of my family. My husband Brian, who has been my cheerleader ever since I came to him and told him I wanted to take on this gigantic task. His support has been unmatched for 30 years. He's kinda my person. To my children, Jackson (does Jake need his own book? I think so!) and Samantha (my personal Mallory and autism warrior). You three are my life and my world. Nothing makes sense without all of you. Please, never stop believing in me.

To my parents. Thank you for encouraging both my brother and me to explore our own individual creativity. It's the job of all parents to help their children grow and become unique individuals. You accomplished this in spades. I also need to thank my Mama Gram Gram, for passing this love of reading and writing onto me. She was a remarkable woman, full of strength and passion. I can only hope to live up to the woman and mother that she was.

And how can I sit down to write this and not thank my friend Delaney? I credit her for reigniting this love of writing that I had buried long ago. She is the one that lit the match and started this fire. I will forever be grateful to her for her support, early critiques of my manuscript, words of wisdom, our weird random telegram messages, but most of all, her friendship.

To my Beta readers: My husband and son, my mother-in-law Patty, my sister-in-law Alicia, Tami, Piper, Delaney (again!), Brooke, Lizette, and my workmates, Lisa B, Lisa K, Lisa F (I know ... lots of Lisa's), Susan, Marie, and Tiffany. You guys pulled out all the stops and understood the assignment! Your feedback, with a balance of praise and criticism, was a major factor in shaping the final version of Becoming Mallory and making the book what it is today. I am eternally grateful!

To my editor, Nevvie. I am so happy that after an exhaustive search; I picked you to be the one to hand over my baby over to. Call it a gut feeling, but I knew you were the one and I'm so glad I listened to that feeling. You used your Jedi powers of editing and made this book shine! Thank you for your time and patience and for being my partner in crime during this process. And if you ever need color inspiration again, you know where to find me.

Finally, I would be remiss without mentioning The Camelot Center. Thank you for allowing me to use the center's name and likeness in the book. I hope the portrayal of Camelot on the page felt as warm and inviting as its real-life counterpart. Camelot changed my daughter Samantha for the better, and just as Mallory did, Samantha started riding and then volunteering. We've never looked back. This equine center provides immense help and support for countless individuals, regardless of their disabilities or lack thereof. If you have the means, you can donate to this non-profit organization. All donations go to the maintenance of the facility and to the care of the horses. It has been in operation as a PATH Premier Accredited Center since 1994, and those doors need to remain open for many more years to come! Check out their website at www.thecamelotcenter.org for more information.

Now, to all the parents trying to raise a child with autism and/or mental illness. I need you to understand that you are not alone. And I hope that this book, in some small way, helped you feel seen and heard.

Finally, I want to thank all autistic individuals and anyone battling mental illness out there in the world. Thank you for being you. I see firsthand, through my daughter, the struggles you face daily. As a healthcare professional in a pediatric hospital, I work with many children and teenagers who are autistic with mental illness. It's difficult living life with one or both. To every one of you, never stop believing that you can. Never stop believing that you will. Let no one tell you that you can't. Always be yourself. And remember, *you are worthy.*

ABOUT THE AUTHOR

Elaine Evans has had a love of writing ever since she can remember. Becoming Mallory is her debut novel and it certainly won't be her last.

When she's not writing you can find Elaine exploring her other hobbies of reading, cooking, and photography. But more than anything, it is the role of wife, mother, and dog mom to her black Pomeranian, Vinnie, that she cherishes the most. Outside of the home, she works as a pediatric Medical Assistant, a job she loves. Elaine resides in Ohio with her family.

www.ingramcontent.com/pod-product-compliance
Lightning Source LLC
Chambersburg PA
CBHW060222030726
47499CB00004B/1157